THIS
BLOOD
THAT BONDS
US

S. L. COKELEY

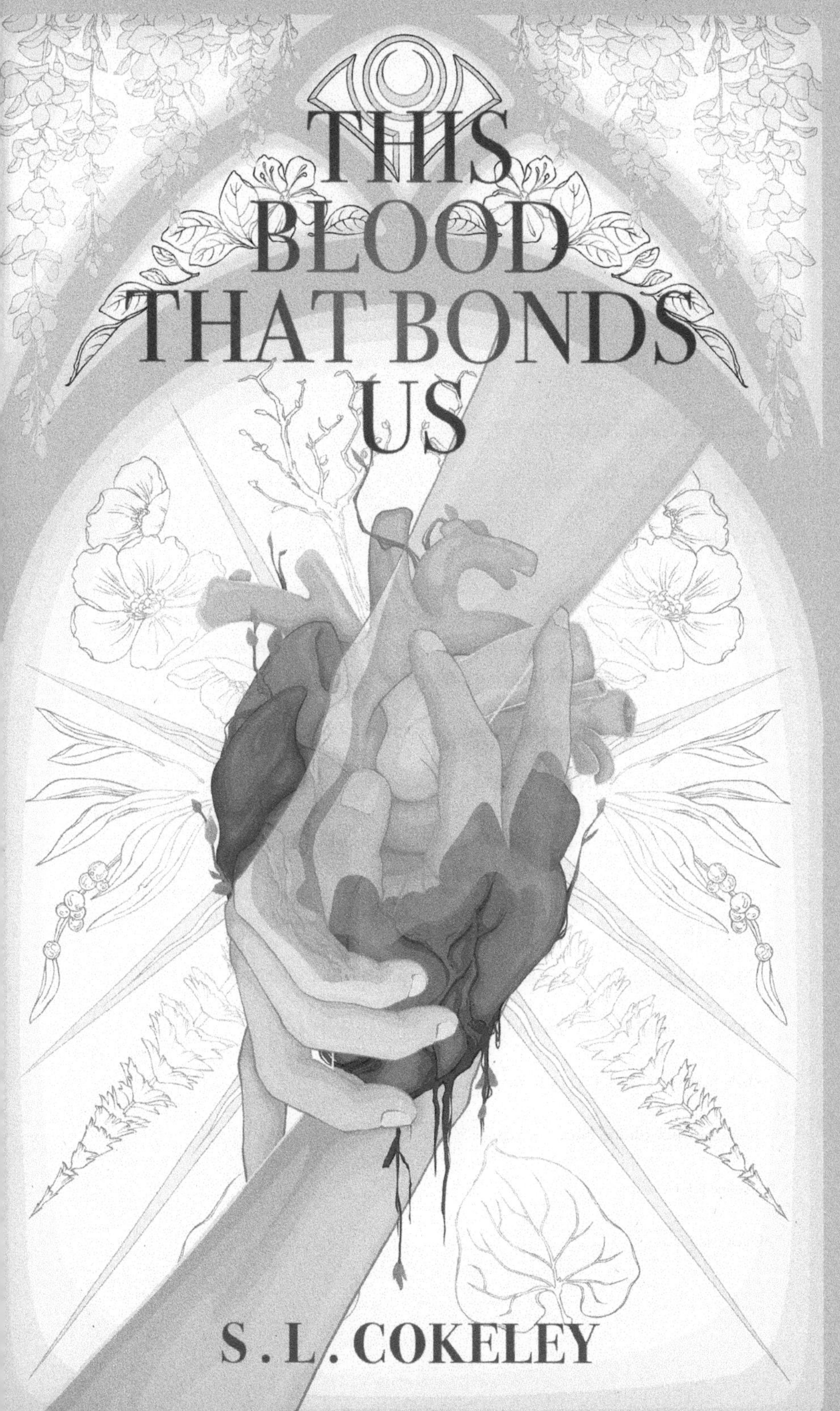
THIS BLOOD THAT BONDS US
S.L. COKELEY

Author's Note

This series contains content that may be triggering for some audiences. You can find an updated Content Warnings page on my website.

Scan here or visit _slcokeleybooks.com_ :

Playlist

Francis Forever by Mitski

Wish That You Were Here by Florence+
The Machine

Evermore by Taylor Swift

Blinding by Florence+ The Machine

Cardigan by Taylor Swift

First Light by Hozier

The Prophecy by Taylor Swift

Everywhere, Everything by Noah Kahan

Blood by The Middle East

WHILE I LIVE, I HOPE.

Scan for more!

*All song recommendations are solely for inspiring readers'
imaginations when reading and sharing the love of music.*

For the dreamers and those who have lost hope—
Spring will find you even after the coldest winter. Don't be afraid to get
your hopes up and dream again. Just try.

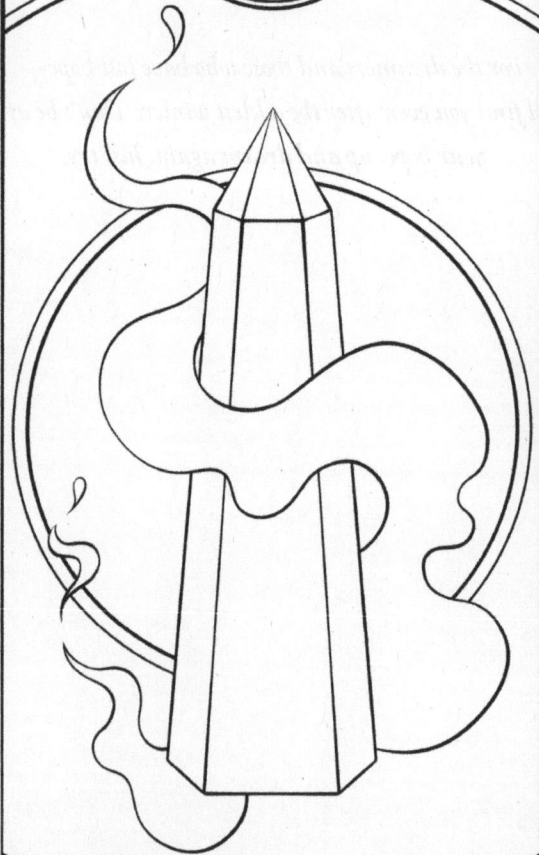

XVI

THE TOWER

PART TWO

PART TWO:
THE LAST HOPE

Prologue

"Don't think you'll be able to keep me from Her, because you won't. I want to go see Her." My little brother was causing a scene in the garden. The fresh scent of rain and the darkness of the night enveloped us.

I was still taking it in and regaining my bearings. The evidence of my fight with Zach was all over my body—sticky, wet blood and bites that struggled to heal.

Presley had shed his soaked jacket and rolled up his sleeves, revealing his forearms scrawled with black ink. The word 'Her' was written over and over, covering every inch of skin, some jagged and long while others were small and hard to see.

Everything was slow with the blood loss, and when I stopped Presley with a hand on his shoulder, I fought to summon the strength in my arm.

1

He was full of Her blood—shimmering and exuding strength while bouncing with energy. She'd taken hold of him, and it reflected back to me in his dark irises.

I'd have killed anyone else for acting like that, like they belonged to Her. Like they, too, could have the same bond as Her and I did, but this was my little brother. My blood, and I felt the draw of something much stronger there.

"We'll see Her in a minute, and we'll be with Her all night. I promise."

My voice sounded soft and sincere. How long had it been since I'd registered my own voice? My own existence? The churning in my gut worried me. Where was Zach? We'd been fighting, and I vaguely remembered why, but it wasn't me. Nothing about that person carried any traits of mine, and I'd have never fought with my brother. Luke Calem wouldn't.

"Tell me what happened with Aaron and Kimberly. Where are they?"

Presley should have never been standing before me. He should be where I left them all, safe and tucked away. *Together.*

He turned away. "They're better off without me."

"They're okay? They're alive?"

"No. They're dead."

He couldn't be serious. He couldn't be so far gone that he wouldn't care. Did I care? The ache in my chest and the heat in my face told me yes.

Presley scratched at the back of his hand.

"You're lying," I said.

Recollection passed over his eyes, like he was seeing me for the first time. "H-how would you know that?"

Because I'm your brother, and your tells have always been obvious to me. Because it's my job. Because I love you.

"They're not dead. Are they?"

He shook his head with his gaze fixed on the ground. All his light was dull. With the bond, I felt the ache of sadness in him. They'd given him more blood, and now we were all equal. It almost felt complete. Like it was whole in a way it wasn't before with just Zach and me. The bond was always moving, surging in and out, but now I felt my brother's pain, and it didn't topple me to the ground. That pain wasn't weakness. It was strength. The three of us were glowing with it.

"I'm sorry, Luke. I couldn't be good. I couldn't do the one thing you told me to do. It was too hard."

His eyes were pure onyx. Not a hint of the warm brown was left in his irises.

"It's all right." I pulled him into me, expecting him to jerk away, but he didn't.

"My chest doesn't hurt anymore. Isn't that great?"

"That's great, Pres."

How could I not hope? Even despite everything, our connection remained. It was just enough to keep me together. I stroked his head and breathed in his scent. He smelled like my mom, like vanilla and laundry soap.

It was repairing something in me. My queen was right. My brother was always meant to be at my side. The Guard could never be just Zach and me and two others; it was always going to be the four of us.

Zach appeared next to me. "She wants to see him."

He seemed different than I remembered. When did the haziness of my memory start? We'd gone through Ascension, then went to the bar and . . . that must have been it. Ascension was the answer.

"She wants to look in his head and see what he's been up to." Zach looked at me with a stern, unmoving expression, but I knew the fear in his voice.

"She wants to see me!"

3

Presley moved toward the cathedral again, and Zach and I both stopped him.

"Pres, listen. When She looks into your head, what is She going to see? I need you to tell me all of it right now."

"Why?"

"Because we need to know so we can protect you."

"She won't hurt me."

I should have agreed. A part of me did. Everything She'd done and we went through was for a reason. We'd run away. We'd deserved the punishment. Things were different with him. It confirmed the prophecy. We were on The Divine Path.

Yet I was still afraid for my little brother.

"I know. Just tell us so we know everything about why you're here."

I already knew. The prophecy. Fate. The Divine Path.

"If I tell you, you'll take me to Her?"

Zach and I shared a look, then we nodded. A little of that dull ache in my chest dissipated. Just enough. I'd protect him till my heart stopped beating. We would be a family again. It's how it was meant to be. The one true path.

One

Three months earlier

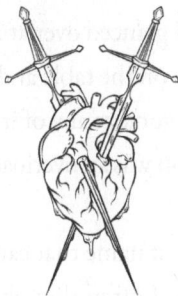

Keep your eyes on me.

Reciting Aaron's words in my head, I studied the wood grain of the bar. My foot tapped on the barstool beneath me, and I picked the dirt from under my nails for what had to be the fifth time in ten minutes. Aaron sat at the front of the bar, with Presley in the only window seat. The streetlight from outside and the glowing blue neon above them illuminated the tops of their heads. I couldn't see Aaron's face or his eyes, only the shadow shielding him from me.

Dive bars were the easiest to sneak into. Mostly because Presley and

5

Aaron were naturals at distracting the ID checker. As I sipped my beer, I hoped I'd be able to tolerate the smell of mildew and smoke for longer than an hour.

"Well, hello." A group of guys, who couldn't have been much older than me, made their way to sit. They shed their large puffy coats and scarves and dropped them to the ground and over their stools.

"Were you waiting on someone?"

The guy was forward. That would make it easy. His dark hair and eyes reminded me of William. Only, he didn't have the same charm William possessed in our first meeting.

"No." I smiled, tucking my hair behind my ear. "No one."

He smiled a toothy, wicked smile and leaned back to whisper something to one of his friends. I glanced over at Aaron, but all I could make out were his clenched hands on the table and Presley tucking his head to say something. I wasn't any good at any of it yet. Focusing on the sound and using my improved vision was an overload on my already taxed brain.

"What's your name?"

"Chelsea." I picked the first name that came to mind.

My old life was gone. But I often thought of Chelsea and wondered how everything had played out for her. I'd sent my letter and hoped she'd gotten it. It was strange being dead to the world I'd once called home. I could never return.

"I'm Jared," he said.

Jared was a talker. He couldn't pull himself from me all night. The more shots he and his friends took, the more handsy he got. It started with a soft brush of his hand and turned into an arm around my shoulder. Every minute felt like an eternity. It was too loud. The voices were a throbbing jumble in my skull with the music coming from the jukebox, and that didn't count the noise of normal human function. Like laughing, chewing, or dropping glasses. The roar of cars driving by or the crash of balls on the pool table set me on edge. I had to grip the trim of the bar to stop from flinching—and that was just one sense. The stench of cigarettes ate away at the last bit of sanity I had, and the karaoke machine had lights that constantly flickered.

I dropped cash on the bar for my tab, chugged the rest of my beer, then said my goodbyes. Heading out of the bar, I didn't glance at the boys when I passed them. The click of my heeled boots echoed on the concrete as I tugged my jacket over my shoulders. A chill ran up my spine, but I didn't shiver. I wasn't always the bait. Presley was better at it. He got the job done faster and was more personable. Aaron on the other hand . . .

I slowed my pace to give them time to catch up. The bar was in a secluded part of town, and the lack of people around was ideal for what we needed. Even with all the right variables, it was never a guarantee that they'd follow. Sometimes we'd have to wait in an alley for the drunkest ones at close.

The doorbell rang, and Jared called out, "Hey, wait! Where are you going?"

I looked back expecting to see just one, but they all followed me. *Perfect.*

As I turned into the alleyway without a sound, Jared was hot on my heels.

"Do you need help?" His tone was sincere, but he grabbed my arm. "Wait."

The alcohol on his breath overwhelmed my senses. He was too close to me, backing me into the wall as two shadows emerged in the moonlight, and our plan commenced.

I yanked Jared by his hood and sank my teeth into his neck. It wasn't as hard as I thought it would be. Feeding was logical, and I'd done it many times. I could think myself through it pretty easily by counting to a certain number and letting go. That was that. The euphoria I got from

7

drinking blood was nowhere near as strong as the nagging of my own brain and its need for control.

There were only the sounds of struggle and muffled yelling as I drank. The boys had found their marks too. We'd formed a routine that had gotten better every time. The first time, we forgot about the screaming and had to run.

Suddenly, Aaron pulled the guy from my grasp and sank his teeth into his neck.

"Aaron, don't." I tried to pry him off, but he wasn't budging. His eyes were black and filled with rage as he shoved him against the wall.

"Presley, help me!"

It took both of us to pull them apart. Jared's heart hammered against his ribs. He'd need an ambulance. I tore off a piece of my jacket to hold pressure on his neck and motioned for Presley to hold it.

Aaron wasn't coming back to himself. His eyes were pure obsidian, and he stood still with rigid shaking shoulders.

"Aaron, you're in control. It's okay." I grabbed his face in my hands. "Fight it."

I turned to Presley. "Go get someone in the bar to call 911."

"But—"

"Please, go!"

I ran my hands through the length of Aaron's hair. "Come back to me. You can do this. I know you can."

There was something caged behind his irises, tearing its way through. He was like this now. Untamed, with his thirst unquenchable.

"It's okay." I placed his hand over my heart and mine onto his. "We can fix this. It will be okay."

Finally, his eyes softened and melted into pools of golden chocolate.

"Shit. I'm sorry. I tried. I'm trying," he said. His eyes widened upon seeing a very pale Jared on the ground.

"It's okay. They'll be fine. But we have to go."

"Wait, what?" he said.

I grabbed his hand, and we ran out of the alley, and Presley followed us as we made our escape.

THIS BLOOD THAT BONDS US

Two

AARON

Kimberly's delicate touch stilled the relentless tapping of my leg. I faked a smile and tried to move my focus back to the road while my fingers pressed into the leather of the steering wheel. The tapping would come back. It always did.

The guy at the bar had lived, I think. We'd waited around long enough to see him get taken away in the ambulance at least. That on top of everything else just added to the weight in my chest and our mounting list of issues.

Snow flurries littered the windshield as we drove through frosted trees. Everything was white. Soft blankets of snow surrounded us. During the day, it was blinding, and at night, it was isolating. I preferred Blackheart. I had preferred a lot of things. The most glaring thing was not feeling like I would lose myself to the monster in my head. At first, I thought it was my grief, but as time went on, nothing about it was normal.

Akira's blood caused a chain reaction of energy and restlessness in my body. The longing ache in my chest never went away and sometimes turned into a deep sadness that made me feel like my lungs would cave in. That wasn't the worst part.

"I'll need to hunt again soon." I sighed, and her hand tightened on my leg.

She nodded. Her best effort at bringing me any sense of comfort, but I knew it scared her, because it scared me.

The hunger had gotten worse. I'd thought it was well on its way to getting better after hunting with The Legion. Until Akira. The unquenchable gnawing in my chest that longed for more blood was constant. No amount of hunting helped, and it was driving me a little insane. The queen's blood in my veins had awoken the beast I'd tried so hard to tame. I hadn't even noticed it until it grew closer to the two-week mark. Then I realized something was very wrong.

I'd wanted more blood even though I'd just fed. I craved the feeling of it. The warmth of blood in my mouth and the rush of euphoria it gave me. Only, the satiation didn't last more than a couple hours.

I didn't know what to do or why I was the only one between my brother and me who seemed to have that problem. I thought of Luke and shuddered. How he'd drank so much of Her blood and maintained his sanity, I'd never know. It all made sense now, the fidgeting and the pacing. He made it all look easy. It had been only two weeks, and I was already drowning.

I looked in the rearview mirror at Presley. His gaze was set on the snow, but his thoughts were anyone's guess. I wanted to ask him if he was feeling okay, but even if it were possible to waterboard him, I couldn't get it out of him. He stopped talking. Fully stopped. And of everything happening to me, that was the most worrisome. He was mad at me because I wouldn't let him drive, but I had to drive. There was no way

I could sit in the car with my thoughts and not think about blood. At least driving kept me occupied.

I failed him before I even started, but I was the one with the map. Luke's message of a sequence of letters and numbers were coordinates. Even in his absence, he led us.

My chest was hollow, so I cleared away my thoughts of them like the wipers on the windshield pushing snow. I couldn't let the grief in. Not until we were safe.

Three

PRESLEY

Aaron was a bad driver, and there was no one to tell him except me. Kim's sweet tendencies meant Aaron's annoying behavior—probably mine too—would go unchecked because Luke and Zach were . . . on vacation somewhere else. Probably doing great and not sad at all.

Aaron liked to do this thing where instead of easing off the gas into a stop, he'd slam on the brakes. It was like I was on an amusement park ride, and not the fun kind. It would have made me want to barf if I still could.

Kimberly took the change like a champ. I'd decided to be helpful by not yelling at Aaron for his poor driving skills, because it was a little too much on her senses at the moment. She couldn't even handle the radio for very long.

I'd decided to be a good boy for her, but the torture of sitting in the car for hours in silence had me drawing a frowny face into foggy windows of the car.

I could have told Aaron all of that. Not like we were playing the quiet game or anything, but for the first time in my life, I didn't feel like talking. No, that was sort of a lie.

I fiddled with the peeling lettering on my pullover. Kimberly thought of everything. She'd made us stop at a thrift store and bought us all new clothes with the money we'd saved from the car wash. I was being forced into blah-gray clothes, but I got the meaning behind it. We needed to not look like ourselves. But clothing was personal and fun, and I looked forward to choosing every day. This had been chosen for me. Though it was probably for the best, I didn't want to make mundane decisions.

"Are we there yet?"

Aaron glared at me through the rearview mirror. I was on my third warning, but Aaron wouldn't do anything. Unlike Zach . . .

I sighed. "I want to stop and get an MP3 or something. I'm tired of sitting in the silence."

I didn't even know if they made such an ancient device anymore.

"We're not spending money on that," Aaron said.

"Oh, so you're the finance man too, huh? You believe that, Kim? He's such a dictator."

She rubbed her forehead. "We need to stop soon anyway. We can check by the hotel."

We'd been driving for miles on a singular road in Alaska. It wasn't exactly high on my list of places I'd wanted to visit. I don't think Alaska was happy to see us. It hadn't stopped snowing since we'd arrived.

The whole car jolted as we ran over something. A puppy—maybe a child.

"Smooth driving there, Tex."

"I'm trying. It's the blizzard. There's debris all over the road." Aaron sighed.

Kimberly rubbed his shoulder—she coddled him too much. "It's okay. Five more minutes."

"I can drive us," I said.

"No. You'll drive us into the ditch."

"I'm a better driver than you!"

"Guys," Kimberly said.

"Look, you're upsetting Kim," I said.

"You're the one who's yelling."

"I'm only yelling because you never listen to me." I grabbed his head-rest and shook it.

"Stop touching my headrest," Aaron snapped.

"What are you going to do about it?"

Aaron tried to slap my hand off. The car swerved into a tailspin, and all three of us screamed as we crashed into a ditch.

"Shit!" Aaron slammed his hands on the steering wheel. Sitting in the ditch, I remembered my previous resolve not to piss my brother off because he'd been acting a little unhinged. Eh, I'd try harder once I wasn't stuck in a car for hours upon hours with the worst heater known to man.

Kimberly rubbed her forehead again.

"Sorry, Kim," I said.

"It's okay." She turned to me with a soft smile, then back to Aaron. "Why don't we stop at the convenience store here on the corner, then our hotel is only a street over."

"What about the car?" Aaron said.

"Let's ditch this one and get another tomorrow," I said.

"We just got this one."

"Yeah, and it sucks."

"Sorry, I couldn't steal you a better car, Pres," Aaron spat.

"Me too."

"Boys." Kimberly stopped us both.

"Sorry," we said.

"I'm going to the store. I have some stuff to get. I'll look for your MP3."

"I wanna come." I pat Aaron's shoulder on my way to follow Kim. "Make sure to wipe down the car real good, buddy."

We'd tried to scrub our stolen cars of prints and things before we left them. Just generally to make it harder for someone to track us. Cops, The Family, Legion. The list was long.

Kimberly rubbed his shoulder again. "Do you want anything?"

"No." He gave her the googly eyes, then glared at me. "Don't spend all our money."

"Sir, yes sir." I gave him a salute with my middle finger.

"Come on." Kimberly wrapped her arm around me and handed me a bigger coat. It was more for the disguise than it was the cold. I fished my sunglasses out of my pocket and put them on. It was pitch dark outside, with barely any moonlight peeking through the clouds, so naturally, I couldn't see shit, but I looked cool, and that's all that really mattered. Kimberly had some too, but she needed them for the fluorescent lighting.

The snow was falling in thick puffs that soaked into the fabric of my coat and wet my hair.

"How are you holding up?" Kimberly asked. She always asked me that. She asked Aaron that too. Kimberly was working hard as our glue. I guess someone had to be, but I felt bad because it wasn't how it was supposed to be. It should have been us taking care of her. That was the original plan.

"So peachy, Kim. Happier than I've ever been."

She gave me her serious brow.

16

"I'd be a lot better if Aaron wasn't so annoying."

"He's trying his best. We're all a little stressed. And he's—"

"I know. I'm sorry you're in the middle of all this."

"Nowhere else I'd rather be."

"Seriously, you're telling me your fluffy strawberry bedspread back at BFU wouldn't beat walking in a blizzard in the dark in the middle of nowhere?"

"That's exactly what I'm saying."

Aaron and I would have killed each other already if it wasn't for her. She'd seen adversity and had a level head. Aaron did too when his veins weren't full of the queen's blood like mine.

It wasn't fair. All of us were going to go somewhere safe. We were going to help her through the change. We were all supposed to be—

She squeezed my arm as we entered the brightest building ever. The convenience store had buzzing fluorescent bulbs and was blaring Christmas music. I rubbed my chest where it suddenly felt hollow. Kind of like when I used to get heartburn from eating way too many hot chips and drinking energy drinks.

A man dressed in a green elf costume looking for donations rang a bell just inside the entrance of the store. Kimberly gripped my arm. *She must be hurting.* The sensory overload hadn't been that hard for me to manage when I changed. It was different for everyone, but for her, the sound was killer. "*Too much noise in my head,*" she'd say.

"I'll take care of him," I whispered to her.

She mouthed, *Thank you* as she pulled her hood over her head to shield her ears.

"Hey, dude. Can I see that bell?"

A large man with salt-and-pepper hair looked down at me and raised a bushy brow.

"No."

"Come on, I want to show you a magic trick. It's worth it. I promise."

I grabbed the bell and covered it with my hands. I'd practiced sleight of hand a lot as a kid who liked to cheat, and it was about a thousand times easier as a vampire. It was criminal that my brothers didn't let me get on social media, because I would've made us so much money as a social media magician. Luke never thought the idea was stupid.

I did the ole behind the ear trick which he wasn't too enthused with. *Tough crowd.*

"Oh my god, what is that?" I pointed at nothing across the store, and as he turned, I chucked the bell outside in the snow as far as it would go.

I was gone by the time he turned around. *Sucker.*

"Hey!" His voice echoed in the store, but I'd already found Kim. She'd protect me. Any man would shiver and quake in the face of an angry Kimberly Burns. Human or vampire.

"Here." She shoved the smallest MP3 player in my face.

"Oh god, it's ancient . . . and gray. No pink? Green?"

She scoffed with a smile. "It's all they had."

"How do I put music on it?"

"There are instructions on the back. Maybe you can use a computer at the hotel."

"It comes with a manual!? We're really in trouble, aren't we?"

We were in a lot of trouble. And the MP3 was a bad omen.

I kind of zoned out after that, watching the door and waiting. The feeling was still there in my chest, like I had slammed three burgers and washed it down with a liter of soda. I expected them to walk through the door like they always did.

The twins were just those guys. They always showed up. Even if they told me they might not make it to a game—I was the best mascot to ever mascot the halls of my high school—my brothers always made it. Christmas, New Years . . .

18

Suddenly, I was reminded of the Christmas music playing in the store. The hollow feeling grew, and I rubbed my chest. I hated the bells. The nostalgia. The stupid sparkly Santa decorations mocking me with their smiles.

"I'm going to check on Aaron, okay?"

She narrowed her eyes. "Will you be good?"

Luke's words danced in the foothills of my mind.

"Yes, ma'am. I earnestly swear to only piss Aaron off a little bit."

I bolted for the door, taking extra care to wave at the doorman before darting out into the night. The parking lot was sparse, with larger trucks and four-wheel drive vehicles. A fresh blanket of snow covered everything, and the swift wind swirled around me. With nothing but darkness overhead, I wanted the snow to lift me into the sky so I could dance there and escape for a minute.

Aaron found me. He had a wool sweater on and a huge jacket that made him look ridiculous, and I had to fight the urge to make fun of him for it. Aaron and I were really bad fugitives. This whole ordeal was making me realize we were bad at literally everything.

"What are you doing out here?" Aaron asked.

"Do you care?"

"Of course I care."

"Coulda fooled me."

"Well, you could have fooled me too. You're being difficult."

"Well, maybe if you'd stop trying to be Luke. We could just continue like we always did before."

"I'm not trying to be Luke. I'm trying to make sure we get where we're going in one piece."

"We'd probably be there by now if we didn't have to stop every other day for you to feed and almost kill everyone who looks at Kimberly the wrong way."

Aaron opened his mouth to speak, then buried his face in his hands and groaned. "I hate this . . ."

"Shit. Sorry. I didn't mean that."

"It's okay."

"No, I was being a dick. You can't help it."

As much as he was annoying, he was trying. We never had that dynamic before. Maybe a little once Zach and Luke graduated and it was just us and Mom most nights, but we didn't have to depend on each other. We'd always had someone to tell us what the hell we were supposed to do.

Aaron nodded and patted me on the back. "I'm trying. I just don't . . . feel like myself right now."

I hadn't given Her much thought before we left Blackheart. For one, why doesn't Ms. Hell Bitch have a name? Who decided referring to Her as a pronoun was appropriate? It made any conversation about Her extremely confusing. I once asked Kilian Her story, and I couldn't get past the first two minutes before deciding not to care. He talked too slow, and it all got jumbled up. I wasn't interested in Hell Bitch's story anyway. She hurt my brothers. Which meant She was dead to me.

Also, why is She a "queen?" What exactly does She rule over? A bunch of mind-numbed zombies? I guess my brothers fell into that category, but in my mind, they didn't count.

This whole treating Her as something otherworldly was so weird. I stopped asking Luke about Her. Aside from his pulse shooting through the roof, he'd get this strange look in his eye that made me sick to my stomach. When his eyes glazed over like that, he didn't look like my brother. He didn't sound like him either. His voice would change and get all serious. Luke wasn't like that. All mysterious and broody. He was fun and loud.

Her blood changed everything, and now it was swimming in my veins too. I still didn't get the hype.

"What does it feel like for you?" he asked.

"Like I have the worst heartburn ever. Kinda hollow deep in my chest like I'm a chocolate bunny."

It made me sad, but I didn't say that. I wasn't ready to hash out my feelings just yet. I wanted to save them up and spew them on Luke when I saw him next. I would see him again, and it would be soon. This was just some temporary madness.

"That's a good way to put it." He did that weird half-smile thing. Normally, it didn't work on me, but he looked wiped. I needed to be nicer to him.

"Do you . . . feel it too?" I asked.

"Yeah, I feel this dull ache. Sadness but mostly thirst. It's stronger than any of that. That's all I can think about. Like it knows that's my weakness or something."

Hell Bitch caused that too.

"Give it to me straight. Are we fucked?" I asked.

"No, Pres. We're going to get through this."

"We're going to find them, right?"

"Yeah, when we get to where Luke wanted us to go, I'm sure he left us some kind of instruction."

I nodded.

He did. I know he did. He always had a plan. This would be no different. We would be together soon. I hoped. In time for Christmas even; it wasn't that far away.

Four

KIMBERLY

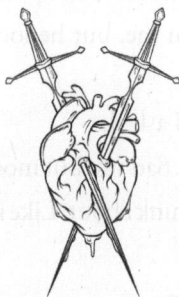

I'd decided to dye my hair. It was too easy to describe a redhead finding her way into bars and luring men into the alley with two blond guys following her around. We might as well have been writing our own crime reports. The incident at the bar had made the local news, and we couldn't risk it.

As I pulled the black dye through the ends of my hair, staining my neck and fingernails, I wondered why I thought it was a good idea. Pools of dye fell in droplets and stained the hotel's porcelain tile beneath my feet. Swirls of blue and gray kept flowing. No matter how much I washed, the darkness kept coming.

I got out and wrapped my hair in a towel. I'd already dyed my brows and couldn't stand to look at the two black bars unnaturally framing my

22

eyes. Staring at myself in the mirror, all I saw were my dark circles. I'd always thought Zach had a monopoly on it. Turned out, I would give him a run for his money.

I wrapped another hotel towel around my body and shivered. It was always cold. My body couldn't be cold. Not really. But I still felt it. This slinking chill in my bones that never went away. I stared at my reflection long enough for my fingers to stiffen and bend around the porcelain. Being a vampire meant I could stand as long as I wanted and never tire. I could stand there for days if I desired it. I liked that part of the change. It made all the uncomfortable parts of being human easy. There was never any ache or pain. I didn't have to take bathroom breaks or stop to eat.

I finally got the courage to pull the ruined towel from my head, then gasped at the tangled mess that fell to my shoulders. Raven-black hair laid against my cool pale skin. It would take years to grow my natural hair back out. Years before I'd see myself again. Did we have years?

A deep gnawing feeling in my chest told me I was staring at my fate. As the Calem boys grew closer to their fate, so did I. It was shrouded in uncertainty and sealed in black blood. The farther we drove, the more it haunted me, drawing me into its clutches and seeping into my pores.

You can't save him.

Akira's words echoed in the silence of the bathroom. For some reason unknown to me, I imagined him laughing in my face. He'd want me to be wavering, sad, and sniffling about our fate. I would save them. Somehow. I didn't exactly know how, but I'd keep trying to navigate them in every way I knew how and helping however they needed.

And oh, how the Calem boys needed help.

A soft knock startled me.

"Are you okay?" Aaron's soft voice was right next to the door. It was a little raspy. He must have been outside.

I didn't answer.

"Can I come in?"

I unlocked the door without a word, and he examined my face. I expected his eyes to widen when he saw how much I changed with the bundle of black hair knotted at my shoulders and the stains of dye along my neck. It was just hair, but then why did I have tears rolling down my cheeks?

I moved to wipe them, and he beat me to it.

He never stopped gazing at my face. Not once did he look at the hair lying on my shoulder or the towel wrapped around me, not even the gray water dripping on his feet.

"Do you want me to help you brush it?"

I nodded and faced away from the mirror. His touch was gentle. So gentle it took way longer than it needed to, but I didn't mind. After he finished, he blow-dried it with the little hairdryer strapped to the wall. I didn't even have to ask. He just knew.

When it was finally time for me to turn around, he rested his hands on my shoulders and let me take it in. I didn't recognize myself. My old life was truly gone, and I'd chosen every step that led me here. I guess that was part of choosing what you wanted. Sometimes choosing your own path meant staring the possibility of failure and ruin in the face. We were safe but for how long?

"Wanna go lay down? Presley's in for the night."

"He's not in our room?"

"No, he said he'd get his own. Didn't think it was worth it to fight about the money. I'll make it up somehow."

"We both will." I grabbed his hand.

Aaron led me to our bed. The room wasn't anything fancy. A queen-sized bed, couch, an old TV, and a mini fridge. I braced myself for the repetition of its buzzing but smiled when I realized Aaron had unplugged it for me. We turned on cartoons, and I nestled into his arms

24

under the comfort of the blankets. The stench of hair dye was clinging to my pores. The curve of his bicep and the strength in his arms as he pulled me onto his chest relaxed me. I got lost in the feel of his heartbeat beneath my fingertips. Aaron Calem was the best foolish decision I'd ever made.

I'd say I felt ten years old again, but I never felt as safe at that age. Despite everything falling apart, Aaron's warmth knit me back together from the top of my head to the tip of my toes. I closed my eyes imagining what it would have been like to know him when I was younger. We sat on a dock, kicking our feet over the edge into a beautiful sparkling lake. We would've met at the water's edge every day, and he would've told me the most amazing stories. Fantastical stories about places and creatures I didn't know existed.

"What are you thinking about?" He played with my hair.

"Running away with you . . . and what you looked like as a kid."

"I was a nerd. Very skinny. Shaggy hair. My mom called it a mop."

"Now that I could see."

"I bet you were a know-it-all. The cute kind." His lips grazed my forehead with a kiss.

"Yes, a little. I was quiet and mostly kept to myself."

"I would have fixed that."

"You would have."

He buried his face into my hair. "I would have taken you all over Blackheart. You could have shown me all the cool secret places. We'd have run away together either way. I think it's written in the stars somewhere."

His arms tightened around me as he pulled me closer, and I nuzzled into his neck.

"I'm supposed to be making you feel better. Not the other way around," I said, pleasantly smushed and oddly whole.

He was the one who just lost his brothers, with no way of knowing how we would get them back, yet he was taking care of me.

"You are. Trust me."

Running away with Aaron Calem was written in the stars. It sounded like the first sentence of a really good book. One that I'd read over and over.

Five

AARON

I wished I could've enjoyed it a little longer, but it was agony lying in bed with her all night. The first hour or two was fine, but the gnawing thirst came back with a vengeance. Like lead in my stomach, it pulled at my skin and brought me to my feet. The need to feed rolled around in my skull until I had to get the feeling to stop.

I couldn't keep feeding every other day. We would never make it to our destination, and I would end up killing someone.

Drink. Kill. Drink. Kill.

The voice. The voice. The voice.

It was louder now. Always in my head. Was I going crazy? No. The queen's blood was *making* me crazy.

My head was a tornado as we packed the car I'd gone out to steal early in the morning. I'd needed something physical to distract me. It had been tempting too, to go off on my own and wait for someone outside. There were so many unexpecting people around who went out at night to do things like smoke a cigarette ...

Because of that, I spent most of my time out in the empty frozen wilderness. I felt like less of a danger sitting on a tree stump and watching the stars overhead.

I'd made it through the night without killing anyone, and that had to count for something. I just had to get in the car again and start driving. It would stop. It had to stop.

The sounds of the cars roared by. More people were getting out now that the blizzard was over. The snow crunched beneath every step I took, and I tried to focus on it while I organized the trunk of the car. It didn't need organizing. It's not like we had that much stuff. But I couldn't get out of my head. Nothing brought my attention away from the emptiness in my stomach.

Maybe being with the queen is the only solution ...

My heart jolted with fear at the thought. That's exactly how She'd want me to feel.

Kimberly appeared beside me and maneuvered the last bag into the trunk of an old 4Runner. My chest ached with guilt. I should've been there to hold her. I should've been coming up with answers on how to find my brothers, but I needed blood and was about to be trapped in another car.

"Are you okay?"

"I ..." I wanted to lie, but I promised not to. I'd have done anything to go back before I drank Akira's blood, and everything in me felt ravenous. Her blood was poison.

What could I say? *"I know you just changed and left everything you've ever known and you're counting on me to protect you, but I feel like I'm going to murder someone in the next few seconds."*

I was at the crossroads to hell. Suddenly, all I could think about was what the queen's blood would feel like in my veins and the want. The heat of it. The taste.

"Aaron." Kimberly's voice was stern, and without another word, she grabbed my arm and shoved me into the back seat of the SUV with her.

The car door slammed, and we sat with our knees touching in the back seat. We were close. Almost too close. I moved toward the door, and she stopped me with a hand on my leg.

"Tell me. Whatever it is. We can deal with it together."

"I don't know how."

"Try."

With my head spinning, I couldn't gather the words. Blood. I needed blood.

"Aaron, you disappeared at 3 a.m., and you haven't said a word. Where did you go? Besides to get the car."

"The woods. I was in the woods."

"Why?"

"Because . . . Because I . . ."

"I know a lot is going on right now—"

"I need to get out of the car."

"No you don't." There was fire in her eyes. "We can fix this."

"We can't! There is something wrong with me. Hunting isn't helping. I'm starting to wonder if it's making it worse. I can't think straight. Ever. I can't do anything without thinking about blood."

That was Akira's plan, after all. To make us want Her. To make us so insane we'd have no other choice but to seek Her out.

"You want more . . ." she whispered, averting her eyes. "You want Her."

The threat of her words stilled me. My sudden urge to bolt disappeared. She was jealous. There was no way I could let her think the queen had any hold on me. Even if She did, it was just blood. It was nothing compared to what I felt for Kimberly.

"Kim." I grabbed her face with urgency. "No. You're the only person I want. You don't understand how badly I need you, and I don't know how to even begin to tell you."

Her cheeks flushed with warmth, making my mouth water.

"You are everything." I looked into the cool blue of her eyes. "It's just. . . I'm making everything worse. I don't know how to fix this, and all I'm doing right now is holding you and Presley back from getting to where we need to go. Maybe we should split up. You both keep going and—"

"How could you say that?" I didn't like the deep frown set on her face. I was worrying her. Hurting her more.

"But I'm ruining everything."

"We don't do things alone. You know that."

"I know, but—"

"Hush. Let me think." She grabbed my hand, probably to keep me from bolting.

I tried to train my attention on her. Her new black hair was pulled into a bun with pieces framing her face. I could tell she didn't like it, but she was breathtaking no matter what color her hair was. She was still my Kimberly, and nothing would ever change that. Vampire or not. She couldn't be more out of her element, yet she was navigating it gracefully in her baggy blue jeans and flannel. I moved my hand up to her cheek to pull her out of the thought spiral she was undoubtedly falling into. She'd try to fix this, and I wasn't sure it could be.

She gasped as my fingers grazed her jaw.

"I have an idea." She wrapped her fingers around my hand. "What if you . . . bit me?"

"Huh?"

"I know that sounds strange, and. . . I don't have much to go on other than it's really our only option to try. If human blood is making it worse, and if it's really Her blood that you want. Her blood is technically in my veins now too."

I shook my head, feeling sick all over again. "Barely, Kim. I'm not biting you."

"And I'm not letting you run off and live in the woods like some feral animal. We have to try every possible solution."

"It's too dangerous."

"Not really. Not anymore. I'm not human, Aaron. Your brothers literally battled in their own blood. I think I can donate to you and be just fine."

I covered my face with my hands. What the hell was happening? There shouldn't have been anything appealing about her proposition, yet her invitation made the hair on my arm stand up. I always wanted her, and now she was offering me her blood. Considering the night we'd met, I'd never let myself think about it for more than a few seconds because it was wrong, but I *did* think about it. Going into her room, crawling my way into her bed, and biting her everywhere she'd let me.

"Will it help?" I asked.

As much as I loved to torture myself, she was right. We had no other options, and I couldn't imagine leaving the car without something to take the edge off the thirst boiling me alive. It was that or running into the woods until the blood lust turned me insane.

Her heart skipped. "I don't know. It's possible it could make it worse, but I don't think so. My blood should be diluted enough. I think it's our best option."

"It can't get worse." My mouth watered as I tuned into the sound of her heartbeat.

She held up her wrist. My unnecessary breathing was already unsteady, and her skin was cool against mine. Everything in me was burning, aching, and ravenous.

She guided her other hand through my hair. "Let's try."

Everything in me shifted like a caged beast hitting the edge of its prison. "I don't want to hurt you . . ."

The yearning knotted in my stomach as I moved a hand over her thigh to pull her closer. Maybe it would make it worse. Her blood was technically connected to the queen's blood. I was in the middle of the most complicated blood system I knew almost nothing about, and nothing was helping. Nothing was okay. My brothers were gone and—

"You can't hurt me. I'm not made of glass anymore."

It all swirled together. Lust. Thirst. Want. Fear.

"What if it's a bad idea and we can't go back?"

"It will be okay. We'll figure it out together."

Her cheeks flushed, and she looked up at me through her lashes. Coy. Anticipating. Her chest heaved like a cornered animal's, and I was overly aware of how it felt to trap her there with me. Nowhere to run. My fingers wrapped around her wrist, and I savored her pulse beneath my fingertips.

"You gotta stop looking at me like that." It was a plea that came from deep within as I used one arm to pull her toward me till she was sitting on top of me. My fingertips dug into her thigh.

There was something so beautiful and right about how warm she was and how it felt to have her body interlocking with mine. I wanted to be closer. So much closer.

"Like what?" She blinked.

I used my finger to trace her jaw. "Like you want me to bite you."

"I-I . . ." I grazed her inner thigh.

"Do you want me to bite you, Burns?"

She let me bring her wrist toward my lips with silent permission, and the world stilled. Her pulse. *God, that sound.*

My fangs slowly descended, and the venom coated my teeth. "Are you sure?"

"Yes."

I savored the moment of surprise in her eyes when I let her wrist fall and threaded my fingers at the base of her neck. In a blink, my lips had found the rushing pulse at her neck, and I sank my teeth into her skin.

The taste of her blood was like ice water on a fire. Her human blood had fanned the inferno of longing of the thing inside my head, but this. *This* was like a cool breeze in the heat of summer. Different than the queen's blood had been. That had only left me wanting. Her blood was poison, and once it was gone, it left the aftereffects of a bad hangover.

I wasn't sure how long I drank. Seconds? Minutes? Long enough for all the muscles in my body to relax. It was better than everything else. It was . . . satiating.

When I pulled away and rested my forehead against hers, I stared into her eyes. A different kind of longing lingered. I needed her under me, clawing at my back, saying my name. There was still something wild breaking through, only now it was directed at her.

"How do you feel?" she asked, breaths uneven.

In one motion, I pulled her under me and spread her knees apart, pinning her beneath me until her hips dug into mine and the pressure hurt. She let out a soft, breathy cry, and I placed my hand over her heart to soothe her. Her breath deepened as I kissed her neck.

The scent of her skin was intoxicating.

"So good, Burns. You taste so good." My lips lingered at her pulse hammering below her ear.

Her panting. Her skin. Everything. I needed everything. Nipping at her skin, I needed more. More. More. More

"I need more," I demanded as I peeled off her flannel, savoring the catch in her breath. Then her bra came off too.

"Aaron." There wasn't any fear in her voice. Only longing for me as she clutched at my hips, drawing me closer.

She was so beautiful beneath me I couldn't stand it. I bit her shoulder, then her arm. Not enough to break the skin, but I wanted to sink into her in every way possible and never let go. I couldn't stop touching her. There were no thoughts left in my head. Presley would be down any minute, but I just didn't care.

She deserved way more than our first time to be in the back of a dirty, cold—not to mention stolen—car, but the unquenchable need to give her more of me was consuming, and every stuttering breath and whimper started a frenzy I wasn't sure I could stop.

Licking her neck was a mistake. I bit her, and she gasped as I sank into her again. Her fingers tightened in my hair. Every beat of her heart sent fresh flowing blood into my mouth. It was *so* good.

A crack sounded, and the window buckled under my hand. It brought me back into my own head, and panic rushed through me in one heated flush.

"It's okay." She held my face, stilling me. "You're safe. I'm safe."

"Are you okay?" Her blood was still fresh on my fingers as I surveyed her neck, but it was already closing.

She smiled with a blush on her cheeks. "More than okay. I'll be even better if it actually worked. Do you feel better?"

"Yeah, I think so . . ."

I did feel better. The racing thoughts had stopped, and all I felt was her under me. Warm and perfect.

"I'm messing this up, aren't I?"

"No, not at all. We're just navigating this a day at a time."

"I hate not feeling like myself."

Now that I wasn't thinking of blood, I was thinking of everything else. My brothers were gone, and I didn't know how to find them. I was wasting so much time. My little brother was annoyed with me, and I didn't know how to make it better. And . . . I'd bitten Kimberly.

"You look like you." She ran her hands through my hair.

And Kimberly was freshly changed and doing everything on her own because I had been too busy walking around in the woods.

"This should be about you, and as usual, I'm making everything about me. Taking up everyone's time . . ."

I just wanted to have normal vampire problems. Why did it have to be so hard for me?

"You can always take up my time."

I smiled and went to pull her in for a kiss when I spotted my brother coming through the parking lot.

"Oh, shit. He's coming."

We made a mad dash to get Kimberly dressed, then crawled into the front seat.

The back door opened, then closed.

"Kim, your hair . . ."

She sucked in a breath, smoothing down the frizzy and out-of-place pieces.

"It looks so badass. Why didn't you tell me you were going to dye it? I would have done mine too."

She sighed. "I'm glad you like it. I'm not sure how I feel about it yet."

"Don't worry. It will grow on you. Style it a little and . . ."

There was brief silence.

"Uh, Kim, I think this is yours." He held her bra up by the straps. "I specifically got another hotel so you guys could have alone time. Do you guys need me to go take a lap?" Presley was joking again, and even if it was annoying, I was happy to hear it.

"No." I smiled, putting the car in drive. "Do you have everything you need?"

They both nodded.

"Hey, why is there a crack in my window? Never mind, I don't want to know."

Six

KIMBERLY

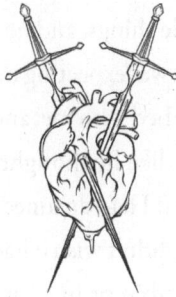

We drove all day. The winters there were nothing like I was used to. There were no tall trees bathing the warm woods in darkness, and the only time I'd seen that much snow was during a rare blizzard when I was thirteen. Blackheart was far away from me.

I sat in the passenger seat with my sunglasses on and let the dull roar of the tires fill the silence. During the day, the light reflecting off the snow was too much. Like the music from the radio was splitting. It was slowly getting better. It was as if all the nerves in my body were firing on full blast. The first few days after the fire were the worst. My head pounded. My eyes hurt. My teeth hurt. My skin. And the sound . . . I couldn't get away from the sound. It made it impossible to think at a time when I really needed to use my brain to its fullest extent. The transition was technically done, but it was taking a lot of getting used to.

Oddly enough, I didn't miss sleep. Since that night in the church with Kilian, I had nightmares that kept me up at night. I thought there would be things I missed, and there were, just not as much as I'd thought. No matter which way I looked at it, being immortal was always better. With it came the safety and assurance I never had before. I'd always wanted certainty in my life, and this came close to reaching it, and it would have if it hadn't been for our vampire cult issue.

It helped having someone who missed everything. Aaron gave me permission to grieve the little things, and he held my hand when it came to the bigger ones. I think he was expecting me to be more upset. The first night I didn't sleep, he lay in bed with me, and we awaited the sunrise. He watched me with such care, like he thought I might break, but I didn't miss dreaming. I was certain if I had dreamed, I would've dreamed of fire.

I'd be lying if sometimes I didn't wish it had been as Luke planned—all of us together hidden in a cabin or in a car—but it felt selfish to want that. Because I'd have never taken the burden of any responsibility from Luke. The twins would still be shouldering it all on their own. I wouldn't have had to be as concerned with every little detail and step we took. The three of us would be free to do something that wasn't so stressful.

I was understanding how unfair that was. The burden they shared while Aaron, Presley, and I ran around Blackheart dancing, going to school . . . falling in love. It had only been around two weeks since they were taken, and I was ready to throw in the towel. Or at least take a long hot bath.

The Calem brothers had become my responsibility. I was choosing for them to be, like they'd chosen me. It was no longer just Kimberly Burns. I had people who cared about me and people I cared about. People I'd risk everything for. And that was a dangerous place to be.

Luke had prepared an icy paradise for us to hide in safety. One with blankets of freshly fallen snow that went on for miles. Frozen branches and buds encased in ice that would never bloom. This place seemed as though it would never thaw. Our paradise didn't hold peace, only a gnawing emptiness at their absence. Presley and Aaron held an unspoken fear in their eyes. Their compass was gone, and it had thrown everything off its axis. I felt how deep the loss was for Aaron and Presley in every one of their interactions. It was apparent with every conversation ending in a heated debate, no matter the subject: a car, where we should stay, how long everything would take.

They were hurting. We all were.

"We should probably stop here if you need to feed again, Aaron. According to this map, it's the last town around for miles," Presley said.

A few buildings passed in my peripheral, and faint music from his MP3 drifted from the back seat. I had to teach Presley how to use the paper map. He insisted on taking over navigation because it gave him something to do.

"I'm okay, actually. I feel good." Aaron smiled at me. His light was back. When he was thirsty, he was fidgety and quiet, and Aaron Calem was anything but quiet. He'd chatted the entire drive, and I'd been able to let my mind rest while he filled the silence with every thought that popped into his head. I loved it.

"You're not just trying to be agreeable and then go fly off the handle and kill a bunch of people by accident, are you?"

"No." Aaron sighed.

I'd been bitten by Aaron before, but each time had been so chaotic and painful I hadn't thought of them as much else. As I grazed over the already healed skin on my neck, my heart beat faster. Something about it made me replay it in my head over and over again. His hands pulled the hair at the nape of my neck tighter to gain better access to my pulse. His heartbeat blended into mine as I fulfilled a deep need for him. We were closer than we'd ever been before, and I wondered if he felt it too.

———— ✦ ————

Our drive dragged into the night. As we got farther from the main highway, streetlights revealed a sleeping town. Dim lamplights shone over a few shops strung together. It was smaller than the college town of Blackheart. We kept driving till we pulled onto a barely drivable road.

My heartbeat surged against my ribs as a little cabin appeared in the twilight.

Presley leaned between our headrests, and we took in the scene together.

"This is the place?"

"Yeah, the coordinates lead here," Aaron said.

"A cabin in the woods? Creepy."

It wasn't just one cabin; there were many hidden in the trees. Some with lights still on, but most of them dark. We were surrounded by wilderness and snow.

"It doesn't say what house?"

"Uh, no. It's not a full address, Pres," Aaron said.

"What are we supposed to do?"

"I don't know."

"You're supposed to know."

"I thought you said you didn't want me to try to act like Luke."

"Yeah, but it would be nice if you knew what the heck was going on."

"Boys. Let's sit here for a minute."

"What happens if we sit?" Presley said.

I leaned back. "Sometimes that's all we need. A little silence."

Presley sighed and we waited. When I said wait, I'd meant wait until we saw a light or some indication of where we were. It wasn't five minutes before the porch light in the cabin in front of us flickered on.

"Probably shouldn't have kept the headlights on," Aaron said as he twisted the key, and the engine turned off.

The cabin door opened, and a woman emerged. Short. Salt-and-pepper hair.

"Oh my god," Presley said with his mouth agape. "It's Mom."

I looked at Aaron as Presley bolted out the door. A weird sense of fear fell over me. I hadn't expected it. A large logical error on my part. It made perfect sense Luke would send us there. Back to the beginning. He was the only one who knew her location. He'd memorized it for this moment.

My mind swirled with the need to please someone I'd never met. How could I let her know how much her sons truly meant to me? What if she hated me? Did it matter if she did?

Before I could suck in a breath, Aaron grabbed my hand and squeezed. Presley ran into his mom's arms, collapsing and smiling. They were crying, laughing, and falling into the snow. I was happy. So very happy. But scared. Why was I scared?

Aaron was still looking at me. "It will be okay. Come on."

He opened the door for me, and we stepped into the snow-covered driveway. Deep bitter cold hit me first. It was only a minute before Presley and their mom came up to Aaron and me. My heart thumped in my ears. Up close I noticed her brown eyes were wet with tears and surrounded by crow's feet.

"Hi, Mom." Aaron gave her a weak smile.

"Oh, baby." She grabbed Aaron and hugged him tight around the neck. Tears continued to fall at their reunion. "I knew you'd come if I was just patient. I missed you so much."

You're fine, Kimberly. This is good. She won't hate you.

"Mom, this is Kimberly. My girlfriend." Aaron smiled at me. He didn't seem worried at all.

"Hello, it's nice to meet you." That's all that came out. My lips were already frozen.

She smiled with tears in her eyes.

"Oh, my wonderful girl. Come here." She wrapped me in a tight hug like the ones Luke used to embrace me with. "Call me Vera."

The hug lasted longer than I anticipated, easing tension in my shoulders.

She turned to Aaron. "Your brothers?"

Her voice broke on the words, and her eyes widened in hopeful excitement.

"They couldn't make it . . . but they wanted to. We can tell you about it."

Aaron looked at Presley, who now had his arm wrapped around Vera's.

"Come on. You must all be freezing! Let's go inside the main house."

"Mom, I missed you so much." Presley skipped around her. "This is where you've lived this whole time?"

"Oh, I missed you, sweet boy. And yes, I've been right here since I got the call."

The call. Neither of us asked what that was. We were all still in shock. Aaron followed close to me while Presley walked alongside Vera. The night was still. Quiet. No bugs. And the sky shined like a beautiful marble of blue and black with thousands of stars.

"You must be starving," she said as she led us through a cabin door. Though it was the middle of the night, the fire roared and candles were lit all around the room. It wasn't a large cabin, but it was big enough to fit an armchair and a couch on what appeared to be a thick wool rug

42

covering the hardwood. It barely fit a dining table with four chairs that blocked a walkway. On the other end of the room was a kitchen, with the top of the cabinets filled with little figurines. It was cozy.

"Uh . . ." Presley said, "we just ate."

"I don't know how. There's nothing around for miles."

"Junk food. We packed it." Aaron caught Presley's eye line.

"That's not a proper meal, and you know it."

"Mom, it's late. Shouldn't you be asleep?" Aaron said.

"Oh. I couldn't sleep. Now I know why. I was just sitting there reading when I saw headlights blasting through my window."

"Sorry," Aaron said. He rubbed my back after helping me take off my coat. Even with just a few minutes in the cold I felt it everywhere.

"I'll put a stew on."

"Mom."

"No arguing."

Aaron and Presley shared a look.

"Soup it is." Presley winked at me.

Seven

AARON

"Don't say anything," Presley said as he pulled plates from the cabinet. We offered to set the table while Mom heated the soup.

"How? She's going to want to see us eat," I whispered, and scrunched in next to him in the tightness of the kitchen. Mom wasn't paying attention. Instead, she whisked her way around the kitchen to pick up things off the counter and ready the food. I'd already told her Kimberly wouldn't care about the mess.

"I don't know. We'll improvise. Just don't tell her yet. Let me enjoy this for a minute."

I sighed, catching a glimpse of Kimberly as she emerged from the bathroom. She'd taken her hair down and combed through it. The hairs on my arm stood up. I couldn't let myself think about her too much, otherwise it was all I would think about. Our previous encounter. Getting her alone. Taking off her clothes. Biting her neck—

44

"Is everything okay?"

"Uh. Don't say anything. Presley wants to keep the vampire thing under wraps."

"How?"

"I really don't know."

She nodded like she understood the assignment anyway, and I guided her to the dining area. Mom set a big simmering pot of soup in the middle of the table. It was old and worn and had cracked light-blue paint on the side with intricate, faded designs that reminded me a lot of *Alice and Wonderland*. Mom's whole cabin was accented in blue. The cabinet knobs, the couch, her shelf that held her trinkets she loved to collect. I eyed a set of cherubs sitting on a shelf above the fireplace.

"One of my neighbors brought the table over. Her older daughter painted it before she left for college." She turned to Presley. "Maybe when she comes to visit, you could meet her. You might get along."

I hadn't fully processed her presence yet. My old world blended into the new, and I'd often wondered if they'd ever realign. None of it felt real. Why did it feel like it had been so long? It wasn't quite a year yet, but everything was different. She looked the same yet different. Her hair was grayer, her dark circles were still there, but now she looked . . . relaxed. I didn't know if I'd ever seen my mother relaxed a day in my life. Maybe once or twice. She was always in a rush. Trying to get to work or trying to get us somewhere on time. We were never on time.

Here, she moved slowly, adding things to the table. Cornbread, butter, linen napkins, and mismatched porcelain china. I wanted to stop her from doing the work, but I couldn't take my eyes off her. I'd wondered if I'd ever see her again, and when we decided to run away from The Legion, I imagined it would be a lot longer, if ever.

Sitting next to Kimberly, I squeezed her knee under the table. This was all new for her, and regardless of what was going on with me, I would make sure she knew she wasn't alone. I saw the wheels turning in her head as she tried to figure out how to act. She was probably worried Mom wouldn't like her, but Mom liked everyone. She'd treated Ashley and Sarah like her own daughters. Plus, it was impossible not to fall in love with Kimberly, and thanks to her, I was able to enjoy sitting with my mom without wondering if I would snap and kill her. Things were looking up.

"Dig in." My mom smiled, and the wrinkles next to her eyes bunched. I'd never noticed them before.

We all hesitated until Presley took the lead, filling his bowl with soup and gathering a large stack of cornbread. The smell filled the space, and my heart ached from the nostalgia of Mom's cooking. Suddenly, I was five again, waiting anxiously while Mom cooked dinner. I think she enjoyed it; she just didn't always have the time. I wished I could eat it.

I'd seen Akira eat popcorn. There had to be a trick to it. Maybe it was small bites. I grabbed a piece of butter for my cornbread and motioned to Kimberly. Maybe she could kill time by pretending to butter her bread.

"I'm so happy to have my table full again." She laid her arm on the table, looking at us longingly. Her eyes flickered to the front door behind me.

"Have you been lonely?" I asked.

"Oh no, there's quite a community here. Lots of retired women. Families. I have the best neighbors. We share food and stories."

"We were in this place called Blackheart. It's where Kimberly grew up. It was on a mountain and had these huge trees with massive trunks," Presley said.

"Oh, is that how you all met?"

Kimberly nodded. "Yeah, we met at college. It's a university town in California."

Mom's forehead dented. "You were all going to college together?"

We all shared a look, wondering what to say. She'd probably imagined something much worse. All of us lost. Scared. Hungry. Unbeknownst to her, we were all drunk in a frat house in California.

"What did Luke tell you?" It felt weird saying his name, knowing he wasn't here. I didn't know where he was, and that wasn't a feeling I'd ever really had before. He was always close enough to visit, but they could be anywhere.

Mom picked up her mug of tea and sipped it. The smell of lavender permeated the air, mixing with the roast. "I got an urgent call from Luke while I was at work in the ER. He couldn't wait. He simply said, 'You asked me to tell you when I needed something. Right now, I need you to go home and pack a bag. We'll meet you.' I didn't ask any questions. I was saving them to ask later, but when I got home your brothers were waiting with a car and a driver who was instructed to take me as far as he could across the country. I asked about you. I asked about them. Luke just said, 'Trust me. We'll keep them safe.' I didn't go easily, but your brothers begged. They said I'd put you all in danger if I stayed and that it was safer for all of you if I didn't follow."

She paused and stared into the woodgrain of the table. "I've spent all this time thinking and wishing I'd done something different. Maybe I should have asked more questions. I thought about how many times I should have stood my ground and stayed. But I knew that look in your brother's eyes, and I trusted him. The day I'd always believed would come had finally come. Something your brothers had been running away from had finally caught up with them, and they were scared."

Mom sniffled and wiped at the redness of her nose. There was a strange pause. A lingering emptiness in the air. Something we all knew but wouldn't say. The Family had poisoned everything. And somehow, even in the glow of the cabin, the cold crept in.

"Honey, the soup will get cold if you don't eat." Mom rubbed Presley's back.

"Oh, right," he said.

I gathered the tiniest bit of broth I could onto my spoon. The soup wasn't steaming anymore, but I blew on it anyway. When the spoon touched my lips, my whole body reacted. Drawing in on itself. The sample was so small I couldn't even get a read on the taste, but the moment I tried to swallow, I gagged. I changed my mind. There was no trick. Maybe Akira's senses had dulled, because my body rejected it like it was rancid.

Presley, who had taken a much larger bite, coughed it up on the table, and Kim held her hand over her mouth, trying to force it down.

"What is it? The meat is fresh. A neighbor just brought it over."

"No." I coughed. "It's not your food."

"Are you sick?"

Presley and I shared a look. "Kinda."

Mom waited, glancing between the three of us.

I shrugged at Presley, not knowing what to say. I didn't know how we could keep it a secret. Or was it even necessary. It's not like my mom would try to turn us into the police or anything. Plus, she deserved an explanation.

Presley smiled sheepishly and turned to her. "Uh, do you remember that movie I always used to make you watch . . . with the girl . . . and the love triangle, and the guy with the hair who could do cool stuff?"

"Of course I remember that. You dragged me to all five of those movies."

"Well, we're kinda like that." Presley looked at me for help, and I shook my head.

"You're a . . . wolf?"

"No, we're like the other thing. The other guy. The sparkly one with good hair."

48

"We don't sparkle," I said. "And we're not cold or anything."

"Are you telling me you're . . . vampires?"

We nodded.

"All three of you?"

We nodded again.

There was a long silence as we waited for her to process.

Kimberly squeezed my leg, and I squeezed back. She'd been able to believe it once. Mom could too.

My mom had gone pale and fiddled with her coffee cup. "You're not playing a prank on me, are you?"

I'd never seen Mom blow up. She was always calm, probably a learned behavior from work, so her silent processing didn't scare me.

"No, Mom. This is real. We could show you . . . if it helps."

"Show me how?"

I motioned to Presley.

"Do you want some honey for your tea?" Presley said.

"What does that have to—"

Presley shot across the room to bring the floral ceramic bear holding a dipper stick. In less than a second, he was back at the table.

Mom's hand shot over her mouth, and she gasped in a ragged breath.

"We're okay. I know it seems scary, but we're actually better than before because . . ." Presley motioned for me.

"Because we're immortal, technically. And we can't get sick, and we don't get hurt easily, so if that's what you're afraid of, then don't worry. We're okay, Mom."

Her eyes were wide as the silence settled between us.

"I was just changed . . . and I can confirm. It's better than being human. Safer," Kimberly said.

"This has something to do with your brothers, doesn't it?" There was sadness in my mother's eyes when she looked at me. "This is the secret."

49

"Yeah. It's a long story. But we don't sleep, so we can tell you if you're not too tired."

"Let me make some coffee." She placed both hands on the table to keep her steady as she stood up.

But Presley shot up after her. "Let me help."

I wondered what my mom thought of me. Would she look at me the same? Was I the same person she knew? She had to know I was scared, because she squeezed my shoulder on her way to the coffee pot.

———— ✦ ————

We told her everything from start to finish. The journey to Blackheart when our brothers changed us, joining the frat, meeting Kimberly, then meeting The Legion. She nodded through most of it but cried when we told her about Sarah. I knew it would be hard to say it out loud, but telling her made it finally feel real.

These two separate parts of my life had collided, and we were left in the wreckage. Nothing was familiar anymore without my brothers. Every minute was new territory for all of us. There was no more Brooklyn and no more Blackheart.

We moved to the living room so Presley could pull Mom close to him and hand her tissues. The fire cracked in front of us as a few logs tumbled and fell into the ash.

"You believe us?" I asked.

"I always knew there was something. And as far-fetched as it is, somehow, your brothers joining a vampire cult makes sense. As much sense as it can for tonight. And Sarah . . . ugh, my sweet girl. Luke must have been devastated, and he never told me." She wiped another tear.

50

"He couldn't, Mom. He didn't know immediately. I think they were scared," I said.

I was scared too. I'd seen firsthand what The Family was capable of. Every day, I replayed that day in the burning forest again. I didn't want to think of what would have happened if we'd all been captured. I also didn't have it in me to imagine where my brothers were. My chest ached again, so I leaned into Kimberly for comfort, and she grabbed my hand.

"I can't believe I let this happen." Mom's voice broke.

"You didn't do this," I said. If anyone should feel guilty, it should be me. If I'd made different decisions, maybe they wouldn't have felt like they had to do everything alone. My whole life I'd let them shoulder all the responsibility.

"Luke didn't say anything to you? About what we do now?" I asked.

I still had hope there was more to this story. That somehow my brother had prepared for our inevitable separation too. Maybe he had a secret way to contact him or a way we could find each other again.

"Luke left you a note. I have it here." She pulled a tattered letter from her cardigan and handed it to me. The envelope was inked with Luke's handwriting—*Aaron*.

"A note?" I swallowed. The familiar ache tore at my insides, which leaped with hopeful anticipation.

"Just for Aaron?" Presley said next to her.

Kimberly squeezed my leg, and I carefully grabbed the letter, overly aware of how worn the paper was.

Aaron,

If you're reading this, that means we succeeded. You're finally safe and reunited with Mom. Sorry in advance about the cold. But I needed it to be somewhere secluded. Plus, I know Mom really likes the snow. This was the best I could do on short notice. Things didn't exactly work out the way I wanted them to. I wish we could all be together. I want you to know that.

I have a lot to apologize for. I'm sure you'll be mad at me. But try to remember the good times we did have. Try to remember the people we were. No one can take that away from us.

Take care of them. I know you will.

Love,

Luke

I let the letter fall to the ground, and Presley snatched it.

My heartbeat was in my ears.

"Aaron?" Kimberly called, but the room was fading around me. "What does it say?"

That was his plan all along. To disappear and go back to The Family and . . . stay there? He didn't plan on ever coming back. He didn't want us to follow. There was no map, or coordinates or cellphone number. My brothers were out there, and we had no way to find them. It finally hit me.

I may never see either of them again.

No one would hand me a grand plan of how to fix it. We were on our own in the middle of nowhere.

"They want us to stay here. This is it. That's all it really says."

It all fell into place. What should have been obvious but I'd never fully realized. The reason Luke constantly asked about our five-year plan. He never had one. Neither of them did. The Family was their plan. Their fate. Their future.

"I opened it after the first three days of waiting," Mom said, "and I cried all night. Your brothers didn't think they were ever going to outrun what was chasing them. Now I know why."

I shot to my feet, feeling hot all over. That couldn't be it. There had to be more.

"Aaron?"

"He didn't give you anything else?" I snatched the envelope to make sure it was empty.

"No. Just this letter and some money."

My chest burned. The room was spinning. It couldn't be it. Why didn't he give me anything else? How could that be it? It was nothing.

"Are you okay, honey?"

All of them stared at me with wide-eyed worry. My whole body was flushed with emotion I couldn't place.

"Can I have a second alone on the porch?"

"Of course, honey."

Without grabbing a coat, I went out the door into the freezing night.

Eight

AARON

Being alone never helped anything, neither did punching trees. I'd trudged straight through the snow that reached my calves, and hit the largest one I could find till some of the emotion rocking through me ran its course and my clothes were soaked from the avalanche of snow that had fallen from the tree.

I'd moved to the porch where snowflakes fell in a light frost covering the deck. The cold air was harsh on my skin, and I stared out into the vast wilderness.

They weren't coming back. My brothers were gone. I'd thought for sure they'd give me another clue. A way to find them. *Something*. But that was a child's way of thinking. I was still expecting them to come and save me but scoffed at the absurdity of it. I wanted them to save me so I could save them.

Burying my head in my hands, a gnawing emptiness hollowed my chest. When I thought of them, it got worse. I wasn't sure I'd ever been so angry before, and I'd directed plenty of anger at my brothers in Blackheart. I replayed it all in my mind. That night at the carnival or any time I'd blamed them for everything that was wrong with my life. They let me paint them as the bad guy and yell and scream.

I thought I'd been angry then, but none of that compared to the anger I felt toward myself. I'd been so naive, letting them believe in a world where they couldn't be saved, and this was the consequence. I'd let them shoulder everything, and I didn't realize I'd done it the entire time. Since I was a kid, I'd let them do it and didn't think twice about how it felt to be responsible for everything.

I thought over our last moments together in Blackheart. Before The Family showed up and ruined everything that day in the forest. They wanted to stay together. We were all going to be together, and they wanted it too, then they had to watch as it all got stripped away from them.

It had taken me so long to see it, and it was two weeks too late. They'd given me everything I could ever want. Safety. A house. Mom, Presley, and Kimberly. But it cost them everything. They were okay with that, but I wasn't. They watched me build a life while everything they wanted got taken away from them.

I needed a plan, but I didn't make plans. The only times I'd ever made the plans had resulted in almost killing someone. So how was I supposed to do this? How was I supposed to find them? Where did I start and how could I make the time go faster so I could see them sooner? If only there was a way for them to know I was looking for them and I wouldn't stop until I found them.

Mom appeared bundled in a blanket and holding another for me.

"You don't have to worry about hypothermia with us, Mom."

"I just want you to be comfortable. You're not used to this kind of cold."

I took the blanket, knowing it would do little to help my wet clothes. The fleece engulfed me, and the smell of vanilla helped ease the tension in my shoulders.

Mom sat beside me, watching the stars overhead before she spoke. "You look so grown."

"I look the same."

She shook her head. "No you don't. You look . . . like you aged five years. I can tell something is different."

"A lot has happened." I didn't want to look at her. A strange invisible wall blocked me from her. Was it time? Was it me?

"I know. I'm sorry I wasn't there."

I stared into the blank nothingness of the snow. The porch light illuminated the fresh powder in front of the cabin as it fell on the hood of our car. The snow was like a blanket that muffled every sound. There were no cars or critters close by. Outside was a void. If I disappeared into the night, I wondered if I'd be swallowed by the emptiness of it all.

"It's okay if you're upset about the letter."

Upset didn't cover it. Devastated didn't hit the right note either.

"I'm not just upset. I'm angry. They deserved better."

"You're right. They do."

"I don't know how to find them. I don't even know where to start."

"There's time to figure it out."

"No there's not! Who knows what's happening to them right now? Luke always had a plan, and I have nothing. I'm not like him."

"I don't think you have to be, baby."

I stood up. "Well, I can't be me. All I've done this entire time is mess things up. I don't know how to form a plan. I can't even protect anyone like this. I'm literally useless. I have to go. I have to save them."

"Just let it sit for tonight. Don't rush things."

"Mom."

"I know. I know." Her voice quaked. "But I just got you back. Can I enjoy it for a second? Will you sit with me for a minute?"

A tear fell from her eyes, and I darted to her, burying her in a hug. I held her close to me and let in everything I'd been trying to hide from. Her warmth and her scent. How it felt to see her almost a year later . . . aged. Different. And I hadn't been there.

"Of course you can. I'm here. I'm sorry you had to wait all alone."

She wiped her eyes. "Don't worry a second about me. I was just so worried about all of you, and I wondered if I'd ever see any of you again. And I wasn't sure if I could live with myself if I didn't."

When Mom hugged me, she wrapped her arms around my head to smother me. Thankfully, I didn't need to breathe.

"I'm sorry, Mom."

"Oh, honey. None of this is your fault. It's mine. I should have done more. I should have—"

"Stop. They wouldn't have wanted you to blame yourself."

As soon as I said the words, I let go of her. Neither of them would have wanted any of us to take the blame. They did it all out of love. Though there were things we could've all done differently, it didn't change the facts. My brothers had been manipulated since they were kids to believe this was their only fate. There was someone responsible for this.

"I'm going to find them and the people who did this. I'm going to end it."

"End it how?"

"I don't know. But I'm going to free them once and for all. And they're going to get to live wherever they want and do whatever they want. They won't have to answer to anyone anymore."

I cringed at my own naivety. I didn't even know what all that statement entailed, but I meant it with every cell in my body.

Mom sniffled and let out a long breath. "I had a feeling you'd say something like that. There was no stopping your brothers and no stopping you. Your grandma had that same type of bravery . . . She'd be so proud."

My grandmother was my mom's favorite person in the world. I didn't remember her, but Mom spent my entire childhood making sure I knew all about her.

"You're brave too, Mom."

She shook her head. "No. Not like all of you. And as much as I want to tell you to stay here and not dare think of leaving my sight again . . . I can't find your brothers on my own. Even if I could, I'm a woman in her fifties, and this is way above what I'm able to control. But I want them home too."

She moved a piece of hair from my forehead. "And I think you're more than capable of doing what you set your mind to. Gosh, you're reminding me so much of your brother. He's so proud of you. I know he is."

You're ready.

Luke's last words to me. Ready for what?

I wasn't a leader, but I had people who needed me now. My little brother, Kimberly, and Mom were all relying on me to be stronger than I'd ever been. To push through. To make plans and to protect them. To save my family.

"I've got people counting on me. I'll make it work."

She smiled. "Like that beautiful girl in there?"

"She's special, Mom. She's . . . everything."

"I know. I can tell with the way you look at her. And I know she's got a good man to care for her." She pulled me into her, and I laid my head on her lap. All my tension left. Even the ache in my chest was kept at bay in the warmth of my mother's arms.

58

"I was afraid I'd never see you again," I said.

"I knew you'd come. I trusted and prayed."

It still didn't feel real, and I couldn't fully enjoy any of it without Zach and Luke.

"This wasn't supposed to happen. They're supposed to be here too."

"I've felt so helpless here. But now that you're all here, I feel hope again. I don't think it's a coincidence. Sometimes it's dark for a while, but there's always light somewhere. This place has long, dark winters, but it also has the most beautiful stars and the brightest summers. You'll see."

Luke wanted me to let them go. That's, no doubt, why he brought us to the one place we wouldn't be found. The moon was the only light tonight. I ignored the stars and wondered where my brothers were and if they were looking up at that same sky. What horrors would await them with The Family?

Zach and Luke were always my heroes, and as I watched the snow fall, I realized my current reality was their dream. All of us were together and safe. It wasn't their only dream.

We're leaving together. That was the true dream.

Something turned in my stomach, then I knew there was no going back. The seed had been planted in my mind and, in seconds, taken root. It had a force of its own that sang through my blood till I felt weightless. I lifted my head as the snow fell on my lashes.

Even at the conception of the idea, I knew it might be the end of me. I would save my brothers, and nothing would stop me.

Nine

PRESLEY

The door clicked shut as I showed Kimberly some of Mom's figurines. She collected the coolest stuff, and even though she had brought none of her old ones with her, she had the same ceramic collections. Cherubs. Check. The birds—who likes birds? Check. Unusual tiny houses. Check. And one of her newer ones. Butterflies.

She'd started collecting them after Sarah went missing. I'd heard her pray over them a couple times.

"Oh. As you can see, not much changes. I just got that one this week actually." Mom motioned to the tiny ceramic butterfly in my hand.

"It's beautiful," Kimberly said.

"It was Sarah's thing. She wears—wore these butterfly necklaces all the time. I got her this butterfly pillowcase once, and it made Luke so jealous he hadn't thought of it first."

As soon as the words left my mouth, that weight in my chest sucker punched me. I swear Aaron winced.

"I wish I could have met her." Kimberly smiled halfheartedly.

"She was lovely," Mom added.

"You would have gotten along," I said.

That icky kind of silence followed, and I knew who would be the one to break it.

Aaron shifted on his feet. "Uh, Mom. You have to be tired. It's so late."

"Oh . . . do you not sleep at all?"

"We do if we need to heal. Like if we lost a lot of blood from a fight or something."

"Right," Mom said, rubbing at the edge of her eye. "Well, I think that's quite enough information for me to handle for the night. I have a spare bedroom down the hall next to mine."

"Dibs," I said.

It made her crack a smile. I missed that.

"We have some dry cabins here in the village you and Kimberly can stay in. I'll talk to the property manager in the morning to work out payment." She moved to a small chest next to the couch and pulled out a pile of fleece sheets and blankets for my brother. "It will be cold tonight, but there should be fresh firewood and a heater in there. No running water though, so you'll have to shower here. It's outside to the left. The porch light should be on."

"No problem. Thank you," Kimberly said.

Mom moved to give them a hug, then wrapped her arm around my shoulder and gave me a kiss on the cheek. The air from the wall heater was hot on my face, and I finally felt thawed for the first time in days. It was heaven compared to the car.

"This is the best day I've had in a long time."

"Us too," I added.

"You'll be good?" Aaron asked, with his hand on the door and his brow lowered.

I rolled my eyes and flipped him off. Lovingly, though. He knew the difference.

The corner of his mouth tugged into a smile. "You know where to find me if you need me."

What could I possibly get in trouble doing in the middle of the night?

———— ✦ ————

I stepped into my empty room. It had a dingy wooden floor and a little bear night-light on the other side of the bed. The room wasn't very big, but big enough to have its own wooden heater in the corner and a twin-size bed on the other wall. I sat my plastic bag full of everything I owned next to me on the bed.

It was quiet. There wasn't anything to look at on the walls except little swirls of wood grain. The only sound was the crackling fire beside me. There weren't any bugs chirping outside or loud parties. Not even any traffic. It was chilly even with the heater. Mom told me it would take some time for it to warm up.

I rubbed my chest. It was just me and the cold and the ache. *Great. Good. This isn't terrible at all.*

It was all fine and not at all a complete and utter disaster.

I stared at the empty space next to me and ran my hand over the chilled quilt. One spot reserved for someone else. Only, he wasn't here. I remembered the last time I'd felt like that—in an empty room at one of the random safe houses before we'd arrived in Blackheart.

I'd locked myself in a spare room. Luke was the first person to notice I was gone. The one who always came looking for me.

"Can I come in?" He'd knocked softly on the door despite the brute he was.

"Sure, if you want to get under the covers and sulk with me."

He opened the door and took the spot next to me. The bed shifted under his weight, and I fell into his shoulder.

He waited. That was one of the best things about Luke. He'd wait and listen. Zach bolted the second things got awkward, and Aaron often would fill uncomfortable silence with babbling. But Luke was never afraid of quiet.

"I'm really going to miss Brooklyn." I sniffled. Unaware that I even cared that much, then a tear fell. *"Oh, great. We can still cry? What's that about?"*

I leaned into his shoulder. *"What about our quilt? Or all the beanies Mom crocheted me?"*

I cried more, and he wrapped an arm around me.

"It's not just the clothes." Though, I'd spent a long time collecting specific pieces from thrift stores, and I knew I'd never find them again. Which was a tragedy all its own. *"What about my trip to Italy this summer? I saved for forever."*

Hours of shopping and time spent dog-sitting for the money for the trip was all wasted. All of it was gone and left back at the house.

Luke rubbed my shoulder, waiting between my blubbering.

"And my love notes!" I buried my head in my hands. *"I wanted to keep those forever. Julie Goodman wrote me the most beautiful poem about the color of my eyes."*

I'd saved all the notes we'd passed during art class. Along with all my old artwork. I'd thought it was all terrible—Mom had put some of it on the fridge though.

"I know." He squeezed me harder.

"This isn't fair."

"I know. I'm sorry."

"Mom will be okay, though?"

"Yeah, I promise. She's safe."

My tears ended. It was hard to keep crying into Luke's shoulders when he was so damn comforting.

I gasped. *"No! I left Mr. Bear in my closet!"*

I'd had all of five minutes to grab things from my room and had forgotten my most-prized possession. Mr. Bear, my favorite stuffed animal, was too important to leave out on a shelf where someone could come into my room and snatch him. Okay, fine, he was embarrassing, but I wouldn't tell Mr. Bear that and hurt his fluffy feelings. Mr. Bear was special because he was Mom's favorite toy, and of all my brothers, she'd chosen me to keep him.

"Well, Mr. Bear knows you had to go on an adventure."

"What if he misses me?"

Luke smiled. *"No, Mr. Bear has plenty of bear friends to keep him company. He told me. And a little bear family."*

Luke was right. Mr. Bear didn't need me to be happy. He was outgoing and charismatic. He'd have company in imaginary bear world. Luke always knew what to say. I wasn't in front of Zach where I had to pretend to tough it out, I was with Luke. The protector of every secret. Nothing was too embarrassing with him.

"You won't tell anyone I cried over Mr. Bear, will you?"

"Never." He wrapped me in a hug. *"It's okay to be sad. This is my fault."*

"I don't care whose fault it is," I said, with my face smashed up against his chest. *"I have everything I need."*

There was another knock on the door, and Zach poked his head in. *"Are we good?"*

Zach cared too. He was just afraid of intimacy. Closed-off bastard.

Everything I need. The thought snapped me back, and I pulled the quilt up and over my shoulders. Suddenly, the room felt a few degrees colder than it had before. There was no knock on the door this time. It was just me and the silence and a night-light that looked strangely like Mr. Bear. I rummaged through my bag and pulled out a few photos I had left. A lot of Zach flipping off the camera. Luke always smiled in his. I held the one of us at the Halloween party in our costumes. Pictures were cruel in that way. They held a moment that was nice to remember, but you couldn't go back.

I rubbed my chest again where the hole grew bigger and bigger by the minute.

We were finally safe, like they'd wanted, but why did it feel like I was missing something? Something I vitally needed.

My coat still smelled like smoke. I wouldn't wash it, but I might hide it so Mom wouldn't do it by accident. As I hauled it from the bag and straightened it out, something crinkled, and I pulled a piece of paper from the pocket.

The ink was smudged, making the zeros look like sixes.

It was a phone number signed off with *–A.*

The only A-named person I knew now was Aaron, and he didn't do things like leave little notes in my pockets. I guess there was one more . .

Akira. My stomach sank at the reminder.

The note could be from Akira. Killer vampire cult Akira. Akira, *I'm really dead now* Akira. He must have slipped it in my jacket at some point. But why?

Hope fluttered in chest. The sick kind you feel when you're on a rollercoaster and then it bottoms out. Whose phone did the number go to? What if it was Luke's or Zach's phone? Did they have phones?

Probably not, or they would have called.

Second thought, they didn't have my number. *Duh.*

But maybe I had theirs . . .

I picked up my tragic little flip phone, then paused because that could be the worst idea ever. Luke specifically said to be good, but what did that even mean? Be good as in help little old ladies cross the street? Or be good as in listen to everything Aaron said? I needed specifics, dammit. He should have left *me* a note.

What if the person on the other end of the line ended up being my brothers? I gave it one more second before I dialed the number, then paced the room as it rang.

"Hello?" a male voice answered. Not my brother's.

"Is Zach or Luke there?"

"No."

"Oh."

"Is this Presley?"

"Uh."

"He told me you'd call."

"Who? My brothers?"

"No. Akira."

I hung up and threw my phone onto the bed. *Shit.*

My heart raced and I paced again. *Bad. Bad. Bad.* It was fine. They couldn't track my phone that fast or anything. *Right.* Everything was fine. I sat on the edge of my bed and stared at the wall till my heart stopped throbbing in my ears.

It wasn't a big deal. It changed nothing. Akira gave me this number and told some guy I'd call him. No. Not important at all. The phone vibrated on the bed, and I jumped. They could call all they wanted, but I wouldn't answer because I was going to be good like Luke said. That was the correct thing to do . . . right?

Ten

KIMBERLY

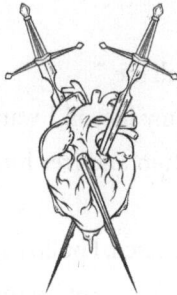

The blanket of snow numbed my senses as we arrived at a little square cabin with a baby blue door. The porch light was dim, but I could make out the 222 on the front post. It was less than a three-minute walk from Vera's cabin.

Cold rushed in as Aaron opened the door. The room was cast in a blue light shining from the kitchen. It was small compared to Vera's, with only a sink, a miniature camping stove, and a mini fridge on one end of the room. However, it was large compared to anything else that had ever been mine. I placed the sheets and blankets on the couch and got to work on the fire. The smell of cedar overwhelmed the modest space.

An eeriness of cold and silence made me eager for a distraction. All the nerves in my body were still firing. I locked the cabin door, like that would help anything. Aaron had disappeared up the stairs to a small loft with a skylight, a floor-length mirror, and a smaller dresser. The only light was a dim table lamp. I flipped on the small space heater built into the wall and sighed in relief when the sound wasn't too shrill.

He'd already made the bed and was admiring the quilt in his hands.

"My brothers used to have this quilt on their bed, and we passed it down when they graduated. It was soft . . . softer than this one." His eyes stayed fixed on the fabric.

He was still in his snow-caked boots and jacket, so I pulled it from his shoulders to hang.

"Come on. Lay down with me."

After the longest day of my life, all I wanted was to feel him close. I hoped it would help thaw him and free him from his mind. Usually, I needed the distraction.

We nestled into bed still dressed. I pulled him to me so hard the threads of his T-shirt ripped. He was so warm. In the midst of all the change, he was still my heater. I wrapped my arms around his torso, and he pulled me in tight, kissing the top of my head. Clinging to him, I interweaved my body with his till we were fully entangled.

My body slackened and my nerves settled.

"I thought the sun would be up by now," Aaron said.

"There are long stretches of night here. The sun will come up late and only stay for a few hours. Remember?" I'd noted it on our journey through Alaska the last few days. He'd probably missed a lot of it with the bloodlust.

"Oh. Right." There was a long silence, and I peeked over at Aaron observing the sky with careful diligence. Something was brewing in his eyes.

"Kim . . ."

"Yeah?"

"I'm going to find them."

"I know."

He shifted to look at me. "No. I'm not going to stop until I find them. Even if it takes the rest of eternity. I'm going to do it."

In the lamplight glow, his irises burned with determination. I'd never seen it so starkly in his demeanor before.

"I believe you."

He squeezed me. "But it's going to be dangerous."

"I know, but everything we do is dangerous."

"Not like this. This is different. It's like I've been cracked over the head with something I should have figured out forever ago. I can finally see it clearly. All the things my brothers went through—the fear and the hopelessness. After everything in the church, I thought I understood it all. I let them continue to take the burden and protect me . . . because they were there and always made me feel safe. But now that they're gone, I know the danger was there all along, and the way I feel now is the way they've felt their entire lives. It's not fair."

"I know."

"Maybe it should have been me and not them."

Even the thought of it made me cringe. I didn't want to imagine not having my arms around him where I knew he was safe.

My fingers clenched. "If they'd have taken you, you'd be with Her right now."

There was no doubting it. He would've never been able to overcome his need for blood. My stomach soured as I imagined a beautiful woman running her hands over his bare chest and leaving kisses over his neck. I wasn't the jealous type, but the thought alone had my heart racing.

"You're right. Maybe this is how it was supposed to be. And now it's my job to save them. They really think no one is coming for them, Kim. And that thought alone makes me want to run and find them even though I have no idea where to start looking."

"We will. We'll find them."

"I don't know if you should."

"You really think I'm letting you do this on your own?"

He pulled his fingers through my hair. "No. I'm just—this is different. This is something I have to do, and I don't know how to do that and protect you."

"You don't need to protect me."

"I do." His eyes glistened. "I need you."

"They're my family too. I made a promise. I know you want to protect me, but . . . some things are more important. You can't save me from everything, and I don't want you to. We're committing to this path together. No matter the cost. That means the mission is more important."

Every day I'd thought of the blood oath I'd made by the fire. I hadn't imagined that bond would be tested so severely, or so soon, but I meant it with every ounce of blood pumping through my veins. The Calem brothers were my family, and I vowed to protect them like they'd protected me.

Without warning, Aaron pressed his lips to mine. It was a flurry of quiet desperation and need. He worked his way up my jaw to my ear, then to my temple, leaving my cheeks flushed and my skin hot.

"Okay. But we have to be good at constructing a plan this time."

"You mean we shouldn't keep secrets and wait till we get captured?"

It had been so long since that day in the church. All of it felt like a lifetime ago, and with everything that had happened, it was. This time last year, I was Kimberly Burns, a normal college girl on her way to graduation. The only thing I was worried about was having too many absent days and turning all my assignments in on time.

"Definitely not. We have to redeem ourselves. No one gets captured."

"Deal."

The cabin was warming, and Aaron buried his head in my hair with a groan. "My chest hurts."

I pushed my hands through his hair. "I think Akira's blood . . . Her blood connected you all."

"Do you think . . . they feel it too?"

"Yeah. I think you're all hurting."

"I guess hurting together is better than being alone."

"You're never alone, Aaron. You never will be." I kissed his forehead. "It's okay to be sad."

"Okay, but in the morning, I'm making a kickass plan."

"At first light, we plan. Now, we can just lay here together and watch the stars."

And we did. We got lost in the darkness of the night and watched the stars through the skylight. After an hour, Aaron finally spoke again.

"Maybe this time, you'll let me be the hero."

I pulled him in tighter. "We'll see."

Eleven

PRESLEY

"I won't go if you don't want me to." My mom put on her lipstick in the bathroom. It was a blast from the past, and the same mauve color she wore every day, even the same brand.

I didn't want her to go to work, and I wanted to tell her.

"I want to stay, honey, I do. But with there being so few staff out here, it's really hard on them to not give notice. They really need me at the ER today." She stopped to look at me. "But if you need me, I'll stay."

Mom was such a good nurse that people actually died when she was away. That's the way I imagined it, anyway.

Aaron appeared in the doorway, getting his nose in my business. "Go, Mom. We'll be here when you get back."

"It's a short shift today. Only six hours."

She wanted to go. Mom loved work. It was something I never understood. No one likes work, but no matter how exhausted she was by the end of the day, she'd come through the door with a smile. Something about helping sick people brought her joy. I didn't get it, but she always said, "*One day you'll find something that brings you as much joy. And you'll understand.*"

Now that was just comical.

"We can't let people suffer because we want to see Mom," Aaron said.

"Debatable. I haven't seen her in almost a year."

"I'll be back by dinner. I promise. Kimberly, if you need anything, I have makeup, clothes, shampoo, conditioner. Everything I have is yours. Go nuts. But boys, stay out of my room."

More nostalgia hit me as Mom neared the door in her scrubs with a packed lunch in hand. Her hair was perfectly slicked back in a bun out of her face. I was certain there wasn't that much gray in her hair last year.

I wanted to talk to her and catch up on everything I'd missed. If there was anything I'd learned, it was that a lot could change in a matter of months. Maybe she had new hobbies or a boyfriend. Or a secret new love of romance novels. Whatever it was, I wanted to hear about it.

"Thank you," Kimberly said right before Mom blew a kiss and scurried out the door.

"So, how was your guys' swanky new cabin?"

"Cold," they said at the same time.

We gathered in the living room by the fire. I'd kept it going through the night while I avoided my bedroom and watched TV till the sun was up.

"Okay. So, Kimberly and I were talking last night, and we agreed we needed a plan. Zach and Luke aren't here, and I'm sure we can all agree it's up to us to find them. The three of us are their last hope."

"Yep." I edged a little closer to the fire. My chest hurt more than it did yesterday. It was so deep I felt it in my back.

I waited for him to get to the point.

"Then the question is, how do we find them?"

I planned on telling them about the phone number in my pocket, I did, but first, I wanted to hear all our options. Aaron would freak out when I told him about the phone call, and I'd silently prepared myself for that during commercial breaks.

"I have an idea that I'm certain neither of you will like," Kimberly said while pulling her hair into a bun—Kimberly Burns with black hair was kick-ass. "We need to find The Legion."

That snapped me out of my daydreams.

"Kim, did you forget about them locking everyone up and kidnapping us?"

"Let her talk," Aaron said.

"No. But I spent all night thinking through every possibility, and I'm certain it's our best option. They've been tracking the coven for centuries. They may even know where their new location is. The Legion knows their histories, their patterns, their strengths . . . weaknesses. We know nothing. Even if by some miracle we find some type of clue to lead us to Zach and Luke, we won't be able to do anything about it because it's just the three of us. We need help."

"We can't trust them. They don't have hearts, Kim. I'm pretty sure Kilian is the tin man," I said.

"You're right. But we need them. And they need us. We're their last bit of connection to the queen. Kilian is closer than he's ever been to bringing them down. Plus, they have Will. And we know that Kilian kept Will safe more than the others. We might be able to strike a deal."

"This is stupid." I stood up.

Aaron growled, "It's not stupid. She's right."

"You don't know that. What happens when they decide to lock us up and do experiments on us? Or they put us in a cage and serve us up as bait?"

I could see it all play out perfectly as they stuffed us in their creeper van.

"This is different than before. Kilian didn't know how important the twins were to The Family." Kimberly's voice was so calm and rational it was giving me a headache.

My blood was boiling over with anxious energy, and I had a lump in my throat that matched the weight in my chest.

"There's got to be a better option than that."

"If you have a better idea, we're all ears," Aaron said.

My phone burned a hole in my pocket and suddenly felt heavier. No. It was a terrible option. We'd trusted The Legion. I'd spent all that time with Thane . . . and we were betrayed, and no matter how much logic they threw at this, it wouldn't change that. We couldn't risk it. I wanted to see my brothers again, but I couldn't do that if they held us hostage, and if Aaron knew about the phone number, he'd never see it as a good option. When things with The Legion failed—and judging by the past, they would—I was holding the only known connection to my brothers, and they'd take it from me like they'd taken and ruined everything else.

"Whatever." I went for the door, suddenly hot all over. My chest thrummed, and I needed to not look at them anymore.

"Where are you going?" Aaron spat.

"Away from both of you. If you want to buddy up to the people that got us into this mess, then fine. But leave me out of it."

"You're not going to help?"

"Nope. You two have fun with your death mission."

I flung the door open, and Aaron jumped to his feet.

"Let him go," Kimberly said as I slammed the door shut.

As soon as I started walking, the anger left. Shit. Why did I just storm out of there like I was freakin' Kylo Ren having a temper tantrum? I didn't get angry. Yet, here I was, standing in the snow. Again.

I kicked a trash can. *Very smart, Presley. Don't help them. Litter instead.*

It's what Zach would do probably.

I picked up my mess and swallowed the guilt for slamming the door. I probably hurt Kimberly's poor ears. Being a jerk to my brother was one thing, but Kimberly didn't deserve it. I'd apologize later to her alone. She was trying her best, even if her best plan was terrible.

Not that I had a better one.

Okay, Aaron didn't deserve it either, but I needed someone to be angry at, and it couldn't be Mom or Kimberly.

I kept walking along the plowed road. The sun was out but did nothing to thaw the snow covering everything. I could have taken the car, but I just wanted to move. I didn't know if it was me or Hell Bitch's blood making me feel like that.

I'd never dramatically stormed out of anywhere in my life. Though in the moment it felt better, every step out into the cold left me feeling sick.

I couldn't remember the last time I'd been sad. Briefly when we'd left Brooklyn, but that was nothing compared to how I felt now. My brothers were gone. It was like they'd died but almost worse because I didn't know what was happening to them, and from what I knew about The Family, it wasn't good. I wanted to sit alone in the snow and mope, but instead, I fished out my phone and stared at the missed call notifications. I didn't call back, but I thought it over for a minute or two.

I finally reached the town after being offered a ride not once but twice. Probably because I was not wearing a jacket and everyone thought I would die. That, and I had to walk directly on the road because the snow berms were so high.

I snatched a coat out of the back seat of someone's unlocked car so I could walk in peace. There were a lot of supply shops before I hit the main part of town with clothing stores and a few restaurants. It was like a cozier Blackheart with little to no people walking around. Only, everything was covered in snow, and instead of being on the mountain, there were a group of them in the distance. If I was in a better mood, I would have said it was beautiful, but I wasn't, so it was ordinary and boring.

A small building with a large dog hand-painted on the window caught my attention. My first guess was a pet store, and I imagined getting lost in the store and holding fuzzy bunnies to make me feel better. Maybe they'd have an aquarium section I could ogle at.

A bell rang as I entered, and the strong scent of wet dog rushed my senses. Dogs barked somewhere in the back, and a large black husky came up to greet me at the door. It wasn't a pet store, that was for sure. It looked more like a hospital lobby that needed upgrades.

"Hi, how can I help you?" A girl with dirty-blonde hair pulled back in a ponytail greeted me.

"What is this place?"

"We're a sled dog rehabilitation center. We also do training and adoption. Are you looking to adopt?"

"No. I'm new in town, visiting my mom, and I was just looking for a place to distract me." *More like hide.*

"Oh, who's your mother? Maybe I know her."

"Her name is Vera . . ." Did she give her last name? I wasn't sure, so I avoided it.

She gasped. "You're one of Vera's sons? She never stops talking about you all. She must be so happy. I'll have to bring you all some cookies later."

"She'd probably like that. I'm Presley, the youngest."

"I'm Sydney, the middle child of three girls." Her eyes sparkled. "Vera said you were travelers."

"Oh. Yeah . . . totally."

She raised her brows like she expected me to say more. "Where did you go?"

My phone vibrated in my pocket, and I jumped. I wriggled it out, and the same number was calling me again. The blood drained from my face, and my heart hammered.

"Are you okay?"

"I-I'm sorry, I'm having an off day." I peeked out the window behind me. *They couldn't find me if I didn't answer my phone.* There was no way someone could be watching me from across the street.

"Well, I could show you the dogs out back? Sometimes that cheers me up."

I plopped it back in my pocket. "Uh, yeah, sure."

I followed her past her desk littered with paperwork and a fresh coffee. We moved out the door into what looked to be a kennel area where a few dogs sat. All kinds but a lot of huskies. I'd begged for a dog as a kid, and Mom never let me have one. She said she preferred cats, but looking back, I think it was more of the money thing.

The kennel hall led to an outdoor area freshly shoveled, with piled snow lining the fence. Ten large dogs ran around chasing each other and scrapping on the ground with their toys.

"They're loving this sunshine," Sydney said with her hands on her hips.

The same huge black dog nuzzled my calf from behind and almost knocked me to the ground. Its long tufts of hair were velvet between my fingers as I scratched its back while its heavy tail beat me.

"What's this one's name?"

"Oh, that's Sarah! She's such a sweetheart. We've had her for almost a whole year."

I sighed and used my fingernails to scratch under her chin. *Of course that's her name.*

She licked my face and barreled into me.

No matter where I was, I couldn't escape my own reality. The buzz of my phone jolted me again—a not-so-gentle reminder that even in our haven we were doomed.

Twelve

KIMBERLY

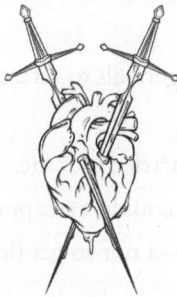

"I should talk to him." Aaron eyed the door Presley left through.

We'd settled on the couch in Vera's cabin, which was covered in various patchwork quilts. The heat from roaring fire radiated through the room.

"Give him space."

"I don't like him talking to you like that." The black crowded Aaron's irises again, so I reached for his hand.

"He can't help it. It's the blood making him . . . different."

"Well, I'm not mean to you."

"No, but more than occasionally, you are in danger of killing innocent people."

He nodded, finally softening. "Right."

"It's hard on you both. The blood confuses you on top of your own grief. Try to give him grace."

"I'm terrible at this." He squeezed my hand. "I'm so thankful you're here."

"You just started. Give it some time." Aaron kissed my cheek, then my neck. I forfeited a breath. Something tightened in my stomach, and I fought to refocus at the sudden warmth in my belly. "Don't thank me yet. We need to figure out how to find The Legion, and I don't have any ideas yet."

Aaron looked down for a moment while tracing over my knuckles with his fingers. His eyes lit up a few seconds later. "We do know how they found us last time. You went to the hospital."

"For an animal bite."

"Exactly. They had to be looking for specific things in police reports. Kilian must have connections to get that kind of information. You know, my mom works at the hospital . . . maybe we could stage something that would get their attention." Aaron glowed with enthusiasm at his new idea.

"Okay, so they find us, and then what? We have to make sure we're prepared. Give ourselves an out, in case . . . they aren't friendly." I didn't blame Presley for not believing in the plan. There was a good chance it could be a disaster, but it wasn't just the best option because of resources, it was the fastest one. Every day the twins spent in that place, worried me more. I'd been there for Luke's panic attacks, and I'd seen the look of silent desperation and fear in both of their eyes when Akira showed up to take them.

"What if we went to the city to do it?"

"Do you think your mom would be able to help us with something like that? Maybe go with and make sure we can actually get out of the hospital once we go in. She could make the police report."

"Only one way to find out." Aaron's smile grew wider. It was good to see him smile again.

We were scheming once again. We'd started long ago in the parking lot of a grocery store in Blackheart. Only now, the stakes were much higher than before and we had no safety net. No one would bail us out and burst through the church doors to save us. It was the three of us—and one of us wasn't on board with the plan.

Presley never mentioned it, but I think, like Aaron, he had a lot of guilt surrounding Thane. I'd assured them both more than once there was no way we could have known. Will didn't even know, and he'd known him the longest. We all wished things had gone differently, but we had to move forward, and I was confident finding The Legion was our only way to find their brothers.

Everything was blue. It was on the accents of the porcelain dishes as I set the table, the linen napkins, and even the little numbers on the cabin doors of the village. That color was a poised ink stain on our bright canvas turning everything that had once been bright yellow, muted and murky. Even the sunrise was mostly gray and covered in clouds.

"Kimberly, do you want to start chopping the vegetables for the salad while I cut up the meat?" Vera asked beside me.

"Yeah, of course." I'd offered to help in the kitchen because I wanted to get to know Vera better. Plus, Aaron needed some time alone to talk to Presley. He wanted to try to get him on board with our new plan. We would ask for Vera's help tonight, and it would be easier if Presley agreed.

Vera clearly knew what she was doing as she pulled the meat from the butcher's paper and plopped it down on the cutting board. I watched intently as she cut away at the fat with quick, clean precision.

She noticed me watching and smiled. "We'll use it all. I'll show you. If you want to get started, you can chop the onion and julienne the carrots."

"Right." I grabbed the carrots and rinsed them thoroughly under the water. I didn't know the first thing about how to cut carrots. The only cooking I'd ever done was in my dorm room microwave. Though I once had a foster mom who liked to bake, it wasn't my thing.

I grabbed the knife and carrot with determination and only a little intimidation. *Julienne must be a special kind of cut.* Suddenly, I'd wished I'd watched more cooking shows so I knew what that meant. I brought the knife down to cut. Did I need to peel them first?

"Are you okay, hun?"

I must have been staring at the cutting board for longer than I thought.

"I-I just don't really know how to cook. No one ever taught me growing up."

"Oh. Don't worry. I can show you. My mom is the one that taught me everything."

"Were you close?" I asked.

"Oh, yes. Not when I was younger, though. I moved away at eighteen and lived in Texas. Which is where my mom was from, but she moved to Brooklyn for a job and loved the city. When she got sick, I moved back. We put down our grudges, and I, of course, got pregnant. We moved in together. She helped me at first when she could, but her health declined quickly. I ended up taking care of her and my boys. Their father wasn't much help. She died before Presley and Aaron were really old enough to remember her. And Luke and Zach, they didn't know the real her . . ." She bit her lip and paused cutting the meat. "I'm sorry. I'm talking your ear off."

I smiled because I could see where Presley got his enchanting stories from. Presley could make anything into an elaborate story, and I loved being his listening ear.

"No, I want to know." There were a lot of things I wanted to say. One being, she'd created the most important people in my life. I needed to know more about their family. "Their . . . dad, what was he like?"

"He was very charming. But his mouth got him in trouble. He drank too much. He'd spend all our money. I thought I was in love, so I kept giving him more chances, and he wasn't worth any of them." The corners of her lips tugged upward. "My mom begged me to have the boys keep our last name. She never married either. It was her father's name, and she was so proud of it. I was stubborn. I almost didn't listen, but when the day came in the hospital, I signed their birth certificates and gave them the Calem name. Their dad protested, but I never regretted it. Now I really don't."

I couldn't imagine him. I wondered if he was tall like Luke or dark haired like Zach. How he'd been able to give up his family over and over again, especially this one, I'd never understand.

"What about you . . . Does your mom know about all this? You don't have to answer if that's too personal. I just wondered if she's out there worried about you. It sounds like my boys are the main culprit that pulled you into this, so I can't help but feel a little responsible."

"I don't have a mom. I was put in foster care when I was four years old. She abandoned me. I just say I don't have one. I aged out at eighteen."

"Oh, I'm sorry. You don't have to worry. If you need anything, you have me. But I won't try to mom you. Don't worry. I'll try not to, anyway."

"I don't mind," I said with a smile. The boys had her smile, and I couldn't help but stare. I was in awe of her and her warmth. She had an aura about her that made me want to sit with her a little longer, like I wanted her to teach me things.

She dried her hands after scrubbing them with soap and water. "Okay. So, you julienne carrots for things like salads or spring rolls. What you want to do first is clean them—you did a lovely job, then we'll peel and cut them into little strips."

I nodded while watching her work. Every cut was confident and sure.

"Luke must have learned everything from you."

Her jaw feathered. "Yes, he was my little chef. Luke loved to soak up all the knowledge I could give him. He even did the dishes after."

"You must miss them."

"Oh, so much. All I want is for them to be home and safe in my arms again," she said with a tight-lipped smile.

I followed her lead, cutting the carrots as she'd instructed.

"You don't have to be perfect here. Lord knows I'm far from it. I'm not a perfect nurse, and I'm not a perfect mother."

"The boys talked about you a lot. They missed you . . ."

"When I first arrived, I was afraid I talked all my neighbors into hating me. I talked about them so much. I never imagined they were partying in some frat house in California. Honestly, it's better than I imagined. That's where you grew up?"

"Yeah, I was fortunate to stay in the area and continue college there. I loved it."

"What do you want to do?" she asked.

"Oh, I haven't thought about it for a while . . . I just wanted to graduate." It all seemed so far away. I'd hardly allowed myself to think about it since the fire. The fact all my credits were null and void since I was technically dead to the world, I'd have to start over if I went to college again, but I'd just be happy to be alive this time next year. "I couldn't decide on a major that felt right."

"Well, think hard, what do you want to do? If you could do anything."

"I like to hike . . . I miss hiking."

"There you go! You could be a park ranger. Won't have to worry about your age with that. We have parks here, but you could move around."

"That's what Aaron said."

"He's smart sometimes." She winked at me. "I already told him I thought he'd be great running a dog daycare or even as a dog sitter. He always loved animals. But maybe now he'll want to find something else to do with his time. He's grown up a lot."

I smiled at that thought. It was something I hadn't let myself contemplate. What happens when we're finally free? I'd gone through the odds. Getting Luke and Zach back wouldn't be easy. And even if we did, that battle Kilian talked about was imminent. This would end in blood either way, and as much as I wanted to believe my side would win and come out unscathed . . . our odds weren't great. If they were, Kilian would have attacked long ago.

Maybe that's why the absence of them filled us all with so much grief. We may not know what went on in The Family, but we knew they were powerful and would not let the twins go easily.

What if we won? Then what would we do with all that free time? I smiled thinking of it, deciding that was the thought I wanted to focus on the most, and hope fluttered in my chest.

"Here, let's pull your hair back so it doesn't get in the food." Vera handed me a clip from her hair.

"You don't have to. I can go fix it in the bathroom." I tried pushing the pieces framing my face behind my ear.

"Nonsense. What's mine is yours." Vera smiled.

Thirteen

AARON

"I don't want to do this." Presley had his arms crossed as he sat opposite me on his bed. His room was as big as Kimberly's and my living room.

He wasn't looking at me, just staring at the wall with a bored expression.

"You don't have to do anything you don't want to do, but that's what we're doing. And . . . I'd like to have your support."

He rolled his eyes, and his jaw flexed.

"Why are you so angry at me?" I was trying my best to understand him. I'd taken a full five minutes to prepare for our conversation by composing myself and thinking of what Luke would do. He never lost his cool and didn't get snippy unless he was extremely stressed out. I needed to be a better brother than I'd been and be patient.

"I don't know. I'm just angry and I'm sad. And my chest hurts. Like all day long, and it just doesn't let up. It's like that all day, and I can't even nap or anything to get a break from it, so I just hurt all the time now. I just . . . I hate it."

"My chest hurts too. It got worse when you left."

"Yeah, I thought it did." He'd briefly explained his adventure with the dogs, but something else was bothering him, and I didn't think he'd tell me.

"You can be mad at me if you want."

"What?" He stopped picking at an unraveled thread on the quilt.

"I'll be your punching bag if it makes you feel better. I just want you to talk to me, and I want you to not run off where I can't find you."

When I couldn't find Presley after thirty minutes, Kimberly had to remind me no one knew where we were. The likeliness of him being taken was slim but not zero. I couldn't even imagine him disappearing. I'd never forgive myself.

He nodded. "Okay."

"It's going to be okay. This is temporary. I'm going to get them back. I promise."

He lifted his head. "Really?"

"I swear. I'm going to make it happen."

If there wasn't a path, I'd forge one. I didn't care what or who was standing in my way. Nothing, not even a vampire queen, would stop me. I had the confidence but not the skill. I was still kind of hoping the skill followed heroic declarations like in the movies.

We moved to the kitchen where Mom and Kimberly had prepped dinner. The smell of thyme and baked bread filled the air. I snuck a kiss to Kimberly's cheek. Now when she blushed, I remembered the taste of her. It was strange, like memorizing the sound of her heartbeat. The strangeness grew with age, I guess.

Presley had given Kimberly a hug immediately when he came home, and she accepted his very solemn apology.

At the dinner table, he took a seat next to Kimberly, and I sat across from him. The simmer pot wafted steam into the air, and the butter melted on the loaf of bread. Mom was still cooking like we could eat with her.

"So, Mom, I have something to ask."

"Okay . . ." She sat at the table, and anxiously arranged her silverware.

"To find Zach and Luke, we need to find The Legion."

"The one that locked you in the room?" she asked.

"Yep," Presley answered.

"Kilian did. He's the leader."

"And this is the one you were trying to escape from before the fire?"

"Right again, Mom," Presley said.

I gave him a warning glance, and Mom sipped her tea.

"Yes, it's risky, but it's the only option. They know all the history of the cult. We need them to help us."

"And you think they'll just do what you say because you ask them nicely?"

Kimberly stepped in. *Thank god.* "No, but they need us because of the connection the boys have to the leaders of the cult. We need them. We won't be able to find the twins without their help."

She said what we all knew. It wasn't just improbable without The Legion, it was impossible. We had no choice.

"What's your favor?" Mom asked.

"We need to go to the city hospital and pretend to have an animal attack injury. Emphasis on the blood loss. That's how they found us the first time . . . because of the police report. You could help us because you're a nurse, and you could help keep suspicions down while we're there. Make sure the report is made and the blood loss is specified in the medical records."

"I do know a few colleagues in the hospital close to Fairbanks."

"Believe it or not, this is the least dangerous option."

"Okay." She nodded and picked at the loaf of bread, like it was the simplest answer in the world.

"Just like that?" Presley asked.

"Whatever we need to do to find your brothers, I'll do it."

"Well, I want to help too. You'll need me. I'm good at sneaking," Presley said.

The more the better. We needed to put out the equivalent of a bat signal.

"If I had to guess, they've been tracking us up the coast anyway. This should be simple. Easy to pinpoint," Kimberly said.

"What have you guys been doing that would get you on their radar?" Mom asked.

I looked to Presley, and he raised his brows and motioned for me to speak.

I could practically read his mind. *You're the oldest. You explain.*

"We kinda . . . roamed bars and fed."

"On people." Presley specified.

"Right." Mom took another sip of her tea. "But you won't do any of that in town, right? Can you venture out?"

"Yeah, don't worry. Plus, it's not time yet. We drank right before we came." Presley rubbed Mom's hand.

Her face had drained of color as she picked up a fork to eat, but with each steaming hot bite, it came back. Blood-drinking would be the hardest thing for her to accept. It was for me. Oddly enough, I'd forgotten about blood completely. A few days earlier, that was impossible. Kimberly's blood worked to tame the need. I didn't know what that meant or how long it would last, but it was a relief. I could focus on what mattered, which was getting my brothers back. Then our only problem would be buying more dining room chairs so we could all sit together at the dinner table again.

"How do we keep Mom safe?" Presley asked. "What if Kilian goes all evil again and uses her as bait or something."

"Good point," I said.

"We don't let anyone at the hospital know we're related. Maybe she found us after the attack?" Kimberly's brain worked quickly.

"Sounds like we have a plan."

This was it. The last hope my brothers had.

Me. A hopeless case who was driven mad by blood occasionally. Not a strong fighter and not a good plan maker. My brother? Childish and about as hopeless and confused as me with the queen's blood, but he could be cunning. Especially if it involved talking. My mom? A brave, strong woman who should not be involved. Then Kimberly. Maybe our actual only hope. I was confident we wouldn't have made it out of the forest that day without her. Not just her smarts but *her*. Presley and I needed her.

This was the last hope we'd all be together again. Something told me there wasn't any more running. Our next encounter with The Family would decide everything, and we needed to be ready to end this once and for all.

Fourteen

KIMBERLY

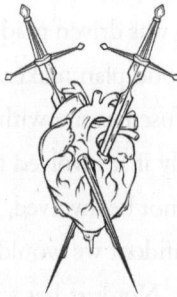

My life had officially come full circle, and I hadn't seen it coming. Not like this anyway.

Aaron, Presley, and I stayed in the cover of trees while fresh blankets of snow continued to fall from the sky. One great thing about Alaska was it was quiet everywhere. There was a low rumble of cars and a few animals in the distance, but nothing too loud. Which was great because I needed all my brain power for what we were about to do.

"Okay, Kim, let's get you looking like a final girl." Presley splashed me with fake blood from the craft store, barely leaving time for me to cover my mouth.

He poured it haphazardly over his hands and moved it over his clothes and hair.

"We need actual wounds," I said, wiping the bit that had gotten in my eyes. "They're going to check us when we walk in."

"Right." Aaron's gaze lingered on my neck, and I swallowed, remembering that rush of heat as he bit into my skin. That, and the way I'd fisted my hands in his hair and pulled him to me. I'd wanted him to keep going.

I shook it from my mind.

We would not be having a replay of the car with Presley present.

"Got it." Presley bit into his wrist, and black blood spilled into the snow like used oil.

Aaron and I shared a look and immediately did the same. I let the blood drain from my wrist like a faucet, and we used the fake blood to smear into our wounds, mixing it into a dark red.

"Not sure this is even believable," Aaron said.

"We just need them to make the reports and then we disappear."

"I don't want to attract too much attention." Aaron eyed me. "The wrong attention."

The wrong attention, as in The Family coming to rip us apart. My stomach turned while they tore at their coats and left behind bites and fake blood. The Family had wanted them at one point. We needed to be careful.

"We won't," I said. "This will be enough for them to get a needle in my arm. Test vitals. We'll be quick. I'm still holding out hope that The Family doesn't want you and Presley at all."

I hoped, but I wasn't a fool. The twins could be enough. They were the ones specifically mentioned in the prophecy. Not that it made me feel better, but it would help if The Family weren't looking for us too. Akira had tried to get the twins to come alone before he decided *he wanted the set*. That meant something was not set in stone with their prophecy. Something crucial was still up in the air regarding Aaron and Presley.

"Maybe we'll get lucky." Aaron winked.

I didn't believe in that type of luck.

I ripped at my cardigan and bit into my arm again, higher on my bicep. Aaron watched me with a furrowed brow.

"Okay, that should do." I was already feeling woozy.

"Alright, Kim, you know the drill by now," Presley said.

I nodded, knowing exactly what was about to happen. Aaron picked me up bridal style and carried me toward the hospital.

Fifteen

PRESLEY

"Please, we need help!" I yelled into the not-so-crowded lobby of the hospital. Alaska was a dead zone.

Chaos erupted around us. Nurses and doctors came rushing in. Mom held me up. She'd met us in the parking lot while we bloodied up, so we didn't get it in her car.

"What happened?" one of the nurses asked as they immediately took Kimberly from Aaron's arm.

He collapsed on the floor, taking a fake plastic plant with him. A mob of nurses surrounded him, and shouts echoed against the white walls.

Aaron might just take my Oscar.

They fumbled to get him up on a gurney, and I resolved to lean into my role harder. I groaned while holding my arm. The weakness in my limbs surprised me as I grabbed for my mother and slipped on the fake blood.

"I found them just off the side of the road by Mulberry Trail," Mom said. "I'm a nurse." I think I was able to stop the bleeding."

"Vera?" one of the doctors said to Mom while trying to cover the wounds on my arm. "I remember you. Do you know them at all?"

"No. But may I come back with them?"

He nodded and pulled me to the back through some double doors into a room full of bright light and the smell of antiseptic and blood. A symphony of machines echoed, along with the rush of footsteps and wheels across the bare floor.

"Someone attacked us. A person bit us. Call the police. Tell someone," I said, channeling my inner Leonardo DiCaprio. I was going for an anguished Romeo in *Romeo and Juliet*. Classic. Specifically, the scene where Leonardo DiCaprio cries in the field. I'd gotten a lot of fake crying practice while being the youngest. Zach used to pinch me to help me channel it to gain Mom's sympathy.

"Where are my friends? Are they okay?" I added a lip quiver for some extra pizzazz.

"They're in good hands. Try not to move." Mom soothed me with a hand on the back while she talked back and forth with the nurses. "I think this one is delirious."

They led me to a bed, pulling me in different directions.

"You have to call someone," I said again. "He's out there."

Mom was off talking to the nurses and hopefully ensuring the police report was made.

The room was oddly slow and dim. My vamp vision was dull, and I couldn't move like I wanted to. Even small things like opening and closing my hands felt too slow. All that power leached from me minute by minute. Though, my wrist wound was almost completely healed. I didn't train like Zach and Luke had, but I thought it was cool and had asked to. They outright refused to let me battle it out in my own blood.

Now I couldn't stop thinking about how they did it.

Every drop of blood on the tile felt like losing power, and I needed power if I would find my older brothers. I needed it all. And feeling it leave me made me angry again. And cold. Alone.

I guessed I wasn't as high of a priority because I was talking, but there were two nurses with me.

"Heart rate is . . . normal, but blood pressure is low. Oxygen is . . ."

An elderly woman looked up at me with wide eyes. "Something is wrong. The machine isn't working."

Gasps came from the next room over. We would need a distraction if we were going to get out.

"Ah!" I grabbed at my side. That gained Mom's attention from outside. She was on the phone with someone.

The nurses' mouths fell as they panned over my wounds. They were trying to hook me up to more machines, but my skin was hardening.

"This is—"

"There he is! He's right there!" I pointed to the hallway and pushed my voice to the brink of hysteria. "Help!"

"I don't see anyone."

"He's here! You don't see him? He's there staring at me."

It was better for them to think I was hallucinating or on drugs. It would be easier to explain what came after. Those nearest, reeled around to gawk at the other end of the hospital hallway, and I popped up out of bed.

"Wait! Sir!"

I sped across the room, not nearly fast enough. One of the nurses almost caught my arm. The hospital wasn't that big. So there wasn't a lot of space to maneuver in. I crouched behind some equipment before they could find me.

"I've never seen anything like this!" someone exclaimed from the other room.

That was my cue. I found something large that didn't look too important or expensive and sent it careening into the wall with a large thud.

"What was that?"

"What is going on right now?"

As their attention dispersed, I weaseled into Kimberly's room and motioned to her to follow me. Only, there were still doctors in there, watching in horror as Kimberly seemingly resurrected off the table.

"Where's Aaron?" she whispered in our hurried fleeing for the door. People were watching, yelling, and exclaiming things I didn't care to listen to.

"Oh, god. I'm so sorry." Aaron's anxious voice came from the hall.

"There he is."

He'd tipped over an IV drip and was getting fake blood over the hallway. We bolted for the lobby doorway and fumbled our way to the exit. I fell into a couple people on the way out, but we managed to hide back in the trees where we'd come from.

Once the hospital was firmly behind us, we collapsed next to the red and black mess we'd made in the snow.

"Uh. This blows," I said. I was now sluggish *and* achy.

"I kinda like it," Kimberly said. "My head feels . . . clear."

"How'd we do, Burns?" Aaron asked.

"Perfect. I think that will be more than enough to put us on their radar. We just need to be ready when they come."

I said nothing. I didn't want to see The Legion again. Especially Kilian. If Kilian hadn't been who he is, we'd never have been separated. So every moment my brothers suffered, how much I suffered . . . was because of them, and I wouldn't forgive that. Aaron wouldn't understand, but

Zach would have.

"Here, let me see you." Aaron grabbed my arm and inspected my wounds that were now closed.

"I'm fine."

He moved past me to pat down Kimberly. "You're okay?"

"Yeah. It wasn't too bad."

Aaron had that puppy-dog look again, and it was working. Kimberly wrapped him in a hug, and he kissed her forehead.

Pain radiated again in my heart deeper and more painful than it had been before, so I clutched my chest.

"Ah." The groan didn't come from me.

"Did you feel that?" I turned to Aaron rubbing his chest.

"Yeah. The ache got all intense all of sudden."

I felt it again and had to put my hands on my knees till it passed. Like someone kicked me in the chest, it stole the air from my lungs.

"What the hell." I could barely get out the words. Then it was gone again. The pain softened back to its heavy, dull ache. "I don't know what's happening over there, but it's not good. That felt like a true Zach kick in the chest. What could be happening?"

The three of us shared the same worried expression. Kimberly's eyes softened like she might cry, and my brother gritted his teeth. And me . . .

"We have to go." I picked our empty fake-blood bottles up off the snow.

I didn't want to be there anymore. I wanted to go home and lock myself in my room. I'd helped them with their doomed plan and needed time to think about my equally terrible one. Alone.

Sixteen

AARON

It was bad again. So incredibly bad. Two weeks and there had been no sign of The Legion. Two. Whole. Weeks. In those two weeks, my hold on my humanity loosened day by day.

My skin crawled with need, and I couldn't think about anything other than Kimberly and her heartbeat. And blood. I needed blood. I needed it so bad my hands were trembling.

I tried to steady them as I cut an onion for Mom's stew. Kimberly and Mom chatted happily while Mom told her one embarrassing story after another.

She was being so cute and helping my mom cook, and I had to hide the fact I was staring at the back of her bare legs and imagining what would happen if I set her free in the forest and watched her run.

I licked my lips and continued chopping. All the while, the image seared into my brain. I was the equivalent of a feral dog waiting outside

100

her door begging for an ounce of her, and it was impossible to think of anything else.

As my knife sliced another onion, I lost myself at her pale legs disappearing out of sight and into the trees. Her bare feet darting through the snow. Her body dodging trees while I pursued close behind. She couldn't run fast enough. There was nowhere she could hide that I wouldn't find her. The sound of her heartbeat was like a siren calling to me.

I wanted her.

My heart raced thinking of the chase. What would happen when I finally tackled her to the ground, stripped off her clothes, and wrapped her legs around my waist. And that sound she makes when I—

God. Someone make me stop.

I was aware of how fucked up that fantasy was, considering our first meeting. It packed guilt on top of my already aching chest. My control over my thoughts was slipping. The bloodlust was too much.

Kimberly smiled at me, and my stomach sank. I scratched at the back of my hand, fighting the urge to pace the kitchen. Maybe I could get her alone for a minute . . .

No. Shit. Stop. You're good. You got this.

My skin was crawling. I needed to move. I had to get out of the house. I needed blood and needed it now.

"Are you okay?" Kim whispered.

I backed away. Fearful of her breath on my neck and the fact it could set me off at any minute. I was seconds away from throwing her over my shoulder and taking her to our cabin.

I was certain there would be nothing left of that sweater.

I just needed some air. Away from thoughts of blood and lust and need.

She stared at me with those cool-blue eyes I usually wanted to disappear into. Now I didn't know what I wanted. What would she think if she knew? If she knew how bad I truly was?

I didn't want to lie. "I need some air."

I stepped out into the snow. There amid the negative temperatures, I could finally think. It was time to feed again, but I wasn't thinking of the pub. I wanted what I'd already had. Kimberly's blood was everything, but I didn't want to want her in that way. I wanted to be a normal freaking boyfriend. Why couldn't I have normal issues?

She'll get sick of you. She'll hate you.

I know.

She didn't mind the biting, but it was wrong. I'd almost killed her twice. Good boyfriends don't almost kill their girlfriends. They don't bite them or hurt them and drink their blood. Normal ones don't, anyway. And she deserved normal.

I needed something to distract me. I didn't take turns and walked straight into the trees. The snow was never ending, like the cold. Though the cold didn't make me shiver or my teeth chatter, I still felt it everywhere. That kind of cold wasn't natural, and even being bundled up, I was uncomfortable. It didn't hurt, but it sank into my body, leaving me numb and chilled to the bone.

You're so pathetic.

I snarled and walked faster. I wanted to disappear. Leave this place behind. Everyone might be better off without me. It was what I thought two weeks ago and had forgotten about. I was holding everyone back. Maybe I was the bad luck we had and that's why The Legion hadn't come for us yet. And this was my punishment. It all seemed to make sense.

I spun around in the clearing, looking for the best place to bolt.

Then I saw it.

A buck walking in the field in the distance.

It wouldn't help. I knew it wouldn't, but at that moment, I had to try. Drinking any blood at all might make the feeling go away.

I ran for it and tried to let the Thing in my head take over, but it didn't. It wouldn't.

I was too fast for the deer, and I made its death quick by snapping its neck.

But everything was too raw. Too vivid. I was too lucid as I brought my fangs out to bite it. I ignored the sirens going off in my brain, at least tried to, before the reality of what I was doing made me choke. All the gamey blood in my throat was tasteless. My body convulsed until the blood splattered over the white snow, my clothes, my hands, and even the dead animal lying at my feet.

It looked like a massacre.

Emptiness consumed me as I realized what I'd done.

I hated when Zach and Presley squashed ants on the sidewalk, and now I'd tried to drink a deer.

I took off as fast as my feet would take me. My feet were numb from the cold. Snow packed in the soles of my shoes and weighed me down as I ran, and I ran until something bright and blue sparkled in the distance. A pond sat cold, frozen, and lonely.

I collapsed at its bank and sank into the snow. My knees were icy when I pulled them to the warmth of my chest. With a shaky breath, I rubbed my chest right over the rapid beat.

Is this what my brothers felt like all the time? So miserable inside they wanted to scream? How were they able to keep it hidden? I couldn't hide this anguish. All I wanted was Luke to come bounding toward me in the snow and put an arm around me and tell me things would be okay. I needed Zach beside me with his snarky smile and his sureness of safety, but that wouldn't happen. All of my problems were mine now, and the only person who could fix them was me.

I stared out onto the water and spotted a broken dock not far from me. Memories of the lake in Blackheart swirled in my mind. Back in the heat of summer, when we'd jumped in the water a hundred times. I could imagine us all there when it was thawed and green. The pain of the memory was enough to bring that echo of discomfort to my chest and to the forefront of my mind.

They'd never get to see this place.

It was up to me to bring them back, and I was curled up on the ground, covered in blood, crying over a dead animal. The voice was right. I was pathetic.

The snow soaked through my clothes as I made no attempts to remain dry.

I let it bury me as I sat alone in the growing darkness. A clambering of footsteps sounded behind me, and Presley appeared wearing pajama pants and one of Mom's faux fur coats. Any other day, I'd have laughed.

I tried to wipe my tears from my cheeks and smeared deer blood across my face.

"Uh-oh. Who'd you kill?"

"A buck."

"Oh good, I didn't want to have to find a shovel."

I sighed and turned back toward the pond. What was worse was having my little brother watch me fail in every way my older brothers had succeeded. I could never fill their shoes. It was pointless to try.

"So, is that what we're doing now? Freezing and crying in the snow? Because next time, I'm going to need an invite to this kinda thing."

I scoffed. "Don't try to make me laugh."

"I'm not. I legit want an invite to this sob story where we cry and make snow angels after. I'm going to have to veto the animal killing, though."

I buried my head into my knees, and he rubbed my back. Something tight in my chest loosened. I hadn't even noticed it until it was gone.

"How'd you find me?"

"Some of it was your footprints, but the snow kinda covers it. I just had this feeling and followed it. I could tell the moment you left."

"What do you mean?"

"I was doing my own thing and then I kinda felt like I was going to throw up all of sudden, and you were the first person that came to mind. When I went to look for you, Kimberly told me you'd been gone for a while. She wanted to come look for you herself, but I convinced her to stay."

"You came for me," I said, rubbing my chest. The ache was still there.

He shrugged. "I'd rather sit and be miserable with you than be miserable alone."

I never thought I'd be thankful to be united by blood, but something about it was comforting. I wasn't alone in my pain, and neither were my brothers, and it didn't matter how much distance separated us, blood didn't lie.

"I like to think they can feel us too, even if they don't realize it," Presley said, watching the sky like someone would part the clouds and fly down in a golden chariot.

"I've been thinking that."

The snow fell silently on the dock in the distance. Who was I kidding? They had felt this way probably more times than they could count. My brothers had been tricked into turning. They'd seen Sarah killed in front of them, then dealt with the mental repercussions all in silence. They'd dealt with the agony of knowing they were going back to that place to be tortured all the more, and I'd never seen them curl into a ball.

Neither of them ran away and cried. If it had happened, I never knew about it and had to worry. As the weight of the cold hit me again, wave after wave, I knew I was being childish. *Old habits die hard, I guess.*

I had people who needed me. It was time to grow up.

"I'm sorry, Pres. I shouldn't have run off."

"I don't mind it. But I know a girl who's probably counting the minutes till our return. I told Mom you went to the store for milk and eggs and then she had a conniption because she buys it from this certain guy in town."

Kimberly. I hadn't forgotten about the bloodlust, but I felt lighter than before. More in control.

I wrapped Presley in a hug. "Thank you."

"Does this mean we're not making snow angels?"

Seventeen

KIMBERLY

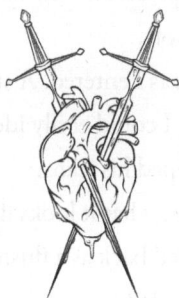

I flipped through the pages of a book, pretending to care. I'd already cooked with Vera, watched her eat, and listened to her stories. I cared, but not more than I cared about where the boys were.

I couldn't stop looking at the door between the paragraphs that weren't registering in my brain.

They were fine, I told myself over and over again, but I'd been thinking over every scenario. The most likely ones were all leading down roads I didn't want to believe in. Legion. The Family. They could be here. They could have taken them somewhere I wouldn't be able find them, then I'd never see either of them again.

I repeated the cycle again. Read a paragraph. Glanced at the door. Spiral.

I was about to start counting the words on the page when Presley emerged with a brown bag and a milk jug. "Here you go, Mom. Aaron's turning in for the night I think."

"What? Why?"

"I think he just wants some alone time." Presley looked at me and raised his brows.

I was instantly on my feet, excusing myself, then out the door. I'd slipped my shoes on the wrong feet, then stumbled my way to our cabin.

A fire cracked in our fireplace, and the flames cast a glow on the wall as I climbed my way to the loft.

Aaron peeled off his shirt as I entered. A strange scent lingered on the clothes at his feet. Nothing I could easily identify. Then I saw the deep red covering him as he dropped his jeans.

He turned to me. "It's not what it looks like. It's deer blood."

"Oh." My shoulders pulled back as a flush of heat ran through me.

I refused to move as he pulled some pajama pants from his backpack. There was still blood smudged over his face and torso where it had stained through his shirt.

I went for a rag on the kitchen counter and a bottle of water. It was mostly frozen solid.

"Sit. Tell me what happened. Where did you go?" I said, cornering him at the edge of the bed.

He stared at the floor while I poured some of the freezing water on the rag to dab it on his skin.

He winced when it touched him. *Good.* I forced the lump down my throat.

"I was feeling overwhelmed with thirst and needed some air and just started walking through the trees. I attacked a deer . . . I knew it wouldn't help, but I was desperate."

I said nothing, moving the towel to wipe the red from his cheek and lips.

"I just didn't want to drink from you again."

I stopped, placing the rag on the bedside table. "Does it help?"

"Yeah . . ."

I met his gaze. The lamplight illuminated the lingering warmth in his eyes.

His pupils consumed me, fixing me in place at his side. He was starving for blood, but I wouldn't let him off that easily.

"This isn't working," I said, moving away from him and toward the dresser.

Aaron's rigid form dissolved like snow in the sun. "What?"

"I mean, you can't just leave. I thought someone took you. You were gone for so long, and I-I . . ."

"I'm sorry."

"You wouldn't want me to go off and leave you in the cabin. You wouldn't want Presley to do that."

"I know, you're right."

"Let me be angry for a minute." I spun around, and he was standing next to me.

"Okay."

"You scared me."

He stepped forward, with all his attention on my face. "I know."

"You need to start talking to me. You need to tell me when something is wrong. I can't help you if you shut me out. That's what they want. They want you to run off by yourself and disappear and go back to Her."

I was surprised by how my voice shook. My chest was tight with worry. I eyed the door, and something stirred in my stomach, telling me to run. I couldn't imagine it. I wouldn't.

Her lips on his cheek. Her breath on his neck.

Aaron moved a hand under my chin. "Keep going."

"You not telling me anything is selfish. If something happened to you, everything would fall apart." *I would fall apart.* "I know you're scared. But we're all scared. And the only way we're going to get through this is if we're radically honest and if we work together."

His thumb rubbed my bottom lip, and I sucked in a breath. The heat of his skin set goose bumps over my mine.

"You're right. I'm sorry. I promise I won't run away again."

He leaned into my lips. Soft as a feather. My hands shook, and as he grabbed them, I realized his were shaking too. He needed to feed but was holding himself back for me.

"I'm not going anywhere." He wiped the wetness gathered at the corner of my eyes. "I'll be radically honest . . . I've never wanted anything else as much as I want you. I want to make love to you, Burns. Real and proper. I want to be near you and to touch you. But I can't think. I can't focus. This Thing in my head won't leave me alone. But you and your blood make me feel like myself again, and it's so confusing. All I've ever wanted was to give you something safe and normal, so taking blood from you feels like I'm . . . corrupting you. It scares me. I don't want to mess this up, and I feel like I am already. You deserve so much, and I'm—"

I stilled him with a finger to his lips.

His forehead touched mine, and I was crushed under the weight of his gaze and the way his hands dug into my hips.

"You don't have to be afraid," I said.

"You're never afraid."

"You know that's not true, but one thing I can assure you is that I'm never afraid of you."

He kissed me again, and I tried to stifle the moan that leaped from my throat.

I pressed myself to him tighter and tighter. We were finally alone, with only the crackling fire in the fireplace downstairs.

Aaron must have sensed my urgency. Because we lost the little space between us. With both hands, he moved the hair from my neck and grabbed the sides of my face. He nipped down my jaw and up to my ear. The feel of his breath on my neck made my core tighten. Slowly, he ran his lips under my ear, and I shuddered. He was exploring me and showing his cards at the same time. Pleasure seared my skin, and I fought against the growing ache between my thighs.

His hands trembled as he continued to kiss my neck.

"You need blood."

"Mm-hm." His attention stayed at my throat where the wetness of his lips turned to careful licks from his tongue.

"It's okay . . . you can bite me. I want you to," I said breathlessly.

He pulled away, holding me so tight his fingers imprinted my cheeks.

"You want me to?" The words tumbled out slowly as the light left his irises a soft, warm honey smothered by shadow.

I did. I craved his closeness. I'd tried not to think of that moment in the car, but I couldn't get it out of my head because I'd wanted to give him more.

I nodded as he towered over me.

His jaw tensed like he might protest again. I thought back to that boy in the forest last spring. He was still him, but he'd had to fight to be the sweet, caring person I knew him to be. He was at war with himself again, weighing his options, but there was desperation in his eyes, and I wondered what it must feel like to have Her blood swirling around with his and tainting his every thought and feeling.

There was one thing I knew for sure: it created a much deeper hunger in him.

A hunger I wanted to fill.

When his lips met mine again, they were greedier. Rushed and hurried.

My back hit the wall, and a feral growl ripped from his throat. This time, I hadn't imagined it. I was pinned with no way to escape. My lip was caught between his teeth, harder than ever before, but it didn't hurt.

He bit into my neck. His venom cooled any bite and left me with gentle pressure, but everywhere else, pressure grew. His knee parted my legs, and I whimpered at the sensation of him digging into me. Sweet and slow, he took his time. A gentle tingling ran down my arms and into my fingertips, and it was far from unpleasant. I savored the feeling of his lips on my skin, longing for me. I wanted to bond with him in a way we could have never done before I changed.

When he pulled away, I knew this time would be different than any time we'd ever been alone.

He wouldn't stop, and neither would I.

"Aaron . . ."

Did my heartbeat give me away? Or was it the flush in my cheeks? My whole body was on fire, and my pulse drummed loudly in my ears. Could he tell how badly I needed him in that moment? Could he tell I wasn't scared?

I gasped as he snapped the buttons on my flannel, exposing my chest.

"Say it again." He kissed my skin, lightly sucking along my collarbone.

My core ached. Burned. I needed him closer. With hands in his hair, I pulled him tight to my chest, and his fangs entered my skin again.

I obliged his request and moaned his name again. He groaned, taking in more of me. It hurt more than the bite on my neck but not enough to stop. The warmth of his lips against my cool skin made me shudder. I felt lighter. Almost like being intoxicated but better.

I'd never felt safer in my entire life.

Everything slowed. All that existed was him, and I fell into his glorious rhythm and the feel of his body grinding into me. The rocking of his hips pulled pleasure from me in waves.

"Are you okay?" His voice was soft against my ear.

Where he'd bitten me was a slight wetness. The wound was closing, and my body was slower, but I wasn't focused on every little sound anymore. My head was finally empty.

I didn't mind the feeling of emptiness if Aaron was there to fill the void.

"I feel . . . human. But I'm glad I'm not."

His lips curled in a smile. "Right now, me too."

With warm hands on my face, he pulled me in for a kiss. Slowly, he came back to himself. And that was good too. Still desperate and full of yearning but less rushed.

How long had I wanted this?

It seemed like forever. The fruition of yearning I hadn't even known I had. All those longing stares. When he'd touched me, and I'd begged him not to stop.

His fingers coiled in my hair as he lay me back on the bed and pulled off what was left of my shirt. With two arms pinning me to the bed, he leaned in close to my lips.

"We could stop."

I didn't want to stop. I'd never wanted him to stop. We just had to.

He'd been a safe place for so long, and I was ready for him to consume every part of me. I'd been ready.

"Don't stop touching me."

Aaron fell into me with a fevered kiss. Soft at first, then harder. I pulled him closer, wrapping my legs around his waist. His fangs entered my neck as his hips ground into me.

I gasped, and the ache between my thighs deepened.

I wanted to be everything he needed. I *needed* to. The room was spinning, but I felt solid.

The dim light of the lamp illuminated his face as he licked his lips.

"You don't need to be gentle with me," I whispered.

His eyes ignited with a carnal thirst, then he pulled me toward him. Hard. With one pull, my bra was off and thrown tattered to the floor. With hot breath, he licked at the wound on my neck.

"You taste so good, Burns. You have no idea."

He moved his thumb over my neck, then to my lips. My blood coated his fingers, and it was still warm when it fell on my own tongue.

"See."

"I-I . . ."

Aaron had never looked at me like that. The ferocity of it stilled me, and I opened my mouth for him.

Warmth pooled in my gut as I licked my blood from his fingers. Our eyes stayed locked with each dizzying second. I wasn't focused on the metallic taste, just the act of submitting to him.

"Fuck, I can't handle this," he said through gritted teeth.

"What do you mean?"

"I don't know how I'm going to stop touching you. I don't know how it's ever going to be enough."

I hung on his every word, savoring the yearning in his voice. It was just for me. Aaron Calem was all mine.

But he was still holding back, afraid I was the fragile girl I used to be.

Slowly and carefully, I traced the lines on his chest. I reached for his pajama pants strings, and he stopped me.

"Not yet. Let me feel you a little longer."

I opened my mouth to protest.

"I can't think straight when you're touching me. And I need more time to make you feel good."

It wasn't up for debate. He kissed down my legs, that were already shaking from the need.

"Don't you want me to touch you?"

"Yes," I gasped.

I couldn't form sentences. The only thing coming from my lips were whispered utterances of his name.

"Here?" He sucked at the tender skin by my knee.

"Please—"

"Or here." The wetness of his lips reached my inner thigh.

I squirmed, and that only made him hold me tighter. His gentle laughter grazed my thigh as I uttered his name again.

There was slight pressure as his teeth bit into my leg. I thrust a hand over my mouth to keep quiet while he drank, and it was quick.

"Sorry, I've been daydreaming about that for a long time." He moved to stroke me between my legs.

"How long?" I said, staring up at the skylight.

"Long. I tried not to think about it because I didn't think I'd ever be able to or if you'd want me to . . ."

I arched into him while his fingers continued to circle where I needed him most.

"It hurt not to be able to touch you like this."

It was too much. And yet not enough. Aaron had wanted me like this.

He'd imagined touching me and biting me. I'd imagined it too, but it was new for me. To want this, and to feel this safe and wanted by another person.

I wanted to open up to him.

The heat in my core swelled in the cold night air. I needed more pressure. Suddenly, I felt empty. Like I so desperately needed something I wasn't getting. I'd never wanted someone to touch me in the way Aaron had until I met him. All that trust and love was overwhelming and pulling at me, urging me to make this moment last and give Aaron a part of me I'd given no one else.

"Don't be quiet. I wanna hear you."

"But—"

In my head, I ran through all the reasons that wasn't a good idea, and I was going to tell him until his kisses up my chest stopped and he sucked my nipple into his mouth.

"Aaron," I gasped.

The suction sent my hips grinding into his.

"You're perfect," Aaron said, his breath grazing my breast.

"Aaron, please."

It felt good. It felt amazing, but I needed him closer. I needed him so desperately I could hardly get the words out. It was embarrassing to admit, but not in the arms of someone I trusted more than I'd ever trusted anyone.

I dug my fingers into his arm and pulled him up to me. "I-I need you closer to me."

He rested his forehead on mine. "I'm yours, Burns."

With carefulness, he lifted my hips to peel off my underwear, and worry drew across his face. His brow creased, and my underwear fell to the floor. I helped him with his pajama pants and leaned back on the bed while he kissed my forehead.

His kiss was soft, less sure than before.

"We can go slow."

"You're still holding back." I cradled his face in my hands, with my bare legs wrapped around his waist.

Then I understood. Beneath his amber eyes was that Thing lying in wait and threatening to overtake him. He wasn't just afraid of hurting me, he feared losing himself.

I knotted his hair in my hands. "You'll always be my Aaron. No matter what."

The light flickered in his eyes before he consumed me. One final moment of permission before taking every liberty he wanted and craved.

It was at that moment I promised myself I would guard his soul from any terror and darkness. Aaron would always be my sunlight. Even if that meant I'd have to rip the moon out of the sky to save him from the dark.

"You have to tell me if this is too much. Don't let me hurt you. Tell me and we'll stop."

"Okay. I will. But don't stop. Please."

"Kim, don't beg."

"I need you."

"I won't stop." He said it with a certainty that had every inch of my body yearning for release, and I wanted it to be him who gave it. "I'll give you everything . . . anything you want, it's yours."

My breath was the only sound. That and my hammering heartbeat.

"I don't know if I can be gentle enough."

His hands shook, and I kissed them, placing them on my bare breasts. "That's okay."

Aaron guided his length to my opening, and I involuntarily tensed. He pressed his forehead to mine. "I love you."

A flush of heat ran through me as he pushed into me slowly.

Then I was stretched and full. A new, unexplored feeling. Not bad—just new. My hands twisted into the sheets, and the need for him burned me alive. An aching that wouldn't relent.

As he moved inside me, I couldn't speak. I couldn't think. It was just Aaron everywhere, and it's exactly what I needed.

He kept his eyes on me as his lips brushed my ear. "Are you okay?"

"I'm okay," I said breathlessly.

I knew I'd needed him, but I didn't know I needed him *there* till he was there. People enjoyed sex. That wasn't a secret. But I didn't know it was like this.

I didn't know anything could feel like this.

"Don't stop."

He groaned into my neck. "You're so beautiful."

My hips moved on their own to bring him farther into me. Every bit of him alleviated the aching that pulsed in my veins. Aaron cursed while placing his hands on the bed frame, and the wood cracked and split under the pressure of his palms.

"This is good. You're so good."

My whole body thrummed with the feeling of him. From my scalp to my toes, he was there. Caressing my head. Squeezing my body. Pinning me to the bed. It was a lot. I'd never been so engulfed by another person.

"I love you." The words poured from my lips between thrusts of his hips.

There was only one way to describe what I was feeling—love consuming me alive. Piece by piece. I'd never known love could feel this good. This safe. The world was on fire. I forgot about the cold. I forgot about everything but this.

Our bodies blended in one glorious symphony of pleasure.

"Stay here with me." I meant it in every way a person could mean those words.

Never leave.

Let us always have this.

Love me like this forever.

When his hand touched my face, it was soft as a feather.

"I will. I'm right here."

He went deeper. Filling me and stifling that part of me that was burning out of control. I wanted to thank him because it was perfect. Blissful. This need was new, and it felt good to have him fulfill it. The thought only opened me up further. Aaron paid more attention to my face, leaving soft kisses along my jaw and up to my forehead.

With one arm, he lifted my leg up, and the moan that escaped me was louder than I'd expected.

"Right there, huh?"

I couldn't think. All of the power I'd had in my body, I'd freely given to Aaron, and now I was weak and woozy, yet whole and content with his arms wrapped around me.

My gasp echoed in the cabin, followed by another incoherent scrambling of sounds.

His name lingered on my lips and only got louder and louder.

"Yeah?" He kissed me with each thrust. "You're so pretty like this."

The pulling in my stomach built with the friction. I gripped his shoulders desperately.

"Aaron. Just don't—"

"I won't. I'm here. Right here." He held me perfectly, keeping a perfect pace.

If I were human, it might have broken bones, but it was perfect. The perfect pressure. The perfect everything.

"Kim," he choked out.

We let go together. I tightened around him, and all that pressure released. Waves of pleasure rocked through my lower body, and we rode every shiver of ecstasy until we were spent.

I didn't know it could be that good. I was full of warmth and happiness.

Suddenly, I was aware of how tired I was. I was sore everywhere, but content. Happier than I'd been in weeks.

He moved the hair from my face while his hips stayed firmly pressed into me. There were no words at first, just kissing and the watchfulness of his gaze.

Our world had changed. Something between us had shifted. It had been different every time he'd touched me, and now . . .

"Hey, Burns."

"Hey," I said, settling into the bed. All I'd forgotten came back. The crackling of the fire, the chill of the wind pressing in from outside, and the cedar smell of our room came rolling into the back of my mind.

"Has anyone ever told you that you're literally the perfect girl? Smart, gorgeous . . . you're everything."

"You're the only one who's ever told me that."

"They're missing out."

Eighteen

AARON

I lay awake all night staring up at the ceiling. Kimberly was more than enough to look at, but the stars in our skylight helped keep me from boredom. I'd warmed some water, helped her clean up, and held her while she dozed off.

I hoped she dreamed of something good. A place far away that was warm and sunny. If only I could have slept too. Anything to get a break from being in my head. With one arm, I squeezed her to my chest. A soft sound left her lips, and she gripped me tighter.

I'd bitten her. Not only did I bite her. I kept biting her. It made me a little nauseous to know I'd taken enough blood from her that she needed to sleep, but the gnawing in my stomach was gone. My body was satiated in every sense of the word. It was nice to have a clear head again.

The need to protect her was stronger than ever. It was the best night of my life, and as I kissed the top of Kimberly's head, I thought of my brothers again. Of every night they too were stuck in bed looking up at the ceiling and not able to sleep.

When Zach slept next to Ashley after he was changed, did he ever watch her sleep and wonder how he would ever tell her? Was he scared when he realized what was happening to him?

When they heard the news about Sarah's disappearance, did they talk all night before they went searching themselves?

And when they got their memories back about Sarah's death, how did they cope together? Did they get time to grieve?

All those secrets got taken with them.

I'd never thought about any of those things before. I was ashamed to admit it, but I thought they'd had it handled. It was their problem, and they'd dragged me into it, so it was up to them to solve it, but these problems weren't theirs. They had always been ours. Or they should have been.

I placed a hand on my chest right over my heart where that familiar weight ached. I'd grown to like the agony of it, because it was like I was shouldering the weight of their pain from however many miles away.

I'd finally taken up my guard post, and I was on the night shift feeling their pain. Hopefully, they felt a little less because of it. I had a lot of time to make up for, but I'd make up for it by being the one to bring them home. As I searched the skies above, I focused on nothing but the thought of fulfilling that promise.

"Hi," Kimberly murmured.

"Hi." I ran my hands through her hair, replaying touching her and tasting her in the way I'd been craving for much longer than I was willing to admit. I was still in awe of it. Kimberly Burns, the girl who'd done everything alone, had given me a part of herself she'd never given to anyone else.

"Is everything okay?"

"I don't know." My thoughts weren't spinning anymore, so I didn't have as much trouble being honest.

She waited for me to elaborate, and I touched her neck where I'd bitten her. "I just . . . didn't really want that to be how our first time would go."

Her features remained unchanged as she fought to open her heavy eyelids. "How did you imagine it?"

"Less biting—actually, scratch that. No biting. Maybe more romance. Candles. Rose petals. The whole nine yards. Not me going animalistic and trying to eat you would have been preferred."

In our brief window of being together as a human and a vampire, I'd thought about it a few times. Everything I'd wanted to put in place to make it perfect, and I'd wondered how long until I'd have enough self-control not to hurt her during. That felt like a lifetime ago, and I was a different person. I liked this version of me better. I was less of a dumbass and a better brother.

She smiled. "I didn't mind the biting."

"I know. I just feel like I made this about the monster thing, and that's not what I wanted. I wanted to give you something normal."

"I don't need normal. I never have."

I touched her soft lips, okay with that answer. I could never give normal. "This is enough?"

She ran her fingers through my fringe. "This is everything."

"Do you feel okay?"

"I feel very relaxed. But sore." She traced circles on my chest. "It's okay, Aaron."

I squeezed her hand. "I know."

———— 🖋 ————

We got up at first light, which was around 10:00 a.m. That would take some getting used to.

The minute I opened the door to the main cabin, I came face-to-face with my little brother.

"Whoa," I said, taking in the sight of his darkened hair. It was now dark-chocolate brown, and the remnants of hair dye had stained his ears and neck.

Kim's eyes widened. "You dyed your hair."

"Yeah, I didn't want you to be the only one. Plus, I needed a change."

Kimberly buried him in a hug and smiled in pure delight. "I love it."

"So, guess you guys made up, huh?" Presley asked as we funneled toward the dinner table where Mom sat reading. The fresh scent of coffee permeated the air.

"Why do you ask?"

"No reason," Presley said. Then he mouthed behind Mom's back, *I could hear you.*

Shit. I explicitly told Kimberly not to be quiet, but god, I loved hearing her say my name over and over.

"Good thing I had headphones."

"What, honey?" Mom said, lifting her head to greet me.

"Nothing," we said together.

"Will you boys help Margret, my neighbor, put up her Christmas lights later today?"

"Mom, we spent all week doing that." Presley groaned. "And we can't even eat the cookies she tries to pay us in."

For the last two weeks, we'd settled into Mom's world. She finally had a reason to use her paid vacation days. We'd met her friends and gone to the weekly town meetings. Most nights, we'd been roped into helping Mom's friends cut wood and put up their Christmas decorations. I knew why it bothered Presley, because it was the same reason it bothered me. We weren't celebrating Christmas this year, and even being around the sounds and sights of the holiday hurt. Physically and mentally.

"I know, but she's elderly and she loves them. I can come by after work and help." She rubbed his hand, and his shoulders dropped from his ears.

"Fine, but don't ask me to do anything more than that. You guys can celebrate the holiday if you want. But leave me out of it."

Christmas was the biggest celebration of the year in the Calem house, and it was never about money or buying gifts. It was about tradition and food. We'd never spent Christmas apart.

A sputtering vibration on the wood of the kitchen table stopped my thoughts.

"Oh, I have to take this. Hold on," Mom said.

"We don't have to celebrate," Kimberly said to my brother. "Maybe we could do something you like on the actual day. That's what I used to do if I wanted to forget about the holiday completely. I'd lock myself in my room, shut the blinds, and watch the same movie over and over again. That way I didn't have to deal with any of it."

I pulled her closer at her admission and kissed the top of her head. I didn't think she realized how sad it sounded. Though it was an experience many people dealt with and could probably relate to, I hated thinking of her alone in her room with no one to call.

My brother seemed to have the same sentiment, as his aggressive tone shifted. "I don't know what I'd want to do though. I hate being in my room."

"Maybe we could go visit the dogs at the shelter? I still haven't been."

That was the only thing Presley liked to talk about, and he'd only been twice. He said it was the only exciting thing in town, and he wasn't exaggerating. There wasn't much to look at or do here other than brave the elements and follow Mom to her community and church meetings and eat. Which was a huge bummer when you couldn't, because the potlucks smelled amazing.

Presley's smile returned at her idea.

Mom set the phone down on the counter and sucked in a breath.

"There's someone at the hospital looking for information on three young adults claiming to be bitten. They obviously weren't allowed to give out any medical information, but I told her to call me if anyone came looking for you all."

"It's them!" Everything in me leaped with joy. Weird, confusing joy that we'd finally been found.

"Did they say what they looked like?" Kimberly asked.

"Just that he's quite tall. An older man, very adamant, but wouldn't give a name."

"That's him, alright," Presley grumbled, and popped down in a chair.

"Can we take the car?" I said, searching for the keys on the kitchen counter.

"Wait a minute. Shouldn't we talk about it?"

"Mom, this is what we've been waiting for. I don't want to risk him leaving."

"Will you be careful?" The fear in her voice stopped my search.

"Yes, I promise. This is a good thing."

It was a worrying step in what was likely a good direction. It was better than nothing.

I turned to my brother. "You're sure you don't want to come?"

"No way. Send me a postcard from your jail cell though. If you want me to be able to find you, be sure to leave me some clues, and they better

126

be really good if you want me to find you."

His confidence in me was slightly insulting but warranted. I'd never given him a reason to believe I was capable of taking the lead, but this was my chance to start, and I was ready for the challenge.

Nineteen

KIMBERLY

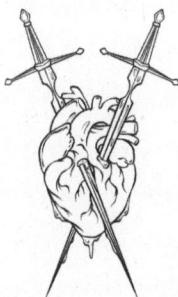

We pulled into the plowed hospital parking lot. Plenty of cars and witnesses around and the daylight helped. None of the cars seemed familiar, but I wasn't sure Kilian even owned the cars they'd spent all that time shuffling us around in. Once I had that thought, I'd spiraled the entire drive with a list of all we never knew about The Legion. Everything could have been a lie. Kilian could be about to take us in a few minutes, and my entire plan could be our downfall.

Aaron squeezed my hand that was gripped, white-knuckled, around the gear shift.

"This is a good plan." He said it like he could read my mind.

"One of us needs to be bait," I said while watching someone wheel an older man through the emergency entrance. I wasn't sure if it was a good plan, but it was the only one that made sense.

Aaron zipped his jacket. "That's my cue."

"Be careful."

He kissed my cheek before I could sigh or frown. "I'll signal if it's safe to come out."

I was still weak from the blood loss, making the whole thing a colossal risk.

Aaron stepped out and walked into an empty lot with his large jacket puffed around his ears. The hairs on my arms stood as I gripped the steering wheel. I'd fight if it came to it. I would let no one take him.

"What's our signal?" I asked.

"Pineapple?" He smiled.

I nodded, and he sauntered into the parking lot with his hands in his pockets. Then I readied myself for whatever was about to happen. At the top of my list was hitting Kilian with my car. I wasn't sure how that would work, but it would at least hurt him.

There was nothing at first. Just Aaron standing in an open lot while regular people went on with their regular lives to and from the hospital. The sun reflected off the roofs of cars and hospital windows, and I fumbled for my sunglasses. If only it were enough to melt the snow.

Aaron walked in a circle, carefully scanning the lot. There weren't any identifying cars or people till a car door opened close by. I couldn't see it, but I heard it behind another car. All my muscles tightened.

Kilian emerged. He was bundled up in a long thick wool jacket and slacks. His hair was cropped and less put together than I'd seen him previously. There was no smile on his face or indication he was there in peace.

Aaron said nothing, only squared his shoulders and faced him head-on. I focused all my attention on the sound of his heartbeat and the crunch of his shoes on the snow.

It was good practice to tune out the cars and the hospital, which was buzzing with sounds.

"You wanted us to find you." Kilian's voice was like molasses.

"Yeah. Not that I know if I can trust you or not," Aaron said. "Do you know where my brothers are?"

"I have information about their whereabouts, but we have many things to discuss."

"The only thing I want to talk about is where they are."

"We can talk about your brothers. Preferably at a different location."

"Why would I do that? I have no reason to trust you."

I let out another breath and willed myself to stay seated. There could be others lying in wait in other cars. I scanned the lot again. Nothing, but it was hard to trust my new senses.

"Aaron, I . . . apologize greatly for what transpired in Blackheart. I misjudged the situation, and I should have been more open to compromise. I understand how my actions have affected you and your family, and I know there is nothing I can do to fully make up for my error."

"That's a start." Aaron flexed his jaw, with his shoulders pulled back. "I'll need more insurance than that if I'm going to help you."

"What do you suggest?" Kilian shifted. "My only fear is that you will take the information I have and flee. And I have no intention of stopping you or hurting you if that is what you choose to do. But I implore you, this is the closest we've ever been to taking down this coven, and I do not think that we can do that without you. Without you, we won't have a chance at saving your brothers or Thane and Will. I am in need of the information that you have since you were the last one to see them alive."

"So, you do care."

"I'm afraid you have a distorted image of me. And for that I can only blame myself. I'd like to start anew. I want us to work together."

Kilian stepped forward, and Aaron let him stand an arm's distance away. It was too close. I huffed, opening my car door with no thoughts in my head other than not letting Kilian grab Aaron and pull him into the infamous van Presley was always going on about. There were no vans around as I got closer, but I was ready for anything. The cold air sliced through my jeans.

Aaron pulled his shoulders back, and his back went rigid. "I'm not the only one who needs convincing."

The weight of Kilian's gaze was strong but not stronger than my resolve. The anxious tension dissipated as soon as I was next to Aaron again. If he got taken, I'd get taken too.

"I couldn't stay," I said.

Aaron stood in a protective stance between Kilian and me, but he kept a cool, collected smile and nodded like he anticipated that answer.

"We don't trust you." I stared directly into Kilian's eyes.

Normally, we'd have a buffer. Zach and Luke mainly dealt with Kilian in Blackheart, but now it was up to us, and a part of me had been dying to tell Kilian what I thought of him leaving Presley and me to die while he held the people I loved hostage.

"I understand."

"Do you? You made a bad deal, and because of you, Skylar is dead and everyone is gone. The twins needed your help. You failed everyone, including Will. We trusted you because we're all too young to know better and we didn't have a choice."

Kilian's armor cracked for a brief moment. His eyes softened, and for the first time, it felt like he was actually looking at me and acknowledging me as a person.

I had no problem wounding him with words like he'd wounded us by his actions. If we'd worked together from the beginning, maybe all of it could have been avoided, but he'd used and exploited us for his own interests. If we were going to move forward, I needed an acknowledgment.

"I will not claim to be a saint." He linked his hands together and rubbed them. "We may have met in a church, but I'm a flawed man who's made many mistakes in his lifetime. A man whose faith holds on by a thread. And you two tumbled into the room and got dragged into something bigger than yourselves. I can't help but believe that in itself is the same fate that brought you in front of me today."

"Is it just more of what we can do for you?" Aaron said.

"I won't twist my motives to soften you to me and my cause. And I'd like to be as transparent as possible moving forward. Many do not believe in our endeavors. My old friends left in The Legion will not help me with this because of the risks. It is only you. And I have no way of knowing where this journey will lead. But I have nothing else. I will not live another day without pursuing them for what they've done. You needed me, and I let you down, and now, truly, you're the only hope I have left."

His voice cracked but his stoic gaze never faltered. The scars on his hands had me wondering how many battles he'd fought and how many times he'd tried this endeavor only to fail. Akira claimed it was because The Family had killed his brother. At one point, I'd have found it preposterous to hear Kilian's pleas at all. But now . . .

I understood how love might make someone do things they weren't proud of. Zach's tired, cold stare reminded me of that often, and our conversation came back to me.

"That's what makes people like me incredibly dangerous. We're selfish."

Zach would never have trusted Kilian if he'd known he had a brother, but like Kilian now, he had no choice. I didn't know why I was asking myself what Zach would do. Something told me if the roles were reversed and we'd been taken, he wouldn't care about Kilian's motives or even an apology. He'd grab him by the collar and make him help.

"Are you even sad that Will and Thane are gone? Are you sorry my brothers went back to Her because of you?" I'd rarely heard that kind of venom in Aaron's voice.

His calm exterior was cracking. He was thinking of his brothers and probably feeling their pain as we spoke.

Kilian pulled his shoulders back like he'd been hit. "More than I'll ever be able to make you understand."

"This was a mistake," Aaron said, shielding me. "Let's go, Kim."

He could be right. He was taking the cautious approach, and it made sense, but I wasn't looking for the cautious approach. Not when our best plan was staring me in the face. I wasn't ready to trust Kilian yet, but the thought of walking away with no other options wasn't enticing. I grabbed his arm to stop him.

"Wait." A car door opened, and a tall silhouette emerged.

"Dom." I said his name more eagerly than I'd anticipated, but he'd saved my life. I hadn't forgotten, like I hadn't forgotten his sister. Skylar was always in the back of my mind reminding me to trust myself.

"Let me speak to them."

Kilian nodded, and Dom walked into the middle of the parking lot. His disheveled dark hair was longer, and the edges of his usually stoic lips tugged into a small smile.

"Kimberly."

I hugged him. He was rigid underneath my arms, but I didn't care. His smell reminded me of Skylar.

"Your hair is different." His voice held the same boredom as before.

I smoothed down a lock of my hair, suddenly feeling self-conscience, and Aaron grabbed my waist to pull me closer.

"How are you?" I looked up to his light-emerald eyes, anticipating a non-answer.

"Fine." Dom looked between us. "But I need you to listen to Kilian."

Aaron squeezed me tighter.

"I'm working directly with Kilian now, and we have plans, but all of those plans involve you."

Kilian stood tall in his beige trousers, with his hands in his pockets, waiting.

"Why us?"

"You're still our closest link to The Family by blood. We've never had that before. And you have cause to fight."

"What about Skylar?"

To my surprise, the edges of his lips tugged upward. "My sister never lived a day of her life with regret. We've known the risks since we first met Kilian."

Aaron and I shared a look of uncertainty.

"We know where the coven is located."

"You do?" Hope stirred in Aaron's voice.

"Yes. We tracked an unidentified plane in the general area, and we've been able to pinpoint a possible location. There are things that must be done. A battle is coming, and we won't have a chance without you."

Kilian sauntered up next to us. "We have a cabin not far from here. Meet us there, and we can finish our talks and discuss our next steps."

"Wait, first tell me where they are. Tell me, and I promise we'll help you."

Something in Aaron's voice, exuding strength and confidence, stirred a memory. He reminded me of Luke, and as I'd been told and seen . . . Luke always kept his promises.

"Northern Ireland on an island. We have to confirm the exact coordinates, but there is a lot of buzz in the area of their return to the queen's home country."

Aaron and I exchanged a look. Butterflies circled in my gut. Good news. The first bit of good news we'd had in weeks.

"We're in," Aaron said, and I nodded.

"Whatever it takes."

The address we were given wasn't too far of a drive, about forty minutes from Vera's. Aaron dialed Presley's number to fill him in. When we closed the car door, we sat in the silence of the car for a moment.

Aaron smiled from ear to ear. The cadence of his heartbeat filled the cold compartment of the car.

"We know where they are," he said, staring at his phone. His ears and cheeks had pinkened, and I'd thought it was from the cold until I saw the glisten in his eyes.

I squeezed his hand. "We're going to get them back."

Twenty

PRESLEY

I couldn't believe they went. No protection, no nothing. The twins wouldn't approve. No way. I hunched over on the side of my bed, rubbing my chest for the thousandth time. No matter what I did, nothing helped. Mom gave me heating pads—the weird rice kind that smelled when you put them in the microwave. Even showers were useless because the water was permanently lukewarm.

What if they got taken? Then I'd be alone with Mom till she died of old age, unless I convinced her to turn—already asked and she'd said no—but it was still early. I could probably still get her to do it if I begged on my hands and knees. Only, then I'd feel guilty because Mom's been talking about heaven for forever. She also talked about missing grandma a lot and how excited she was to see her again one day, so taking her away from that kind of made me feel like a selfish loser. Would I be alone for the rest of eternity because I wasn't brave enough to take risks?

Then it would just be an eternity in a cold barren wasteland. *Oh God.*

I popped up to my feet to pace my room. What was I thinking? I should have gone to help. I should have done something. Now I would turn into a lonely hermit, but not the cool kind like Yoda. It would be the bad kind. The kind that lives in a cave and talks to himself and tries to trick people with riddles. *I'm terrible at riddles!*

My phone ringing broke my thoughts. A shrill pop song I'd picked because I had nothing better to do. I sighed at the sound of my brother's voice and listened intently while he explained the meeting with Kilian.

"Ireland?"

"Yeah, he said it's an island, but they're still trying to find the exact coordinates."

"Well, that's not too far. Right? We can go?"

"We will. I promise. We're going to the cabin to talk about the details, and I'll fill you in. I'll send you that address just in case."

"Don't go into any basements!"

"I won't, don't worry." Aaron's voice was oddly calm and comforting. "I'll text you updates and when I'll be home."

When he hung up, I thought I'd feel relief. I should have felt a little happier about the occasion, but all I could think about was how long until Kilian stabbed us in the back.

We needed to get to Ireland.

At least I had a little spot on the globe I could look at. Rummaging through the closet, I found what I was looking for: a world map that was tattered and should have been thrown away a long time ago. It's probably been there since they built this cabin in the freakin' 1970s. Mom said none of the furniture was hers and belonged to whoever was renting.

I sprawled it over my bed to take in the full view. An ocean apart was not that bad. I could probably swim there if I had to. Not ideal. Very cold. But I wouldn't drown or anything. I mean, probably not. I didn't exactly know all the vampire rules, but I didn't think lungs full of water would feel that great.

Maybe we could hop on a boat and go over, but Northern Ireland was big and had a few parts that looked like islands. I wanted to look it up, but Mom was the only one with internet on her phone, and it was incredibly slow.

Suddenly, my phone felt heavy in my pocket. I could help another way.

We needed a backup plan when this thing fell through, and all our plans tended to do that. It wouldn't hurt to think about it for a second or two.

The note was left to me for a reason, but I wondered what that reason might be. What did Akira see in me, anyway? Why did *I* get the note? Akira didn't trust The Legion either. I guess we had that in common. He said a lot of stuff I didn't remember, but I remembered that part.

I opened my phone and stared at my call log. The number had called me back numerous times, but I'd let it ring. No messages though.

Maybe Akira knew something about The Legion we didn't and the number was supposed to help somehow. He didn't hurt us when he could have. He was strong enough to kill us all that day at the farm. He'd obviously let us win so we would drink Hell Bitch's blood, and that was not very trustworthy.

I just need to choose.

If I wanted to do it, I should just try it and see who was really on the other line. It wasn't my brothers, but it could give us another clue. It wasn't like I needed to tell anybody. I could make good decisions on my own.

That weird emotion bubbled in my stomach again. My body flushed and I felt . . . angry but couldn't pinpoint why. Just the heat of the emotion rushing through me.

Another memory resurfaced before I could block it out.

Zach and I were in my room in Blackheart.

"Aaron is being such a baby," I said to Zach after Luke had explained I couldn't taunt Aaron anymore by fake flirting with Kimberly.

"I don't think Aaron would actually hurt you. Luke just wants to be safe."

"No, I mean with Kimberly. He's being ridiculous."

"Ah." Zach plopped down on the bed and rested his head on his hand. *"This doesn't have anything to do with Ellis, does it?"*

I stopped folding my clothes on the bed. *"What? No. Why would you say that? I haven't thought of him in forever."* At least thirty minutes.

"Hmm." Zach watched me with those piercing laser eyes, like he had cut me open and started dissecting my insides. He had little pliers to pick out all my hidden parts, like that board game with the loud noises. He was really subtle about it.

"Don't do it. Don't psychoanalyze me. You know I hate that."

"I'm not."

"I know you and Luke sit around all day and worry."

"Do not."

"Well, maybe you should be talking to Aaron. Someone's gotta tell him how brainless he's being. Kimberly is the perfect girl, and he's going to ruin it. He's going to ruin his chance to have a relationship with someone who is literally his soulmate. He doesn't even see how lucky he is. It's like talking to a wall. A big stone wall that doesn't do anything but just stand there and listen to no one and . . . Uh, I don't where I'm going with that."

There was silence while Zach watched me fold shirts terribly and made no effort to correct me.

"It's okay, you know . . . if you want to be angry."

"How did you get that from what I just said?"

He sat up, letting his shoulders fall. *"Changing you took a lot away from you, and that's our fault. I know, especially right now, dating is pretty out of the picture with everything going on. I've thought about it. How . . . I'll never get married. No chance of having kids. So, it's okay if you want to be angry at me."*

"I'm not angry."

"You're not angry at Aaron for having something you don't?"

"I'll be angry if he leaves her. Wait." I held up my finger and pointed. *"Ah. you're doing it! I said no."*

He smiled. *"I'm just saying, if you want to be mad, it's okay to be mad at me. I can take it."*

"Why would I be mad at you? It's not like any of this is your fault."

"It is my fault," he said quickly. Cleverly leaving little room for argument.

"Well, too bad. I'm not mad at you."

He got up and hit me on the shoulder. His equivalent to a Luke bear hug.

"If you ever want to talk about that thing that didn't happen with Ellis, I'm all ears."

How did he even know? Leave it to Zach to recognize something as seemingly insignificant as my monster crush on my formal date in Blackheart.

I pulled myself out of the recollection before too many of the memories crept in. My chest already hurt. I didn't need to make it worse.

Aaron thought I was the younger brother with no perception skills, but I could be helpful like everyone else. I was good for more than sitting around in my room waiting for things to happen.

I dialed the number, with the heat still in my cheeks. Pacing the cabin floor, I waited as the phone rang.

Maybe I was wrong. It wasn't something Aaron would do, that's for sure. Aaron would tell me to burn the note or something. Rubbing my chest right over my heart, I didn't see any other alternatives. If things fell through, I was the only one who might have a way to find them.

When a voice sounded on the line, chills ran down my spine.

"Hello?"

"Is this Presley?"

I stilled, contemplating my decision. "Um. Yeah. This is Presley."

"Why did you hang up on me and not answer?"

"Uh, I don't know. You're kinda scary." I mean, why not be honest?

"Nobody has told you anything?"

"Nope." *A common occurrence.*

"Well, I was given this phone a while back and told to have it on me at all times until a Presley called me. I have some stuff for you. We need to meet up."

"That seems sketchy." *Really extra sketch.*

"He said you'd say that."

"Well, I'm not really in a place I can travel."

"I'll come to you. What's your nearest town?"

"Why would I tell you that?"

"Because you need what I have? He said to tell you 'All roads lead here.'"

Of course, more cryptic vampire shit. These people needed to be stopped. It was actually ridiculous.

"Can't you just tell me what it is first?"

"No. I don't make the rules. I just follow 'em. And you should too. We can grab a drink."

"Fine." I swallowed the lump in my throat. "But it might take me a bit to arrange."

"Just tell me where and when."

"Fairbanks, Alaska. I'll let you know a good time."

An hour away. Far enough away to keep my family out of it. *I hope.*

"Okay, I'll make arrangements. You just make sure you answer my phone calls."

"Maybe just text me next time."

I was asking a mystery man to text me and was going to go meet him in another city. My older brothers would murder me.

Twenty-One

AARON

The sun disappeared behind the snow-covered trees by the time we made it to Kilian's cabin. A strange sense of déjà vu fell over me. It was just another cabin in a different place, but this time, it was without my brothers.

Only, it wasn't a cabin but a house with large glass windows. It was surrounded by trees drowning in snow. One big colorless rectangle with a modern staircase leading to a porch and a second floor.

I texted Presley our address. That way he'd at least know where to look if things went bad, but I was hopeful about the whole thing.

Ireland. They were in Ireland. I could find them, even if I had to search that whole country on foot. Technically, I could. That fact alone, even if impractical, helped ease the tension in my chest.

I was able to differentiate when the pain was mine and when it wasn't. With one hand, I pat my chest, hoping it reached my brothers. Whichever one needed it. They just needed to hold on. We were coming.

I was the first to get out of the car. One reason was to open Kimberly's door, but the other was to scan the area. With a sharp inhale, I let the cold air fill my senses. Snow muffled everything. It made sounds and smells murky and watered down. Everything in Blackheart was loud and sharp. The smells of pine and dirt were constant, and I'd learned to tune them out. Instead, I'd just smell Kim's perfume and anticipate her proximity. That was more fun.

I was smelling for anything dangerous, like blood or people in the trees. While walking around the car to Kimberly's door, I focused harder, and the only sound was my footsteps crunching in the snow. Kilian and Dom were already out of their car. I worked on memorizing their patterns: the sounds of their feet and their heartbeats each had a specific cadence.

All I heard was the TV in the house mixed with faint whispering but not a crowd, just a few people. I noted a few other cars built for snow in their driveway.

Kimberly's blue eyes steadied me as I opened her car door.

"Are you good?" I pressed my lips to the warmth of her hand.

She had that faraway look in her eyes, like she was trying to solve an impossible puzzle. Kim's brain gave her questions with impossible answers. It was a never-ending list of possibilities in her head. She explained it to me like constantly being bombarded with every outcome there could ever be while simultaneously only believing in the bad ones.

I squeezed her shoulders to ground her back with me. She liked it when I did that.

"I'm okay." The corners of her mouth tugged but never made it to a smile. Smiles weren't as common as they used to be for us.

I leaned in to kiss her on the lips, and that did it.

She melted into me, and we walked hand in hand after Kilian and

Dom into the house. I could see no one else from the outside. Just a living room with a leather couch and fireplace.

The house smelled of firewood and a candle that reminded me of the sauna back at BFU gym. It was a massive upgrade from his place in Blackheart. No wonder he'd spent all that time in our library. That dingy cabin was a shack in comparison.

"I thought you weren't loaded with money," I said.

"This is a friend's. She let me use it for the time being."

"What are the odds of that?"

He said nothing and continued showing us down a long hallway with freshly polished hardwood floors. It was kind of a red flag but not enough to make me bolt.

Halina and Felix stood in a dining room with a piano and a long mahogany table surrounded by chairs. They stared as we came through the door, and I wrapped my arm around Kimberly.

I had spoken little with Felix since our poker incident in Blackheart, but I remembered his words about Kimberly's imminent death. He had a toothpick in his mouth and his hands behind his back, but he wasn't scowling this time. He and his sister had white-blond hair. His was short on the sides and spikey at the top, and hers was long and straight and flowed down to her hips. Halina's features were sharper, and her brow lowered as we entered.

They weren't the only ones in the room, but the only ones I recognized. I spent little time learning names in Blackheart and was starting to see where I'd spent most of my attention—pursuing the girl under my arm. I didn't regret it, but I needed to think differently going into this situation. There was no safety net. I was Kimberly's protector. What would my brothers do?

They'd take charge. Zach would scowl. That was easy. Luke would square his shoulders and puff out his chest. He'd probably listen too. *I should listen.*

The TV in the other room played the local news and talked about the weather. More snow was coming. A few feet stomped around upstairs but nothing fast moving.

"Are we going to have that rematch round . . . cheater?" I smiled, trying to make it the right amount of standoffish. I wasn't going for Zach's level of antagonism, but just enough. Felix's teeth snapped his toothpick.

"We're happy to have you. You could sit. Make yourself at home here," Kilian said.

"Not likely," I whispered to Kimberly.

We were outnumbered, another new feeling I was still processing. Being one of four brothers was never lonely.

"Okay, we're here. We're listening. We need to know your plans," Kimberly said.

Kilian stood next to a long window that stretched to the ceiling. I'd almost forgotten how tall he was until I saw him next to it. Halina and Felix chose to sit.

"Your disappearance was . . . unexpected. We've spent a considerable amount of effort in finding you all. I was surprised when we got such an obvious sign of where to find you. I'd been focusing most of our resources on not losing the leads we did have on The Family. It was Felix's idea to keep an eye out for outgoing flights in the area and to track it."

Felix interjected. "You're welcome."

"Once we had that likely location, we focused on following your trail up the coast. Right now, I have employed scouts in Ireland surveying the area and using any means necessary to get a layout of the island. They appear to run tourism there, and we're working diligently to see if we can get a detailed map of the town and the castle grounds."

"My brothers are living in a castle?"

"Most likely. I have not confirmed appearances of anyone we're look-ing for yet. But that is our hope. It appears they've owned the castle for centuries. It might be the original place where Cecily Dooley was born. We'd never been able to find the exact location. Though, we didn't *need* to find it before due to their location in the United States."

"When do we get to ask questions? You're not the only ones who need information," Felix spat.

"How did you all kill Akira? Was Will there?" Halina asked, her eyes sparkled with something new. Desperation.

Maybe that's why they were looking at us like that. The death of Akira was a big deal, and I'd hardly had time to process it all. They didn't know the story. Will and Thane were supposed to fill them in when they met up with Kilian.

"How did you know we killed him?" Kimberly asked, a question I hadn't thought of.

We'd left the building in flames. They had no way of knowing.

"The flight in the area came from Ireland. We have reports from our scouts that Ezra was away on business. They would never leave the queen with one member of The Guard without good reason. If Akira had lived, there would be no reason for Ezra to disappear." Kilian's voice stayed steady.

His calming voice helped me to focus. They had more resources than I thought, and I wondered if my brothers knew.

"Will helped us fight. Everything was great until Ezra showed up in the forest and took them. They would have taken all of us . . . but Will sacrificed himself so me, Presley, and Kimberly could get away."

Felix's blue eyes seared into mine. "How did they know where you were? We didn't even know."

"Thane. He was . . . taken over. He betrayed us. He must have been keeping tabs for them the whole time."

Halina shook her head. "He wouldn't."

"I don't think he chose it. Akira got to him somehow and used him."

Felix and Halina shared a look. My stomach dropped. I guess twin telepathy was common. With a white-knuckled grip on the table, Felix's hand shook.

I ran them through the rest. How Will snuck us out of the frat house and we'd found my brother and Kimberly. I told them about the fight with Akira and the blood my brothers and I consumed in order to kill him.

"So it's going to be a battle, then? As you said before in the diner . . ." Kimberly brought us back to the plan.

"I'm afraid so. It will not be easy. And we are likely outnumbered, outmatched, and at a disadvantage," Kilian said. "But as I said before, we have reason to hope and believe that this is the most advantageous time we have. There is a celestial event I have a feeling is closely related to the queen and Her power. I'm awaiting more intel. But there will be a solar eclipse in that region in March."

"March," I spat. March was so far. Too far away.

"It's tentative. But I believe the event is important enough that we need to figure out its purpose. We need the time if we're going to acquire victory."

"You said celestial event . . . What does that have to do with this?" Kimberly asked.

"We've been collecting data for centuries, and one thing we know for sure is that Her strength is closely related to the moon cycles. Though She is the most powerful in regard to psychic and mental abilities that far exceed even the oldest vampires, we believe She does not always possess Her powers every day. On the night of the full moon, She's the strongest and gradually through the waxing phases loses that power."

"The . . . moon?" I scratched my head. "You're saying that's what Her power comes from?"

"We don't know for certain where it comes from, but we have charted Her abilities with the moon cycles. I know it's hard to believe. There are many things that were not pertinent to tell you before. I never imagined you, Aaron Calem, would be helping us in a battle. Keeping vital information about the queen hidden is what I've been trained to do for centuries."

"Right. Okay. So we need to track the moon. Got it. And that's going to help us defeat Her?"

Kilian nodded and lowered his head. "There's something I want to show you. Just a moment."

He went upstairs, leaving us in silence with Dom and the others. Kimberly and I shared an equal look of confusion as we processed Kilian's words.

"So, Calem, how's life treating you without big brother?" Felix didn't smile. He seemed genuinely curious. Something about him was softer and open. And me . . . I was harder.

"Been better."

"You changed your hair," Halina said to Kimberly while looking her up and down. "It's . . . interesting."

Kimberly's brows furrowed as she took on the weight of that comment, and I kissed the top of her head. She was so beautiful, and I'd never let her forget it.

"My sister would have liked it," Dom said, looking down at his shoes and running his thumb over his bare knuckles.

"That's not the only thing that's changed, it seems." Felix licked his teeth while he eyed Kimberly. When I squeezed her closer, he turned his attention to me. "I'm surprised you changed her."

"It was my decision. And yes, I do like it. More than being human, anyway," Kimberly said.

"Anything's better than being human," Felix said.

The sound of Kilian's footsteps flowed down the hardwood steps, and we quieted as he entered the room with a wooden box. It resembled the one that once held the black blood that had brought my brothers to their knees.

I flinched when he opened it. There was no vial of black blood but a silver dagger the size of my forearm. It had a floral pattern engraved on the silver handle, and it led to a pin-straight blade that looked freshly polished and sharp.

All the movement in the room stopped. Everyone's eyes were trained on the blade.

"What am I looking at?" I asked.

"This is one of the last daggers. The daggers were crafted and are believed to be the key to bringing more queens into existence. Much about the first creation of the first queen and the creation of these daggers is unknown, but it's believed through ritual text guided by the fates the queens were formed. Each blade is carved with a unique Latin phrase, and there is blood harbored in the handle from the victim of the ritual. In this case, Cecily. It's kept sealed with an emerald on the end of the handle."

"You could have mentioned a magical dagger."

"The existence of the daggers themselves is lost to many around the world, and we desire to keep it that way. It's how we've kept the forma-tion of more coming to fruition. We've worked tirelessly for centuries to eliminate the daggers from existence. There are only two remaining, and the other one is with The Legion's archives."

"Why keep them? Why not destroy them?" Kimberly eyed the dagger with wide eyes.

"Because it's our greatest aid in killing them."

"So we can kill Her . . ." I said, my throat dry and hoarse.

"Yes, these daggers are believed to hold power. At every fall of a queen, one of these daggers were present. Queens historically are hard to eliminate, not only due to their Guard but also the physical effects of being near them. Humans are not strong enough to kill them, and anyone who has been turned has the power of Their blood in them. It's easy to overpower and bring them into Her thrall. But it's believed the blade can pierce Her skin without the loss of blood."

"Do they know you have this?"

"Yes. This dagger was taken in the battle where my brother lost his life. It's the last hope for many, especially those in this room."

Dom interjected. "Everyone here has committed. We have close to twenty souls that are willing to fight."

"Working on more," Kilian said.

"How many do we need?" I asked.

"It's impossible to estimate how many they have right now, but my intel should help."

"Can't you just turn more people and make a little army or something?"

"Don't ask questions about things you don't understand yet," Felix growled.

"It's a good question," Kilian said. "I can promise any idea you have has been tried before over the centuries. Finding people who have a reason to fight is crucial. Changing people for the purpose of our cause hasn't worked in the way we'd hoped. It also leaves us vulnerable. The Family has been known to use the ones we turn and bring them over to their side."

"What about your friend who loaned you this house? Are they included?" Kimberly asked.

"No, unfortunately. There is something you both must understand about me and The Legion in general. This dagger is unknown to anyone outside of this household, and I have kept it so for a reason. The Legion as it stands is very secretive. They don't take risks, and they don't fight on whims and feelings. They work more on principle and rules. I have prior interest in this endeavor with the coven of your brothers, and due to my closeness to the situation, many will not help."

"They think it's a suicide mission. And it is," Halina said.

"I don't get it. Why wouldn't they want to band together to take them down?" I asked.

"Many will not intervene unless they believe they propose a large risk to the public. The ones that have were taken out. But not without a great deal of sacrifice to our cause."

"Wait, so you're not even Legion? You're a weird rogue branch?"

"I am. We share the same ideologies. I just . . . have a prior interest."

He was a fraud and a liar. My palms flamed, and I clenched my fist. I wondered what would have happened if we'd met someone from the real Legion. The type that wanted to keep to the rules. Something told me we'd have never made it out of the church. I wanted to be mad at Kilian, and I was. He'd done nothing but lie and bend the truth. He used me and my brothers for his own gain. And still, he may be the only reason we were alive. If they'd never picked us up in Blackheart, Akira would have taken us all back to Her.

"Is this because of your brother?" Kimberly asked Kilian. I hardly remembered that bit of information.

The color leached from Kilian's face. "Yes. My brother was inquisitive and curious. He had invested interest in this queen. And now, so do I. We tried once before to take them down, and we were unsuccessful. Though we did bring down a member of Her Guard, my brother couldn't be saved."

My chest tightened. I couldn't even think of losing one of my brothers. When I looked at Kilian's solemn face, my perspective shifted. It didn't change the things he did, and I didn't agree with his methods, but there wasn't anything I wouldn't do to get my brothers back. That feeling could lead anyone down a dark path. If I didn't have Kimberly firmly pressed against me or my little brother to look after, things might be different.

"I'm sorry," I said, knowing it was stupid. I probably should have hated him more than I did, but I wasn't an angry child anymore. All the anger I had would be better disbursed on the people who took my brothers from me and were currently holding them.

Kilian nodded. "We need you. Both of you."

He looked at Kimberly, and I felt prickly all over.

"We've never had a woman with such close connection to the bloodline. Now that you've been changed, we want to test some things. One thing we need for the battle is an advantage. Right now, with the queen's abilities, it will be easier for Her to see us coming, who we're bringing, and more options for our attacks and our most likely day of arrival."

"What kind of tests?" I asked, my muscles tightening.

"This might be hard to believe," Kilian said.

Kimberly and I shared a look and shrugged. There wasn't much we wouldn't believe.

"The full moon is tonight, and with this dagger and Kimberly, I believe we can access some of that power and use it to our advantage."

"How?"

"On the night of the full moon, She feels the most connection to Her power source. We will tap into it and hopefully be able to use it, possibly Her clairvoyance. I have not been able to test any of my theories until now."

"Through Kimberly," I said flatly.

I didn't like it. He had that look in his eye again that glowed with something more than hope. It was hard to trust a desperate man.

Backpedaling was an understatement. Suddenly, all those thoughts about not being angry were gone.

"What would I need to do?" Kimberly asked.

"I will try a few incantations. I'm not certain it will work, but I've never been able to try until now. The queen doesn't change women, and the ones She did, died long ago. Skylar's blood was too far removed, as is Halina's. I've tried it on myself, but I'm a mutt by blood as well. I theorized that it may only connect with women. The entity has always favored women."

"Kim, I don't like this," I said, knowing they'd hear.

"This is not a coincidence. Us meeting on this day. Meeting here of all places. This is destiny. From the moment we first met, everything was aligning for this purpose."

I hide to fight an eye roll at that one.

"Can we have a minute?" Kimberly asked.

"Of course." Kimberly grabbed my hand and guided me to the front porch. It was snowing again.

"We can't trust them," I said.

"I know. But Kilian is just desperate enough that I . . . believe it."

"We don't know what the ritual is."

"I know. But I'm willing to try it." She looked off into the distance before staring deep into my eyes. "Aaron, if you want to find your brothers and save them, it's going to be hard. And it's going to cost. I don't think we'll always like what it costs, but I think we need to try. We need to take risks. If we play it safe, I don't think we'll find them."

She was right.

"I don't want you to do anything that could hurt you. And they wouldn't want you to do that either."

"And I'm telling you it might, and I'm okay with it."

I sighed and wiped a fallen snowflake from her face. There wasn't any use arguing with her, as that determined look in her eyes scorched me from head to toe.

"And if I'm not?"

"You can't tell me what to do." This time, she smiled.

Twenty-Two

KIMBERLY

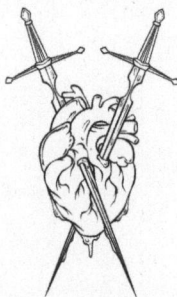

"Are you sure?" Aaron eyed me with a thin-lipped frown. It didn't suit him.

He flinched away from a candle on a bookshelf next to his head. The shelves were lined to the ceilings in books with cracked spines, and the smell of parchment filled my senses.

I understood Aaron's hesitation, but I was confident I was up for the task, whatever it might be.

Meeting Kilian again took me back to the church where everything began. I remembered it all. The smell of wax and cedar and the salt air tinging the saliva on my lips. Since we'd been trying to find The Legion, I'd thought of that day repeatedly, and the moment I couldn't forget—Zach and Luke bursting through the church doors. They'd been prepared to die, even in my place as a practical stranger. *"I'm glad I met you,"* Luke had said. They both looked death in the face with a smile. In comparison, tapping into the queen's power was easy.

Touching the cool blade of the dagger resting in my lap, I smiled at Aaron.

"Let's do it."

We weren't alone. Halina, Dom, and Felix were scattered around the room in various fabric-lined chairs. I'd expected more pushback from them. I remembered their scowling faces back in Blackheart not that long ago, but everything had changed for them and for us. All that old resistance separating us was no longer important because we'd all lost people. We'd been only kids in their eyes before, and now we were important to them. With Thane, Will, and Skylar gone, their mission to kill the queen was all they had.

The time for games and laughing was over.

"I'm going to read over the phrase on the dagger as it's listed in the text."

"How long is this going to take?" Aaron's knees were touching mine. He'd finally stopped pacing to take the chair beside me.

I hated to worry him. I wasn't exactly thrilled with the unknown of Kilian's plans either.

"It could take all night, or it may not be useful at all. I'm not certain the passages referencing the dagger are accurate. It will be trial and error. Ancient texts were created of the ritual during the first queen's creation to document the discovery, but many of those passages are gone. There's power in them, and The Family has gone great lengths to keep the information to themselves. Much of it has been destroyed by The Legion as well. But we were able to take these from the monastery during our last altercation. They have promise."

"We should start then," I said.

"Wait? How will she know if it's working? What will it feel like?" Aaron said.

"I'm not sure. This is an experiment."

"Okay, but what if it's painful or something?"

"Aaron, we're trying it regardless." I squeezed his hand resting on his knee.

He nodded. "Whatever happens. I'm right here."

His eyes sparkled with unending confidence, and I was sure I needed no other assurance than that.

Kilian wet his finger and flipped through a few pages while sitting on a desk a few feet in front of us.

I nodded, and a long string of words trickled from Kilian's lips. It almost sounded like a song. Latin. I felt nothing other than the cold silver of the dagger.

"Should we take a break?" Dom asked after two in the morning.

We'd been there for hours wondering if it was possible the moon's position in the sky had any bearing on the ritual, or even our proximity to them. But my new body didn't falter or ache. It was strange how quickly I'd forgotten how pain and tiredness felt in the body. It made time pass quickly and without fuss.

Aaron rubbed my leg, awaiting my answer.

"Just a little longer."

There wouldn't be another moon like this for weeks, and time was precious. Too much time had already passed. If the twins were with The Family, there was no telling what was happening to them. I tried not to imagine it, but Luke's panic attacks came to mind. His fear and inability to focus because of Her. The thought alone sent my heart aflutter.

We were missing something.

"Maybe it needs blood," I said. "I mean, this entire thing is about blood."

"Wait, is this not the exact same thing that created the queens? Is this Thing going to reach in and possess her?" Aaron asked.

"Good point," I said.

"The entity—"

"Thought you said it was a demon."

"Whatever its origin, I can guarantee it will not be able to harbor itself in your body. The text is clear about one thing. It must be a human woman. Kimberly has already been changed and taken on the entity in her body. She can't be a vessel because she is no longer pure."

Aaron shook his head and raked his fingers through his hair, clearly not believing Kilian. I didn't trust Kilian, but if something happened to me, Aaron would bail and all of Kilian's plans would be ruined. Which meant he thought it was a viable option.

I bit into my thumb and ran the blood along the blade. Aaron's frown deepened.

Kilian spoke again in Latin. It sounded like all the other things he'd recited, yet this felt different. My hand was tingling.

Come closer.

I flinched.

The Thing in my head never spoke to me in the way Aaron had described it. A distinct voice. But this must have been what he'd been referring to.

"Are you okay?" Aaron said.

"Yes, keep going."

Closer.

I wrapped my hand around the dagger, wincing at the slight sting as I gripped the sharp edges. Then there was a pulling sensation that turned into a sinking feeling. Like the floor was giving out and I was seconds away from falling.

And I did.

The world disappeared around me, and a strange weightlessness settled into my blood. Like my body was pumped full of helium, I fell into pure bliss.

And there was . . . nothing.

Nothing for me to fall into.

Nothing to feel. Everything was a void.

I wasn't afraid it would swallow me. This place was safe for me. Even if I felt like someone was watching me.

Show me. I pushed, no longer feeling my hand on the dagger but knowing it was there.

Help me. Show me something.

It was hesitant. There was no way for me to know that. Nothing to see or physically assert, but I could feel the truth in my head like It was speaking, but it sounded more like . . . singing. Singing that was a low whisper in my ears.

Perhaps It wanted me to beg. I dug in harder.

Help me help him. I thought of Aaron's face. His golden-blond hair and his warm eyes.

With that, a flash of light overwhelmed me. The brightest light I'd ever seen. Something that could only exist in a void.

And then I saw . . . Aaron running. Faster and faster. It was the view from the back of his head, and he didn't turn back. At first, I thought he was being chased, but this was different. He was running toward something.

What did it mean? As soon as I contemplated it, the image morphed.

My stomach grew sick. There was something I needed to see. A warning. No. *Just a different path.*

The bright light faded until I saw the Calem brothers. All four stood next to a large ornate throne dressed in all-black suits. Seated between them was the queen. Long white hair and piercing eyes. Presley was at Her feet pulling at the hem of Her silk gown to gain Her attention. Her head was inclined toward Luke, while he whispered something in Her ear and She ran Her fingers along his chin. On Her other side, hovering with a white-knuckled grip on the chair, was Zach. His expression was cold, unwavering, and devoid of any semblance of the person I knew. And then there was Aaron, *my Aaron*, holding Her hand and kneeling to kiss Her cheek.

The shock of it felt like a punch to the stomach. No. Worse. The worst thing I could imagine. Worse than death. With nothing but pure despair left for me, I willed the image to turn.

When I blinked again, I was on the floor surrounded. Aaron held me in his lap while caressing my head, and around him, everyone who'd been in the room was leaning over me. Cool, intoxicating relief washed over me as if I'd awakened from a nightmare.

"It worked," I said.

"Step back," Aaron said to the crowd surrounding us, with his eyes darkening.

I felt for his arm and rubbed it softly. He was still with me. Still mine.

"It's okay. I'm fine. What happened?"

"Your eyes rolled back, and you stayed like that for a minute, then you just fell," Aaron said.

I let him pull me up. The disorientation left as I got to my feet. A line settled between Aaron's brows and dented his forehead.

"I'm okay. Really."

At my words, he softened. He surveyed me with carefulness that brought a flush to my cheeks, as if there weren't four other sets of eyes on us.

"Where did you go?" he asked.

"I was in this . . . strange nothing place. I couldn't feel my body, but I felt something with me."

"What did it feel like? Did it seem malicious?" Kilian asked.

"No. This was . . . neutral. Whatever it was, something watched me until I asked for Its help."

I told them all the details while Aaron ushered me into a chair. Though I kept the details about the Calem brothers with Her to the minimum of what they needed to know. I didn't want to think of it, especially the vacant admiration in all their eyes.

Aaron didn't even flinch when I said it. His hand tightening in mine was the only indication he'd heard me.

"This is an amazing progression." Kilian smiled from ear to ear and looked at Dom. "Do you feel any lingering effects?"

"No, I feel good. Should we try again?"

Aaron shook his head but awaited my response.

"I wouldn't advise. I'm not sure of the side effects of tapping into Her power. Unfortunately, that means we won't be able to try again for another month."

Something cracked in Aaron's expression—deep disappointment.

"But I wasn't shown anything useful. What about the prophecy?" I asked, feeling the same disappointment, but it made my blood burn hotter.

"It might take time. This gave us a significant clue. There is still much we can do. We'll train, form a plan of attack, and teach you both to fight. Will your brother be joining us?" Kilian asked.

Aaron and I shared a look. That was unlikely but not impossible. Presley's distrust of The Legion ran deep, and my theory was because he was deeply loyal to his brothers. The kind of loyalty that even if Kilian could help us, he probably wouldn't want the help. I didn't agree, but I understood it.

"So a battle, then?" Felix's eyes glowed with exhilaration, and he popped his knuckles.

"We're ready," Halina said.

Dom made eye contact with me and nodded.

"This is better than I'd hoped." Kilian stood before us. I once thought him to be frail, but there was a newfound strength in his voice. "The end is near."

I looked at the dagger sitting on the desk and felt the weight of his words. A battle is what it would take to get our family back together. In Blackheart, I'd thought Aaron and his brothers would have to fight alone and I'd be at the mercy to watch, but that silver dagger was our only true connection to the twins, and I would get everything out of it I could.

Twenty-Three

PRESLEY

A fluffy blanket rested on my head while I watched *Lion King 2*—arguably the best *Lion King* movie, and I'd fight anyone on that till the day I die, which, of course, would be never. Therefore, I'd win. Within thirty seconds of the opening song, I was crying. Luke and I used to watch the movie together over and over. I had a not-so-subtle obsession with Kovu—still do. I endlessly clicked the different tools on my fidget toy Mom picked up for me in town, and combined with the movie, it helped get my mind off things.

The fire had been burning all day long and the cold still crept into the cabin like the plague. How was that even possible?

The clock on my sad little flip phone told me how late it was, and Kim and Aaron weren't home yet. I'd tried to get my mom to stay up with me, but she said she was too old to stay up past 9:00 p.m. I'd even made her extra strong coffee at 7:00 p.m. for her nightly drama. It didn't work.

So it was just me, alone—again—and crying into my blanket that smelled like a fire pit.

The front door opened, and I jumped to my feet, wiping my eyes and turning off the television.

"Hey guys. Took ya long enough."

"I heard *Lion King 2*." Aaron smiled as he helped Kimberly with her coat, then frowned. "What's wrong?"

"Nothing. Just listening to the beautiful song and lyrics and seeing Kiara be brought into the world."

"Oh. Right."

"Good. We can tell you all about it." Kim sounded tired, and her hair was unusually frizzy.

"I'm surprised you both came back in one piece."

Dude totally had a basement where he did freaky shit. No doubt about that. I tossed the throw pillows to the floor, and Kimberly and Aaron went to join me on the couch.

"Ah." A sudden wave of pain sliced through me. It was quick at first, then it grew.

Aaron grabbed his chest too. "What the hell is that?"

That was usually the end of it, but this time, the pain grew. I gripped the edge of the couch as the pain slammed into me again and again. It was like a wave pushing and pulling me under.

One look at each other told me we knew the answer to that question. Which brother was it? It had to be both. There was no way one of them could produce that much anguish at once. Gripping my stomach, I hunched over with a groan. I wished for the time when I felt only Aaron's emotions and it was only nausea. It was better than feeling like I was put in a vat of hot oil.

"What can I do?" Kimberly looked between us frantically.

"Uh," I spoke through gritted teeth, "sedate me maybe."

I fell back into the couch, and Kimberly rubbed my back, and her heartbeat thrummed loudly in my ears. A nice distraction. Aaron braved through the pain with his head in hands.

Then it stopped, but I felt like I had a weighted vest strapped to my chest that was on fire. Somehow still tolerable.

I melted into the couch. "Uh, thank god."

"Something happened," Aaron said while Kimberly helped him to the couch.

"They need us. We have to go to them now."

"We can't go yet, Pres. We need time," Aaron said. "We have to have a plan."

"Well, the plan is taking too long already. It's obvious something terrible is happening to them."

"Don't you think I know that? I feel it too. But this isn't something we can rush."

"How is it rushing? It's been like a whole month. We're past Christmas."

I couldn't sit anymore. My body needed to move. I had to go and save them.

"I know."

"If you know, then let's go. We know where they are now."

Aaron shook his head with a sigh. "It's not that simple. If we lose here, it's game over. There's no reload screen. We don't get more lives. Us losing means them taking us all."

"And killing me," Kimberly added.

I groaned. It made sense, but that didn't mean it was right. In front of the warmth of the fireplace, I rubbed at the tenderness of my chest. My brothers were out there hurt. I couldn't imagine the things happening to them. Would The Family torture them? Were they even being nice to them?

Heat resided beneath the ache. Like someone lit a match in my chest. I didn't know how, but I knew it was Zach. I just did. Somewhere, someone had pissed him off, and I held onto it.

The fire cracked in front of me, matching the simmering heat in my chest, and I blocked out the conversation happening between Kimberly and Aaron. My brother was angry. *Maybe I should be angry too.*

JANUARY

Twenty-Four

"I can't believe it," I whispered as I marked off yesterday's date on the kitchen calendar.

It had been almost a whole stupid month since I'd felt that strange pain, and though nothing had felt as intense as that day, the weight in my chest had gotten gradually worse. Not exactly sure how that was possible. I'd tried to explain it to Aaron in terms of his rock collection. Aaron had a ton of rocks back in the day. Lots of small ones in little plastic containers, then some bigger ones. Mostly ones we stole from places we should not have taken them from, but there were some bigger than my fist that I had to hold with two hands. That's what it felt like. Like five of those sitting on my chest. Every. Single. Day.

I didn't think Aaron felt it as much as I did, and I wasn't sure exactly

170

how I felt about that yet. On one hand, good for him. On the second, how was it fair I got all the weird vampire phantom pains? It had to be because of how much blood of Akira's I drank. I wasn't sure I regretted that. I'd never tasted anything like it and knew I never would again.

"Ready?" I motioned to Aaron, who was standing in the kitchen fidgeting with some breadcrumbs on the counter. He was dressed and ready for a snowstorm, but there wasn't one. Not that week, at least.

"Yep."

It was time to hunt, and this time, it was just Aaron. Aaron and Kimberly had been kind of shady about their blood-drinking endeavors, but I honestly didn't care. They could keep their damn secrets. I just didn't want to go alone.

Mom came through the front door with her hair disheveled, stomping the snow from her boots on the welcome mat.

"Hey Mom. Aaron and I are going out. Need anything?"

"What about Kimberly?" she said as she dropped her empty lunch container in the sink.

"I think she's resting in the cabin," Aaron said.

"Okay, I won't bother her, then. I think I'm going to go see a friend tonight anyway."

"Got a hot date we don't know about?" I asked.

"Wouldn't you like to know." Mom snickered.

"Please tell me I'm not going to accidentally walk in on you and your lumberjack boyfriend named Hank, am I?"

Two things I'd noticed: there were a lot of Hanks here and all the guys were buff, blue-collar working men, and I wasn't mad at it.

"Of course not . . . we're going to his place."

"Mom," Aaron and I said it at the same time. Disgusting didn't cover it.

"Kidding." She left down the hall with a chiming laughter.

I shivered and immediately threw that thought out of my head.

I needed to focus on something way more productive, and there was one thing I was looking forward to. My phone buzzed in my pocket, and I reached to check the text.

Mystery Man: Everything still on?

Me: Yep.

The cold as we stepped out on the front porch chilled me. My blood was hot with the anticipation of getting to meet the phone guy soon. It had taken weeks, but I'd finally arranged a good time.

Maybe I should have felt guilty for not telling my brother, but when I started to, I remembered that day and the searing pain. If there was anything my older brothers had taught me, it was sometimes you had to take risks.

Luke wouldn't have liked it, but Zach would have understood.

Twenty-Five

AARON

Two minutes in and I regretted my decision. Presley and I posted up outside a bar without a single working sign. All of them were missing letters. My jacket kept the cold out, but my body shook for a different reason.

"Shoulda just asked your new besties to come with you," Presley grumbled.

"You wanted me to come with you, remember?"

He responded with a puff of smoke in my face before pressing his cigarette to his lips for another drag.

He was trying to pick a fight with me again. Presley and I fought in Brooklyn too. This was worse. He just liked to be angry at me. I offered to be his punching bag, but that didn't mean I enjoyed his animosity.

I needed to feed again and didn't want to keep taking from Kimberly. It was hard to compartmentalize it as an okay thing even though she didn't mind. If I could make things normal again, that would be ideal. I had mentioned none of it to Kilian yet, and I didn't think I would.

"You're still coming this weekend, right?" I asked.

"As long as you keep your end of the deal."

I'd been trying to get Presley to come to Kilian's for weeks. That's where Kimberly and I spent a lot of our time learning and training. Even if he didn't want to train, I wanted to get him out of the cabin. It wasn't good for him to be stuck alone all day, but it didn't matter how much I begged, he refused. I didn't like what all that alone time was doing to him.

"Of course, but you have to be nice and try to listen."

"I won't be nice to Kilian."

"I meant me."

"Fine. And you'll be less of a fun suck and let me enjoy the city a bit?"

I sighed. Presley wanted to go to Fairbanks—the biggest city near us. He talked about a few bars and things he wanted to do and see. I'd promised we'd go together if he agreed to at least see what we were doing with Kilian.

"Yes. Now let's play the quiet game."

"Fine by me."

Presley didn't talk again as we waited. It was strange. I'd always hated his carefree spirit when we hunted in Blackheart, but now I just wanted him to smile and crack jokes again. Granted, I asked him to stop talking, but usually, he wouldn't listen.

He finished his cigarette and was on his way to another until a group of guys left the bar. I didn't get the smoking thing. He'd done it a few times in Blackheart in social settings, but he never chain-smoked. When I asked about it, he shrugged.

"Hey!" Presley moved his way into the group. "You guys look like you need a ride."

"We could use one. We were just going to walk home across town," one said while falling into me. They reeked of smoke and sawdust.

"Don't worry. We've got you covered." Presley motioned to the other one, and I flanked him.

"I don't know. I could probably drive. Where are my keys?" the one next to me said, his large fingers fumbling in his jacket.

"Nonsense. We can take you home."

I hated being bait.

Something in my brain wouldn't let me talk to people I was going to bite. The guilt got to me. I'd feel sorry for them and let them leave or it ended like last time when I practically took a chunk out of a guy's neck. It was easier to let Presley take the lead.

The pulse next to me was so achingly close. I was afraid to drink human blood again, but the voice was quieter than ever, and having Kimberly donate to me occasionally was working. Still, how long could we do that for? Was it even sustainable?

I needed to test my theory. Maybe drinking Kimberly's blood helped, and I could go back to my somewhat shitty normal.

There was only one way to know.

Presley led them to an empty parking lot covered in snow. I couldn't even find the sidewalk. Everything in Alaska was empty and barren. In California, there were people everywhere and it was normal for people to walk places.

"Which one's yours?" the tall one said.

"Sorry, dude. This is probably gonna hurt in the morning." Presley pushed the taller one in my direction while he went for the shorter one.

I pulled him by the collar, not giving myself any time to think any harder on it, and sank my teeth into his neck.

The blood hit my throat, and I pushed him off with the remaining strength and sanity I had. Because The Thing in my head practically grabbed me from behind and pushed itself into my body.

I couldn't feel my hands.

It wouldn't let me move my feet.

I was drowning again and didn't know if I'd be able to find my way back to the surface ever again.

You're mine.

Twenty-Six

KIMBERLY

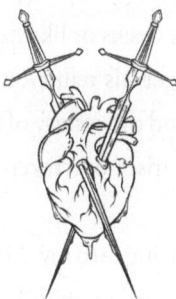

I shivered as I entered the shower. The water was warm, but the heater was never enough to thaw the chill in the bathroom. The glass shower door and the white tiles lining the floor were always cold. I huddled under the water, reciting my new list of things to do. A full moon was coming, and I'd been anticipating it all week, clawing at the chance to place my hand on that dagger again.

I wet my hair, and the door clicked open, then I turned in time to see Aaron opening the shower door.

"Aaron? Did tonight go okay?"

He pressed his chest into mine and pushed me back while shutting the door.

"What are you—"

"Kim." His voice was drenched with longing. The whites of his eyes were tinged like black ink. "I found you."

"You need blood," I said breathlessly.

His trembling hands vibrated my arms. "I need you."

I nodded and wrapped my hands in his hair, pulling him toward my neck. That's all the invitation he needed to sink his teeth into my skin. After a few seconds, his lips were on mine. It was forceful but not too hard. Every second that passed, he took a little more. His tongue explored the inside of my mouth, and his hands tangled in my hair. He was kissing me like he hadn't seen me in weeks or like he thought I might die.

"Aaron." I could barely get his name out. The combination of the water running off his body and the ecstasy of his touch left me speechless.

He reeled back, with his irises overtaken in darkness. "Sorry, is this okay?"

He panted, and his fingers dug into my skin with desperation. Human blood wouldn't fix what was wrong with him—what She was doing to him, and I'd do anything to free him from it. I answered by pressing my lips to his.

A groan echoed around us as he pressed me up against the shower door. The fog on the glass made it impossible for me to get a grip. I gasped and wrapped my bare legs around him as he lifted me effortlessly.

Every second, I fought to gain control of the growing tension building in my core.

The new position gave him greater access to the bare skin on my chest. Like a feather, he used his tongue to wipe any remnants of blood from my neck and down my chest. My heart beat in my ears as he followed the trail of water down to the top of my breast and bit me again.

The soft lightheadedness combined with the steam of the shower had me melting into him. It soothed every stiff muscle, and I realized how much I enjoyed being there for him. I used the railing on the inside of the shower door to keep me steady as I gave him everything he needed. For once, I wasn't cold and everywhere was burning hot.

He didn't see how tamed he was, even when he felt out of control. The pressure was never too much. He held me perfectly. Slowly adjusting for his own pleasure and for mine.

Every time he dug harder, I bit my lip to stifle the sound threatening to leave my mouth. He dropped me to my feet and kneeled before me as if I was an altar. With every touch of his lips and tongue, he sealed his devotion. He kissed my legs all the way up until he reached the apex of my thigh. It was quick yet perfect. Then he placed one leg over his shoulder and sank his teeth into my inner thigh. This time, I couldn't hide the whimper escaping my lips, then pushed my hands through his hair. I'd come to enjoy the feeling of being the thing he needed more than anything else.

My core was on fire, tight and yearning for release. He moved over the bite with his tongue and didn't stop when he grazed over my opening.

Everything in me grew tighter. The feeling of his tongue sent shivers of pleasure through me. He held me to the tile wall more firmly, and I rolled my hips into him until I was certain I would go over the edge.

He didn't have to, but he wanted to. It had never been like that before. Ravenous perfection, like every inch of me was the best thing he'd ever had the pleasure of tasting.

"Aaron, I—"

Something deep in my stomach crested and my knees buckled with pleasure that cascaded through my whole body.

He steadied me as he stood to face me. The darkness was gone, and all that was left was his soft-brown eyes devouring me. I sighed. He was back.

Swiping the water from his face, he realized what he had done—gotten in the shower fully clothed.

"I—"

I pulled off his jacket and his shirt. "Don't. Just stay. Shower with me."

He complied, letting me help him strip, then he drew me into a hug and held my head to his chest while the water ran over us.

"Is this working?" he asked, his voice still filled with worry.

"Yeah. It's good." His heartbeat fluttered in steady cadence beneath my ear. "This is perfect."

Twenty-Seven

AARON

"Really, Aaron, in my mom's shower?" Presley smirked as he handed me dry clothes at the door.

I'd had to beg. It wasn't pretty.

"Shut up."

"I didn't think that's why you wanted to come home so quickly. Shower sex was that tempting for you? You couldn't even take a few seconds to not drench your clothes."

"Let's never talk about this again."

"Oh, brother, you owe me now. Kim still owes me too, by the way." He wiggled his eyebrows as Kimberly appeared beside me in some old flannel pajamas with her hair wrapped in a towel. She avoided eye contact with my brother, but the fight was futile because he was blocking the door. I was just glad I had my sanity back.

"I'll be conjuring up what your favors will be, and I'm going to make them extra interesting now that I have to put headphones on to drown you guys out." Presley shielded his eyes and turned away from Kim. "Nope. No manipulative pouting is going to help you now, Kim. You owe me big time."

"But I'm not doing anything," she said.

"No, you totally do this thing that makes me feel bad. But you're a Calem now. You must reap the consequences of being annoying."

"Can you let us out of the bathroom, please?" I tried to push past, but he had his arm propped up on the doorframe.

"I'm sorry," Kimberly muttered, "you're right."

"Don't worry. I'll give Aaron all the worst punishments. He'll do all the embarrassing stuff, and we can watch and laugh."

I think that was the fastest I'd ever seen my brother fold. At least he was enjoying himself.

"Please move," I said, not entirely hating that mischievous smirk on his face.

I kissed Kimberly's hands as we lay twisted in our fleece sheets. I didn't know a bed could feel that good. The stars made the sky more light than dark as they blinked and danced in our skylight. With a feather touch, I traced the lines on her hands and kissed each tip of her fingers.

I still wasn't over it. The smell of her all over me. The way she looked in nothing but my T-shirt. We spent every night soaking it in, just us in our little cabin in the woods.

Sometimes, I liked to pretend that's all our life was, living in Alaska with no other problems to speak of. There was plenty of hiking and places to explore. Mom loved the company. There was even a community college within driving distance. I imagined the lush green of summer when the mountains in the distance would be the only memory of the cold and snow.

It didn't last long; once I looked up at the sky, I felt the weight in my chest again.

"Are you sure you're okay with everything?" I asked.

I was thankful to have a clear head, but it came with a high cost. All the wildness I'd had coursing through my blood a few hours ago was a bad memory that had been replaced by her head on my chest and the reverberation of her heartbeat.

"You worry too much."

"You're one to talk." I chuckled while I played with her hair. "I worry about hurting you. That's something to be concerned about."

"I feel great." She draped her bare leg over mine, and I grabbed it to pull her closer. "I just wish we knew what was happening to you. What does it feel like?"

I'd had so many bad experiences with the Thing in my head I'd lost count, but there was a common theme. It thrived in chaos and destruction. It wanted not just blood and to kill but to find my weaknesses and hurt me.

"This is different than before. Before it felt like this Thing was just messing with me. Taunting me. When I drank that guy's blood today, It didn't want it. It wanted something else. And It wanted to use my body to get it. Like the Thing in my head is looking for something . . ."

"It's looking for Her."

Her words accompanied the quickening of her pulse, and a shiver ran down my spine.

"Well, I was looking for you." I squeezed her. "It was weird. I smelled for you and tracked your footprints in the snow."

I hunted her, and the memory of the elation of finding her in the shower made me question my sanity.

"I just don't get it. Luke had more blood than me. Directly from Her, and he had no problem with human blood. It doesn't make sense."

"Her blood seems to affect you all in different ways. There's a reason. For you, maybe . . . you're supposed to drink from Her. Maybe it does something. It's just a theory, but it seems like The Thing in your head is seeking Her out for a reason. Do you feel like you want Her more? Do you . . . think of the queen a lot?"

"No."

She looked up at me with her head still on my chest. "You can tell me the truth. It won't hurt my feelings."

The only lie was hers.

I couldn't resist cupping her cheek and rubbing my thumb over her bottom lip until her worry lines vanished.

"Honestly? Never. Only when I'm worried about what She's doing to my brothers."

I actually tried not to think about it too much. The fear of the unknown on that subject was enough to make my chest feel like someone was trying to pry open my rib cage.

"I think we should tell Kilian."

I answered with a groan and buried my head in her hair. It had dried and smelled of vanilla and honey shampoo.

"I know, I've just been thinking about your brothers and their secrets . . . Being here gives me so much time to retrace our steps. If your brothers hadn't kept their secret, or even if you and I hadn't had any in Blackheart, if we'd all just laid it out, how different could things be? If we never got as close as we did and ended up in the church. If you'd had told your brothers, and you all left, or maybe if Kilian hadn't seen what he saw in them. These secrets . . . have often made things worse for everyone.

Maybe he can help, and he'll know what the problem is."

"You spend a lot of time thinking." I shifted till the weight of her leg dug into my hips.

"It's helping."

"It is. It's great. I just don't want you to get lost in there. I need you here with me." I kissed her temple, then her cheek till her anxious grip on me loosened, and she was back to melting into me. There weren't words for how I needed her. Her blood was low on the list.

"I'm here." She laughed softly.

"We'll tell him. I think it's a good idea. No more secrets. But that does mean we'll have to tell him I've been drinking from you, and I'm not ready to have that conversation with my brother. Doesn't need to be a secret, just not ready to deal with the questions. Plus, he's already struggling with the changes."

"That's fair. Maybe we'll go see him before Presley comes this weekend."

"Yeah, but we have to get him out of the house. How many times can someone watch *Lion King 2* and sulk?"

Even Kim couldn't convince Presley to get off the couch, and she'd tried just about everything.

"I spoke to your mom about it this morning. I think she's going to make him volunteer at the dog shelter during the week."

She was already ten steps ahead of me.

"I wonder why he wants to go to Fairbanks so bad," I said.

"I'm not sure, but it can't hurt to take a little night off. For all of us."

I'd denied Presley's request for so long because I didn't want any nights off. I wanted to spend every minute working toward getting my brothers back, but I didn't need to tell Kim that, she knew.

She drew little circles over my bare chest, and I shivered. It brought my attention back to the weight in my heart.

It was weird to get used to it. My own grief physically embodied. All our grief lived in my body as a constant reminder of what was lost. Like I needed the extra reminder. Every night I looked up at that night sky, thinking about the distance and wondering what they were doing and how they were feeling.

"Where does it hurt?" She flattened her palm over my chest.

I grabbed her hand and guided it to the middle of my chest. "Here. It always hurts here. Like someone punched a hole in my chest and it's just empty. It's deep, like I can't get to it."

I moved her hand to the right. "And here it feels like stabbing sometimes, and then I'll feel it in my back."

"Want me to rub your back?"

I smiled and guided her head back to my chest. "This is better."

Nights kept me together. I couldn't imagine sitting and staring at the ceiling alone.

In the warmth of the cabin, I could tell Kimberly everything. Every good thought, every bad. We had no secrets anymore, and more importantly, nothing to hold us back from each other. Blackheart felt like a distant memory. I'd held myself back from her, and I was sure it caused all our suffering, because being with her was the easiest thing I'd ever done. Loving her came naturally, like it was something I was meant to do and it was the one thing I was ever any good at.

I gasped as a star streaked across the sky. One single ray of light carving a path through the darkness.

"A shooting star." I'd only ever seen one, and it was with Kimberly. That's where I'd made my first wish, and it had come true.

I'd gotten to stay with her, and she was undoubtedly mine. I pulled at her as if I could get her any closer. There was one way, but it was still early in the night.

Kim placed her hand on mine. "Let's make a wish together."

I squeezed my eyes shut.

I want us to win. Please let us all get to come back here together.

The sight of seeing my older brothers step out of the car in the drive-way and greet Mom seared into the back of my mind. It was so vivid, and I believed it would come to fruition.

I'd get them there.

I kissed the top of her head and continued to gaze up. The only rule was we couldn't say our wishes out loud, but believing together had worked before, so maybe it would again.

"You know the same moon we're looking at is the same one your brothers see. We're looking at the same stars and the same night sky."

I smiled at the thought, wondering if they ever got time to go outside and gaze up at the stars. I hoped so.

Twenty-Eight

PRESLEY

I finally cashed in a favor. Kimberly's punishment for her crimes was watching movies with me all day in the living room, and Aaron wasn't allowed to join.

Romeo and Juliet, the 1996 version, played on Mom's pitiful TV. We had to use the DVD player, and I'd hit it a few times to make it work. We were lucky she had *any* movies. Mom said she'd picked that one up at a garage sale because she knew I liked it and it made her think of me. It was my favorite because Leonardo DiCaprio looked like the embodiment of an angel the entire movie—even if I had no idea what he was saying half the time.

"You and Aaron should wear that next Halloween."

Romeo was starstruck in his suit of armor, staring at Juliet in her angel

188

costume. A turquoise fish tank glowed between them. Aaron's hair was a perfect match, and Kimberly would look radiant dressed up in white and angel wings.

I regretted the words as soon as they were out of my mouth. My brothers would be back by then. Things could go back to the way they were in Blackheart, and nothing would be different. Right?

My stomach sank as I remembered the intense pain in my chest. Things were already different.

"That's a good idea. You can help me with my costume."

I shook my head. "No. It's bad."

"What?"

"I shouldn't plan for things that far ahead. We'll probably be dead by then."

"You don't really think that, do you?" she said with her mouth agape. I shrugged.

"No. I wouldn't let anything happen to you." Kimberly hugged me without warning.

"I know." Maybe that was part of the problem. Everyone wanted to protect me, but what was I doing? Lying in bed and watching old movies was about all I was good for. She moved to block my view of the TV.

"You don't talk to me anymore," she said.

"I do."

"Not like before."

"I don't have anything to say." More like everything I had to say was depressing.

My older brothers were gone and likely being tortured or something terrible by Hell Bitch. Physically, my chest hurt so much I forgot what it was like to feel good, and Kimberly and Aaron were buying into Kilian's nonsense. I wasn't entirely sure *they* weren't being sucked into a different cult, and even if a miraculous phenomenon happened and Kilian was right and we had some great big ole battle to get my brothers back, how would it end?

We were so *fucked*.

"You don't have to talk. I've just been worried about you." Her cheeks were red from the fire.

The alarm bells went off in my head. Kimberly had a lot to worry about. I didn't like being something else on one of her lists. I'd always imagined having a sister growing up, but it wasn't like I thought it would be. With brothers, I could cause them pain with little to no remorse, but with Kim . . . I couldn't stand to see her upset. All that time wishing I had a sister, and it turned out to be harder than having a brother.

"Thanks Kim. I, uh, I'm excited to see the stuff you're doing with Kilian this weekend."

I wasn't. There was a weird protectiveness that came with having a sister too.

"I'm glad you're coming. I have a good feeling about everything."

I cringed at the thought of her being around Kilian, but I trusted Aaron's judgment when keeping her safe. Sometimes, I couldn't stop imagining Kilian wrapping his boney little fingers around Kimberly's neck and squeezing the life out of her right before he locked her up to use for his stupid ritual.

Why couldn't vampirism be a fun random thing that happens sometimes? The fact there were cults and blood ritual things made it objectively less fun.

My phone vibrated.

"What's that?" Kimberly asked, but her eyes stayed glued to the screen.

"Oh. I have a timer. I have to do something for Mom. I'll be right back."

I jetted into my room. Luckily, the wall heater was on in accompaniment with the TV, so she likely couldn't hear me.

I flipped up my phone and brought it to my ear. "Why are you calling me?"

"Just confirming our location for the meeting."

"I told you to just text me."

"Yeah, but I have to be thorough and make sure I'm still talking to you."

I sighed and picked at the flaking paint on my nightstand. "As opposed to?"

"It's my job to make sure to give you this stuff. You're not going to bring anyone else, are you? Because that would be a bad idea."

"Are you threatening me? Because that won't have the effect you think it does. I just won't show up."

"I have what you need. You'll show up. And as long as you come alone, you have nothing to worry about."

"I don't know. I'm starting to wonder if this is a good idea."

"Having second thoughts?"

I said nothing. I had no idea what I was doing.

"I asked about your brothers."

"What? Asked who?"

"I don't know him. Name's Henderson. But he knew your brothers."

He was probably lying, but my body buzzed with the news.

"He said Zach was an asshole, but he's a good fighter." It was real. That was *my* asshole brother, all right. "And that Luke was growing on him. He told me they're always together. Annoyingly so."

"Where do you want me to meet?" I asked.

"I have a place in mind. It's public, don't worry. I'll text you the address. I'll see you on Friday."

I didn't know what The Family wanted from me, but they knew where my brothers were. This guy held the key to seeing them again, and soon, I'd know what that was.

Twenty-Nine

KIMBERLY

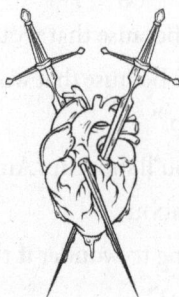

The light of day had dimmed by time I found Vera outside. There wasn't much out there except for snow, but there was a covering for the stack of lumber and a stump for splitting wood. In one swing, she axed through a stump with graceful ease. Hard-working was an understatement, as she'd just gotten home from her shift and was still in her scrubs and a thick coat.

"Mind if I try?" I murmured, so as not to startle her.

"Of course. Here." Vera wiped her hands on her pant legs and handed me the axe.

It would have been heavy for me before, but I could hold it with one arm now. I tested the weight while Vera watched in amusement.

"Was it hard for you? The change . . ."

I grabbed a piece of dried wood and wiped off the stump before placing it down.

"It's been great, actually. Not expected, but I figure I've probably had it better than most of the boys." At least I chose it.

I swung the axe, and the entire chopping block split in two, leaving the axe wedged into the hard ground. I needed to work on pressure.

"I'm still getting used to it." I dislodged the axe in one pull.

"Yes, I've been thinking about that. How it might have felt for all of them, including you."

I tried to piece together the remnants of the chopping block so I could try again.

"I think Zach and Luke had it the worst. They were tricked. I can't really imagine what they went through together."

"I'm just glad they had each other, I supposed. That always seemed to be what they both wanted the most growing up. They shared rooms and toys, even clothes at one point. Since they were teeny tiny, they were on their own planet. The most chaotic toddlers running around getting into trouble together—and oh, how they lied and covered for each other."

"They're still like that." I laughed.

I thought long and hard on the version of them that I knew and the one their mother knew. Two bright-eyed children ready for the world but poisoned under her nose. She never knew.

"I wanted to save them from this. I didn't even know how or what. They wouldn't tell me, no matter how hard I begged or punished them. I could tell they were scared . . . but they wouldn't tell me why. You must think I'm a terrible mother."

I stopped to look at her.

"Oh, no. You don't have to worry about me judging you. I don't have a mother. She didn't even bother to try to take care of me. I think you've done a great job. Being a mom is . . . really hard I've heard."

I couldn't imagine her life. Four kids—the Calem brothers at that—and taking care of her mother. All the while still making time for her career that required everything from her. I didn't know how she'd found the energy.

"Oh, hunny." She squeezed my shoulder. "There was room for improvement. I can't believe I accepted their stories when they'd tell me they were picking up groceries from their school's food drive. Or that they had part-time jobs mowing lawns, and that's how they'd somehow have an extra twenty dollars to help with bills. I never asked, and I didn't talk about money, but they knew. It was hard as a single mother . . . but I supposed that's my fault for letting their father back into my life so many times. I was young . . . I thought I loved him. And if I hadn't, I'd have never had Aaron and Presley."

I shuddered at the thought of them not existing. Those two were my life.

"If I could go back, I would have asked. I would have moved when I realized things were dangerous."

"The Family would have killed you if you'd moved. It's not your fault this happened. We're going to fix this. We'll bring them home."

"You're so much braver than I ever was."

Vera's stories of the twins lingered in the chill of the air. We needed something solid this time. The dagger would show me something. I'd make sure of it.

"Are you ready?" Aaron asked, his hair was fluffier than normal and growing longer at the sides. "Mom, I told you to let me do the firewood."

"Don't worry. Us girls got it just fine." Vera winked at me.

I set the wood down and swung again. This time, I focused on the muscles in my biceps and my forearm. I'd give it only twenty-five percent effort. *Gentle.*

The wood split in the blink of an eye, and the axe handle with it.

"Oh, I'm sorry." I held up the splintered wood. I'd need to try ten percent next time.

Aaron grabbed the axe handle from me with a relaxed smile. "Don't worry. We'll get a new one."

Thirty

AARON

"I can't feel my arms." I groaned, then Dom released me from behind, and I crumbled to the floor. I didn't know how my brothers did it. Battling in blood was the worst thing I'd ever done. My entire body was achy and weak, and add in the pain in my chest, and it felt like I was fighting the flu.

"Do you need a break?"

"Kinda." I groaned and lay back on the mat. The room spun around me. The basement was large and full of mirrors. Like the whole house, it was a major upgrade from what we'd had in Blackheart. While the other was makeshift, this room seemed intentional by whoever built it. Underneath the mats were black concrete and a drain system that made it easy to clean up. Everything was new and wrapped in plastic like it had laid in wait for a moment like ours.

I could barely sit up to stare at myself. Black blood stained the edges of my hair and soaked my chest.

"You're doing well. It takes practice."

"Yippee," I said.

Training wasn't all of it. I needed to learn how to navigate advanced blood loss. Though it was important and I needed to learn to build on basic defense, Kilian was certain my role would be less about violence and more about getting through to my older brothers and getting them to fight on our side.

"*They may not recognize you,*" he'd said one day, and my chest hurt so much at the thought my heart skipped.

"*What do you mean?*"

"*It's possible She could wipe their memories of your time together. It could be some. All. It's all unknown.*"

"*Are you saying they may attack me?*"

"*Yes. You need to be prepared for your brothers to be different when you see them. They most likely will be changed, and not for the better.*"

"*If She wipes their memories, how do we fix it?*"

"*By killing Her.*"

Dom's large hand in my face snapped me back to reality. He held out a blood bag for me to drink. The sloshing red liquid was tempting, but I knew better.

"Here."

I hesitated. "I don't need it."

"You need blood."

"I'll be fine."

Dom didn't argue, clearly not caring if I chose to be miserable.

"Can you help me up?"

He pulled me up with ease, and I held onto his forearm to steady me. "I'll let Kilian know you want to speak with him."

Dom spent half of his time training, then the other half away doing more technical type preparation. He'd mentioned once that he had the skill to fly planes and choppers. It was the only hobby I'd found of his. I was a little jealous that he got such a cool job in the whole thing. Kilian said he was the last known pilot they had on the team.

I followed him up the steps and willed my legs to move. Like I had cinder blocks tied to my feet, I took every step slowly, and Dom waited for me with not an ounce of annoyance on his face. Being around him reminded me of Blackheart in a way that added to the collective pain in my chest. I remembered the little things. The times he picked the lint off Skylar's clothes or the two of them whispering in the corner. The way she'd ask him if she had lipstick in her teeth and he'd answer honestly every time. He had to be in pain, but not an ounce of it showed.

"Can I ask you something?" I finally reached the top of the stairs, and we walked toward the library that unfortunately required another set of steps.

Oddly, I trusted Dom. He saved Kimberly, and that meant something to me. It was more than anyone else there had done.

He nodded.

"Why do you trust Kilian? When he locked us up, Thane mentioned something about Will being the only reason he didn't kill you and Skylar, but I've been trying to figure out if he just said that to get us to turn on Kilian. But even then, why? Why follow Kilian after what happened to your sister?"

"Kilian's true intention was apparent. We were never fearful of him. Kilian is an open book. He wants one thing. I knew he'd want something from me and he'd be hard to please if he didn't get it. I didn't provide much for him. My time with The Family was brief. I was changed only for service and never fully integrated like your brothers. Important enough for them to kill my mother but not enough for me to see their main operation. I was changed by a rank much lower than your brothers'."

I nodded, thankful conversations with Dom didn't require me to say much.

"I believe that's the only reason Akira left me alive. He hoped that I would return. There have been many Legion lost to The Family and not by death. Akira thought of it as a game. He enjoyed turning Kilian's men over to his own side."

We reached the door to the library. Felix passed us in the hallway and grunted at me before I entered. Kimberly sat in an armchair with her hair pulled out of her face while she read and scribbled notes in her notebook. The tired ache in my body disappeared. She looked adorable in research mode, and I almost forgot about how stressed out it made her. She hid it well, but she was quieter in Alaska; she talked less and worried more.

"I'll be right back," Dom said, closing the door behind him.

Her eyes shot up to me. "Aaron. Oh my god."

I flashed her a toothy smile. "It's just a little blood."

She didn't smile. Only blinked a few times as she stood to survey me. "What's wrong?"

She stared with wide eyes. "It . . . I think it scares me to see you this way."

"Oh. I'm fine, Kim. I have to learn how to deal with the blood loss. It's good practice."

"Are you sure? Can I help . . .?"

"That depends, do you want Kilian catching us in the library to be the way he finds out about this?"

"Aaron, you're dripping blood on the floor."

With a feather touch, she brushed the blood on my shoulder.

"Builds endurance," I said, like the room wasn't wobbly.

"Can you be quick?" Her doe eyes beckoned me, and all my blood rushed south. She *wanted* me to bite her, and anything Kimberly Burns asked me to do, I really wanted to do for her.

"I-I . . . Yeah." I pressed in till her back hit the bookcase. "Can you be quiet?"

She nodded, and I took her wrist and tuned into the sound of her pulse. Getting to drink from her was a gift. A grotesque, bewildering gift. My teeth tore the flesh of her wrist—the same wrist that held the scars I'd given her as a human—as I held her eye contact, and the heat of her blood filled my mouth. Her heart beat fresh blood into my veins, and I could see more. *Feel* more.

A small gasp escaped her mouth, and I pressed into her again as a reminder to stay hidden. I wrapped my other hand behind her head so I could hold her while our hips crushed together. Something about the pressure of her always felt right. Like her blood did.

After a few more seconds, I licked the remnants of blood away. She hadn't trained, so her wound closed quickly. With a quick kiss, I let her hand fall back at her side.

"You look so beautiful when your cheeks flush like that."

Her smile was back.

"I just like this." I pressed my forehead to hers. "I hate how much I enjoy this."

The taste of her blood lingered on my lips. How long had I wanted this, and now I could have it? What was the consequence or reason?

She gripped at the hair on my neck. "You're not the only one."

The door clicked and we separated. Dom and Kilian funneled into the room.

"Ah, happy to see you both. Dom told me you want to see me. I apologize. I've been out at a meeting."

"So, uh, we have something we need to talk to you about."

Kilian and Dom shared a look.

"Do I need to leave?" Dom asked.

"No, you can stay," Kimberly said.

"Yeah . . . sure. Stay. Um, I'm just gonna say it. Ever since we beat Akira, the thirst got worse."

Kilian's brow bent. "You need to feed more?"

"I thought that at first. But human blood made it worse. I fed more and it just made me feel like I was losing my mind. Until I . . . didn't have another choice but to try another option, and I drank Kimberly's blood."

Dom's and Kilian's eyes grew wider. I didn't think I'd ever seen that much emotion on Dom's face.

"Is this . . . normal?"

Kilian shook his head and stood straighter. "No. I've never heard of such a thing happening. And Kimberly's blood keeps you satiated?"

"Yeah, for the same amount of time human blood did."

Kilian rubbed at his forehead in a way that showed all his wrinkles.

"Should I be worried?" I'd never seen Kilian speechless.

"I do not know. I think it's good you've found a suitable solution."

It was physically painful to tell Kilian something so personal.

"Maybe there's a reason . . . Do you remember any texts or anything talking about this?" Kimberly asked.

"No. We'd have to look for any specifics. But it is bringing up a thought." He rummaged on this desk some, moving stacks of books and papers.

When he didn't find it, he went for the shelves and ran his finger over creased, cracking spines till he pulled out a little black book. It was leatherbound with worn pages strapped together. The engraving on the front was barely visible. It appeared to be a crest with two swords on either side, a harp and an owl in the middle, with four Latin words on the bottom.

"This is the coven's crest. Not all of them have one. But Cecily was born in a time period where having family crests was common."

"What do the words on the bottom mean?"

"That's what interested me the most about this. At first, I believed them to be just words that The Family valued, but now I believe the four words represent a trait of each of The Guard: strength, loyalty, desire, and protector."

"What do this have to do with my blood problem?" I said, shifting under the weight of Kilian's gaze.

"We've spoken about your brothers' issues with Her blood before. It affects you all differently. I've had a lot of time to contemplate why that might be. I met The Guard when we attacked long ago and they fit these roles. We surrounded the monastery with fire. I suspect Ezra must have taken the queen to safety immediately. They were accompanied by Sirius. Only Eros and Akira stayed behind to fight. My brother wanted to stay. He wasn't going to let Eros out alive, and vice versa. The entire place went up in flames and took their mangled bodies with it. Eros . . . he was stronger than all of them . . . I wonder . . ."

"And your brother . . . What happened?"

"He was able to find a chip in that armor. We found their hideout and ambushed them. Much like now but less prepared. They didn't have near the numbers, and we didn't have the dagger. He locked me out of the monastery before I could go after him. By the time I escaped, they were all gone and the building was ash. Ezra stayed closest to Her—the lover, symbolizing Her desire and lust for connection. They took Sirius with them, and at first, I believed his trait to be loyalty, but after talking with the twins, it makes more sense for him to be strength. Akira was undoubtedly loyal. And that leaves Eros . . . the protector."

"These traits would be brought out in me and my brothers, then? Since they think we're the new Guard."

"Yes. You'd likely be a better judge of that. If you find your role, it might help better understand what's going on with the blood."

"Luke is the lover," Kimberly said, quickly writing all four words down on a piece of paper.

"Agreed." Luke talked about the queen like he was in love with Her, so likely, that was his trait.

"Zach could be strength or loyalty or protector," I said, staring at the remaining words. "But there's no way I embody strength."

"There are different types of strength," Kimberly said.

Kilian interjected. "This particular word also could pertain to courage or bravery."

"Definitely not."

"That leaves strength for Presley or Zach," she said. Kimberly was already moving the pencil and writing *Loyalty* under Presley's name. "I have a feeling about this one. What do you think?"

"It fits. Then Zach is strength and I'm . . . the protector?"

"Yes, *Presidium* represents guardianship. Being the ultimate protector."

We didn't have the words in the right order. I didn't fit into any of those roles well.

"How would drinking from Her make me a protector?"

"Something for us to contemplate, indeed."

I thought about my brothers' dreams again. That place was all they'd known and all they believed in. They were forced to fit into those roles. It was like there were two roads before me. Maybe I was their protector, but not as a member of The Guard. I could be the protector of our dream of freedom.

Thirty-One

PRESLEY

All I had to do was get to the pub across town without Kim and Aaron knowing. It would be a bit of a challenge, but the love birds were easy to distract, Luke wasn't there to pick up on my lying, and Zach wasn't there to be overly protective and want to follow me everywhere. It sucked, actually.

It was snowing again. I still didn't understand why Luke couldn't have picked a place in the Bahamas or something. At least a place that wasn't constantly overcast.

My thrifted shoes weren't made for the snow, and every step packed more snow into the treads.

"What did you want to do first?" Aaron asked, pulling Kimberly between us so we were all shoulder to shoulder. We were overdressed for the cold.

"I was thinking we'd grab a beer or two and hit the museum."

"It's 10 a.m.," Aaron said, like it mattered.

"Yeah, but we're vampires, so it doesn't matter. Come on, the plan is to get day drunk and have a good time, you know, since everything sucks and the world is ending."

"I get it. Yes, okay. Pub it is."

"Whatever you want. We're doing it." Kimberly smiled.

"Oh, Kim's getting drunk, then?"

"If it pleases you," she said.

She did need to relax. She was always journaling and reading. I'd snooped once. It was all these old books about the moon cycles and their meanings, along with constellations and Irish history. That wasn't even the weird part. She'd make lists filled with pros and cons, different scenarios. There were notebooks full of her scratched-out thoughts. Even as we walked, her hands were smudged with ink as she tucked a piece of hair behind her ear. She was trying to fix our problems again.

After I met up with my stalker, I would help too. Hopefully then, I'd have some information that would get us to my brothers. I could give it over to Kilian, and everyone would be better off for it. Lying and sneaking around could be a good thing.

I convinced a hot guy with hazel eyes to buy us drinks at a random bar. Two scotches deep, I was finally warm. He'd gone back to sit with a friend, but his attention lingered on me.

Focus, Presley.

Hot guys could wait. I checked my phone. One missed call.

"I'm going to go outside to get some air. Maybe you can take Kim to the museum over there."

The bar was part restaurant and part shopping mall. Groups of people—mostly older couples—funneled in next door. It was probably something boring like historic stuff.

"Yes!" Kim's eyes lit up, then she frowned. "Do you want someone to come with you?"

"No, I'm going to smoke. I'll be right back."

"Okay." She was still frowning.

"Don't worry. Enjoy the time with your lover."

I liked the way Kimberly looked at my brother. Like he hung the sun in the sky for her every day. Which she needed because the sun set at 3:00 p.m.

Aaron wasn't holding his liquor as well as I was, so he slurred a bit. "You're sure? Because I'll come out there right now and protect you from whatever. I've been training."

"I got it, ace. Chill here with your girl."

He gave me a thumbs-up.

Once I was finally outside, I lit that cigarette and pulled my hood over my head. I didn't like the taste of cigarettes, but I liked that they made me feel a little closer to my brother, wherever he was. I liked to imagine every time I lit one, Zach did too.

I called the number back. Blinking a few times, I fought to steady myself. I was buzzed and going to meet a mad man. *Perfect.*

"Hi," I said while passing a street sign. I didn't know where I was going, but I just walked toward the sounds of more people and cars. He'd given an address, but no smartphone meant no GPS and I had to find it myself. The city was barren the farther you walked from the more popular stores.

"You're late."

"I know, but I can't just disappear without anyone noticing."

I said it in hopes it would be a warning because I wasn't entirely sure I wouldn't get kidnapped. I tried to take a turn down an alley toward the sounds.

"No. Keep walking straight."

"Wait . . . how do you see me right now?" I stopped, suddenly feeling sick from too much scotch.

"I'm just up ahead. You'll run right into me."

I looked ahead and saw much of nothing but a busy street and a crowd of people.

"How do you know what I look like?"

"You dyed your hair. It's not that hard to spot you. I was given a picture as proof. Couple videos."

My heart stayed in my throat as I walked, and I really wanted my brothers to come busting through that alley. Luke would wrap an arm around me, and Zach would take the lead and kill anything that breathed wrong. I missed that sense of safety. It was bad to sneak off and follow secret notes all while being tipsy and useless, but my feet kept moving.

Once I was across the street, I spotted a man with tattoos lining his neck and arms while dressed in an all-black suit.

He might as well of had a sign pointing to a dark alley saying *Cult This Way*.

I could practically hear Luke lecturing me in my head. Getting back to them was the only thing that mattered, and I would finally have some answers.

I stopped in front of him, and he held out his hand for me. Not in that regal way, but more like bros in the frat house did.

"Ready to grab that drink?" He seemed nice enough, with dark hair and broody eyes. Also, very hot.

"Totally."

We descended a set of stairs into a dimly lit room that reeked of cigarette smoke. The smoke poured out into the frosty air, leaving a dim haze. It was mostly empty except for two others at the bar paying us no mind. Something told me it wasn't the type of place to check IDs.

The guy led me to a booth at the back where we had a good view of the door. *So far so good.*

"Name's Reg."

"You already know my name," I said.

Normally, I'd give pleasantries, but the guy had been practically stalking me. I didn't think I needed to go that far.

"I do. Mind?" He pulled out a cigarette and offered me one, and I declined.

"So, how long were you instructed to look for me?"

"As long as it took."

"And you're . . . part of them? The Family."

He looked at me for a long second before tapping the ash in his tray. "No. Not really. I do work for them. But I'm not like you."

"Like me?"

"Special."

"I'm not part of them either."

"Well, you must mean a great deal to them either way. I was given your name, description, and a phone. He told me to wait until you called. In the meantime, I gathered up what he asked."

"You didn't ask why?"

"Above my pay grade."

The only thing I was still unsure of was why me? Akira didn't seem all that interested in me back at that farm when he shoved Kim and me into a freezer.

"You're getting paid for this?" I asked.

"A great deal."

"To sit and have a drink with me."

"No, to give you this." He reached into his breast pocket and laid out a pocketbook. I didn't wait for permission to grab it. It was three passports and new driver's licenses for Aaron, me, and even Kimberly. I guessed it made sense they'd want her there. Not for a good reason. The pictures looked real, and I grabbed one of the licenses and moved it in the light to check. All of it was legit. So much for trying to find fake IDs online.

"But I don't know where they are. I can't use any of this. I don't have any money."

Mr. Mysterious was pissing me off a little. Taking all this time to arrange this meeting and fly out here to give me new documents I couldn't use was so annoying. *Does everything this cult do have to be so secretive and perplexing?*

"I don't know what I'm supposed to do with all this."

"Looks like he's testing you."

"Yeah, well, he's dead so . . ."

Reg's eyes widened at my words.

"Yeah, yeah. I killed him." I tried to make that information as convincing as I could. "Does that change your mind about helping me?"

It was technically true.

He shook his head. "It helps prove my theory. If they haven't killed you for that, they must really want you for something. I told you everything I have, though. They did leave one other thing. Look in the back."

I flicked through the passport books again and found another envelope.

"You have another clue." Reg smirked.

I read it aloud. *"Go to the place where the sky meets the see."*

Riddles were the worst thing ever invented. Mostly because they could have a thousand meanings, and I would have to find the exact right one.

209

It was cruel and unusual punishment.

I sighed. "How is a dead guy leaving me clues?"

"Listen, kid, I've worked for these guys for years. Now that they've moved overseas, everything here is running slim. But if they sent someone to leave you these clues and you killed the guy I talked to, my guess is they're testing your loyalty."

"Test? What kind of test? I just want to find my brothers."

"Chances are, they had their own loyalty tests. This is yours."

"Well, thanks for that drink." I slammed the rest of my drink back. "Love to stay, but I have people who will have a panic attack in about two minutes when they can't find me."

He nodded. "Good luck finding your brothers. May fate guide you."

I stumbled through the snow back toward the museum. For the first time in my life, my head was empty. I stared at my feet crunching in the snow.

Kimberly and Aaron were still at the bar. I spotted them through the foggy window with large letters painted on the glass. They giggled and laughed like they had no other care in the world, and maybe they didn't. It was hard not to be a little resentful, but I think I just wanted someone to share my pain with like they had. They were there for me, and I knew that, but it wasn't the same. I wanted to be the one with the partner to lay my head on at night. I didn't even have Mr. Bear to hold anymore, or someone to make me laugh and reassure me that even if the worst happened and they never came back, I wouldn't be alone.

At the same time, maybe I didn't.

My brothers didn't need to know everything. I only told them stuff when it needed to be said. Like Kimberly being taken by a vampire and possibly being dead seemed like the right time to reveal that little secret I promised to keep.

They didn't need to know I almost told Ellis, my date to the fraternity formal, I was a vampire.

I didn't say it, but I wanted to and almost did.

It was that night after the formal. Ellis met me back at the frat house to make sure I was okay. He wanted me to go to the hospital, and I'd refused.

"Let me see." He shut the door to my room.

"I'm okay. Really."

"Fine. Then you won't mind me checking."

I hesitated as his hands grazed my waist as he lifted my shirt. There was nothing. No bruised ribs. No broken skin.

I watched his hands. His beautiful, strong hands with the veins that led to his forearms.

His thick brows knit together. *"That's strange. It doesn't hurt?"*

I winced. *"Ah. Cold hands."*

"Sorry." I genuinely missed that cute subtle smile on his face.

"You're looking at me like I'm the one who beat the shit out of someone."

"No. I . . . There's no way you don't have at least a bruise."

"Well, I'm lucky, then."

"No. Not lucky. Luck doesn't exist."

Ellis thought through everything. He liked to know the why of everything that had ever been invented.

"It does in my world."

"This isn't funny. I tried to come in and help you, and I couldn't. They pushed me to the ground, and I have a scrape on my elbow. They were hitting you so hard, and I don't see a scratch on you."

"What do you want from me here?"

"To tell me the truth."

"And what if I told you something crazy, like I'm superhuman?"

"I'd tell you to get your head checked."

"Seriously? You wouldn't take my word for it. This could be the start to

a beautiful love story, and you're killing the vibe."

"You're concussed."

"Guess I'll need you to watch over me then."

My joking usually made him laugh, but he was still searching for signs of a scratch.

"Are you done?" I asked, pulling at the edges of my shirt to get him to stop.

"Yeah. Now get your ass in bed." He smiled.

He stopped answering my texts after that, only asking for a few days if I was okay. Things were cool, but it was never the same.

Had things miraculously worked out with Ellis and he was as cool as Kim, he wouldn't be safe.

What would it cost to get my brothers back, and what was I willing to give up? A foreign concept. Everything was a foreign concept, like someone had given me a final test with no prep. Luke and Zach paved the way through every experience in my life, but I was on my own path now, and I was sure I wasn't making good decisions. Maybe I had to make the bad ones, all the hard decisions the others couldn't.

Aaron and Kimberly had more to lose.

So maybe that's why I stared at the note in my hand a few seconds longer before shoving it into my pocket, resolving not to tell them a thing. Or maybe it was because I was getting used to doing things on my own. I couldn't tell anymore.

I was surprisingly sober enough to feel the ache in my chest again. As soon as I did, Aaron's head shot up like he'd felt it too. His eyes darted to the door, then the window, and he smiled when he saw me.

Thirty-Two

KIMBERLY

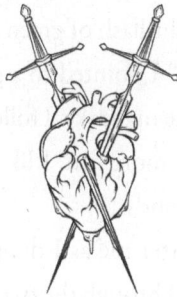

I'd sobered up long before the boys had, and as I did, all my fears and thoughts came tumbling back one by one. We took our time on our way back to the car. At least the alcohol had lasted long enough for me to brave through Presley's second favor. All three of us sang karaoke in a nearly empty bar in the middle of the day. I'd have done it regardless, because it was good to see him smile.

The boys sang Avril Lavigne at the top of their lungs as we walked back toward the car. The sun was gone, but it wasn't late yet. Only 5:00 p.m., but it felt like midnight in the pitch-black cold that encircled us. The soft rumble of cars on the nearly barren roads eased my worries, and the snow-blanketed trees covered us. We were alone there, and it was comforting when it was just us three.

Presley grabbed the edge of a streetlight and jumped on the base, spinning around in his drunken state while Aaron kneeled to the ground and serenaded him on one knee. The plastic base cracked, and I prepared for it to fall. It was the normal Calem ridiculousness that I had missed. We hadn't had a carefree night in what felt like months. I didn't like to count how long it had actually been, but I had a calendar. I knew the time down to the day—the hour even. I never talked about it, but I liked to know in case it could be useful somehow.

The boys spun around in the snow, lightly grabbing me and blending me into their shuffle. A bright flash of green sparked in my peripheral.

"Whoa, do you see that?" I pointed to a green hue that blurred and bended in the darkness of the night sky. I followed it, running in my new body that had started to be more fun. I liked that when I saw places I could go and be there in seconds.

"Kim!" the boys called after me as I disappeared into the trees, but their footsteps stayed close. Through the trees, the lights of the city grew dim and the green hue in the sky got brighter. I went for an opening in the trees. My boots weren't made for the amount of snow covering my calves, but it didn't stop me from following that light until I stared in awe at the wispy green light bending in the sky.

Presley tackled me from behind with a laugh. "Don't tell me you're dragging us into the mountain of snow to see the green gas in the sky."

We fell into the snow, and Aaron came in shortly after.

"You've never wanted to see the northern lights?" I asked while laying my head in the blanket of snow. The boys followed suit, nudging their heads close to mine as they stared at the sky.

"I kinda forgot it existed, but you're right. It's so cool!" Presley exclaimed.

"Have you always dreamed of seeing it, Burns?" Aaron's hand found mine in the snow.

"Kind of. I imagined I'd come out here and hike. Alone."

"Typical Kim. Always trying to get herself killed somehow," Presley said.

The laughter settled between us. Seconds turned to minutes as we watched the light twist and bend in a swirling pool of green and blue.

Presley broke the silence. "Remember that shitty picnic by the lake when we almost killed you by making you jump in the lake a hundred times?"

"Kimberly's birthday," Aaron murmured.

I could never forget. The hike there and our time spent at the lake. All five of us with the unwilling William to accompany us. The Calem boys serenaded me as my birthday present, and I'd never stopped thinking about it. The sight of all four of them and the love they shared over-whelmed me. Silently, I'd hoped it would rub off on me.

My face warmed and tears stung my eyes. "Luke made the best cake I've ever tasted."

"I really miss Zach's pissed-off scowl. He'd be so annoyed we decided to run off and lay in the snow," Presley said.

"Luke would love the lights," Aaron said.

"He'd probably tell us to journal this moment, to write about it in our diaries and tell all our feelings."

We all laughed. I couldn't see their faces, but their grief fell into mine. We'd broken our golden unspoken rule to not speak of the twins.

Presley's laughter sputtered to an end, but a roughness stayed in his voice. "Do you think it was worth it? Sometimes, I wish Blackheart didn't exist because then it wouldn't feel like this."

That place wasn't their beginning, but it had been the start of some-thing for them. Zach and Luke were secretive, keeping a distance, but finally we'd worked together as a team. They'd pulled back the veil and let their brothers in. It left a mark on them, and it certainly left a mark on me.

"It was worth it. It was just the beginning, Pres. Not the end."

"You really believe that?" Presley asked, voice breaking.

"More than I've ever believed anything else." Aaron's voice was strong as he squeezed my hand tighter. "We're going to get them back. I promise."

"But what if it costs . . . everything?" Presley asked.

"I'm all in," Aaron said with a finality and sureness that startled me. I'd needed that answer from him, and his brother did too.

"Me too." I grabbed Presley's hand just above my head.

We would get them back, whatever it took. The thought should have scared me, and I knew it would haunt me late at night, but I couldn't be scared holding the hands of the people I loved most in the world. Instead, as I stared at those bending lights, I felt what could be described only as unfortunate, powerful hope.

Thirty-Three

"This looks exactly like the Cullen house in *Twilight*," I said as we pulled up to a building surrounded by fluffy white trees.

If only Kilian was Carlisle Cullen. That would have made my life way better. Why couldn't Kilian be a hot vampire doctor? *Such a shame.*

"It does." Aaron ogled the house like it was the first time he'd made that connection.

I let Kimberly and Aaron show me the house while I noted all the exits and looked for hidden passageways or secret basements.

"Presley, it's a pleasure. I'm appreciative of your support." Kilian held out a hand that I refused to take.

I looked to Aaron for help, and he patted my shoulder reassuringly.

"I'm only here because I want to get my brothers back. Aaron said I don't need to be nice to you."

"No politeness needed."

"Well, I'm here. Can you give me the super speedy version of what's going on?"

"Right now, we are gathering intel and getting a clear view of the area your brothers are being held. We will have a map of the island soon and hopefully something for the castle grounds. We have witnesses who have seen your brothers. And we're still evaluating the amount of people they have at their disposal."

"You've seen them?" My heart was beating me up already.

He nodded. "Yes, we have a visual confirmation."

"Why didn't I get that job? I could have totally been the infiltrator."

"No," Aaron said. "You're going to be with me. Kilian thinks we'll be best used if we go ahead of the main assault and try to convince Zach and Luke to fight with us."

"Oh. That sounds awesome. When can we go? Tomorrow?"

Kilian interjected. "We'd need to be ready first so we can come at a prompt time. Our main objectives now are ensuring we can gain every advantage we have, that is why the rituals are important. Winning requires more than hope. It must accompany a plan."

"We're going as fast as we can, Pres," Aaron said.

"I get it."

"Aaron, do you want to show your brother downstairs?"

I shook my head. The basement was coming.

"Come on." Aaron pushed me toward a doorway.

"What about Kim?" I asked.

"She's getting ready for tonight."

"No, I meant . . . what's Kim doing in the battle?" I never asked her about things like that. Not when I'd much rather talk to her about literally anything else.

"Oh. She'll be a part of the assault on the island. So right now, the plan is for her to come after us—a week or two. But she's trying to use the dagger to figure out a way to help us in battle or give us an advantage."

Yes, the *ritual*. Seemed like another one of Kilian's ploys if you asked me. It probably shouldn't have been that far-fetched that the queen had power from the moon, considering I was a vampire and all, but moon worship just felt strange.

"And you're okay with that?" I asked.

"No, but feel free to try your hand at persuading her otherwise."

No thank you.

I agreed to come to be helpful. Aaron ran me through the logistics of their little operation and led me to a room that reminded me of the basement in *Fight Club*. Only, what a rich person would have for a basement. Kilian was conducting a suicide mission to Ireland. According to Aaron, their numbers had grown in a month, but they weren't sure if it was enough.

"Do you want to spar with us today? Dom's taught me so much stuff. Felix has turned out to be great too." Aaron was way too excited.

"I'll watch you."

He nodded and readied himself to get on the mat. The whole room lingered with the scent of blood. I stuffed my headphones in and sat against the wall. The only thing I'd been able to download at the hotel was the entire Avril Lavigne *Under My Skin* album, but I wasn't above asking ole Kilian to let me use his likely ancient computer to get more music. He owed me as far as I was concerned.

Aaron threw off his shirt and rolled his shoulders. The confidence in his stance caught my attention. Aaron wasn't confident or athletic, even when he tried baseball. With a bite on the wrist, his blood dripped to the floor, and my brother squared his shoulders as Dom charged him.

I'd watched him spar plenty of times in Blackheart—he was kind of shit—but my mouth nearly fell open as he dodged Dom's advance. He was fast, way better at countering than he had been before. More than that, he was determined in a way I'd never seen him. In baseball, he mostly sat in the dugout and ate too many sunflower seeds.

He countered a lunge by Dom and spun in enough time to catch his leg. Dom fell to the ground in a loud thump.

"Good. Very Good."

Aaron was going all out for this. He would fight in this war, but where did that leave me? I was no closer to figuring out my clues, but I hoped to see something that gave me confidence this would work. Maybe I didn't need to do that anymore. Aaron's plan could work.

Thirty-Four

AARON

After I showed Presley some of the training and had him meet a few of the others, we settled into the library to do what I did when I wasn't training. Kimberly was with Halina getting extra blood so she could be ready for the ritual.

I kicked my feet up on the ottoman in Kilian's study. The fire sent a satisfying crack into the silence while I skimmed the pages of a book, carefully at first. I was a little afraid I'd rip the pages, but as time went on, I cared less and less.

I still wasn't sure what I was looking for but hoped I'd know when I saw it. We still needed answers about what was happening to me, but more importantly, Presley and I needed to find something to aid us in helping our brothers.

"This is boring." Presley groaned as he turned a page.

"I know, but it's the most helpful thing we can do. A lot of these books reference The Family, and we need to look for anything that could help us."

"This one is just gibberish. I don't even understand what I'm looking at."

I held out my hand. "Let me see?"

It was a thick book with leather binding. Upon inspection, the entire thing was written in Latin. I'd seen enough of them to know what it looked like.

"Kilian, can you look at this one?"

Kilian had his head buried in a book but looked up at my request. The sun was disappearing and lit up the study in a warm glow.

"Hm." He held the book and flipped a few pages till he landed on one. "It's an account of poems. Many are illegible."

"Anything helpful?"

"This one roughly translates to: Life belongs to Her."

Presley rolled his eyes, picking up another book. "At least this one is in English."

The mention of Her brought sickness to my stomach and a dryness to my throat.

"Do you think . . . she's mean to them?" I asked a little too absent-mindedly. I probably shouldn't have asked in front of my brother, but I wanted Kilian's answer. "I keep trying to imagine what it's like for them. What would they even have in common with Her? What would they talk about?"

"I imagine She'd use whatever She could to create a relationship. The Family is all about the relationships they form. That's how they manipulate them how they want. I'm more confident since Kimberly's dealings, that the entity that makes the queens uses the memories and feelings of their vessel. I'm curious as to if there are times when that energy is stronger in the vessel and if it changes with the moons as well."

"So, Cecily . . . She's in there. She talks to my brothers."

"I'm not sure. It is likely It uses her humanness to appeal to them."

What did that really tell me?

"It's all theory. How the thing connects you and I, connects us to the queens and the queens to their guards. The more we uncover, the more I believe that this entity needs their vessels."

"I assumed you'd know more since this has been your obsession for hundreds of years."

"Yeah. You're so old. How don't you know everything there is to know about every subject ever made?" Presley didn't look away from his book.

The corners of Kilian's mouth tugged into a smile. "The mind can only hold so much information. You think I'm knowledgeable, but my brother was even more so. The myths of Her in Ireland haunted us. My brother . . . was obsessed with hunting Her. He had a strong sense of justice. I often thought of him as purer in heart than me. He's the reason we ended up in The Legion. From there, we gathered as much information that we could. Ezra, her closest, was thought to be the knight of Cecily."

"Like he knew her before everything?"

"Yes, I believe he is the first She turned after Her transformation. The others are less known. Akira is said to have traveled a great distance to find Her. While Sirius and his brother are the most mysterious. These four were selected for a reason."

His gaze flickered between me and my brother, but Presley was busy skimming pages with the same vacant, bored expression.

"Prophecy. Do you believe in it?"

"I have seen many things come to pass through prophecy."

Of course.

"However, I think we have more power than we think. I believe fate is a strong wind, not a solid like stone. This power that the entity draws from, I'm not sure what it is. My brother believed in its power, that's why he gave his life for the cause."

"And you? What do you think?"

"I think I wish I'd died for him when I had the chance."

Just as his words echoed, I stopped on a page. There was no reason for it. It was one natural pause that drew me to a paragraph scribbled in cursive ink at the bottom of a page. The room seemed to disappear.

Blood forges the way to freedom.

Lifeblood gave way, a high price to pay.

Fate does not guide us.

We carve our way.

We settled down in the library, where Kimberly had a stool to sit on by the fire. I squeezed her hand as Kilian placed the box that contained the dagger next to her. Things would work more quickly than last time. We'd found the right incantation, and now all that was left was to tap back into the power.

Presley watched from an armchair over from me while picking the black nail polish from his nails.

"Are you ready?" I rubbed Kimberly's leg.

"Yeah. Definitely." She looked at Kilian. "We'll make progress this time."

After biting her finger, she smeared the blood along the length of the blade while Kilian started his chant.

I hated all of it. Letting her open herself up to something dangerous made me physically ill, but there was no arguing with her once her mind was set. It was her choice.

With fingers clenched around the blade, she closed her eyes. Her brow bent in eager determination, then her head fell back. I went to grab her again, but she slumped forward with her eyes open. Her blue eyes disappeared and misted over in a white haze. I still had my hand on her leg, rubbing her gently. I'd be there to pull her out if needed.

Minutes passed, and she blinked.

"No. No!" The desperation in her voice put me on alert.

"What's wrong? Are you okay?" I asked.

"What did you see?" Kilian asked.

"Nothing. I asked for it to show me something, and nothing happened." She pressed her palms into her eyes.

"It's okay. It's not your fault."

"I don't care who's fault it is. I'm not waiting another month. Can we do it again?"

"I'd advise against it," Kilian said. "The entity can't possess you, but this is new territory. I don't know what could happen to you."

"But can we try? Will you recite it again?"

"Kim," I said.

"No, Aaron." She grabbed my arm with pleading eyes. "We can't wait another month to make progress. This is already taking too long. We need answers so we know how to win."

"I know, but not at the expense of hurting you."

"I have to do this. I can do this."

"Hold on. Family huddle," Presley said. "Everyone give us a second."

Presley got up from his chair to lean in front of Kimberly. "Kim, we can help my brothers in another way. You don't have to do this."

"I know I don't have to. But I want to."

"Dude, they wouldn't want you to do something that would get you hurt," Presley said.

"He's right." I rubbed her leg, but she pushed me off.

"No! I have to do this. They wouldn't want us to be doing any of this at all. They told you both to stay here and leave them there, but . . . I have to do this. It's my decision."

Her tone pricked at me, and it frayed in a way that wasn't normal for her. There was anger in her eyes, and the usual blue pools were darker.

"Let's go again." She looked at Kilian.

"I really do advise against—"

"You know, I don't care what you advise, Kilian. Please. Start the chant again."

Presley and I shared a worried look. He stayed at her feet next to us as she grabbed the dagger again and closed her eyes.

The chant started, and my muscles tightened. I didn't know what to expect, and my imagination ranged from Kimberly turning into the mega Hulk and hurling me across the room to falling into a coma. I forced myself to stop thinking and focus on her heartbeat instead. It beat steadily and picked up speed when a white film overtook her eyes as she stared off into the distance. One of her hands gripped the dagger, and the other was on my forearm. Minutes passed again, much slower this time. Slow enough for me to notice the feet shifting on the floor and a grandfather clock in the other room ticking away.

A sudden change in her heartbeat pulled me back to her.

In seconds, her chest heaved and tears streamed down her face, and those tears turned into a sobbing.

"Kimberly." I grabbed both shoulders and shook her. "That's enough."

She kept sobbing, shrieking, and shaking while she white-knuckled the dagger in her hand.

I grabbed her face in my hands. "Come back to me. Please."

I was seconds away from ripping the dagger from her grasp when she blinked and her blue eyes returned. She fell into my arms sobbing.

"It's okay. You're okay." I held her tightly and stroked the top of her head, but she wouldn't stop crying.

Was she still in pain? Was it something she saw? Something It did to her?

I kissed her forehead, soothing her the best I could manage. "I'm sorry. We should never have tried this."

"No," she said between sobs, clutching my shirt. "Aaron . . . I saw the future. You were dead."

My stomach sank at her words. I probably should have been more concerned than I was, but all I cared about was how upset she was. I'd never seen her so undone.

"You can't go there. You can't."

"Hey, I'm right here. It's okay." I pulled her off the chair and guided her out of the room. "We're done here."

"Wait," Kilian called.

"Touch her, and I take that arm," I warned him. Every nerve in my body was on fire. The room remained silent, aside from Kimberly's sobs. Presley was next to her, also trying to soothe her, but her heart hammered erratically.

I needed to get her away from here. Away from everything.

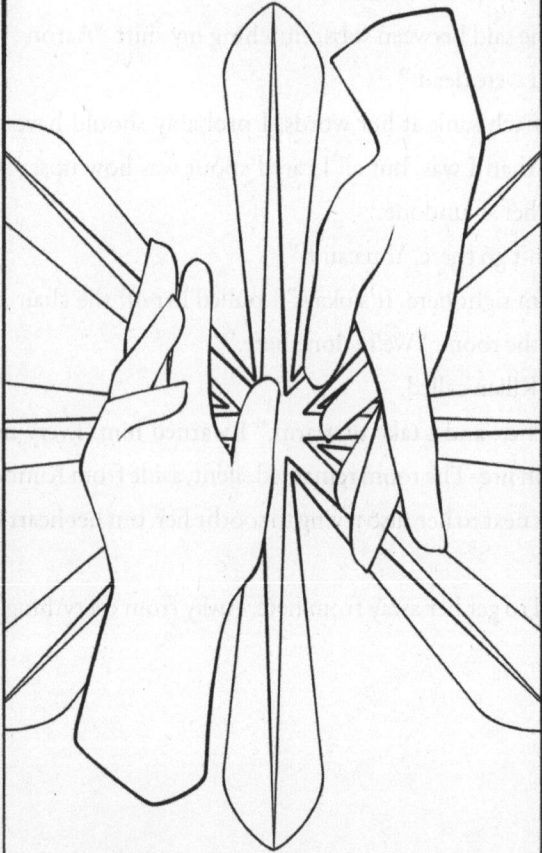

VI

THE LOVERS

Thirty-Five

KIMBERLY

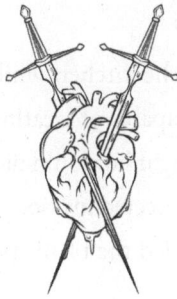

I cried the entire way home, with my face buried in Presley's sweater while he rubbed my back. The tears were relentless, and any attempt to stifle them was futile. Nothing in my life had ever broken me like the image of seeing Aaron dead and cold on the ground.

The image was too vivid and specific to be fake. It was real.

Aaron would die.

None of us said anything on the drive back to the cabin, and I was surprised how quickly the time had passed when the car door opened.

"I'll take her." Aaron opened up Presley's car door, and we funneled out into the snow.

I wanted to make sense of it. To find something to say or think that would bring any comfort, but my worst fears had been confirmed.

Everything would end in death, and the person I loved most in the world would be taken from me.

I'd had it wrong. We couldn't defeat Her. The events had been set in motion long before I was born. Fate had the Calem brothers in its clutches, and it wouldn't stop until they were dead or Hers.

Aaron led me into our cabin, and I sulked my way up the stairs and into our bed.

I wanted to hide. I wanted to sleep. I wanted to run.

It had to be a bad dream. That couldn't be the future. Why had I believed things could work?

There was a rustling in the kitchen while I cried onto my pillow. I didn't think my body was capable of creating that many tears.

Everything meant nothing if he would die. I hated that stupid dagger and the stupid Thing that infected my body. Most of all, I hated Her.

"Come here." Aaron pulled the blankets back, and I squinted from the lamp on the side table.

I complied and sat up while he steadied me, but looking at him hurt. I shielded myself from the warmth of his skin, knowing it would be a distant memory. One day, he wouldn't touch me again. He wouldn't be able to smile at me and tell me he loved me. The battle was over before it began. The singular crack in my armor was torn open, and it felt like my heart was bleeding all over the bed and onto the floor.

A warm rag grazed my cheek, wiping the tears that fell. His hands, strong and sure, wiped my tears and the remnants of my makeup away.

"Are you sure you don't want to shower?" Aaron asked with no hint of sadness in his voice, just patience.

I shook my head, and he kneeled to the floor, pulling the boots from my feet that I'd failed to shed. There was no rush as he unlaced them, placed them on the floor, and replaced my socks with a new, fluffier pair.

Grabbing his forearm, I let his warmth in despite the memory of how cold he felt in the vision.

Aaron made his way into bed and sat up against the headboard. In one motion, he placed me in his lap and cradled me to his chest. I wrapped my arms around his neck and buried myself in his scent. There were more tears at first, but I couldn't cry in the arms of Aaron Calem for long. I thought I'd known love when I told him for the first time. I was so sure then, but this felt like something else entirely. My insides were shredded, yet every tender kiss he left on my face and the top of my head stitched me back together.

It was utterly appalling to feel that way about someone else. So foreign and fantastical, it didn't seem real. He didn't seem real, but Aaron was well-versed in the magic of the world. He was pure radiant magic himself.

"Do you want to tell me what you saw?"

The memory surfaced, and I pushed it away. "No. I can't."

He held my face in his hands and kissed my forehead.

"You don't have to. But . . . I think if you keep it in, it will eat at you. You'll keep thinking about it, and you'll make all your theories and your lists till you won't be able to do anything else." Another tear fell as I listened, and his warm thumb rubbed it away. "But if you tell me, then I can take it from you. And every time you're tempted to worry, you'll just know I've got it. I'm holding it for you."

"Aaron, that's nonsense."

"No, it's not. You're just sharing the burden. You tell me, and I'll carry the weight for you."

I rested my head against him. "Okay . . . I was back in that place. The in-between place, and I willed the power to come to me so I could see. I asked It to show me something specific this time—the future. And then I was in another church. There was fog everywhere, so I couldn't make out everything, just the floor. It was intricate marble and had this long crack. When I followed it, I found you with the dagger in your chest.

And I couldn't hear your heart beating anymore."

My voice broke again, and he squeezed me tighter. When I felt the strength to speak again I said, "You're not scared?"

"No. I don't believe in that stuff." His fingers traced along my jaw.

"Just because you don't believe it doesn't make it not true. It was so vivid . . . it felt so real."

We settled into bed, and he pulled my leg over him until we were intertwined. With my head on his chest, I kept my gaze on the skylight above our heads. My body melted into his, and every breath became deeper and deeper.

His hand rested over my heart. "This is the only thing I believe in."

The thrum of his heartbeat was powerful and roaring in my ears.

"This love is the only thing I care about. It's the only thing that matters. Prophecies be damned."

"You were so cold. There was blood everywhere. It felt real. It felt sure. I was screaming for you . . . and you were gone."

"How do you know it's showing you the truth? It could be showing you just what It wants you to see just to scare you. We don't even know what you're tapping into. We can't trust everything we see at face value. We don't know what the visions mean, let alone who is sending them. Even if it was the future, who's to say that's the only outcome?"

"But what if it's true? What if you die? What if it's . . . written in the stars?"

The stars twinkled above. They usually brought me comfort, but I wanted to hide Aaron away where the stars couldn't touch him. Away from the stars, the gods, or whatever else wanted to take him from me. Because this love was the kind that would haunt me day and night. The absence of Aaron Calem would leave me empty and nothing could ever fill it again. I'd caught the sun, felt it burn in my hands, and if it went out I'd never get another.

"Then I'll change it. I'll make my own constellations. I'm not scared of the stars. They should be afraid of me."

I was awestruck at the fire in his eyes. Who was this infinitely hopeful man, and how did he muster the courage?

"How are you so brave?"

"I learned it from you."

I shook my head. I didn't feel brave anymore, and I could scarcely remember a time when I did.

"No. Not anymore. Every time we get a little closer, the less control I have of the future. I wish I could fast forward to know the end because it feels like I'm about to lose everything."

Love had sucked the courage from my bones and left me hollow in its wake. I no longer felt the fire. Only a brisk emptiness of sorrow in the face of all I'd come to love being torn from me. To know love was to know true pain. It was a fragile, fickle, flickering thing in danger of being snuffed out despite my strongest efforts. I couldn't control it. There was no certainty in love.

"You've been brave every day of your life. And you did that all on your own. It's my turn to be brave for you."

He was braver than I ever was. He'd known love his entire life and was at risk of losing it all, yet he smiled.

"I'm not going to let anything kill me that easily. I've got a girl that needs me."

I squeezed him. "She must be special."

He made me feel that way. Special. A word with no meaning before I met him. I'd just been Kimberly. A girl. Never a favorite. Or the best. I was never chosen first for anything. I was never anyone's first phone call or thought in the morning.

No one picked me.

But Aaron did.

"She is. She's everything. And I'm going to show her things can work out."

Finally, the fear released me, and when I looked at the sky, I could appreciate the stars again and their glow in the dark sky. They were infinite, like our possibilities for a different future. A better one.

FEBRUARY

Thirty-Six

PRESLEY

Another day, another minute of contemplating robbing a bank to buy my plane ticket to Ireland. Robbing the bank would be the easy part. The bank in town wasn't the most high tech, and I was confident I could break into anything.

My stomach ached at what Luke would think of my willingness to commit a federal crime. Maybe that's what he meant by being good.

I was being punished. Maybe Hell Bitch wasn't a demon and She was a god and knew I spent every minute in my room thinking of how much I hated Her, so She was smiting me. I thought of Her—too often, likely not healthy—I felt anger, and I think it was my brother's anger. Probably. It was hard to tell. After a while, all the strange internal sensations started to feel the same.

That's the only explanation for why two weeks felt like two days—hence the bank robbing plans.

The only thing preventing me from committing a federal crime was knowing even if I made my way there, I didn't know their exact location because I couldn't figure out the stupid riddle. I was no Bilbo Baggins. Also, no money. I never acted on my thoughts, but sometimes in the dead of night, I'd go to the kitchen, grab the car keys, and toss them from hand to hand.

Everyone tried to make it better, but that's what made it worse. I was feeling like Aaron when he was whiny and annoying, but I wished everyone would let me be sad. I'd let the sadness swallow me if it would've made time pass quicker. Aaron and Kimberly were off being heroes, and I was sitting in my room in the dark.

There was a knock at my door, and I refused to let go of my pillow and tear my gaze from the lamp.

"Hunny? Are you ready for me to take you to the shelter? I have time."

"I'm not going," I called.

"Can I come in?"

When I didn't answer, she entered. I awaited the blinding switch of the light, but instead, there was a shift in the bed and a hand on my back.

"Do you want to talk?"

"No."

"Work will help." Mom's hand felt good against my back. It was nice not to hurt in at least one part of my body.

"I don't want to work. I want to sulk and be sad, and I want everyone to just let me waste away. Not like I'm any help, anyway."

What was I going to do? If this big final battle finally came, I'd do what? Stand around and hope for the best? It made no sense for me to be there and no sense for me to try. I was waiting for Aaron to ask me to stay home and confirm what I knew: I was the useless little brother.

"You know . . . when I first arrived, I stayed locked away in my cabin for weeks. I did nothing but think of what a terrible mother I had been and everything I should have done differently."

"Now I know where I got it from. Thanks, Mom," I mumbled.

"That was until my neighbor suggested the clinic. It's been the only thing that's gotten me through. Being at the shelter will help pass the day-to-day while you see what the next step is."

"Feels like doing nothing."

"Sometimes we have to wait for the right moment. And you'll know when it is. We all help in our own way. Maybe your moment just hasn't happened yet."

Mom believed in me for some strange reason. It helped to look at her and to lean into the comfort like I used to. I wished things hadn't changed and I could enjoy that comfort, but every time I thought about it, I remembered my older brothers needed comfort too, and they weren't here to have Mom rub their back. They needed it more than me.

"This is going to interfere with my plans to watch *Tarzan* at least ten times today."

She smiled while moving a lock of hair from my eyes. "It will be waiting for you when you get home. I'll watch with you."

With that, I finally found the strength to get out of bed and turn on the light.

———⚬⚬⚬———

"Come on, Sarah. Good girl, come on." I ushered the all-black husky out of her kennel.

Her name was further proof I was being punished for something.

I tried not to like dog Sarah at first, but she was always following me around being cute. My coworker, Sydney, said I was Sarah's favorite and before I came around she'd lay in her kennel all day and mope. Then when I came along, she magically liked to play and eat all her food. I think we needed each other. Being sad was our favorite hobby.

Sarah trotted along to the playpen for her outside time. She was popular with the other dogs but only if I was watching her. If I left to go fill up the food, she'd wait for me by the door. It was annoyingly adorable.

"I didn't know you had a shift today." Sydney came around the corner, sporting another ponytail. That was her thing.

"I took an extra one. Needed a break from my family. I just needed a break."

Probably the only time I'd ever said that sentence.

"Oh, I get it. My sisters piss me off all the time. Love them, but damn."

"Exactly. This is the only place I have that's normal."

Sydney smiled, and it eased my guilt. Barely. "Come with me on break."

I agreed. I didn't mind the company. Since I didn't eat on my breaks, I'd usually just watch soap operas till my time was up.

"Sarah, stay," I said as she ran to walk out the door with me.

Her whining echoed in the hallway as we went for the break room.

The break room smelled of wet dog and had two blue sofas and a tiny TV next to a mini fridge. I was one of three volunteers. Sydney said if I stayed for a while I could eventually get paid.

She ushered me into a story about her sister Callie and their fight over the hair straightener and how even though Callie was older, she always took Sydney's clothes. Usually, I'd be all over small talk, but my chest was achy and it was harder to focus than usual.

I pulled the note from my pocket when she went to take a bite of her sandwich.

"What's that?" Sydney asked with a mouth full of bread. "You're always staring at it."

"I've been trying to figure out this riddle. It's for . . . this class I'm taking."

"A riddle for class?" She raised a curious brow.

I wasn't giving lying my A game anymore.

"Can I see?"

I handed it to her, hoping she wouldn't see how worn it had become. "*Where the land meets the see* . . . s-e-e."

"I have literally no idea."

"Is it supposed to be local?"

"Uh, maybe."

"Well, we do have Seer's Point. It's on the other side of the lake."

"What? No way."

She smiled and took another monster bite of her sandwich. "Way. You didn't Google search it?"

Damn shitty internet.

"I, uh . . . I'm going to leave early today."

"Got a date with Seer's Point?"

"Something like that."

"Well, you better go spend some time with Sarah before you go. I think she gets depressed when you're not around," Sydney called as I reached for the door.

I sighed. Her and I both. I already felt better. Mom was right. Of course she was.

Thirty-Seven

AARON

I fell on my ass again, but this time, I was prepared. I leveraged my body weight in just enough time to send Felix careening into the mat.

"You're getting good," Dom said, barely loud enough to hear.

Felix tackled me from behind as I tried to get up. "Not good enough."

He pinned me to the ground with his forearm. "Don't turn your back on an opponent."

"How is that even possible?" I grunted as I maneuvered his arm from my neck and used his weight to push him off balance. My body was slower with the lack of blood. Every day we trained in Kilian's basement, I got more used to the feeling. It was all defensive maneuvers—keeping away from hands and not giving anyone the chance to bite me.

"You need eyes in the back of your head. Use your senses," Dom said while I struggled under the weight of Felix's forearm.

I was glad Felix and I had buried the hatchet. Or he might have tried to kill me already.

In one fluid breath, I slid from under him and took him in a headlock. Slipping from the wetness of the blood, he struggled to pull me off.

"Good. Keep him down," Dom said.

Felix stumbled to his feet, and I kept my grip locked around his neck. He attempted to sweep my leg, but I dodged it. Squeezing harder around his throat, I held him down and bit into his arm.

"Alright. Alright. I forfeit."

Felix fell to the ground when I released him, and I reached out to help him up.

"I think I'm done," he said.

"Wait, why?"

"Don't you get tired, Calem? We've been going all day."

Dom interjected. "Thirty-two hours."

I still had energy left to burn. Every day that past, Ireland got closer. Like the island was physically moving toward me hour by hour. I needed to use every minute to its fullest. Whatever fate had waiting for me, I needed to be ready, and Dom and Felix were helping.

I must have looked deflated because Dom said, "I'll spar with you. After your break."

Our numbers had grown. Our once-sparse basement was flourishing with people. Most made no effort to talk to me. They liked Felix and Dom though. Everyone liked them. The Legion was made up of tiny little friend groups or families all merging for one purpose.

I settled my attention on one in particular. Kimberly had just started sparring. She was faster than me. I couldn't help but smile watching her with Halina.

I caught the tail end of their conversation.

"Yeah, I like you way better as a vampire." Halina helped get Kimberly off the ground.

Kimberly grabbed her hand and jumped to her feet. "Me too."

She must have felt me watching her because her eyes met mine, and she blushed.

My heart kicked my ribs. I had to fight to keep my mind from wandering into places in which I'd pull her aside and do things with her that would deepen that flush.

It was addicting to flirt with her.

Lucky for me, the door opened and a commotion came from the outside hall. Everyone stilled as they entered. Kilian walked next to a woman with brown hair I'd never seen before.

And they were . . . laughing?

"Ah, Aaron. I'd like you to meet Anzola. She is one of my dearest friends. She sits on the council for The Legion. She's the one who has graciously allowed us to use her home. Anzola has been alive since the first known queen was created. She's come to train and explore our operation."

Anzola flashed her teeth in a sultry smile directed at Kilian. Her jaw and cheekbones were sharp, and her olive skin was clear. Her body seemed to be close to Kilian's in age.

"Never reveal a woman's age, Kil. You should know better." She winked at him.

I didn't know what was weirder: Kilian smiling or them having nicknames.

"Aaron Calem." Anzola smiled at me with pristine white teeth. "Pleasure to make your acquaintance."

"The pleasure is mine." I held out my hand, and she nearly took it off with the strength of her grip. I forced a smile despite the ache in my hand.

"Kilian here brought me to see the operation and get a good feel for things in his absence."

"In case he dies," Felix whispered, and I inched away from his breath on my ear.

"Do not worry. It's only a precaution. Someone will need to take over his archives and carry on his work. Hopefully, it won't be needed. The council wants to ensure preservation of his life's work is in order."

There was a gentle calm about the way she said it that made me feel like she wouldn't care in the slightest if Kilian did meet that fate or if we all did, but maybe that's how The Legion was. An old organization filled with people whose only real goal in life was to take down The Family, so friends and family came second. It wasn't personal. Just strictly business.

Kimberly came up beside me. Her proximity allowed me to put my arm over her shoulder and hold her to me.

"Kimberly, it's a pleasure." Anzola opened her mouth like there was more to say. "Looking forward to speaking with you later about your endeavors with the dagger."

"Oh . . . okay." Kimberly shifted.

"Are you going to help fight?" I asked, partly joking.

"I came to stay for the foreseeable future, not just for cataloging old relics . . ."

With graceful elegance, Anzola removed her jacket, revealing tight overlapping leather underneath. The only thing I could equate it to was a video game character.

Kimberly and I shared a wide-eyed look. I wished Presley were here to break the silence. Kilian did the same but revealed his bare chest and lean and sharply carved muscle.

In my head, Kilian was a fragile older man. The only time I'd seen him move quickly was the night he pinned me up against the door in OBA. I reeled as my perception I'd built up over the months shifted in a matter of seconds.

"Kilian needs a sparring partner that can keep up." Anzola's eyes glistened as she stalked forward to face him.

The rest of us stepped out of the center mat, giving them room.

"So, you're definitely fighting too, then?" I called to Kilian.

He smiled. "Did you think I was too old?"

I bit my cheek, saying nothing. *Definitely.*

I expected it to be quick. For Kilian to be slow and sloppy, but he wasn't. Anzola was a great challenge. They first sparred clean at full power. Their full strength split the mats and cracked the concrete floor underneath. I couldn't stop staring. Kilian wasn't just good, he was great. It had to be the years of training, but all I'd ever seen him do was sit down and read. *No wonder Akira left us that day in the forest.*

If I had to guess, they were closely matched.

"Take your jaw off the floor, Calem." Dom stood beside me.

"You knew?"

"Of course."

The air in the room grew heavier when Anzola got a bite in on Kilian's arm and blood littered the ground. There was something sinister about it and brutal in a way that made my stomach churn. I rubbed my chest thinking of Zach and Luke, and hoped they weren't doing that very thing.

We had strong fighters, and that meant we were finally a match for The Guard.

Thirty-Eight

KIMBERLY

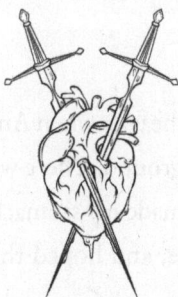

Halina and I took a break from sparring after a few hours. I enjoyed the distraction. We settled into the living room that held an electric fireplace, and various large and small plants littered the space along the floor-to-ceiling windows. The remaining light of the day bathed the leaves in sunlight.

"He kept all of Will's old plants." Halina reached for one of the leaves and rubbed it between her fingers. "We take good care of them . . . He was so particular. I remember all the instructions."

"You miss him . . ."

"Will was—is a large part of what held us together. I don't think he knew that though. And if he comes back, I won't tell him. And Thane was a friend. One of the only people I had to talk to. Not sure if you've picked up on it, but my brother isn't very talkative, so it gets lonely. And Skylar, well, Skylar and I butted heads, but it was nice to have another girl in the group."

"Do you want me to help with them?" I motioned to the plants on the floor and windowsill.

"Sure. You can water and I'll prune some."

I worked through the plants, doing just as she mentioned and checking the soil between each one to make sure it was completely dry. All while I thought of William. He'd hate me touching his plants. I wondered what the four of them were doing but pushed any thoughts away that told me they'd been killed or hurt. I wanted William and Thane to come back to their family as much as I wanted it for mine. Perhaps Will would smile when he returned home to see his plants alive and thriving.

"Hey ladies." Aaron strode in with glowing confidence. An influx of laughter and voices came from the hallway as the boys took their break and walked from the dining room to the kitchen.

Aaron's gaze stayed fixed on me. His bare chest and the fresh flush in his cheeks made me weak in the knees.

"After this break, Dom is going to work with me for another hour, but tonight, I'm all yours." He touched his lips to mine and lingered there till my entire body flushed with heat. He leaned close to my ear. "All night."

I simply nodded. Those golden eyes never faltered, and he winked at me before going for the door.

It took a second longer for me to compose myself.

"God. He's different." Halina's eyes devoured him in an instant, admiring what I, too, admired. The veins in his arms, the curve of his biceps. His messy hair.

A strange heat in my stomach traveled to my throat and almost tore through my clenched teeth. I cleared my throat.

That broke her concentration.

Aaron had changed. What the ritual had torn from me, had fueled him. He hadn't shed a tear. Every day the sun passed overhead, only seemed to pump him full of radiant optimism.

"I'm sorry. Respectfully, I'm very envious of you right now. It's been so long for me . . . and the way Aaron looks at you—well, it's hot."

Halina never talked to me like a friend, though she'd softened to me. We only talked about logistics. Things like: *How long have you gone without blood before? Is this how it was for you? Did you just let me win this match because you feel sorry for me?* Never dating.

"I heard he's been drinking from you. You have to tell me what that's like."

"You mean . . ."

"The sex. It's got to be something else entirely."

"Uh . . ."

Suddenly, I missed Chelsea. Not that she'd have loved a conversation about Aaron's and my love life, but she would have listened if I needed someone to talk to. In Alaska, the only person I could talk to was Presley, and considering Aaron was his brother, that topic was off the table. It was too personal of a subject for me to discuss with Halina.

"It's . . . There aren't really any words to describe it."

Halina wouldn't let me off the hook. She placed her hands on her hips, waiting for more. I'd need to steer in another direction.

"Have you ever . . . had anyone?"

"The dating pool is extremely small when you're like we are and you hang out with your brother all the time. People think we're dating. It's gross. More than that, it's not like I can pull someone into this suicide mission."

"Right."

"Sorry. I shouldn't say it like that." Her long blonde lashes fluttered. "Skylar will undoubtedly make me pay from beyond the grave for saying that to you."

"You really don't think we're going to make it?"

"I don't know about you . . . but I've been prepared to die since the minute I was changed. Everyone who hangs around with Kilian is prepared for death. It's always been a suicide mission. Felix and I were changed for the cause. Like Aaron asked before, we signed on with complete knowledge. Like most people who aren't afraid to die, we didn't have a family to worry about, but we got to see firsthand how The Family steals our recruits. They convinced Felix's best friend, someone I was very close to, to change sides, but it's never enough for them, they bled him out. Let him die. Slowly and painfully. All to prove a point. I fear everyday what they're doing to Will and Thane . . ."

I realized Halina never hated us. She hated watching us live life carefree while this had always been a life-or-death battle for her. In her shoes, I might have hated me too. In Blackheart, we'd been foolish and carefree, and though I couldn't bring myself to regret it, I wished I'd known the secrets and horrors that everyone held close to their chests.

"Do you think William and Thane are a lost cause?"

"No. But I think this is the end. In a lot of ways, I've always felt like I was born with a half-life. Though I've lived over a hundred years, I've never truly lived."

I felt the pull of her words and the truth in them. Fate had its hooks in me. Luring me, it tugged at my skin and my thoughts every minute of the day. There was somewhere it was taking me, and I was afraid to reach my final destination. The queen was beckoning me to Her, and I knew I'd meet Her in the future. Our paths were merging.

"Destined to die . . ." I repeated, averting my gaze.

"Skylar didn't believe that for you, though."

"What?" I stopped my watering to look at her.

"She was adamant that you'd get to live and make your own decisions.

She talked about it a lot actually. It used to get on my last nerve."

The memory of our talk by the fountain almost brought tears to my eyes. I moved to wipe them, expecting Halina to scowl or scoff, but her brows softened, and she offered a sympathetic smile.

"She liked looking after you. I think . . . she liked watching you all have a life we didn't.".

"I miss her."

"Me too. But I have a feeling I'll see her real soon." Halina nodded while tucking a long blonde hair behind her ear. Her attention went back to pruning the dead leaves from William's plants.

As the dead leaves fell, she snatched them up one by one. Halina had made peace with death like it was just another part of life. Fighting would require great sacrifice so life could thrive and go on to live, and I still wasn't sure I'd made peace with that fact.

"Kimberly, I'd love a word with you." Anzola's low voice startled me.

I'd been getting ready to leave and had showered the blood off and was brushing my wet hair in one of the spare bedrooms. She had settled into a long velvet robe like she, too, had the same idea. It broke down my image of her. She conducted herself with the same carefulness as Kilian, and suddenly, she was just a woman like me.

I moved to sit on the bed.

The weight of Anzola's gaze was heavy on my face. Her presence itself was heavy enough. Something old and official.

"Kimberly, I want to be direct with you. Kilian has informed me of what you've been working on with the rituals. The sheer fact that you're able to access the power of the dagger is unprecedented and something that's never been done before. Your very existence on this plane in time is very interesting to me. I plan on being there for the next ritual, and I hope to aid you in your endeavors. If only I could tell the council about you . . ."

"The council doesn't know Kilian has one of the daggers, do they?"

"No, and if they did, they'd take it in an instant."

"But you won't say anything?"

"Kilian and I have a long history. I know he does not take such a responsibility lightly. And if he's able to succeed in his life's mission of taking down the coven, all the better."

I had many questions lingering on my tongue but none I'd ask aloud. The council was nothing I cared to know about unless it would aid us, and it didn't sound like they cared to help. Therefore, their history and their story meant nothing to me, and like Kilian, they couldn't be fully trusted.

"And if Kilian fails? Will you help then? If your precious dagger is lost." I was surprised by the conviction in my voice, but I was tired of being everyone's spectacle. It made no difference to any of them if my family lived or died. They would go on holding their trials and judging those like the Calem brothers and sitting in the shadows waiting for others to make the first move. What would the council of The Legion say at the postmortem meeting of all our stories? Would they tell tales of a battle that ended in catastrophe? I could see it now. A group of hopeful kids thought they could defeat them, but they failed miserably, and only in that failure did they decide to pick up the pieces after. *"If only they'd waited."*

If they didn't want to help, they were no longer of any use to me.

"Very intuitive. The council believes the coven still possesses it."

"And they don't care? What if more queens are made?"

"The ritual requires very specific texts, and they've all been destroyed or are in our possession. And many aren't interested in sharing any of their affections with another queen."

"Anzola, I appreciate you helping at all, but all I care about is getting our family back together. That's the only reason I'm doing this. Whatever it is you want from me, I'm only doing it for the sake of my own. I have no interest in conversing about the council and The Legion."

"That's why I will help. The council will not. It may not mean much, and I do not wish to persuade you to trust me, but regardless, I am here to help you, and I believe I can help you better access the power in the dagger. Kilian tells me you've used it a few times."

"Yes, but I don't think I'm doing it right. It's inconsistent. It shows me brief images, and I don't know what they mean."

"The Family believes in Divine power. They believe the power in our blood given to us by queens is a gift. But I believe it to be a malevolent spirit. To them, their queens are God in the form of a woman. The equivalent of a messiah sent to help them form relationships and bonds that the greater powers cannot create themselves. The council has their own varying religions and consider their practices blasphemous."

That must be where all the council business Kilian picked up came from. The trial and the prayers Aaron had spoken about.

"And you?"

"I've wavered throughout my life, much like Kilian, but I do believe in something greater . . . on most days."

"Well, I don't much care what It is. She could be a fairy or a god or a demon, but it doesn't matter to me." I turned my attention to the hairbrush in my hand, feeling the wood grain and gripping it just as I had the blade of the dagger. "I want Her gone. I want my family back."

I would find a way to be useful in the battle. Aaron and Presley had their roles, and I'd be close behind them when the time was right, but the dagger held the key to something. I just couldn't figure out what and how to use it to help us in battle. If Anzola wanted to help, I wouldn't say no.

What kind of person are you? Zach's words rang in my head. I finally knew where I fell in line with the Calems.

I'd do anything for my family. I'd be anything. Even if it meant not being so nice. The love we shared was worth it.

Anzola smiled with perfectly straight bright-white teeth. "Spoken like a true warrior."

Thirty-Nine

PRESLEY

Since everyone thought I was at work, it was easy to get away. Although, I had no car. I searched to see if any services would take me around the lake, and all I found was a public bus.

I stared out the window as the bus meandered along at a snail's pace. The old lady next to me kept trying to chat me up and smelled of perfumed powder.

What was this test about, anyway? What did The Family want with me? I remembered Akira's words about some prophecy I'd ignored at the time. Akira said a lot of things and probably more than he should have said. He believed in a grand prophecy that my brothers and I were a part of. *Bullshit*, I'd thought at first, but now . . .

There was obviously something they wanted me to know or to see.

The vampire cult that kills people wanted me. The one that killed Sarah. The unease built in my stomach on the ride there, and my heart nearly burst when I reached my stop.

The sun was leaving. *Typical.* With it, the temperature dropped.

Little flurries danced in the streetlight at the bus stop. I had to imagine I was playing a video game. An adventure where the guy had to put together the clues to find his family again, and each level got a little harder. That would explain my sudden anxiety, which I never got. I didn't use to fear anything. When your brothers are there to beat anything and anyone up and you're immortal, what was there to fear?

I could think of a lot of things now.

That thought brought me to the trailhead at Seer's Point. I looked over the worn, faded infographics on the sign. Mostly, it stated things about not leaving trash, and there was a little map.

What would video-game Presley do? I moved my hand along the top and bottom of the sign. No one was around. I couldn't imagine a ton of people walking the trails in the winter. My bare fingers caught something under the bottom edge. An envelope like the one from the pub. Inside was a large see-through piece of paper I unfolded and held up to the light. The biggest landmarks were marked, so I lined it up with the map. A large black X marked a place just off the main trail.

They overestimated my ability to remember things. I took my sad little flip phone out and took a picture just in case.

The snow left water seeping into my pant legs. Was it part of the test? To see how far I'd be willing to walk alone in the snow? It was all a little too much for my liking. Like, wouldn't one note suffice? It could've been an email or a text, but they'd made it into a game.

Of course. Akira loved games. He'd have no trouble having someone on standby to leave me clues before his inevitable demise.

Still, they didn't have to do all this. So dramatic.

It was a cave. Why a cave? The light on my flip phone was dull and virtually nonexistent, yet I went into their creeper cave. I was shaking.

I smelled for blood or anything rotten, but there was just stone and dirt that grew stronger the farther I went.

The cavern narrowed, and a light appeared ahead. A battery-operated lamp sat in the dirt and illuminated a small area. There wasn't much. Just a cardboard box, a duffle bag, and a small folding chair.

I plopped down, thankful my demise hadn't been waiting for me.

Open first was painted in red on the black canvas bag.

It was a trap, and I was being such an Aaron. I'd thought he was an idiot for walking into one in Blackheart, and I'd just willingly done the same thing.

Thank god no one was there to see it.

I unzipped it while fearing the worst. A severed head. A bag full of snakes. Dead puppies—Now that would be vile.

Only, it wasn't dead puppies. It was cash. Stacks of cash. The cardboard box was next, and at the bottom was a pile of pictures. My heart sank as I flipped through them. They were all of us in Blackheart. My family. Weird angles from the forest or the windows. Some of us laughing and others with more intimate moments. I noted the trees. Not all of them were from fall. Some were in the summer at the waterpark. Maybe earlier.

A weird unraveling started in my stomach until a tremble twitched in my fingers. They'd studied us. We were always within their grasp.

All the football games. All the parties. They were there patiently waiting for us. There were close-ups of my brother's faces. Kim and Aaron in his room. Thane and me playing video games. So many of Zach and Luke. Like they were obsessed with the backs of their heads.

I stopped on one that differed from the others with a regal wallpaper I didn't recognize. Luke and Zach were in black suits talking to one another.

I almost didn't recognize them with their cropped hair. Luke's eyes were hollow. He looked like someone kept him in a basement for five years. And Zach . . . had a lifeless stare that made me drop the picture.

I sucked in a breath. The Family knew where I was. They knew what I was doing. They were waiting for me. That reality had never been clearer.

It was bad. *Bad Presley!*

I had to stop. They may have known the general location we were in, but as long as I wasn't tracked, they wouldn't find my family. Luke and Zach would be so pissed off at me for putting everyone in danger while I played detective. They'd given up everything to keep us safe, and I'd led The Family right back to us.

They were obsessed with us. Suddenly, I didn't feel like pretending I was an action-adventure hero. I wanted to run away and hide. The intimacy of the photos and the feeling of dread was plastered in my mind. The anger and sadness on my brothers' faces . . .

They wouldn't give up until they had us all.

It was dark by the time I left the cave. Up ahead, there was a star. Burning brighter than any other. I reached up, wanting to touch it and transport there. Something about the light made me feel like . . . like it would make this burning, throbbing, aching feeling in my chest stop. So I started walking.

I kept my eyes on the sky and let that invisible string pull me into the night until I wasn't walking anymore. I was running. Faster and faster toward that light. It was there. I swear I felt lighter.

What was this feeling?

Was it them?

Was it Her?

Whatever it was, I needed it. The closer I got, the more it eased the pain in my chest.

Then I was standing in the dark, in the cold . . . alone.

It wasn't a cosmic revelation to feel alone, but it was for me.

It wasn't fair that they got all the responsibility because they were born first. They'd done everything for me, and I'd done nothing. How was I supposed to deal with that?

Getting older sucks.

Crumbling into the snow, the tears assaulted me until I was sobbing into my hands. It made my chest hurt worse, but it felt good to let everything fall out of me.

It would have been easier to make my brothers the villains in their story, kind of like Aaron did at first, but they weren't the villains in my story, not in this lifetime or any other. My brothers were both heroes in my book. They'd fought their fate with everything they had.

The pain in my chest throbbed out of control. It was the only connection I had left to them. When I didn't feel it, it scared me, like maybe one day I wouldn't feel it anymore.

I didn't want Mom to tell me everything would be fine. I didn't want Kimberly to try to fix my problems. I wanted my brother to tell me everything would be okay. I needed a hug that would erase my errors and sins.

Forty

AARON

After almost an hour of driving, I finally reached the park. Presley had called me sobbing, and I'd replayed his words over and over again as I drove.

"I really need you to come get me."

All at once, my body went rigid. What hurt him? Who hurt him? And more importantly, what would I do once I found out who?

"What happened? Are you hurt?"

"No. But I need you to come get me right now."

"Okay we'll—"

"No, you. Just you, please."

I tried not to overthink it on the way. Kimberly had already texted me twice. As I drove down an abandoned road, I analyzed the dark, frozen lake to my left. Only a few lights peppered the way. Sitting in the glow of light was Presley alone on a bench with his head in his hands.

His now-faded brown hair was disheveled. I hurled my coat over my shoulders to shield myself from the annoyance of the wind. His cheeks grew red until his eyes spilled tears, and he pulled me into a hug.

"I don't want you to die."

We hadn't talked about it. I tried, and Presley had literally run away at the mention of what happened during the ritual.

"I'm not going to."

I wrapped my arms around him. Frozen still. I'd seen my brother cry many times, but not like that. Not with his tears staining my shirt and desperate heaving breaths. He never opened up to me.

"Tell me what's wrong."

"I did something bad. Really bad, and you're going to be so mad at me," he said through strangled sobs.

I reeled back to inspect him. "You can tell me. I won't be mad."

"No, you will. You're gonna hate me."

I rubbed the top of his head to ground him. It worked with Kimberly. I couldn't help but remember Luke comforting me as I cried on the forest floor when my own world crumbled after Kimberly went missing. I was so afraid of his opinions of me.

"Do you really think so little of me? Whatever it is. I can help."

He wiped his face with his palms as he composed himself, then led me to a black duffle bag.

My eyes went wide as he unzipped it. It was full of stacks of cash and photos. All from Blackheart.

He explained it all in one hurried breath. The note from Akira and the number he'd called. The man he met in Fairbanks, and the clue he hadn't been able to figure out. When he was done, he was crying again.

I couldn't look away from the photos. There were so many of us in Blackheart. We looked happy with all of us together, but the ones of Zach and Luke were different. The ones where their faces showed they were tired. Angry. Maybe I should have been angry at my brother. Or shocked that The Family had gone such great lengths to lure us to them, but all I felt was Presley's grief in my chest. It was so visceral and real that it was like someone was carving into my heart with a knife. He'd shouldered it all that time, and I'd been too busy with the idea of saving my brothers, I hadn't seen him. I was sad too, but I didn't let it swallow me because I had hope that I'd get to my older brothers soon. Presley had none all that time. He'd been drowning.

"Will you hit me or something? Just say anything."

"I'm sorry, Pres."

"No, this is my fault. *I'm* sorry. I've been so unhelpful and mean. I hate it. Why don't you hate me? I put everyone in danger."

I stood to smother him in a hug. "I couldn't hate you. I understand why you did it."

"I've been so useless. You're doing all this, and I'm . . . I'm . . ." He crumbled into me again, and I squeezed him tighter.

"I'm sorry you felt like you couldn't tell me . . . I'm sorry if I made you feel like you were alone."

His sobbing doubled, and I waited patiently through every wave. There was nowhere else in the world I'd rather be than with my little brother. There was nothing he could do that I wouldn't sit with him through and weather the storm. I wondered if that's how Luke had felt.

"I miss them so much. And I'm scared."

I placed my hands on his shoulders to give him a comforting squeeze. "Why are you scared?"

His voice trembled and tears fell from his eyes as he said, "I don't want you to die and leave me here alone. I'm going to be alone and have no one. I'll be a hermit who lives in an ice castle for eternity. And there will be no one left to talk to. Everyone will be gone."

My brother and his movie references.

I pulled him to me again. "I'm not going anywhere. And there's no way in hell I'd ever leave you alone. That's just not going to happen, okay?"

"Promise me you can fix this. I'll help. I'll do whatever I need to do. I don't want to be useless anymore—"

"Stop. You're not allowed to use that word. You're so important."

"You're lying to make me feel better."

"No." I pulled away to stare him directly in the eyes. I didn't even care I was about to say the cheesiest thing I'd ever said. "We've always needed you. Just you and that humor that gets on my last nerve. You just being you is enough. You don't have to do anything special. You're important right now. Hell, I'd die for you in a heartbeat."

"Don't. Don't die." He squeezed me hard, but his tears were finally slowing.

"I'll make sure you're always taken care of."

Call it wishful thinking, but I meant it. Somehow, I would make this impossible thing possible. I would save my older brothers and make sure the two people I'd sworn to protect made it out too. No one would end up alone, and I wouldn't get taken out because some stars in the sky told me so.

As I stared at my teary-eyed brother and held out my hand for him, I realized Presley and I never had that relationship before, but he needed me to step in and give him strength, and I was ready. Just as Luke had said in his last words to me—I was ready to protect them and be the one who kept going and believed in a better future, even when everything was so dark. I once hid in my room from the horrors we faced, but with each passing day, I didn't want to run. I didn't want to hide. I wanted to fight. To pluck my brothers from the hands of The Family once and for all. I wanted it to end.

It was a strange sensation, like fire in my blood. It urged me forward with an undying optimism. If fate was waiting, I'd happily meet it face-to-face.

Presley placed his hand on top of palm, and I smothered it with my other hand.

"Can we not talk about how embarrassing I've been lately? When we scrapbook and journal about this one day, let's leave this part out."

I ruffled his hair, which I knew he'd hate. "Sure."

"Can I still come and help?"

"I'd like that. But first, we need to bring this stuff to Kilian. We need to tell him everything tonight."

"He's going to be so mad." He groaned.

"No, I don't think so. And if he is, I'll protect you."

Forty-One

PRESLEY

I kept *one* photo—the most important one.

I wished I'd never seen it.

It was just a photo, and one little secret wouldn't hurt anyone.

Forty-Two

AARON

"How is he?" Kimberly asked while folding clothes on the dresser.

The cabin was aglow with warmth and the smell of the fire burning.

I took a moment to admire it—the mundane—and how I was the luckiest person in the world to get to see Kimberly Burns folding *our* clothes. Our shirts were mingled in one basket, along with our underwear and socks. I'd have killed for that moment a year ago. Back when she was a stranger who I couldn't have feelings for, but I did. I had a lot of feelings, and mostly, I wondered what Kimberly did behind closed doors. Now I didn't have to guess. It was our room. Our life. I liked her things with my things. Her hair pins on the dresser and her socks in our bed. Makeup smudges on the bathroom mirror.

"Yeah, he's okay. He really perked up on the car ride back."

I'd put her on speakerphone while I helped Presley tell Kilian his story. We sat in Kilian's living room, and Presley took the seat closest to the door because he was sure Kilian would flip out.

"Kilian really wasn't mad?"

"You know how he is." Kilian was actually excited The Family was attempting to lure us. It opened a new avenue for him to access them and incorporate it into his battle plan. He didn't seem to have any real concern about them taking us against our will. He got that faraway look in his eye when we went to leave, and that meant he'd be retreating to his study to draw it all out. I was looking forward to helping with it, but first, I had other things on my mind.

She wasn't facing me, but I saw the muscles in her jaw flex into a smile while she folded my socks into little squares. My mouth salivated when I tuned into the soft thrum of her heartbeat.

"We should do something together tomorrow. We'll . . ." Her voice trailed off as I came up behind her, teasing the skin on her neck with my lips.

"We'll spend the day tomorrow doing whatever Presley wants to do. But I think right now he needs some time alone to rest. You do too. It was a long day."

"I'm not tired."

"You will be." I kissed the soft skin where her pulse drummed.

Biting her didn't always lead to sex. Okay, maybe it did, but it didn't have to. It came naturally. Tasting her blood brought us closer on a whole other level I was certain didn't exist in human capacity. I missed being human a lot less when that's what I got to have instead.

I savored the way her shoulders dropped as I wrapped my hands around her stomach and continued assaulting her neck with my lips.

"Mrs. Calem, you look intoxicatingly beautiful tonight."

She drew in a breath. "You've never called me that before."

"I'm testing it out. Seeing how it feels to say," I said with my lips at her ear.

Girlfriend was a nice title, but it wasn't enough. It wasn't anything close to what I truly felt for her. I'd already thought ahead, and every day that passed, I looked forward to the end of the cold and the end of our pain. I would take her somewhere sunny and bind her to me for everyone to see. All of my brothers would be there and likely obnoxious and embarrassing, and I couldn't wait.

Her hips moved back and into mine while I slid the sleeve of her shirt down to expose the skin on her shoulder.

"What's the consensus?" she asked while I kissed her shoulder.

"I love it. Are you partial to Burns? You can always keep it."

"No. Not at all . . ." I grabbed her stomach and pulled her harder into my hips. The pressure of her sent my mind racing. I wanted to strip her, but I had to be patient.

My mouth salivated as my fangs descended. "I think I'd miss calling you Burns. But I like Mrs. Calem better."

"Me too."

A part of me wanted the blood-drinking to stop, but a much larger part of me didn't. I wanted to taste her, and I loved being the only one who could. I liked having a part of her no one else got. Her blood was mine.

She fell into my rhythm as I grinded into her from behind and sank my teeth into her skin.

It didn't have to lead to sex, but I couldn't stop myself from gliding my hand up her shirt to caress her chest as I drank. Her bare breast filled my hand as I teased and touched her till she moaned for me. The sounds of her set my blood ablaze. I wanted to mark her. She opened herself up to me, arching her neck and letting me take more of her blood. The warmth of it on my tongue sent me into a frenzy that had me squeezing her tighter.

Her yearning sighs sent my blood south. We spent a lot of our time working toward an unknown future, but this was our time. It overwhelmed me till my head swam with images of need.

Training and The Legion didn't always leave us enough time to enjoy each other's company. I missed all of it. The nights sitting on the roof at OBA. Secret getaways to the pool. There wasn't time for any of that with the battle looming closer and closer. There were only stolen moments that reminded me of what we were fighting for.

When she turned to me, her face was flushed. "For the record, I'd love to have the Calem name."

I pulled her to my lips again, this time harder. "Sorry, that was just so hot. We can stop."

"You want to stop?"

"No. Definitely not, but . . . I still don't know how I feel about everything, and this seems to lead to sex, and I just want to make sure you feel comfortable—"

"Aaron."

"Yeah?"

"Just touch me."

"Okay."

She didn't need to tell me twice. I let her take my clothes off, and the blush in her cheeks deepened. She took her time, and I stroked her slowly and deliberately, careful to brush next to the most sensitive areas on her chest and thighs. I knew where she wanted me to touch. It ended with an index finger underneath her jaw and my thumb on her bottom lip.

"Do you ever think about it?"

"Think what?"

"About marrying me."

I pulled her underwear down, and she gasped.

"Yes."

She barely got the word out as I grazed her core, and the wetness on my fingers told me she was ready for me.

"Are you sure you're not just saying that to make me feel better?" I asked before kissing and nipping at the skin on her chest. I placed my hand at the small of her back and pressed her to me.

"Stop teasing me."

She let out another small gasp as I ran my tongue along the curves of her breasts. I was starting to memorize her body. The curve of her hip bones and all the little marks on her skin. All the dips and the sensitive parts that made her dig her fingers into my back.

I lay her back flush on the bed so I could admire her.

"But it's so easy."

My lips grazed a beauty mark on her rib. A mark I'd doubt many had seen. I was the only one who she'd ever trusted enough to touch her. It made me want to be gentle and ensure she enjoyed every second.

I moved my attention to the thin white scar diagonal to her belly button. It was so faint you'd need to be close to see it. Her blood was in my veins, and her hands were in my hair. There wasn't a universe in which I wouldn't enjoy every breath and sigh that poured from her lips.

I licked her scar, and she shrieked, pulling me to her until I was staring into her blue eyes again. On her wrist was the mark of my own doing, barely visible in the dim light, and I kissed it.

"Tell me more about your visions of marrying me." I lingered at the pulse in her wrist and fought the urge to bite her again.

"I . . ."

I ran my hand between her thighs.

I was getting better at self-control, but it was hard when we were naked and she inched closer every second, squirming and asking for me. *Wanting* me. It took everything in me not to go too fast. She deserved deliberate love.

"No words for me?"

"I want you to stay" was all she said while I moved my hand to give her the pressure she needed, and she rocked into me. "I want you to be mine."

"I am yours."

I plunged two fingers into her, and she gasped my name. She was already close. I was learning her body like my own, and I knew the pace she needed and where she needed more pressure and movement.

"Always."

I curled my fingers, and she fell over the edge in seconds while I admired it all—the intimacy of our own bedroom and the feel of her orgasm as she was wrapped around my fingers. Once wasn't enough. I *needed* to give her more.

"Stay with me forever," she said as I moved to lay on top of her and pin her to the bed. I drank in the sight of her beneath me. Vulnerable and open. My Kimberly.

I pinned her arms above her head.

"Oh, I'm here." I slid into her, stifling every word lingering on her tongue, and placed a kiss in the corner of her mouth. "I'll stay till you're sick of me."

I couldn't look away as she writhed beneath me, her hands in mine while she moaned my name softly.

"You're so pretty, Burns."

With each breath, I sank into her deeper and deeper. I wanted to take my time with her. To feel every brush of her skin and the surge of euphoria when I moved within her. Now that her blood was drumming in my veins, the wildness in my blood was soothed and dormant.

"Call me the other thing."

"Mrs. Calem." I leaned to whisper it over the cool skin of her chest.

That had her rocking into me harder. Hard enough to take every other thought in my brain with it. Our bodies connected in a way that left nothing to be wanted.

"Aaron . . . please."

I couldn't take the begging. It lit every cell in my body aflame to tend to her. I'd give her any part of me that she needed. I would tear my heart out of my own chest if she wanted.

"Tell me what you need, Kim." My fingers traced right under her belly button, and she arched into me while I was buried inside her.

"I don't know . . . I just need you. I just want you."

"Relax. I'm here." I pressed into her deeper and placed my hand right below her belly button. She gasped.

"I'll always be here, Kim. I'm not going anywhere."

That seemed to be exactly what she needed because her fingers ran down my back, and she tightened around me as her orgasm shook through her.

I still wanted more. More of her saying my name. More of her breath in my throat. My blood raced with the need to satisfy her. To fill her completely with warmth and stifle all her desires.

I was eager.

So eager.

I'd do anything.

I moved her hair over her shoulder and whispered, "You're perfect."

With my tongue, I teased the skin of her neck, and she tugged my head closer. I would, of course, oblige her request. My fangs pierced the vein in her neck, and her blood poured into my mouth. Then she rocked into me, moving and moaning, and I couldn't last.

She let go, seconds before I did, with a soft cry as she tightened around me. Nothing in the world could compare. My head rested in the crook of her neck while our breaths synced and our movements calmed.

"Burns . . . I . . ."

I couldn't form words yet. How could I even begin to describe the

271

feeling of being that close to someone? It was more than sex with the girl I loved. It almost felt spiritual. I didn't think there could be anything else that good.

"Are you speechless?"

"Mm-hm," I said before licking her neck to clean the blood off.

That brought a giggle and a smile to her face.

"This is . . ." *Otherworldly.*

"Intimate." She played with the strands of my hair.

"Yeah, that."

Our hearts beat steadily in the dark. I didn't know where I ended and she began anymore. We were one heartbeat. One vibrant pulse. Her blood was my blood.

"You should ask me," she said.

"Ask to marry me? Right now?"

We were bare and connected still.

"No. I mean. Yes, if you want. I used to think having a husband would be nice eventually. Maybe if I had to. But this . . . this is different. I like that you want me to be your wife. And it makes me want to . . . be a good one. Or be the best one. Like maybe that could be my thing too."

"On top of being a master hiker? And a brilliant, successful woman that's going to dominate everything she puts her mind to."

"Yeah. Maybe I could do all of that and . . . be your wife. And maybe that could be my favorite thing."

My heart skipped. I could be one of her infamous favorite things. That was special. I could even be *the most* favorite thing. The thought had me buzzing with excitement. I had to fight the urge to get up and start pacing and planning it all out and imagining her in a white dress.

Instead, I caressed her cheek and savored her heart slowing. I wanted to ask her. To claim her heart in that interesting new way. For her to be mine even more than she already was.

"I'll need to get you a ring first."

"I don't need one." Probably because she understood how little we had and how all we had was going to our combined cause.

"Oh, you do. Can we forfeit our no stealing rule?" I smiled, hoping she'd know I was kidding.

She smiled too and shook her head.

"That's okay, I have something else in mind."

I moved to separate from her so I could help her clean up, but she bit her lip. Her attention had moved to something else.

"What are you worried about? You can tell me."

"I'm just afraid . . . the queen will take you from me, and I don't think I could endure seeing you with Her. Because I want you to be mine. Just mine."

"Kim, I'm always yours. Only yours. Forever."

The queen was nothing but a blurry memory. Even the memory of Her blood in my veins didn't compare to the love I felt for Kimberly. How much more of myself could I give her? I didn't think there was a way to be closer to her, yet we kept finding new ways. There was so much I still wanted to do for her. I was learning to be the man she needed. I just needed more time.

Forty-Three

I underestimated my brother. That or he'd changed. Instead of being an annoying cry baby, he was actually cool. The Zach and Luke kind of cool. The kind of cool I let drag me out of bed into the snow in the middle of the day. We'd driven at least two hours to get here, and I didn't know where here was, but it was beautiful. The mountains on either side almost distracted me from the fact that I was hiking in snow. I didn't even like hiking, especially not when there was snow involved.

"Where are we going?"

"Almost there, don't worry."

"I'm not worried. My socks are just wet."

Kimberly came up beside me and wrapped her arm around mine. She was absolutely beaming, and the sun had her natural red hair peeking through the dark brown. It wasn't fair she looked so good in different hair colors. I smothered my brown hair with a beanie, and I guess I understood why Kim didn't like her hair. We weren't ready for the change.

Kimberly was back in her element. We didn't have the clothes for hiking, but it was easy not to slip in sneakers when you were a vampire.

I needed a day without creeper Kilian breathing down my neck or The Family texting me. I'd given Kilian my phone and gotten a new one, then I felt a lot lighter without a cult stalking me. I'd forgotten what no responsibility or problems felt like.

We walked up a hill until there was a clearing in the trees. An enormous frozen lake glistened in hues of bluish-green marble. It expanded far into the mountain encased in snow and powdered trees.

"I thought we could use some fresh air," Aaron said, taking off his gloves and wrapping his arms around Kimberly's shoulder and mine.

Our little trio.

"It's so beautiful!" Kimberly exclaimed.

It reminded me a little too much of our last hike together. The day everything changed and got terrible.

"It's water. You know we have a pond by the house, right?" I was being an ass, and I hated it.

My brother only smiled and squeezed me. "It is water, but I wanted to bring you both here because I have something important to say. And I wanted to say it in a place where I could make you a promise and have that promise be measurable."

He stood in front of the cliff, the hills and the entire mountain waiting to hear.

"The next time we come here in the spring, it won't just be the three of us anymore. We're going to come back to this exact spot and look out on the unfrozen lake. All five of us."

Kimberly nodded with a soft smile.

"You brought us up here to say all that," I said.

"I brought you up here to spend time with you and to initiate this."

He presented a crumpled piece of paper and a pencil.

"Are we writing love letters?"

"No, we're starting a list of things we want to do when this is over. I figure once we don't have a cult on our backs anymore, then we'll have a lot of time to spend together, so I started a list. A forever list."

The vastness of the mountain swallowed me. I was ready for winter to end even more so if it meant Zach and Luke would be standing next to us. I missed normal. I missed Blackheart and all that stupid stuff we used to do. It was brief, but it was everything I'd ever wanted.

Suddenly, I wondered what spring would hold if my brothers came back. The image of them in the photo was carved into the back of my mind.

Would they be different? Would everything be different? Could it ever be as good as what already passed?

The thought made me feel sick to my stomach again. Like the nausea that had transferred in the bond from Aaron to me. Now I was the one making us both sick.

"I know it's hard to see now, but it's going to happen," Aaron said to me, and I pushed down anything else snarky that came to mind. "I already started. Number one: go back to the lake. You guys pick something. Nothing is too far-fetched."

"We could all go to Italy. Like the summer trip I never got to have."

There were a couple things I hadn't let myself daydream about since my brothers were taken, and any thought of vacations was one of them, but Aaron's excitement had my mind turning with the thought of us all on the beach lying in the sun. Visiting the museums . . . riding in the gondolas . . .

"That's good!" He placed the paper on his leg to loosely scribble it down.

Aaron's excitement jolted me out of my previous gloom and into the present.

"What about you, Kim?" I nudged her.

"Sometimes . . . I imagine we'll buy a piece of land and have our own cabins. We could build them and decorate them all and live close to each other, kinda like we do now, but it will be ours. Not sure if everyone else likes the idea."

"It's great. I'm adding it."

"You'd really want me close to you guys, asking you for things like milk and sugar?" I joked.

"Yes. Always." She squeezed my shoulder.

"Will you help me decorate?"

"I'll try my best."

I loved the idea more than I wanted to admit. All of it sounded exciting.

After a few minutes of admiring the view and adding random things to the list—I added skydiving, and Kimberly looked at me like I hit her—she added us making our Halloween costumes, and Aaron mentioned we should head back before we got caught in the dark.

Just as I went to start back on the trail, Aaron stopped. He stood in front of Kimberly and kneeled on one knee.

"Holy shit." The words rushed out of me.

"First . . ." He gazed up at Kimberly with a few hairs in his face. Admittedly, he looked too cool to be my older brother.

Kimberly's cheeks flushed. "W-what are you doing?"

The scene behind them was storybook worthy. I waited with my breath in my throat for him to say it. To ask her those four little words—

"I'm just . . . checking my shoe."

His soft, expectant expression deteriorated into that annoying grin.

"Dude. I hate you." I rolled my eyes.

"You're such a tease." Kimberly hit him in the arm.

"Not cool. Come on, Kim." I placed my arm around her and steered her away from my brother. "Seriously, if he does that again, you have to say no when he really asks you as punishment."

Kim's laughter soothed all the weird sad feelings I had earlier. "Deal."

"Better yet, marry me instead. I'm more fun than Aaron."

"Hey! Wait," Aaron called to us as we descended the mountain.

"Got this one for you."

I handed Aaron a little blue rock I'd found as we continued down the trail. It wasn't bright blue, more like a gray, but it stood out among the brown and white pebble rocks around our feet.

"Wow." My brother grabbed it from me. "I love it. I'll add it to the growing collection." He pulled a few other rocks from his pocket. All various shapes and sizes. "Kimberly gave me this one."

Between his fingers was a heart-shaped stone, almost completely smooth.

"She really loves you, dude."

Kimberly was out of earshot, far ahead on the trail. She was soaking it in, I think. Like hiking was a drug straight into the vein.

"I am going to propose, you know," Aaron said, eyeing the back of Kimberly's head.

"Soon?"

"Yeah, soon. Thoughts?"

He said it like he really wanted my opinion. Like it mattered. It was something Luke would've done—ask me about something to make me feel included.

"I think you better get her a good ring. She deserves it."

"I know. I will."

"I still want to be the officiant. And you better give me a heads-up for the actual proposal because I want to bring the camera."

"Done."

The silence stretched between us, with only the sounds of our feet crunching in the snow and a few birds.

"They'll be here too, Pres. I'll make sure of it." He rubbed my back as my chest ached.

I hated that I believed him. Aaron wasn't someone I counted on growing up. He didn't commit to anything and never took charge. He panicked in a crisis, and I didn't blame him because I also panicked in a crisis. We were largely in the same hopeless panic boat.

Something had changed, like he'd leveled up way quicker than me. He defeated a major boss and gained all the XP. Only, it was invisible. I never saw the mega boss monster. I never grabbed my sword to fight it. Or I didn't own one.

If I'd known about a monster, I'd have hidden instead. Old Aaron would have hidden with me, but he was turning into one of those badass heroes in video games. The ones with the armor and the cool catch phrases. Kimberly too.

I was still the same. Just sad Presley trying to make it through another day. At one point, we were all sad and purposeless together, like an unspoken agreement, then it was just me. Alone.

"You okay?" Aaron asked, watching me. He had to feel the new pain rolling in my chest.

"Yeah. Thank you . . . for this whole day. It's nice. Sorry if I was an ass."

"Not more than usual. Either way, I can handle it."

I know. I let my brother's laughter comfort me and looked up at the trail ahead with only the power of his hope to keep me moving forward.

Forty-Four

I held out as long as I could from seeing Kilian again, but since I'd agreed to help, I couldn't exactly stay away from them.

Anzola had the same creepy vibe Kilian gave off, only slightly less. Her eyes at least reminded me a little of Mom's. Not like Kilian's, which seared into my soul and sucked all the life out of the room. He needed contacts or something. Someone had to tell him, and it wouldn't be me.

They even had a piano no one knew how to play—one of them had to have seen *Twilight* when decorating that house.

Aaron and Kilian said their pleasantries to the others, then we gathered in the dining room at the grand table that took up almost all the space. The moon joined us through the windows, and I averted my gaze to the little piece of string on my jacket.

"I'm glad you're all here. We've made great progress in our reconnaissance. With the help of drones and a few locals, we were able to come up with a map of the castle grounds as well as get a map of the whole island."

Kilian nodded to Dom, and he spread out a large piece of paper.

"*This* is the island . . ." Aaron said as he gawked.

It was detailed and larger than I'd imagined. When they said island, I thought about something you could easily walk across, but this had a whole town, a harbor by the castle, and a bunch of hills and houses.

I was more interested in the other map. The one that showed the castle. I studied it over and over. The labyrinth and the garden, a cathedral, and a church. It didn't seem real that my brothers were in that place as their new home, but I had the proof embedded into my memory from the photograph.

"The only unknown is that we do not know what the inside of the castle looks like. There are no known records, only a few vague descriptions and a few pictures from tourism in the area. But we can assume that there are numerous hiding places. That brings me to my next idea that I wanted to present to all of you."

This should be good. It was likely he wanted us to run into fire or something.

"With Presley's involvement with the phone, we could create a diversion for them. What we need is for them to let their guard down. Every one of you that they capture will feel like a win to them."

"You mean use my little brother as bait?" That familiar darkness flickered in Aaron's eyes, and his nostrils flared.

I was kind of honored Aaron was about to blow a gasket but for me this time.

"She will not hurt him. That much is clear. It will be a temporary distraction, and they are expecting him. They will likely believe it to be a part of their future plan."

"I'll do it." Finally, something I could do that would actually be help-ful.

"No." Aaron shook his head, his shoulders stiffened.

"I'm a grown man. I can choose."

"I know, I . . ." Then he gave me the puppy-dog look—I changed my mind. It was lethal to everyone, not just women. "Family huddle."

"We can hear your huddles," Felix stated as the three of us retreated to the corner of the room, next to a huge monstera I remembered as Will's.

"This is a bad idea," Aaron said.

"I told you I wanted to help."

"I can't let you go off on your own and be bait."

"What does Kim think?"

Kimberly's jaw was set like she was thinking.

"I . . . think no matter what, one of us will have to be the bait and neither of us are going to like it. It could be me."

"No," Aaron and I said practically at the same time.

"See? We're all going to hate it. We just have to . . . trust each other."

Aaron nodded. "Trust the dream."

"We did say whatever the cost," she said.

"Fine."

"I'll do it," I called to the others.

Aaron interjected. "On one condition, I come with him. I'm not leaving my little brother at the mercy of the queen. I don't care if She won't hurt him. I have to be there."

Kilian nodded. "I will see what I can come up with. I'm still finalizing our battle strategy. It appears they've made no move to leave the island, and I've been trying to figure out why that might be. There's no doubt they know we're coming and that we have the dagger."

"Would they not want to . . . you know, hide Her or something?" I asked.

"I agree. But I think there are a few reasons they might want to stay. Including the solar eclipse. They likely need to stay in the path of totality to get whatever benefit they're looking to receive. I have intel that they're planning a party the night before the eclipse, and it's a public event. I suspect it's likely to keep us from coming to interrupt the eclipse."

"Okay, so why don't Aaron and I go early, like right now? We can get a jump on Operation Convince Our Brothers Not to be in a Cult." *Plus, a party.*

"It's not favorable. Leaving you alone with them for too long with the connection you have to Her blood, you'll be easily overcome."

I sighed.

"There is another caveat. I'm thinking it may be best to keep details off our specific battle strategy from the three of you. With the two of you going beforehand and the unknown possibilities of the role Kimberly will play, I think it would be best in the event you get to the island where She searches your memories. They already have many advantages, including the queen's clairvoyance. She'll be able to access the most likely future of The Guard, Will, and Thane. Possibly your brothers'. I've been trying to find a way to remedy this."

The three of us grimaced at the thought.

"In order for the decoy to be helpful, I think it would be best to feed you false information . . . which means I would need to erase your memories of this moment and of anything I deem may aid Her. You must decide now if this is something you want to do."

"Let's do it," I said.

"Pres." Aaron used his scary voice.

"We agreed whatever the cost. If Kilian turns me into a mindless vegetable, then . . . whatever, I guess."

Felix and Halina snickered in the corner while Dom stayed his casual stoic self.

"Not whatever. This is a big decision," Kimberly said.

Kilian was a loose cannon. Our permanent wild card. I would never trust him, but I didn't think it mattered anymore. I was ready to take the risks.

"We are reaching the point of no return. I know I have not made it easy for you to have faith in me, but have faith in the fact that I want this plan to work more than you can comprehend. I've been dreaming of this moment for centuries while for you it's been a short few months. I need all three of you to do this."

I held my hand over the table to him.

"Ready when you are."

Kimberly and Aaron shared a look. They had some kind of telepathy too. The lover kind where they communicated with nods and brow movements. After a few moments, they offered their hands too.

A little more than a month away. I could do that. I hoped Zach and Luke knew we hadn't forgotten them, but more than that . . . I hoped as they walked the castle day in and out, they hadn't given up yet.

Forty-Five

KIMBERLY

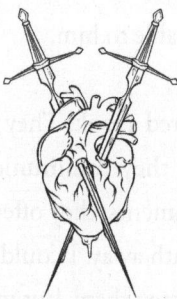

The crisp sounds of the fireside in Aaron's and my cabin soothed the vibrant chatter in my head. It reminded me of home, and the closer I sat to the heat of it, the more I remembered the smell of the pine. With a blanket wrapped around my shoulders and a book balanced on my knees, I flipped another page. The book had a cracked binding and tarnished pages. I deliberately turned each page with care. Applying the right pressure was easier, and in Alaska, my senses felt healed. I could listen to music again.

"Are you reading that again?" Aaron let in the cold wind as he stepped through the front door.

"Presley got me hooked after making me watch the movie." I marked my place and shut my copy of *Romeo and Juliet*. Kilian had one of the early editions of the plays.

"Ah, classic. I've seen it a couple times. And by that, I mean Presley has forced me to watch it many, many times. You never read it in high school?"

"I did, but I thought it was absurd at the time."

"And now?"

"Now I understand it more, I think. I can appreciate it at least. Two people loving someone so much that . . . they'd want to die together."

The first time I read it, I believed it all to be juvenile. It was foolish to let love take over oneself. Even more so to die for nothing, but I'd had it wrong. To be a lover meant believing in the impossible and loving without limits or fear and uncertainty. It was wild, irrational, and untamable.

"What part are you at?"

"The part where Juliet stabs herself in the heart."

"And not a single tear." Aaron sat beside me with his jacket on. The light glaze of snow melted next to the fire.

"I've read it over a few times."

Something about reading about love was comforting. It reminded me no one was promised another day. My plight wasn't unique. It was a fear regular humans lived through every day. I'd only never felt it because I'd never loved something worth losing.

"Come on." He jumped to his feet. "Enough depressing stuff."

He led me to the door and handed me my coat.

"Aaron, it's so cold."

"Humor me a second."

Everything about him was glowing as I followed him outside into the night. We went along the back side of the cabin where a ladder led to the roof.

"After you." He winked.

I ascended the ladder, and a pallet of blankets sat in a carved-out portion of the snow. Surrounding it were lit candles casting shadow onto the pillows.

"I didn't even hear you up here." I had to intentionally close my jaw.

"You were too engrossed in this." Aaron waved it around as he made his way next to me. "I missed our rooftop nights at OBA and wanted to make a new memory."

We settled into the blankets. They were set on a tarp to prevent the melted water from seeping through.

"You . . . keep surprising me." I grabbed at the edges of his coat. "There's still so much to learn about you. I feel like I'm just scratching the surface."

"What better time for me to tell you all those things you want to know about me. Or . . . you could read to me. Or I could read to you."

"I vote all of the above. The night is so long."

He pulled me close, and I wrapped my arms around his torso as we fell back onto the blanket. The roof was hard and frozen, but I was cuddled into the softness of his chest. I missed the lights of the football stadium, the sounds of laughter, and that feeling of weightlessness I used to have.

We must have been reminiscing about the same memory because he said, "I saved it, you know. The money I set aside for you and me. I keep it in the most secure place ever. My shoe."

"Oh yeah? And what will we do with it?"

"Anything . . . everything."

"I like the sound of that."

I pushed myself up to kiss him. I loved the smell of him, the lines in his forearms, and the way he never pushed me away. He leaned in, scooping me closer.

"Kim, I want you to promise me something."

My heart drummed faster, and I pulled back to meet his gaze as he grabbed my hand to rub his thumb over my knuckles.

"Okay . . ."

"If something does happen to me . . . I want to know you're going to still try. No *Romeo and Juliet* sacrifices."

"You think I'm going to stab myself in the chest?"

"If one of us dies, we have to try to keep going. You have to promise you won't give up. You'll keep going."

I stared into his amber eyes, and a lump gathered in my throat. What a strangely horrible thing to ask of me.

"What if I don't want to . . . What if I can't?"

"You can." Aaron's palm was hot against my cheek. "I know you can. The world needs Kimberly Burns. My brothers would need you . . . like I need you."

I fought against the emotion of his words. I didn't want to open myself up to the possibility. Even a second of doubt would send me down a bad road, so I shoved it down.

"But what if I need you. We all do."

"I guess I'll just have to make sure we all survive then." He said it with one easy breath and no hint of doubt, just a calm reassurance that it had to happen.

"I just don't want this to be the end."

I couldn't think about lasts. Last kisses. Last dates. Last laughs. The mere mention brought tears to my eyes.

"It will never be. No matter what, I'll find you again. Somehow, I will. Do you believe me?" The warm brown of his eyes beckoned me into the future. To warmer days and sunshine just up ahead if I'd believe.

I nodded and held my hand out to him. "I promise to try. But you have to promise too."

"Kim, if you die, that means I'm already dead."

"You don't know that."

"I do."

"Promise me anyway."

He leaned in to kiss me, and I savored it. The softness of his touch and the warmth of his breath. The way he smelled . . . Aaron was mine. No matter what happened. Death couldn't take him from me. Our love would still be there.

"I promise."

Forty-Six

AARON

The eclipse was coming, and things were changing again, but some things never changed, like Mom sitting on the porch sipping her coffee. It was the only time she'd ever looked relaxed back in Brooklyn.

When I was home for the evenings, I made sure to spend my mom's last hour awake with her. Sometimes, it was hanging out and watching TV or her watching me play the only video game we had available—a Nintendo Wii given to her by a friend—but at night when it wasn't too windy, she'd light a fire in the furnace on the porch and we'd swing together. Sometimes, it was all three of us and sometimes, just us two, but on this night, it was just Mom and me sitting in the silence.

"You look tired," she said, eyeing me while sipping her coffee. She moved a salt-and-pepper strand behind her ear and laid her head back to watch me.

I tried to soak it in and make up for all the time we'd lost, but time

291

always slipped away from me in Alaska. The faster I tried to grab it, the faster it fled. The daylight was brief, and the moon was more of a companion than it had ever been.

I hated when the days went quickly, but I also knew it meant I was one day closer to seeing my brothers again.

"It was a long day. Things are progressing. I think we're going to leave soon. Kilian says next month there's a solar eclipse happening, and it means something important."

We looked up at the sky. The moon sat between us like a lingering reminder of my brothers and their absence but also the thing that separated us. The queen and Her power lingered in the atmosphere.

"I know you're working hard." She took another sip, no longer looking at me.

It was hard to talk to her about it. Even though I told her most of what we did at Kilian's, I never told her everything. Especially not the part where Kimberly foresaw my death. Even though I didn't believe it, the last thing Mom needed was the additional fear that more of her sons wouldn't return home.

Every minute, I understood more and more of how my older brothers felt, yet I also realized I would never fully understand the pain and the secrets they held. They'd shielded me from more than I'd ever know. The years they spent talking with Ezra and hanging around with The Family in the city, I'd probably never get those stories. Like I'd never know how it felt to know Sarah was missing and find out they'd been there for her murder, only to be accused of being the one to end her life. Some things would stay buried forever.

My fingers dug into the wood of the chair.

"We'll get them back," I said.

She smiled at that. "You really don't see how much you've grown? I'm just so proud of you. Sometimes, I feel like I missed more than just a year of your life."

I cringed thinking of the Aaron she once knew. The one who'd had his brothers do everything for him. The one whose hardest thing he'd ever experienced before Blackheart was high-school drama.

"I like this version of me better. He's there for people who need him."

"You've always been that person. You boys have amazed me with your love for each other. Even when you were younger, I realized I wasn't always enough . . . you boys needed each other. You have a bond that I frankly don't think I could understand if I tried."

It didn't surprise me. Mom was an only child.

"I'm thankful we've had you as our mom."

She rubbed my hand and let out a sigh, signaling she had more to say, but she let it go into the brisk cold air. What more could we say that hadn't already been said?

I knew it all. Everything was up in the air, and she wanted us to stay. As if someone else would magically go and save my brothers, but no one was coming to save our family. We needed to win. It was at the forefront of my mind every day, and every good moment there, was tainted with one thought. *Losing isn't an option.*

There was a brief silence, and I used it to build my courage for the next thing I needed to say. It was easier to push forward than to look back at all my fear and uncertainty.

"Mom . . . I want to ask Kimberly to marry me. And I was wondering if you had a ring. Maybe one of grandma's."

I didn't remember my grandma much, but I didn't have to. I saw how much my mom loved her mother, and that was enough for me to love her just as much. She told me all the stories of how my grandmother had loved her until her last breath.

When she turned, her eyes were sparkling with tears.

"Oh, Mom. Don't cry."

"I'm not. I'm not. I'm just so happy for you." She wiped a singular tear and beamed at me. "I was waiting for it, but you caught me off guard tonight."

"You were waiting?"

"I knew when I first saw you two together . . .You stayed with her and waited to see how she felt about everything before you even let yourself feel anything . . . you were so calm. And I knew then you'd found someone you were serious about." She grabbed my face and kissed my cheek. "Stay here. I'll be right back."

I waited. Was I excited? Absolutely. Giddy even. I couldn't afford a ring, and Kimberly would rather have something I didn't buy anyway. In the darkness far in the distance, a faint green glow illuminated the night sky.

The door opened again, and the porch creaked beneath Mom's boots. In her hand laid a worn small velvet box.

"What do you think of this?"

Inside was a rose gold ring that appeared to be hand forged with little branch-like tendrils encasing a raw stone. It was different hues of blue and green with little bits of pink. I held it up to the faint northern lights in the sky and marveled at it in the porch light.

"It's raw opal. This was your grandmother's favorite ring. She didn't like to wear it because it was so precious to her. I think it would make her smile to see someone else wear it. Do you think Kimberly will like it?"

I held the thin band in my hand. Not able to hide my excitement at the thought of all those daydreams becoming my reality. A few months ago, I was sure Kimberly would marry someone else. Now I was sure it would be me.

"She'll love it," I said.

Mom pulled me in for a hug that warmed me in the same way my brothers' had. Of all the people I wanted to talk to about the moment,

Zach and Luke were first on that list.

It was bittersweet, but it only made my resolve that much stronger. I stared up at the moon as I rested my head on her shoulder.

I would come for them very soon.

Forty-Seven

KIMBERLY

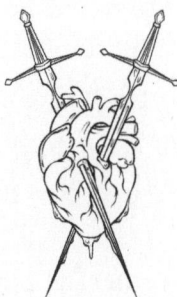

"You're not nervous at all?" Aaron sat next to me cross-legged on the floor.

The memory of what happened a month prior was burned into my mind. Aaron strewn across a marble floor without life in his features. However, when I looked at Aaron smiling, confident, and carefree, I realized I, too, was starting to believe we could win.

We couldn't trust everything at face value. We were tapping into an unknown source of power, and there wasn't one way to interpret anything.

I needed to have an open mind.

I needed to be brave.

"It's going to be okay," I finally replied.

Dom sat in an ottoman next to me. "Everything is ready."

"You're sure?" Aaron said, rubbing my knee.

"Positive. We still need something if we're going to win."

I looked next to me, wishing Presley were on my other side, but we all agreed since we needed to know less about the plan, it was better he didn't come or know more about the rituals. Probably Aaron too, but there's no way he would let me go alone, and I didn't want to. I grabbed Aaron's hand and squeezed it for comfort.

"Have you tried talking directly to Cecily?" Anzola rested on the windowsill. "During that time, there was a frenzy among nobles. Everyone wanted to obtain power and influence, and they were willing to sacrifice anything to get it. Even their own daughters. Many members of the council believe that once a queen is created in the body of a human, their soul is sent to hell. But I believe they're trapped and their souls stay within the body. The dagger you're holding has the blood of Cecily embedded in its handle. It's what created Her."

"This stuff is so weird," Felix grumbled.

"Hush." Halina nudged him.

Felix was right. We'd grown accustomed to the strangeness of things that involved vampires, but this stuff was different. Using a physical object to tap into "power from the sky," as Presley would say, was new territory for my family and theirs.

"I'll give it a shot." I ran my finger along the handle.

"We're ready." Kilian nodded from his desk chair. "Try to stay as long as you can."

I nodded and reached for the cool blade of the dagger, pricking my finger and smearing my blood on the blade.

This time, there was barely any pause.

When I blinked again, I was on my own in a pure white room that went on forever in all directions. There was no warmth. No cold. No worry or pain. It was infinitely neutral.

I waited, unsure how fast time was passing in that space. It was dream-like, but I could still recall things. Like when Aaron mentioned he felt forced into the back of his own mind. Maybe that place was my own mind.

"Cecily. I need to speak with Cecily," I demanded.

When I turned around, I stood face-to-face with a mirror. It went on for miles on either side. As I went to touch the glass, I gasped. Behind the shining glass was the queen.

I only knew from Aaron's vague description. Long white hair and ghastly pale skin draped in layers of white satin fabric. Only Her eyes weren't white, hazy, or even gray. They were bright green.

I knew who was in front of me with no hesitation, like the fact had been whispered in my ear and I was simply repeating it.

"Cecily."

She turned toward me with a pale finger pressed to her lips to silence me.

"She's close." Cecily's voice was thick with an Irish accent. "Can you see me?"

She looked through the mirror as if she were staring through me.

"Yes," I whispered.

"Who am I speaking to?"

"Kimberly."

"Kimberly Burns. Anything She knows, I do. You must be here about the Calem boys. Is that right?"

"I . . . Wait, if I tell you, will She know too?"

"No. This isn't real. It's just a piece of me you're speaking to."

"Where is this place?"

"I call it the In-Between. She holds a piece of my soul and splits me in whichever way She wishes. A part of me is here forever. How are you speaking with me?"

"I have one of the last daggers."

"You're with a Kilian. Listen to me, *you* must use the dagger. It is vitally important, and they know Kilian has it. They know you will come, but you can't let it stop you. You must make sure you all go."

"Tell me what we need to do. Help us. Show me the future. Show me the possibilities you can see."

She shook her head. "I can't. You're not a vessel."

"But the dagger showed me visions before."

"The Divine only showed you brief visions because It wanted to."

"Then tell me, how do I save Aaron and his brothers? Tell me how to win."

"I can't. All of the threads run together. It's nearly impossible to follow one all the way down to a desired outcome. And I cannot tell you too much or it won't come to pass."

Of course not.

"What can you tell me?"

"First. You must speak the truth. What do you want most? Do you want to save him, or do you want them all to be free? I need to know because it determines what I tell you next."

I hesitated. Could I not have both? It should have worried me, but I still felt nothing there. I knew my answer regardless.

"I want them to be free. I want Her to not have access to them anymore."

She smiled. "You don't usually make it this far . . . In most futures I saw, you died before you were able to make it to the island. This is a good sign. You're in Her blind spot. I do not know what awaits you, but I will warn you . . . you likely won't make it out alive."

I paused for a moment, feeling out the weight of that sentence.

"But it saves them, all of them?"

"We can only see what pertains to The Family. Futures that affect us only. I see all of the most likely futures of the boys. And there is only one in which you get your desired outcome, their freedom. It wanes in and out. Sometimes, it is the most prominent, and sometimes, it doesn't show up at all. But that is all I know. I can see that they fall away like falling off the edge of a map. I can't see beyond that. Only that they no longer belong to us."

"There's just one . . ."

"Yes."

"I need details. I need something. We were going to go on the day of the eclipse."

"No! They're expecting you."

"But it's a new moon . . . the day She's the weakest."

"It does not matter. With the eclipse, the power is stronger. If you go on the day of Ascension, you will lose. They will not let anything stop Ascension."

"Wait, what is Ascension?"

"The day the Gemini twins are inducted into The Guard."

Zach and Luke would be inducted into The Guard . . .

"But we have to stop that from happening."

"No. Listen to me, if you try to stop it, you will lose. Wait for the lights."

"Lights?"

"Yes, you must go to the island. But wait for the lights. That's all I can tell you."

"What about Zach and Luke? Tell me how they are. Tell me they're okay."

The sides of her mouth twitched. "This is the last moon before they start to deteriorate. It happens to all who sit upon The Guard. But I-I have been trying to keep them at peace when I can."

I hardly knew what that meant, but there was worry building in her eyes at the mention of them.

"Deteriorate." I wanted to ask the meaning of that word, as, even in this place, it struck me with fear.

"How long will it take for the lights? How will I know what you're talking about?"

"I can't tell you. But you will know. Please remember *you* have to go. Fate will not change if you don't. I want to this to be over, the same as you."

"But—"

"No. You've been here too long."

"I just got here."

"Leave." Without looking, she put her hands through the glass, grabbed my shoulders, and shoved me.

Forty-Eight

AARON

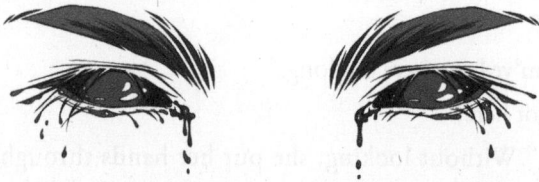

"There's something I need to tell you." Kimberly sat on the edge of our bed.

I already knew what she would say. The entire drive home she'd been quieter than usual. She was torturing herself in her head. Thinking of ways, A to Z, on how to fix something that the power in the dagger had shown her.

It was something she was too afraid to tell Kilian, which meant it was another warning.

Chaos broke loose when she came to after the ritual. The whole room roared with talk after hearing the changing date for the battle and the unknowns that came with Cecily's vague description. I'd called Presley on our way home to tell him the news that we weren't leaving as soon as we'd hoped, and well, I was giving him the night to cool off before I talked to him again.

I didn't agree with it either. I wanted to stop Ascension too, and I struggled to process the fact that Ascension was happening soon and Cecily mentioned that my brothers weren't safe, but Presley and Kimberly were drowning, and I had to be there for them first. I'd work through it with Kilian all day and night if I had to.

"What did she say to you?"

"She said . . . that the only way for me to save all of you is if . . . I go to the island and that there is only one good way this ends." Her attention shifted to her feet bundled in wool socks. "She said . . . I'll likely die."

My chest tightened at the mention, but I let the thought go as quickly as it came. There was nothing surprising about any of it anymore. If there was one thing I wouldn't let happen, it was Kimberly's death. Her death wasn't an option.

"Oh." I leaned forward to kiss her cheek. "Is that all?"

"Well, yeah. Aren't you upset?"

"Kim, do you really think there's a world where I let you die?"

"No, but—" I kissed her jaw and moved my index finger along her hairline and under her ear.

Her breath deepened, and her shoulders relaxed.

"Go on. I'm still listening," I whispered.

"I . . . I just wonder what we should do. What I need to . . ."

I made my way to her neck, kissing slowly.

"You don't need to do anything. I'll handle it," I said, keeping my focus on licking and sucking on the soft skin of her neck.

"This is serious, Aaron."

I pulled away to look directly into her eyes. "Rest assured I take any threats to your life very seriously. But you don't need to worry about this. I would never let anything happen to you. It's dangerous. We've known that. It changes nothing. There's nothing to fix. Let me handle it."

"Let you handle it . . ."

She seemed to be contemplating my words as I continued my exploration of her body with my tongue.

"Why are you distracting me?"

"Because it's good for you." I exhaled against her neck, and she leaned into me. "Because your heartbeat slows. Because you let go and focus only on me touching you and on things like how good I can make you feel. It gives you a break from that war in your head."

"I'll just remember after you stop touching me."

"Oh, I can keep you occupied all night. I'm not worried about that."

I wasn't using my hands yet, only my mouth to tease my way down her neck and to her chest. Every second, she opened up to me, shifting closer.

"I don't know. I want to help. I want to—"

"There's nothing to do about it. Just trust me. Just let me love on you. Let me help you relax."

I continued but stopped short of peeling her shirt off. "Or we could stop if you want to."

Her hand moved to my cheek. "No, don't stop."

I smiled, pulling her shirt off and vowing to ease any tension and doubt she had lingering in her mind.

MARCH

Forty-Nine

All night I watched *Tarzan* and cried. Normally, I'd just sulk in my room, but early in the morning, my hands started to hurt. A pinprick sensation started at my fingertips and moved into a burning sensation that ran down my entire arm. I swear the pain in my chest got worse too. I spent thirty minutes with my hand in the snow. It didn't help.

I sat on an old stump outside Mom's cabin inspecting my fingernails. All were clean and just as invincible as before, yet they burned like when you get menthol in your nail beds. I'd resolved to deal with the weird phantom vampire pain for the rest of the day till suddenly it stopped. Like a wave, peace rushed over me. I lay back on the old stump and enjoyed the weightlessness of it while staring up at the trees.

Winter would never end. We were stuck in a time loop doing the same things over and over again.

It would always be me alone staring up at the dull sky and missing them.

Rubbing my chest, I sighed in relief when the familiar pain returned. My brothers were still with me somewhere. With a flick of my lighter, I lit up a cigarette and let the warmth of the smoke fill my lungs. I grabbed the photo from my pocket—the one I wanted to pretend didn't exist. My brothers were next to a stained-glass window, and Luke *did* look tired, but after studying for a bit, I recognized the curl of his lips. It was that face where he tried to not laugh at something my brother said. Zach was angry as always, but he was looking directly at my brother. They were getting through it together.

I sighed and went to put it back in my pocket when I noticed small black writing on the back.

Havenville Church

666 Wildbend Rd.

Oh no. There was another test. A new location.

I wasn't going to go. Absolutely not. I went to tear the photo but stopped.

What if I needed it?

It would be fine in my pocket. No one else needed to know. It was just a photo with an address on the back. It meant nothing. Not important enough to alarm everyone with. I secured it back in my jacket pocket. It wasn't a bad secret if I didn't act on it, and I definitely wasn't going to do that.

When I went for the door of the cabin to return to my hopeless pile of blankets in front of the TV, I was greeted by a dozen balloons in my face.

"Happy Birthday!" Mom, Aaron, and Kimberly shouted simultaneously.

They stood like statues waiting for a reply—probably a happy one—but at the mention of my birthday, I was reminded of the timing I'd wanted to forget by tearing the calendar off the wall. It had been mocking me, and I swear it whispered to me at night.

Two weeks. Another two weeks had passed with no ending in sight.

"I forgot," I said, feigning a smile. If Luke could smile through his pain, so could I. "This is so . . . great."

My delivery needed work.

I eyed the sage-green balloons—my favorite color. They'd taken my absence as an opportunity to hang a tattered banner and some streamers. None of it looked new. Mom probably borrowed it all from her friends. I swallowed the lump in my throat when I saw the cake. Light blue and covered in sprinkles.

"I know I'm not as good of a baker as your brother, but I figured it didn't matter because you couldn't eat it anyway." Mom smiled and rubbed my arm.

Smile, Presley. You can do it.

"I love it. Thank you."

My heart was beating me up from the inside. I really hoped I could avoid the "Happy Birthday" song. Zach and Luke had been to every birthday party since I was born. I wasn't really wanting to hash out how it felt to not have them there singing in that weird way older brothers do.

"I did buy candles." Aaron looked at me with that smile that used to not work on me, but something about him putting in all this work to be a leader made me want to humor him. Sue me.

"Fine. Let's do it."

Kimberly handed me a colorful paper hat while biting the inside of her cheek. "It will be cute for pictures."

Oh no. Why would anyone want to remember my birthday? The first birthday without Zach taking me on one of our forbidden excursions.

The first time Luke wasn't there to wrap his big arm around me and squeeze the life out of me.

I let them have their song. Their picture. I used to love that type of thing. Maybe I still loved it, but I couldn't focus on anything other than the cause of the weird pain in my hand earlier and the very real clue I had sitting in my jacket pocket. I waited it out and went for the door at the first sign of a pause.

"Okay, well, I'm going to go to warm up the car for work."

"Wait! We have a surprise for you." Kimberly shared a tentative glance with my brother.

Joy.

"Wait here." Aaron smiled.

The birthday celebration was almost over. I would accept the gift, then I could forget it. Super easy. Then I'd be at work for a few hours where I wouldn't have to feel guilty for being quiet.

When Aaron opened the door, the sound of panting excitement came with a blur of black fur, and Sarah the dog came bounding toward me.

"We adopted her for you. I know you've always wanted a dog, and well ... thought she could keep you company."

Sarah was haunting me with her cute, fluffy ears. We couldn't escape each other. She circled my legs, and I kneeled to scratch behind her ears.

"You can rename her whatever you want. If you want to." Aaron spoke slowly and watched me like I was a ticking time bomb.

"I set aside some money so we can go get her a new collar and some things today." Mom had the same anxious expression.

"I ... don't know what to say. She's ... perfect."

I'd begged for a dog growing up. I'd made slideshows and wrote it on every Christmas list, but Mom and Luke especially drilled into me the responsibility it would be.

"She can keep you company in your room."

All that acting in the hospital was paying off. I was able to put on a decent enough smile to where everyone's shoulders relaxed and their anxious shifting stopped. They needed me to be okay and have a good birthday, so that's what I would do.

"What do you think? You wanna stay with someone like me?"

She licked my face, and I rubbed her belly.

We could be sad together.

———— ✦ ————

"Care if I join you?" Kimberly came to sit beside me on the porch steps. Mom and I were waiting for the car to warm up so she could take me to the shelter.

"Sure." I was on my second cigarette and loving the sense of calm I felt from it.

"Did you not like your gift?"

"What gave you that impression?"

"You just seem . . . off."

She had a blanket wrapped around her shoulders and snuggled close to me. It was a nice contrast to the cold chill creeping into my clothes and biting my ankles.

"I love the gift. I've just been thinking a dog is a big responsibility that requires me to be here and take care of it, which is exactly what Luke would want. All of this is exactly what he'd want."

"And that's bad?"

"I'm not staying here." The words poured from my mouth before they registered in my brain.

I'd asked myself over and over again the *why* of it all. Why did Luke think we would just forget about them? Why couldn't he have said something before all this happened?

Why? Why? Why?

There had to be a reason, and maybe . . . it was me.

"It was Aaron's idea, you know . . . He was so excited because he knew you'd been asking for one since you were a kid. He told me he planned to get you one for your next birthday. Before you were both turned. We just want you to have a good birthday. And Sydney at the shelter mentioned how much you loved Sarah . . . the dog."

"I know . . . I know. And I do. I'll probably give her another name, though, when I think of a good one. Feel like that will trigger Luke when he comes back . . ." I paused at the weight of those words. My brother would come back. We all would. Kimberly rubbed my back. "I kinda like her name for now. It makes me think of Luke all the time. And Sarah . . . the human Sarah. She liked dogs. She had this cute little Pomeranian that would get out, and we'd have to go look for it. Luke's gonna love her. He likes dogs just as much as me."

The thought hit me suddenly. I tried to push it out. The memories of Luke and Sarah and our collective childhood. We'd all grown up together. Sarah was going to do something great. She'd been so excited to go to college. Her whole family was abuzz with the celebration, but she never got to go. All those dreams she'd had, everything she'd hoped for, had been snuffed out.

A tear fell from my eyes and ran down the tip of my nose, but I wiped it before it could fall.

"Oh, gross. I'm sad again. Don't tell Aaron."

Aaron was in a good mood, and I didn't want to be the reason he wasn't anymore. I'd been mad at Luke for doing the exact same thing to me. We were all too alike.

"Your secret is safe with me."

I offered her a cigarette, and she took it. I couldn't fight the growing amusement as she surveyed it and sniffed it.

"Don't give me that look. I've never tried one."

"They taste awful, but it's not about the taste. It's about the feeling of it."

I lit her cigarette, and she inhaled, looking as badass as ever with her dark hair.

"What about you? How are you holding up?" I asked.

"I'm fine."

I waited.

"I don't want you to worry about me. I want to be encouraging for you."

"Eh, that's Aaron's job. You can be whatever you want. Be sad with me." I nudged her.

She nodded and took another puff, grimacing but powering through. "Do you think . . . I'm weak?"

"Huh?"

"This thing is happening to me, and I thought it was a good thing at first, but . . . I'm so scared all the time. I swear I didn't used to be scared."

I blew out a puff of smoke. "You're one of the strongest people I know. Seriously, do you remember that day in the forest you were panicking about telling my brothers?"

I imagined it all. Back in that memory, everything was warm and happy. I almost forgot what any of that felt like. The dirt and the trees were vibrant, and Kimberly's cheek was red. I couldn't remember that without remembering my older brothers and their secrets.

"Yeah, I remember."

"Even then, I remember thinking about how brave you were. And then you went toe to toe with a killer-crazed vampire and still came out on top. You changed, knowing you might not make it. I wish I was like that . . ."

She hugged me without warning, so tight she squeezed the breath from my lungs.

"Kim, you're hurting me."

"Sorry. You're just perfect exactly like you are, and I don't want you to ever think that you're lacking somehow."

"Aaron's really rubbing off on you, huh?"

When she pulled back, there were tears in her eyes. "Is it that obvious? I didn't cry before, not even during sad movies."

I smiled. "It's kinda cool. It suits you."

We stayed snuggled together as we admired the snow-covered trees that surrounded our property. That place never changed. I couldn't imagine it not being covered in snow, but every day, we got a little closer to spring.

"Do you ever wish I would have just turned you away at the OBA party when we met?" I asked, finally finishing my cigarette and putting it out on my shoe.

"Do you?"

"No. I just think about that moment a lot, and I wonder if I could have . . . changed things. Maybe you could have avoided the Calem curse."

"If this is the result of some *Calem curse*, I'm okay with it."

"You really mean it? The whole . . . cabins on a piece of land thing? Or is that more of *in a better world* thing."

She grabbed my hand and squeezed it. "I meant it. I want us to always be together. We're going to get them back, and everything will be different. But it will be good too."

The sadness was back. Clawing its way into my chest. I wondered if she believed her own words.

"You do know what you're asking, right? I'm literally never leaving you guys alone."

"I never much liked being alone anyway."

Fifty

AARON

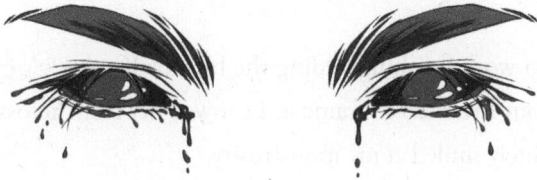

Presley's birthday celebration ended at the dinner table. All four of us sat between a table covered in various colored paints, crumpled newspaper, and paint brushes. We each had a canvas. I tried to paint Kimberly. Thankfully, my terrible attempt was hidden where she couldn't see. The smell of a vanilla candle on the kitchen countertop reminded me of late nights in my childhood when we'd all play games at the kitchen table.

Presley turned his canvas around, revealing a black dog with a little daisy painted on the ear. "It's Sarah."

I still wasn't used to the dog's name, but my brother didn't seem in a hurry to change it.

Sarah stirred at the mention of her name before lying her head back down. Her long fur was like a heater against my socks.

"You didn't tell me you could paint." Kimberly marveled at his work.

"Oh, yes! He even won an art contest in high school."

"Mom," Presley groaned.

"Oh, hunny, it's your birthday. Humor me. He was second best in the showcase. He got fifty dollars."

"I wasn't that good. I just took four years of art in high school."

"He was really good," I said.

"Now you're just sucking up," Presley said.

It was true, I'd never told him how good they were before. It's not like he wanted to go to art school or anything. He just liked painting and was good at it, and high-school Aaron never liked to compliment his little brother.

I went to work finishing adding the blue to Kimberly's eyes. It was atrocious, but I wanted to frame it. I showed her from across the table, and she politely smiled at my monstrosity.

Mom moved her paint brush along her canvas. "When your brother and Kimberly go, we can paint to pass the time. I have some time off I've been saving."

The three of us froze. We hadn't told her yet.

Presley shook his head like he wanted me to keep quiet, but she deserved to know. I put down my paintbrush and readied myself for tears.

"Mom . . . um . . . we're all going now. I don't know the exact date, but it will be soon. Presley and I will go first and then . . . Kim shortly after." I'd rather skin myself alive than have the conversation with her, but there was no way around it.

"Oh." Her eyes shifted to the table where an array of blue paint laid in front of her.

She had too much practice hiding her emotions. Probably where Zach and Luke got it from.

Presley got up to hug her. "I'm sorry, Mom. Please don't cry."

"No. No, it's fine. I knew you probably would. I just keep imagining you all driving away, and how I'll never have the strength to watch you leave."

"You can look forward to the moment we all come back. And this time, we won't come back empty-handed. Aaron's got a good plan. You don't have to worry," Presley said.

She kissed his forehead. "I know."

"Have your boyfriend take you on a vacation. You'll be so busy you won't even recognize we're gone," I said.

That at least made her smile. I hadn't met him yet. Mom was good at avoiding the topic. She spent most nights with us, but the ones she spent with him always left her glowingly happy.

She huffed, and her face grew red while she pushed her hands through her hair.

"Alright. That means I'll have more to look forward to when you all come back."

My mom never broke in front of the family. I never realized it as a kid, but it was obvious as she regained her composure and resolve. She'd mourn about it in private and never let her sorrow touch the three of us. The solar eclipse was soon, and even if we wouldn't be leaving like we'd planned, it was the start of something. Our time in shelter was ending.

The battle was almost at my doorstep, and I was ready.

I wished there was an easy thing to say to my mom to make her feel better, but the best gift I could give her was stronger than any words—the gift of my brothers coming home.

———

"Where did you get those?" Kimberly's eyes widened when she saw me make my way up the stairs to our bedroom.

Finding peonies in Alaska was a million times harder than in California. I had to bribe one of Mom's older neighbors to get them from the city, and it wasn't cheap, but her timing was perfect.

"Doesn't matter. They're for you." I plucked off a petal and smelled it, trying to inscribe it into my brain forever.

Kimberly smiled. I hated how stressful her life had become. It was hard not to take the blame, but everything was almost over, and soon, very soon, we'd all be at that lake breathing in the sunlight.

She wore my shirt and high wool socks that grazed her thighs. My favorite. There was no way she couldn't tell my heart was beating harder, but if she'd caught on, she hid it well. She was just about to pick up her notepad as I plopped on the bed beside her.

"Burns."

Her eyes met mine, and I was taken back to the smell of the peonies on our college campus and to last spring when everything was fresh and new. When she was a stranger and we were both afraid of getting too close, but now she was everywhere. In my bed. In my veins. In every part of my life that mattered.

I'd never been more sure of anything.

I pulled my grandmother's ring from my pocket and hopped off the bed to get on my knee. "Kimberly."

Her eyes went wide. "Aaron . . . where did you get that ring?"

"It was my grandmother's. Mom said it was special, and that means . . . it was waiting for you, I think."

I was down on my knee holding her hand, and at my words, tears formed in the corners of her eyes.

"Kim . . ."

"Wait, are you doing this because you think we're going to die?"

"No. The opposite, actually. I think we're going to win, and I have to think ahead. And I know we're not in a hurry. But I'm so unbelievably sure that I need you to be my wife. I want the title. I'm greedy. I can't spend another minute on this earth without having you as my fiancé. I need it all. And once this is over, I'm taking all of your days and nights."

A soft sob left her throat, and she let me place the ring on her finger. It fit perfectly. I wasn't even worried it wouldn't. It was all too perfect. The ring and the moment were made for her.

"Kimberly Burns, will you—"

"Wait."

My chest hurt from my heart punching me in the ribs. Why was I so nervous? Maybe she would say no. It was too fast. She needed more time. Maybe—

"Ask me after it's over. Ask me when it's over so I have something to look forward to."

I let out a breath of relief. She needed hope for the future, and I was happy to be that for her.

Standing, I placed a hand on her cheek to wipe the wetness from the corner of her eye. "Okay. Then . . . forever?"

"Yes. Forever." She smiled, and I tackled her on the bed to bask in her warmth. "Can I still wear it?"

"Of course. It's yours. It was made for you."

My grandmother would have loved Kimberly, and she'd take good care of her favorite ring. There was no one better to carry it and to take on the Calem name that my grandmother had been so proud of.

I thought about it another minute. "I wouldn't wear it in front of Presley though, unless you want my brother to freak out."

"You're right. Our *harmless* secret. I'll only wear it in the cabin."

Kimberly held her hand up to the ceiling while the stars shone beyond the skylight. The opal twinkled in the lamp light. It felt official, and I couldn't wait for the world to know Kimberly Burns was mine forever.

Fifty-One

PRESLEY

"Are you sure you don't want to come out?" Mom called through my bedroom door. "We can do whatever you want today . . ."

I'd shut the blinds and turned off the lights, with only the fire illuminating my room. She didn't know what day it was, or she'd be bedridden too. The day of the eclipse, a.k.a. Doomsday.

"No," I called, and she sighed and walked toward the kitchen.

We were making a mistake. While Aaron and Kimberly were playing "ring around the dagger," Zach and Luke were about to be offered on Hell Bitch's altar. They could be making them slaughter animals for all I knew—*the horror*.

I tried to tell my brother.

"So you want us to do . . . nothing? The weird witch lady in your dream

320

tells you they're getting inducted into The Guard, and none of us are going to try to stop it. We're just pretending it isn't happening?"

Aaron gritted his teeth. *"That's not what I said."*

"Oh, it sounds like you're saying we're going to do nothing, and we still have no idea when we're going to Ireland, and you want to listen to everything the mystical dagger says."

I felt like a terribly angry husk of my former self. A dried-up tumbleweed drifting around in the wind hitting people occasionally because it had nothing better to do. There wasn't anything funny about it.

"That's not fair."

"You don't get it. You don't care! You never get sad."

"Because I don't want to sit around and be sad, I want to fix it. Every minute of every day, that's all I want to do."

"Fine, I guess. Don't talk to me unless you're telling me it's time to go."

I stormed away . . . then apologized a couple hours later because Aaron's worry was making me sick to my stomach and I couldn't even enjoy my normal crying movie time. The bond had to have been getting stronger.

Grief and anger were good friends . . . no, *best friends*. Twin flame soul mates.

I sighed. Rubbing dog Sarah's ears as she lay at my feet by the fire.

Or maybe it wasn't our fault.

Maybe it was Zach's and Luke's fault. All our suffering was because they couldn't just say how they were feeling. They couldn't even write it out on a note or something? Drop it on an etch-a-sketch? Did it all have to be one big secret?

I found the crumpled picture of them next to me and studied the glow of the fire. *They did this to me.*

I took it in one last time before I held the edge of it next to the fire. Watching it crack and peel was supposed to make me feel better. The secret address was etched into my mind. Hopefully, it would fade before I needed that clue to find them. No more secrets. Secrets did nothing but tear us all apart.

Closing my eyes, I focused on them and the place they were. I imagined the castle, there were likely some obnoxious patterns and furniture, and it would smell old, like a thrift store smell. Then I imagined how they felt. And after a few minutes, the word to describe the growing agony came.

Abandoned. That's how they felt—no one was coming for them, and they were giving up.

My older brothers.

My heroes.

All alone.

I didn't know how I knew. Chalk it up to mystical daggers and magical blood bonds, but it was real. It crashed into me, and my head fell into my hands as I cried. Crying was an annoying side effect of being here, but the longer I cried, the more I wondered if it helped them.

I held on to the weight of it and rolled into bed. Sarah jumped up beside me and licked my tears. I buried my head into the fur of her neck. She needed a new name, but dog Sarah reminded me I could never forget the real Sarah and the person she was. She needed me to remember her.

Maybe that's how I helped my brothers . . .

Maybe I needed to cry so they didn't have to.

Maybe I need to be sad so they could keep going.

Then I'd cry all day and sit with all the anger.

It had to be *someone's* fault. There had to be a reason the pain wasn't ending and wasn't getting easier. I didn't want to think about what Hell Bitch was doing to my brothers.

I wanted them home.

Fifty-Two

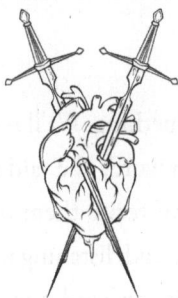

How much longer did I have? Finding a way to help everyone in battle was the most important thing, and still, I had nothing. Anzola must have known I was desperate. Desperate enough to gather on the day of the eclipse and try the dagger one last time.

The whole house was in a flurry. The usual group gathered with us in the library. Felix, Dom, and Halina. Kilian was seated as usual and studying with careful observation. It was quiet. The usual casual chatter disappeared weeks ago. The battle was close. It could be any day, and we were all tired.

Tired of gathering in the library.

Tired of rituals.

Tired of planning.

"I think . . . this energy will be different today. If I'm correct, it should be just as Cecily said. Stronger." Anzola had set up candles on the floor, and she moved to each with precision and a whispered prayer under her breath. "Lay here."

Aaron helped me to the floor. He was oddly quiet, and his attention stayed on Anzola as she glided from one side of the room to another.

"We'll wait for the eclipse to head directly over the island. It should be any minute now."

Anzola kneeled in front of me. "I want you to recite the words this time."

"Me?"

She nodded. "Testing something. We'll recite them together."

I recognized all the Latin words she said even if I didn't know what they meant. I'd heard Kilian recite them over and over, and I'd been practicing them. I did as she said, listening for the exact pronunciation.

Aaron placed the dagger in my hand, and I grabbed the handle, focusing on the weight. The sharp memory of the hilt sticking out from the middle of his chest sliced through me.

I hoped Cecily could show me something better.

With a smearing of blood on the dagger, I did as Anzola had taught me. I lay back on the floor with the dagger in my hand and recited the words. It sounded like an old song—ancient and lyrical.

I closed my eyes and willed it to take me. *Cecily, I want to speak with you. Show me where you are.*

Minutes must have passed without my recollection because when I opened my eyes, I was somewhere else. At the bank of a pond surrounded by fog and a bluish-green haze. The pond was surrounded by lanterns burning with fire and men lined up by the water.

A haze of white thrashing came into my view. Cecily was restrained and shoved into the wet grass that dirtied her legs and dress. She screamed and flailed as they tied a rope around her hands and dragged her toward the water.

The crowd muttered in a dull roar.

"Will it work?"

"What will she give us?"

Another man yelled with exuberance. It sounded like the equivalent of a feral animal. "Behold your queen."

"Why?" was the only word Cecily said.

"Sister, did you think you were fit to rule? You don't have the stomach." He pulled out a silver dagger and sliced her palm before licking a drop and drenching the rest of the dagger in it. The blood oozed into the hilt. "But you're not useless. You may bring us prosperity yet. Your husband agreed. You're the perfect sacrifice."

He motioned to another man with thick, broad shoulders and brown hair, but his features didn't hold the same carnivorous desires building in Cecily's brother's eyes. Instead, he averted his gaze to the water behind her.

She opened her mouth to speak, but someone grabbed her from behind and stuffed a cloth between her lips. The chant started, and there was movement everywhere. The crowd surrounded her and pushed her toward the water.

With her hands tied behind her back, her brother's hand forced her head underwater. The light from the fire illuminated the surface until the trailing air bubbles from her muffled screams stopped.

This was her death.

She'd been betrayed by her brother, and he'd used her fiancé to create a coup. Everyone she'd trusted had betrayed her. I waited for the memory to fade, but then she emerged wet and dripping. Stronger.

The men's eyes widened in horror.

The one she called brother didn't move. Her hand reached for him, and he dropped the dagger as she snapped his neck in one easy motion. I expected the others to flee, but they stared at her in awe.

A groaning alerted her to the grass, where a bloody Ezra had dragged himself to the edge of the pond.

"My queen."

"My Love. I can make you well again," she said as she bit her wrist, then brought it to his lips to drink.

The memory evaporated, but Cecily and I remained. Her green eyes snapped to me. "Why are you here?"

"I'm sorry..." What could I say? It was cruel. I'd never seen something so horrific in my lifetime.

"It tricked me. That's why you must end this. The Thing will try to scare you, but you have to go to the island. I'm stuck here. Reliving this moment over and over. It's my punishment from that Thing."

"I promise. I'm going."

"Use the dagger to draw Her out."

Cecily opened her mouth to say more but stopped. Her eyes widened. "She knows you're here."

There on the banks of the river stood a convulsing woman. She hadn't been there before. I had the instinct to run. I felt the danger. The menacing aura.

The head of the figure snapped around to face me. Before I could move, it slithered toward me in jagged movements. I wasn't prepared for what stared back at me.

It was me...

"What do we have here?" A strange voice strangled out of the figure that looked like me. Same dark hair and face but with black eyes and gaunt hollow cheeks.

I turned to find Cecily, and she was gone. The figure followed the motion of my head, standing nose to nose with me.

"The lonely girl has come to play." It wasn't my voice but a distorted sort of noise.

"What *are* you?" I asked.

"Compared to you, I'm a god." The Thing in front of me was unnatural. Its expression could be described only as something out of a horror film. A grin twisted into a look so sinister it was unnatural. In the real world, I'd have been scared, but here, I could feel no emotion.

It eyed me up and down. Analyzing.

"You would have made such a beautiful queen. You have enough hate."

I said nothing. Every attempt to move only brought it closer to my face, centimeter by centimeter.

"The lonely girl destined to be alone for eternity."

The laugh that left its chest sent a jolt of electricity through me. I couldn't be scared here, but I knew I needed to run.

"What are you saying?"

"If you had taken the gift I offered, you'd feel nothing but bliss. And instead, I get to play with you and take away everything you care about. Lonely girl."

"Stop that."

"Lonely girl. It's written in the stars. Can you read them? I can. Kimberly Burns. You live many lifetimes feeling empty and unwanted."

"It's not true."

"Isn't it? Can you read them? No, you can't, mortal. But I do. I read them over and over. And you are the most nothing I've ever seen. You don't matter. In every timeline, you mean nothing. You die alone. And them . . . those boys you call family . . . are mine. I take them from you, and it's oh so good. All the goodness and love and innocence. It's mine. And I'll have fun squeezing it out of them. Every delicious drop until my thirst is finally quenched."

"No."

"Yes." It smiled back at me. "And your Aaron is my favorite. The things that man can do . . . He is quite the lover. And soon, she'll have her hands all over him. Or we will. It's all the same."

I shouldn't have felt anything, but suddenly, my body was hot. Burning hot.

The Thing motioned to the water I'd hardly remembered we were standing by. Cecily was there face down. This place wasn't real. It was all an illusion. I was seeing what It wanted me to see, and I needed to get out.

It was close again, and my skin grew warmer.

"You really thought I wouldn't find out about you using the dagger to try to speak to the stars."

"It worked," I said. "They do speak to me."

It frowned. "In normal circumstances, I'd make you a deal. Like me and Cecily have. She didn't have to accept the ritual. None of them do. They can choose death instead. But she had so much hate. Beautiful, glorious hate. And now she tortures men for eternity, and I get what I need."

Blood. Love. Goodness. This Thing devoured life itself. That's what fueled It. She needed them like we needed blood to survive.

I spoke slowly. The heat under my skin only rising by the second. "It bothers you, doesn't it? That I lived? Something is happening that you're afraid of."

"Why would I be afraid of something as insignificant as you? Are you not hearing me? It's written in the stars. They are mine. You can't save him. Or . . . maybe you don't want to do the things that would keep him safe. What if your precious lover's only chance at surviving is spending eternity with me? Did you ever think that?"

"I think . . . you want me to be scared because you're scared."

The figure said nothing. Its long hair tickled the skin on my face, but I didn't shrink or cower.

Then I understood. As long as I had the dagger, I was connected to the queen.

They couldn't leave the island because they needed *me* and the dagger, and all Her servants needed Her. We had them cornered. They had nothing to do but wait for us to arrive.

"I'll see you soon," we said it at the same time.

It reached for me, and I reached for It, then the room was black.

When I opened my eyes, Aaron stood before me. His back was turned, and his shoulders were tight and rigid while he gripped the dagger and eyed Anzola. The entire room was . . . destroyed.

Everyone was on the ground. Halina was helping Felix out of a bookcase that was cracked in half. Anzola stood behind Kilian, who stood on the defensive.

I tried to grasp everything faster to find the danger Aaron had detected.

"What happened?"

At my voice, Aaron dropped the dagger and fell to his knees in front of me. The darkness and gray in his eyes dissipated.

"She tried to keep you under. And I made her stop. I'm sorry," he said, wiping some wetness from under my eyes and my nose. Blood. Black Blood. *Mine.*

"Is that mine?"

His voice shook. "Yes. You were bleeding. I got scared and panicked."

"That's panicking for you?" Halina said.

"I think you owe *us* an apology," Felix grumbled as he dusted off his clothes.

Aaron had knocked them all down. The bookshelves, the desks, all of it was broken on the ground, and all their eyes were on Aaron, not in fear but in wonderment and awe. Even Kilian was speechless.

"It's okay. I would have done the same," I said.

He touched his head to mine like there wasn't a slew of eyes watching us. With a firm grip on my shoulder, he pulled me in for a hug.

"You scared me."

"I'm sorry." I rubbed at his back.

"Do you feel all right?" Dom was the next to speak.

"Uh. Yeah. I feel fine," I said.

They were still staring.

Anzola's exuberant excitement concerned me the most. "Remarkable. Absolutely remarkable."

Fifty-Three

KIMBERLY

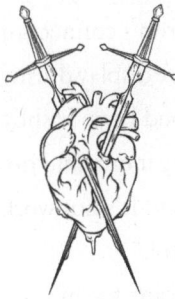

I struck the matchbox in my hand, and the stick's fire burned ablaze. I'd come to love the silence that once felt smothering, because it reminded me of my nights camping and my hikes alone. I didn't miss my old life while every current moment felt fleeting and too short.

The last thing I wanted was to be alone.

I missed the green and the smell of blooming flowers, but it was still winter. Those things would come back. I hoped they would. As I lit another candle, I dared to think of the future. A life where we weren't hiding or running anymore.

At battle's end, I wanted us all to be together again, walking through the trees and laughing. No smoke or fire, just the scent of fresh blooms and the roaring of the waterfall. I didn't care where as long as it happened.

The glow of the candles in the room of our cabin reminded me of the burning stars in the sky and that there might soon be a day when every kiss and touch wouldn't feel like our last.

The front door opened below, and Aaron threw off his coat and boots in a slurry of snow on the ground. I already knew the problem from the rigidness in his shoulders and that urgent look in his eyes. Meeting him at the foot of the stairs, I steadied him.

"Kim, I need blood."

Kilian was convinced Aaron's connection to the queen meant something, and after his inordinate display during the eclipse, Kilian was eager to test it out with a few blood bags. It showed us nothing of use. We'd been unsuccessful in figuring it out, and now . . . we were out of time.

"It's too much, I can't do it. It's not working. I just, I . . . I need you."

"It's okay. You're in control."

I feared for what that meant for him going to that place. If he was injured and needed blood and couldn't get it. Or even worse . . . him not resisting the temptation for Her blood.

He closed the distance between us in one leap and grabbed me by the waist.

"Off." He pulled back briefly to look at me. "Take your shirt off. Now."

"Are you demanding me?" I smiled, unfazed.

"Yes. Now." His brow bent, and his smile was gone.

Heat flared in my body at his touch and the intensity of his gaze.

"I don't think I like it when you tell me what to do." I teased.

"If you keep talking, I'm going to rip this off you." His eyes darkened as he took a fistful of my shirt, then he stopped. "But—this is your favorite shirt. I really don't want to rip it."

Presley brought me home a shirt from the shelter. Aaron remembered

I'd mentioned how soft it was, and likely, how often I wore it.

Savoring the want in his eyes, I peeled it off slowly. It was payback for the teasing he'd given me. He groaned, pulling it over my head and throwing it across the room. Before he could grab me, I ran up the stairs to our bedroom.

I didn't make it past the doorframe before he lifted me and tossed me on the bed. I gasped. He growled, pinning down my arms and biting into my neck.

The pressure swelled, and I arched my neck to give him better access. Losing blood felt like floating on a cloud, then landing in the safety of the arms of the person I loved the most. It was full surrender.

When he pulled away, his eyes were still charcoal.

"You're mine."

"I'm yours," I said, moving my hands through his hair until his rigid muscles let go.

I marveled at how lucky I was to love my best friend and to have him love me back. Lover. Not a title I'd ever thought I'd carry. Scientist, psychologist, friend. Something. Anything, but never lover.

Suddenly, being a lover was the most important thing. Something I'd die for. I never thought much of marriage. It didn't occur to me that being tied to anyone mattered that much. It was just something people did and spent too much money on. I thought a husband might be nice in the far future, *if he was helpful*.

I didn't know it could be like this. I was convinced I wouldn't be satisfied till there wasn't a place on my body that Aaron hadn't touched. His tongue. His teeth. His lips. I wanted to be tied to him in every way possible. I wanted his last name.

The candles on the bedside table and chest of drawers glowed a deep yellow that cast an orange tint along the wall of our room. Vanilla and cinnamon filled our small space.

He let out a slow breath. "I don't think it's getting better."

His fingers caressed my cheek as the warm brown came back into his irises.

A thought I tried to push away came up again. What would it be like to taste his blood? How would it make me feel? Could it help in some way, like William drinking Luke's blood to cleanse it? He needed to get better, and I would try anything. Usually, I never said it but . . .

"What if I . . . bit you?"

He was still leaning over me. "What? Why would you ask that?"

"Because I . . . I wondered what it's like for you. And maybe that's what we need to do to cleanse your blood. Maybe it will help whatever is happening to you."

"No." He moved away from me and onto the bed to sit.

"Why not?"

"Because this is my burden. Let me carry it. Alone."

"Since when do we do things alone? It could help you. This Thing is all about blood sharing. I want to help you."

In the dim light of the candle glow, Aaron's expression softened.

"Kim, you can't. We don't even know if it works like that."

"I'm not too scared to try."

"I know. But I am. What if it hurts you somehow? What if . . ."

I stroked the hair growing longer behind his ear. "Tell me."

"I don't want things to change between us. You've given up so much for me. You changed, and I just . . . I'm afraid one day you're going to realize that I'm the reason for everything bad in your life. You'll see I corrupted you, and you'll leave."

"Corrupted?"

He'd used the word before, but it was only at that moment I realized what he meant.

He continued, "We both know this Thing inside us isn't good. And you would never have taken It if it wasn't for me. One day you might regret all the things you've done for me. All the things you've given up. Becoming like I am . . ."

I scooted closer, pulling him to me until we were face-to-face.

"Do you really believe that?"

"It's just a fear. I wouldn't blame you if you did."

"Aaron, you could never corrupt me. The Thing inside us—whatever it is—doesn't matter. This is the only thing that matters." I pulled his hand over my heart. "I didn't fall in love with you because I was lonely or . . . because you were some mystical thing, I fell in love with how you make me feel. You make me feel so safe and special. And nothing can change that. Not even a little blood. I'll choose you every time."

His lips found mine, and I marinated in the smell of him and the feeling of him on my tongue. I wanted to show him I was his. That I wasn't afraid of the thing inside of us. Because it would never matter with the love we shared. Blood was just blood. This was stronger.

"Okay . . . let's try," he whispered in my ear.

"You're sure?"

He nodded, with his heart stuttering.

I grabbed his wrist and brought it up to my lips and kissed, and he watched me with careful concentration and soft eyes. The light illuminated the side of his face. With one gentle bite, I took in Aaron's blood and braced for the taste, the disgust and the strangeness of it, but there was nothing but the growing urge to consume more. He was everywhere. Everything. How many ways could I tie myself to him? How far could I go?

He groaned as I drank deeper. Moving his hand to my neck, he threaded his fingers through my hair, silently urging me to keep going. His blood filled a dark place inside me I never knew existed, and now it was whole and bright. I looked up at him, with his blood in my mouth, and he watched me with soft, amber eyes. Completely entranced.

After a few more seconds, he rested his head on my shoulder, moved the hair from my shoulders, and sank his teeth into my neck. I didn't stop. I didn't want to.

Every second brought our hearts closer until we were one.

If his blood was poison, then I prayed it would kill me slowly. I wanted the pain to be long and torturous because then it would last. Like ink spilling to page, his blood became my blood. I wanted all the darkness in his veins, even if it knit its way into every cell of my body and left me a dull shade of mauve.

I pulled away, with heat in my cheeks and a burning in my stomach to keep going. "How do you feel?"

The flames of the candles flickered in his eyes, and he moved his thumb over the blood lingering on my lips.

"So unbelievably in love with you."

I smiled, pulling him into an embrace. He was so warm, my own radiator in the cold night. In seconds, his shirt was off, and I traced the veins on his wrist and kissed his collarbone.

His breath deepened, and I followed that magnetic feeling of his skin on mine. A need burned in my chest for him. For nothing more than to be closer to him. It was a yearning that had been there for ages waiting to be awakened.

I needed him. In silent invitation, he offered me his other wrist. I let my desire burn, and my kiss turned into another bite. My bite compared to his was likely painful, but he didn't pull away. He pulled me to his chest and threaded his fingers in my hair while I drank.

"Take all you want." His breath left goose bumps on my skin.

I couldn't get enough of the warmth filling my throat and finally understood that need.

The ravenous, insatiable beast within that yearned for him just as he did me. How did he ever stand it? How had I denied myself this feeling?

When I pulled away, I wiped the blood running down my chin and let our new reality set in. This is who we were. Together.

He kissed my neck before laying me back onto the sheets. I moaned as his hips pressed into me to give me the pressure I needed and hadn't yet realized I wanted.

With feather kisses, he teased the skin on my neck and nuzzled into my jaw. Every touch was intoxicating. *Closer. Closer. Closer.*

"I'm so in love with you I can't stand it." He leaned over me. "Especially the way you taste."

With eyes full of lust, he lifted my chin to meet his gaze, and I watched in silent acceptance as he kissed my wrist, then sank his teeth into my skin again. It was hungry. Frantic. Like every second he needed more of me and even blood wasn't enough.

My attempts to remain levelheaded around Aaron Calem were excruciatingly difficult.

Everything he did was exactly what I wanted. Blood on blood. We were whole, and I didn't know if anything could be that perfect ever again. My head felt lighter, and I welcomed the tingling and weakness in my body.

His tongue licked at my wound on my wrist, and his attention went to the droplets that had fallen on my chest. In long strokes, he licked them while sucking softly on my skin.

Aaron wasn't holding back anymore. Every stroke of his tongue and bite felt like a promise that he wasn't afraid. His teeth sank into my skin lightly, over and over with just enough blood to lick away.

He wasn't as nice to my other pieces of clothing when stripping me. In one motion, he turned me around and pulled me to the edge of the bed. His tongue teased down every vertebra as I arched into him. Like every time before, his touch was gentle and calculated. He made sure I was ready and took his time. Even with the sounds coming from me, pleading for more.

Aaron's lips caressed my neck, and he offered me his wrist again.

As my teeth tore his skin, he moved into me slowly. Gentle. Always gentle. The friction. The blood. It all tore me from my calm, soft state to something more desperate and wild. Our bodies rocked in harmonious rhythm, and I couldn't stifle my moans. The tension tightened in my core until I was on the edge of release. It was so fast, so intense.

"Wait."

Aaron stopped. "Are you okay? Is this too much?"

I shook my head. "Lay on the bed."

His eyes widened at my advance, and he complied, crawling back onto his forearms to face me. I moved up to pin him this time and straddled his torso. He was studying me with soft eyes, like a precious piece of fine art.

"Can I bite you again?" I asked.

There was no thirst. It wasn't like the strange ravenous feeling when it was time to feed on human blood. This was a need for him that overwhelmed me. To feel the warmth of his blood in my mouth and his heartbeat in my head. Human me might have thought the whole thing very morbid, but we weren't human anymore. There was something in each of us that dared to consume, but we consumed each other. It was bloody, slow, and perfect.

He smiled, grabbing the side of my face softly. "You don't have to ask. I'm yours. I'd let you drain me dry right now if you asked."

I smiled. "Don't."

"Drink your fill." He pulled me to him until my lips touched the vein in his neck. I bit down and savored the feeling of his blood surging within me. It was intoxicating how natural it felt.

He kissed me, with his blood still on my lips.

"I don't know why I ran away from this for so long. Why didn't we do this before?" His soft laughter filled the cool area around us. His words were filled with elation and . . . relief. Like all the fear he'd once held had dissolved in front of his eyes.

"You were too busy not listening to me."

"Haven't we learned you have all the best ideas."

"You do. I was scared, but I'm not anymore." He squeezed my cheeks in his palms. "I never had to be afraid of loving you like this. You were always meant to be mine."

My cheeks heated with the adoration in his soft gaze. And I moved myself to take him in, in every way possible. I was stretched and full but needed more. I kissed his wrist before biting him again. With a circling of my hips, I felt him everywhere. Deeper and deeper. Fuller and fuller.

"I'm not going to last with you doing that," he breathed.

"You don't have to."

He stopped me with a hand on my hips. "No. You first."

"Together."

Our bodies moved in a not-so-gentle cadence that sent pleasure rolling from my hips into my abdomen. He kept his firm grip on my waist while we rode out wave after wave of pleasure as one. I shattered completely with a soft cry, but he mended me with his blood, then again when he pulled me down to lay on his chest.

We remained speechless for minutes, and I listened to the rapid beating of his heart until it calmed.

"See, there are candles," I said. Our limbs were still tangled.

I wasn't prepared for the transition, but it had happened right under my nose. He knew me before we were lovers, and now I didn't think anyone could know me more intimately. I never thought I'd be so known. So open. So bare before anyone. There weren't any more layers to peel back; this was me.

I understood it now. That thing that made people do unthinkable things.

I never wanted to leave the warmth of his arms. My heart skipped at the thought of what was to come, and I remembered we couldn't stay locked in the safety of our cabin forever.

"Do you still think you're closer to a funeral or a wedding?" he asked.

"Both."

"Why are you still so pessimistic?" He moved hair from my eyes and tucked it behind my ear.

"I see the writing on the wall, Aaron. And it says . . . give up because your odds of surviving are low. That nothing ever turns out the way you want it to."

He laughed into my neck, and the warmth lifted the hairs on arm. "Are you sure? Come on, Burns. Believe with me."

"I'm afraid of the disappointment."

"But what if . . . what if everything works out the way it's supposed to. And we walk out of that place changed and maybe bloody but alive. You don't think that's a possibility?"

No. Not a likely one.

"I want to believe it. Help me," I pleaded.

"Close your eyes."

I did, and he ran his fingers over my lips. I shivered.

"Repeat after me. I, Kimberly Burns, am brave."

I said the words slowly.

"And I choose to believe in things that I can't see despite when my brain tells me how unlikely it is."

I repeated it, squeezing my eyes as if willing and wishing would make the words true.

"I have hope."

"I have hope," I said.

I pulled him into me for another kiss. I wasn't done with him for the night. Not even close. Each kiss left me wondering if the longer he kissed me the more I'd get a glimpse of that hope his heart held. He filled a deep part of me with optimism. My radiant sunlight warmed me with every touch that dragged in the night.

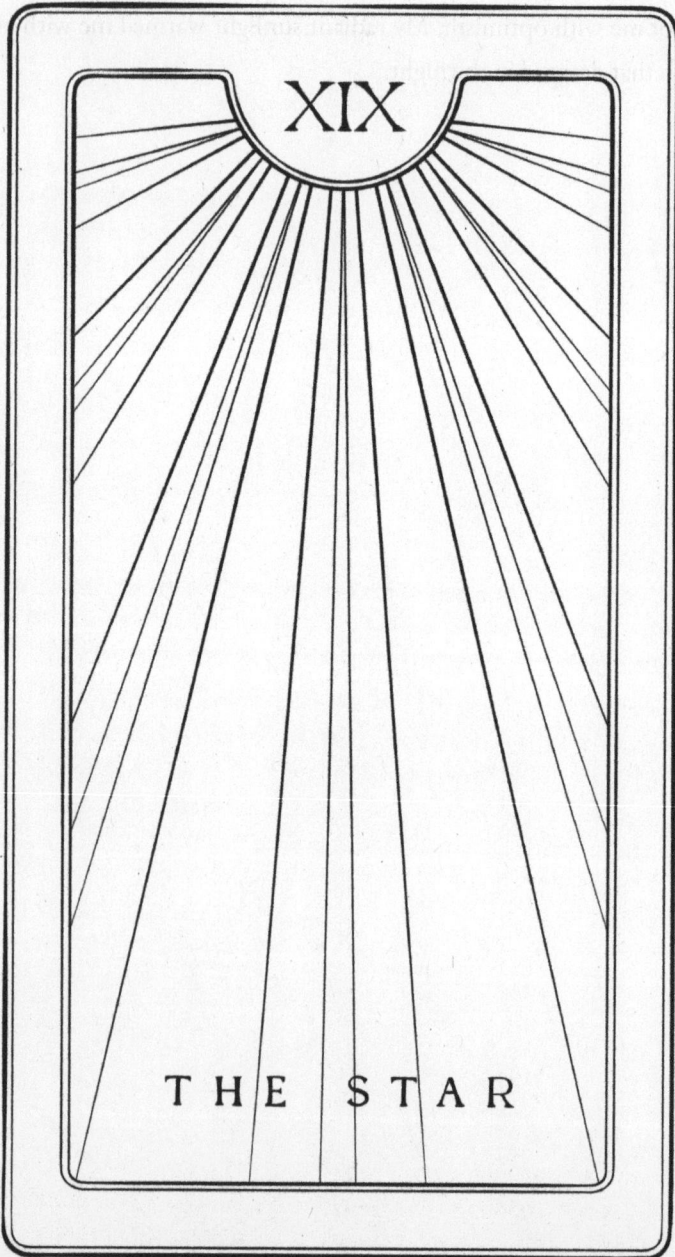

XIX

THE STAR

Fifty-Four

AARON

A numbing cold surrounded me as a set of hands tugged at the back of my head.

"My Love." An all-encompassing voice of a woman sounded in my ear with hints of longing and lust.

When I pulled away, I saw Her. White hair and glossy gray eyes. The queen. Any glance at Her only brought bile into my throat. My eyes watered from the smell wafting off Her—a putrid odor that stayed in the back of my throat.

"Sorry. I'm not really into this," I said.

She tilted Her head in confusion. Like a magnet drawing me away from Her, I spotted a door.

"Where are you going?" She called, more anxious than before.

"I have to go. I'm sorry. I'm not supposed to be here."

She was hot on my trail, running after me when I slammed the door behind me. Instinctively, I pulled a golden key from my pocket. It was glistening and pristine and fit perfectly into the lock of the door. When I turned the key, a sharp bang shook the doorframe, and an angry snarl ripped through the air.

Moving into the hallway, the smell was familiar. Vanilla candles.

I was in our home in Brooklyn. On the wall hung old pictures, the three of my brothers arm in arm smiling and playing in the mud. Christmases and birthdays were encapsulated on glossy film. One of Luke and Sarah swinging with red popsicles in their hands hung in a blue frame. I smiled, wanting to linger in the hallway with the dim glow of warm-yellow light, but the banging brought my attention back toward the place I needed to go.

I was looking for something . . . someone. I stopped just before I passed a matte-black door.

The basement.

I'd avoided going there at all costs as a kid, but something lured me. I turned the knob, then stared at the darkness awaiting me. There was no light to illuminate the room or the bottom of the steps. With clumsy hands, I found a light switch on the wall and flipped it. Nothing. I hesitated on the first step, fearing the unknown but pushed on, knowing it was the right way. As I descended, a glow radiated from my palms first, then encompassed my whole body.

Two boys huddled into a corner on the concrete floor came into view, and they couldn't have been older than six.

"Luke," I said, knowing my brother's long dirty-blond hair anywhere. He had his arm wrapped around Zach, who also had longer hair tucked behind his ears. "Zach."

They shrank away from me when I kneeled in front of them.

"What are you guys doing down here?" I asked.

"We can't get out," Luke said, his cheeks stained with tears and dirt.

"It's too dark," Zach whispered. His attention stayed on the stairs.

"I can help you. I know the way out."

"No. We can't. We tried. There isn't a way," Luke said.

"I know the way."

"But She's out there. She'll find us."

"I already took care of it. She won't bother you anymore." I stared into Luke's glistening brown eyes. "You can trust me."

Zach's body shook. "Don't, Luke."

"Take my hand. I'll protect you. I promise."

I reached for his hand, and after a moment, he placed his hand in mine.

A brief flash of light enveloped me. It was brighter than I ever thought possible. Brighter than the whitest light that existed on earth. When it dimmed, I settled on an expanse of glistening blue water and tall mountains. The soft scent of pine and dirt comforted me with nostalgia. It felt . . . safe.

A flash of red caught in my peripheral vision.

"Hi." Kimberly's voice was loud and clear next to me, but not louder than her vibrant heartbeat.

I wasted no time bringing my lips to hers to gain the taste of her.

"I had the weirdest dream just now. My brothers : . . they were trapped somewhere."

"Aaron!" Luke called as Zach and he ran and jumped from the edge of a wooden dock into the crystal-blue lake. Presley followed soon after with a roaring yell.

"Not anymore." She squeezed my hand. "We won, remember?"

The happiness of it filled my chest, then the relief from it leaked from my eyes.

In a blink, the baby blue sky filled with cotton-candy clouds was gone and replaced with a navy sky. The vast lake met the horizon, but it seemed to go on forever. A glassy marble of twinkling stars surrounded us. It was just Kimberly and me.

A soft angelic sound caught my attention, and I examined those twinkling stars.

It was . . . singing. Soft, incoherent singing came from the sky, along with whispering too low for me to hear. I listened harder, and soft giggling echoed around me.

Aaron Calem is here. Aaron Calem. Tell him. Aaron Calem.

The stars said my name over and over again.

Kimberly's hand tightened around mine as she watched the stars dance around us.

"How did we win?" *I asked. At that moment, it seemed like the only important question.*

"I was the opening, and you were the key."

"I'm the key . . . What does that mean? If this is a riddle, I promise I'm not smart enough to figure it out."

Kimberly smiled and placed a delicate hand on my cheek. "You'll know what to do . . . bond breaker."

I awoke to her lying on my chest, and my movement stirred her. We were tired from the blood loss and must have drifted to sleep.

"Did you have a dream?"

I said nothing, letting the emotion of seeing my brothers again wash over me, but most of all, the peace and the sadness that it wasn't true.

"Was it a bad dream? What did She show you?"

"I didn't dream of Her. It was of you. All of us together. We . . . won."

Her lips curled into a sleepy smile, and I kissed her forehead.

I'd spent so long being terrified of getting too close to her. Afraid I might snap. I pondered why I'd run away from it for so long—afraid to love her to the fullest extent.

I wasn't afraid anymore . . . of anything.

As we repositioned and I stared up at the sky, all of it surged through me.

Hope and love danced like the stars in the sky.
We would win.

Fifty-Five

AARON

I whistled as I slid into the kitchen in my socks, with a new sense of excitement and vigor. The birds chirped outside in a chatter, and the smell of coffee hit me like a freight train.

"Someone's happy this morning," Mom said as I swooped in to kiss her cheek.

"Oh, very."

I picked up various things in the kitchen while she washed dishes.

For the first time in a long time, everything felt clear.

Kimberly sat at the table with her head in her notebook, scribbling down something. The plan was to go to Kilian's and continue finalizing our plan. I came up beside her and kissed her forehead before sitting across from her. The blush on her cheeks brought a smirk to my lips.

"Hey family." Presley came through the front door carrying a paper bag.

"Did you get the popcorn for movie night?" Mom asked.

"Extra butter just like you . . ." The bag hit the floor, and its contents scattered and spewed onto the hardwood.

His eyes widened and he keeled over, holding a hand to his chest. Tears formed in the corner of his eyes until he was sobbing.

I was already near him, holding him and trying to get him up to speak to me, but he was inconsolable. Only uttering under his breath.

"Something's wrong." He looked up at me with red eyes. "Something happened. Something bad."

"Did something hurt you?"

"Not me! It's them! They're hurt. It's Zach or Luke . . . or both. I don't know. Something is wrong." He fell into my chest again, sobbing harder. "It hurts. It hurts."

His hands fisted in his hair as he writhed in agony.

Fear coursed through me at what was happening to him, urging me to find the solution.

"It's going to be okay, Pres. I'll fix it."

"You don't feel that?" He hiccuped. "Why don't you feel it?"

I hadn't noticed the weight in my chest was gone. That constant pain had vanished. I felt nothing at seeing my brother cry, other than normal sadness and the urge to kill whatever was causing him that much pain. There was no ache of any kind. No stabbing or aching.

I didn't feel the bond anymore.

"They need help. Something is wrong. We can't leave them there."

I squeezed him tighter. "We will. I promise. We're going to be together soon, and this will all be over."

Presley sobbed into my shoulder for at least twenty minutes. Then Mom went into protective mode and scooped him up and had him sit with her next to the fire.

All three of us sat with him until he quieted, but when it stopped, he wasn't the same. This was different from the times before. Presley's eyes had gone vacant as he stared into the fire. The only thing that shook him from that state was Sarah nuzzling his legs.

Something was wrong, and I had to find out what. No more waiting.

Fifty-Six

AARON

Kimberly squeezed my hand as I recited play by play back to Kilian. This time we sat in the living room without an audience. Everyone else was too busy preparing for the battle that could begin at any notice. *Wait for the lights.* A helpful note, but how long could we wait? My brothers needed me.

"Then Presley freaked out and grabbed his chest from the pain of the bond. He said it was so intense, and I felt . . . I felt nothing."

Kilian stalked toward me. "What does it usually feel like for you?"

"Like pressure. Like my heart is bruised. And it's gotten worse before to the point I've been on my knees. But this time I didn't feel even an ache. It was like . . . he had all of it or something."

Kilian nodded and excused himself without another word while Kimberly and I sat alone on the couch hand in hand. The clock on the wall ticked by slowly. Outside the window were blankets of snow cast in shadows from the clouds. *The lights. Maybe it was referring to the weather.*

All my extra seconds went to figuring out my dream riddle or the cryptic message Cecily had said. I'd entertained it at all because it came from Cecily, and after hearing Kim's interactions with her during the ritual, I was willing to try to believe her words.

Kilian shot into the living room quickly enough that Kimberly and I flinched. In his hands sat another wooden box, and I knew what was coming because I'd seen it before.

"You kept the vial of the queen's blood." The sight of it had nearly brought my brothers to their knees.

"I want to test something."

It wasn't a question. He cared very little about my protest as he went to open it.

"Wait!" Kimberly choked out.

I braced for the magnetism of the queen's blood, but as the box opened and my gaze settled on the black liquid, I felt . . . nothing.

"I don't feel anything."

"Nothing at all?" His eyes widened. "Would you taste it?"

"Aaron, no." Kim grabbed my forearm, her brows knitted with worry.

"It's okay. It's just a little. I can handle it."

I had to try. The look in Kilian's eyes was beckoning me and told me he was onto something. I hoped it was good.

From the bottle, I drew a singular drop onto my finger. I sniffed the open air, then licked it off. It might as well have been water. There was no reaction from my body at all.

I shook my head. "It doesn't taste like anything I remember."

Kilian's nostrils flared, and he let out a laugh. Crazed and exhilarated.

"What's so funny?"

"I didn't think it was true. There was no way to know. No way to test it out."

"Test what?" Kimberly pulled at my arm, away from Kilian and the blood.

"There was a poem. The story of a man obsessed with a beautiful, mystical woman, but when he gave his heart to another woman, he was able to break the curse and fled with his lover. I believed it to be unrelated, or perhaps I was misinterpreting it."

"But how? We've been together all this time," I said.

I'd given my heart to Kimberly long ago, and I'd still felt the effects of Akira's blood.

"Has something changed between you two?" Kilian's eyes narrowed. "Anything."

Kimberly and I shared a glance. There was one thing. I wondered if I should say it. Kilian already knew more about me than I cared for him to know, but I guess that was part of the sacrifice.

Kimberly spoke first. "We . . . did share blood recently. That's new."

"The mingling of lovers' blood . . . You created a bond. A bond that is stronger," Kilian mumbled.

He studied us, probably putting the pieces together in his head. It all sounded far-fetched for me, something out of a story book, but everything in my world was like that.

"So, this means . . . Aaron's immune to the effects of the queen's blood," Kimberly said.

"More than that. He will be immune to Her completely. He'll likely be able to be around Her with no issues."

"This is good, right?" I asked.

"This is monumental." I swear a tear formed in Kilian's eye. "And it just confirms what I already knew. It's time."

He turned to address only me. "This is what I was waiting for. This is how we will save your brothers. She has no power over you anymore.

353

The risk of bringing you to the battlefield has finally been alleviated."

I looked at Kim, whose eyes widened in relief at the news.

"Then it's time. We're going." It wasn't really a question.

"A last-minute decision is our best route. We should expel your memory of the knowledge of this before we make way."

"Wait. No," I said.

"It will be dangerous for you to both go with that current knowledge."

"But then you'd have to take our memory of the night that we . . . did share blood, right?" Kimberly gripped my arm.

Kilian nodded.

There was something about that night that I wasn't willing to forget. We'd had many nights together, but not like that. I hadn't been able to stop thinking about it. It was more than the sex. I'd never felt so connected to anything, let alone another person. Kimberly shook her head at me, confirming my decision.

"No. I'm sorry, I can't."

"We've given The Family too much already," Kimberly said.

"Very well. We will make do." Kilian was only briefly disappointed before his lips curled upward again.

I squeezed Kimberly's hand in mine and glanced outside at the shaded area. No lights, but we couldn't wait anymore. The remnants of my dream played again in my head.

Luke . . . Zach. I'm coming.

Fifty-Seven

PRESLEY

I did a bad thing. I said I wouldn't, and I did. The car was barely enough to cut through the falling snow lingering on the road. Wiping my eyes with one hand, I gripped the steering wheel with the other. The car slipped on every turn, but I couldn't slow down. My chest. My chest. My chest.

Pressing the pedal, I forced the car faster down the snow-packed road. I'd packed a bag with cash and my passport. I hadn't left The Legion everything . . . because I knew I'd need it.

I couldn't take it anymore. If I crashed the car, I'd run on foot. Nothing would stop me from going to my older brothers anymore. Not Hell Bitch, not Kilian and his cult, not even my family.

They would be so disappointed when they realized I was gone. It only made the pain worse. It was the most agonizing feeling I'd ever felt. Ever. And it wasn't going away.

I tried to focus on anything else, but my face was hot with tears. Focusing on the road was out of the question. I needed to pull over before I hit someone or derailed into the ditch. That's what Luke would say, but Luke wasn't here. He was hurt somewhere; I could feel it. Or maybe Zach or maybe both.

Whatever it was, it was bad.

They needed me. Which meant I couldn't stay at the cabin anymore. I had to go.

Did that make sense? Yes. It was logical.

They would do it for me. They'd have never stopped searching.

Aaron would flip. Mom and Kimberly would cry. I threw my phone out the window a few miles back. If they called me, I'd cave.

I had to be strong. Determined. Brave. Like my brothers.

Fifty-Eight

AARON

I couldn't wait to tell him. Presley would be so happy. I'd tried to get him out of his slump all week. He was quiet again, but the only solution was getting my brothers back.

And it was finally time.

My mind reeled with the new information. Kimberly and I cried tears of relief in the car. Things were finally moving in our favor.

We didn't make it back to the house until late. The sun had disappeared behind the trees, and the car was gone from the driveway. *Maybe Mom took Presley somewhere to cheer him up.*

When I opened the door to the cabin, my mom was at the kitchen table with a cup of coffee. My heart drummed faster at the thought of telling her our time together was over. Sarah greeted us with a soft cry and by nudging my shin.

"Where's Presley?" I asked. "I didn't think he had a shift today."

"I checked on him a few hours ago. But he hasn't come out of his room."

My stomach sank.

"But the car is gone . . ."

Mom's head shot up, and I went to his room, but the door was locked.

"Pres." I gave it only a few seconds before I broke the handle and made my way inside. Sarah followed at my heels.

In the dark, I made out a singular piece of paper resting atop the blankets.

I'm sorry. I tried. I really did. I have to go to them. They need me.

Love you forever,

Presley

The hopeful, joyousness I'd felt just minutes before ran out of me.

"He's gone. He left."

I'd done it again. I'd been focused on my own ideas. My own goals and ambitions. I'd missed the one that formed in my brother's mind. He'd kept some secret. They must have given him another clue.

He was going to The Family to be with my brothers.

"What?"

"Where did he go?"

I could barely hear Kimberly and my mom's panicked voices and could no longer feel the touch of them trying to comfort me.

My heart was sputtering. The walls were too close. My brother was gone. My *little* brother. I was supposed to take care of him, and he'd slipped through my fingers.

"He's gone," I said, still staring at the paper. "This . . . this is my fault."

My world went colorless as I walked out of the warmth of the room and headed for the door. The cabin was too hot. I think they were calling for me as I made my way into the snow. They were crying. I was too.

Why did this keep happening? Why did The Family continue to take everyone I cared about? I'd allowed it to happen. I thought I was doing enough but wasn't. All of the work I'd done meant nothing if they took him.

I fell to my knees, and Kimberly was there to keep me from crumbling completely. The Family had found my weakness. That was their plan all along. To target him and bring them over to their side. I wasn't sure what it meant. They could be hurt, but without the bond, I wouldn't know.

"Aaron." Kimberly's voice was a mix of shock and surprise.

I still couldn't look at her through my tears, but I let in the warmth of her embrace to save my body from the icy cold creeping under my skin.

"Aaron." Her voice was strong enough to bring me to look into her eyes, and she motioned to the sky. "Look."

The entire sky was lit up in vivid pink, blue, and green. The aurora borealis was brighter than I'd ever seen and covered the whole sky. It was always a distant, faint thing, never bright and filling the entire sky.

"The lights . . ."

"We're going to win." Kimberly's cheeks were wet with tears, but she smiled. I leaned my forehead against her chest, and her heartbeat slowed. I inhaled the hope she carried in her heart and let it in again. All the pieces were falling into place, and the stage was set. It was a minor setback, but maybe how it was supposed to happen. Nothing would stop me now.

It was the three of us sitting under the lights.

"We're going to get him back, Mom. And we're all going to be together just like you said."

When I heard my voice say the words, I knew it was true. As if by speaking it, I willed it into existence. Maybe I did. I remembered my previous resolve. The stars should fear me and so should the queen. I was done with secrets, and I was done with Her taking my brothers away from me for Her own gain. They would all meet their demise.

Fifty-Nine

PRESLEY

Of course it was a creepy church. Where else would the blood cult ask me to go? I guessed I was lucky it wasn't an underground cave or the sewer or something. They were lucky I'd gotten good at reading a paper map.

I checked none of my surroundings as I walked through the snow into the church. Nothing mattered when it felt like my heart was bleeding. Putting one foot in front of the other, I opened the double doors. Everything was well lit. Modern. Like those kinds you see in the wedding magazines with the perfect hanging fixtures and the soft see-through curtains.

Only, no one was there. The whole place was empty with no echoing heartbeats or even rats in the ceilings. The company would have been

360

nice. I walked slowly down the aisle, passing lit candles on the edges of the pews. As I reached the front, the stage light illuminated a large altar bowl full of black liquid. Definitely blood. A gold plate sat on the edge of the rim, and on it, was a word that had been etched haphazardly. *"Drink"*

I sighed. *Dramatic much?*

Everyone said I was dramatic, but those cult vamps had it down. They could've done all of that from the beginning rather than give me the run around. Then, I guess I wouldn't understand *loyalty*. I realized I might have turned out exactly like Akira intended. Like he knew the person I was before I did.

The black blood mocked me. It was a bad idea. Like flashing red signs that said *Stop Now or Turn Evil* type bad, and I was about to collect 200 dollars and pass go. I couldn't leave the church. My feet were glued to that tile floor, and my only option was to drink or turn back.

Was it that infamous fate everyone was always going on about?

What would it be like to be king for a day? To be on the side that was constantly three steps ahead of us . . .

That was a bad thought. I didn't need Luke to tell me that. He wouldn't want me to think that way, but he wasn't here.

There was a silver goblet next to the bowl, and I grabbed it. More theatrics. Wouldn't a SOLO cup have been more practical? Probably didn't fit the aesthetic. Okay, maybe I was stalling a little bit. It was a bad idea. A *really* bad idea.

Drinking the blood meant possibly giving up a part of myself I couldn't get back, but it was the cost to get back to them, and I was oddly okay with it.

I couldn't wait another day. Another minute. Another second. I wanted to be with them because maybe it would change something. Maybe I could do something this time.

And maybe submitting to this thing calling to me was worth it.

Whether it was Her or fate, at least we'd be together. It probably looked like I was giving up, but it didn't feel like giving up. It was my choice. I wanted to go see my brothers, so I was going to.

There wasn't a way to know for sure if it was the worst idea I'd ever had.

Ah. Fuck it.

I filled the goblet to the brim, threw it back, and the blood chilled me to my core.

Oh, shit.

Sixty

AARON

It was almost time to get up and say my goodbyes to Mom before heading out. I was looking forward to that as much as I was looking forward to parting ways with the girl lying on me. I just needed more time.

Presley leaving only proved that my time in Alaska was over, and in only a few hours, I'd be on a plane to hopefully meet him where he was headed.

I played with Kimberly's hair while she lay on my chest. Her heartbeat drummed steadily, and I focused on that soft sound. My mind drifted to the night we met under a blanket of stars and a canopy of trees. There was a fire then too. Our crackling fire downstairs was slowly dying as the night dragged into the early morning.

"Why do I feel like this is goodbye?" Kimberly stirred. She'd been silent for some time.

"It's not. I promised to never leave, remember?"

"Then promise . . . promise this isn't goodbye. That this isn't the final everything."

I wanted more than anything to promise that. To promise I had all the answers and that our plan would work out exactly like we wanted it to. That everything would be over soon, and we'd come home with my brothers.

But one of the many things Luke had taught me was not to make promises I wasn't sure I could keep.

"I can't." I pulled her chin up to see her face. "But this will work. I believe it. You're going to blink, and then we'll all be on our way back home together. Then we'll really celebrate properly. Together."

"But . . . what if, Aaron. What if?" There was a crack in her voice.

I grabbed her face in my hands. "I'll find you again. That I promise."

Nothing could keep me from her. Not even death. Some bonds were stronger than death, and ours was one of them.

It had occurred to me it could be the last time I held her in my arms. That the peonies sitting in a vase on our nightstand could outlive the both of us. So badly I wanted this dream with her. I'd wanted nothing more in my entire life, and it was guaranteed if I'd just stay. My older brothers had lain in bed with likely the same thoughts. I wondered if Zach had ever held Ashley knowing he'd say goodbye . . . for us. And now I was the one making that sacrifice.

"What if this is how it always ends for us . . . in every timeline?" She sniffled.

"Then we'll keep trying till we get it right. I'll find you again and annoy you till you talk to me. I don't think you ever have to look for me . . . but I always search for you."

"I wish I could see those infinite worlds in your head, Aaron Calem. All the places of light you see."

I kissed the top of her head. "Just ask. I'll tell you anything."

"The wildest one."

"You're a mermaid, and I'm a do-gooder pirate who saves you from a perilous fate."

"Mermaids?"

"Come on. If vampires are real, somewhere out there, mermaids are real."

Her soft laughter was warm against my neck.

"Fine. Tell me your favorite one."

I hesitated and twirled a piece of her hair. "Well, in my favorite one, we're both human. We met in grade school, and I got to grow up with you. We're best friends, and you're blissfully unaware that I'm in love with you . . . but I finally work up the courage to tell you in college, and you feel the same way. We get married and have kids. My brothers love being uncles. We grow old and die together . . . We're never apart. We're those old people that cry when they have to leave for a day."

She laughed. "I knew you'd say that."

"Am I that predictable?"

"You're just soft. I . . . love it."

I let the silence settle as I gazed at the stars in our skylight maybe for the last time. The entire sky was dancing with the lights. Mom said it was a geomagnetic storm that was causing the northern lights to flair for the next few days. The news showed pictures of it all the way in Florida.

They were our lights. Our storm.

"Aaron . . . this is my favorite one."

"The vampire one?"

"The one where you are warm and here. The one where you're holding me and you never let go. And we never have to say goodbye."

"I like that. No goodbyes." I pulled her up to kiss her. "Are you sure that there isn't a way for me to make you stay here? Where I know you're safe."

"Probably another timeline. But not this one." She smiled again.

I buried my head in her hair to breathe her in. I'd never known love like this existed. There weren't words for it. Only the undying urge to bind myself with her in every way possible.

"Kim . . . please marry me."

Her muscles stiffened, and she moved to look at me.

"You know I will. I want to . . . more than anything."

"No, I mean, right now. Marry me. I can't go another second without being married to you. I want you to be my wife. I promise I'll give you more to look forward to than just a proposal. We have so much we're going to do. I'm going to take you all around the world, and I'll build us a cabin. We can still have a wedding where we can celebrate with everyone. Just marry me right now."

She stuttered out a short breath. "But how? Don't we need . . . official things?"

"No. We just say our vows to each other under the stars, the gods, or whoever is looking down at us in the sky, and then we're bonded. Forever."

Bright excitement grew in her eyes.

"Okay . . . but I didn't prepare any good ones."

Our noses were nearly touching, and I stared into her eyes. There was no nervousness like when I'd gone down on my knee. Everything else that seemed important before, suddenly didn't matter. It was her and me and the stars above, along with the smell of fire and the beat of our hearts; I couldn't ask for anything else.

"It doesn't matter. You always say the best things anyway. It's my turn." I couldn't stop touching her, tracing her lips and up to her brow. "Kim, I promise I'll always protect you and I'll take care of you forever. I'll be your shoulder to cry on, and I'll plan the best dates. You'll always be celebrated with me, and I promise to make sure you feel special because you are. I knew it the moment I met you and you walked away from me in the courtyard. I swear you've had your hooks in me since that day, because . . . you are the bravest person I know. And then I got to know you, and you're kind and funny and *so* smart. I'll follow you anywhere. Wherever you want to go or whatever you want to do, I'll be right there beside you, and you'll never be alone again."

She laughed with tears streaming down her face. "How am I supposed to follow that up?"

"You don't have to say anything. I already know how you feel." I pressed her closer to me.

This time, she grabbed my face to stare into my eyes. "Aaron, I love you more than I've ever loved anything. You've taught me so many things . . . but my favorite thing is that you taught me how to live and not just for myself but for other people too. I didn't think I needed anyone, but . . . I think I was just waiting for you to find me."

She wiped the tears falling from my face and onto our pillow.

"Kimberly Burns, will you be my wife through life and death . . . forever?"

"Yes, through life and death. And will you, Aaron Calem, be my husband forever?"

"Yeah." I answered with a kiss.

I wanted to remember the taste of her long after the night ended and remember the sound of her heartbeat so I could recall it in our separation.

"Presley's going to be upset. He really wanted to be the officiant," she said, like he wasn't likely on his way to Ireland to join a cult. She believed in our dream.

"He will be. He can officiate. Sing. Dance. I really don't care as long as we're together again. Don't you agree, Mrs. Calem?"

Her arms squeezed me till it hurt. "Mm-hm. Say it again."

Dear Luke and Zach,

Can She be everywhere at once? Is it like this for you too?

Eternal agony. Please let me get there faster. Why did you hide me from Her? Her. Her. Her. Why did you separate us?

I can feel Her. Her. Her. She's written into the walls. On all the floors. Can you see it too? She's crawling in my skin. She's in my lungs and underneath my fingernails. I feel Her everywhere I go. I can't think. I just need Her. Her. Her.

Please tell Her to wait for me. I'm almost there. Tell Her I'm sorry I'm late.

She'd always been guiding me. She'd been pulling me to Her since I first came into the world. Even before that. She was mine. And I was Hers.

I'm sorry I stood in your way of something this big. But now we'll be together. I wish the plane would go faster.

They gave me more blood, but it wasn't enough. I'm finally going home. Why did we ever fight this? It hurts to be away from Her. Her. Her.

Please tell Her I'm coming. You probably won't get this. But I'll see you. I'll tell you in person.

-Presley

Sixty-One

AARON

I pulled at the collar of my shirt. The damned thing was too tight and a little itchy.

The Family had been waiting for me at the airport like they'd known I would just show up. I'd bought my ticket and took my passport. Four guys dressed in all-black suits waited beyond the gate with a change of clothes for me.

"This way, sir."

I followed them as we boarded a small plane. I'd never been called sir before. Like I'd never been on a plane before, but I wouldn't say that.

I wasn't entirely sure how to talk to them, even though the two looked to be around my age. They didn't let me have the window seat and chose to sandwich me between them. I wondered if they thought I'd make a run for it.

I let my mind wander as their silence dragged on. Mostly of home. Of

370

Kimberly. Of saying everything but goodbye.

"So, dinner. Your place. Two weeks," I'd said.

"I'll cook your favorite."

Mom wiped a tear, and I buried her in a hug. It was hard to leave when she hadn't stopped crying since Presley left, but she had a community to support her and a boyfriend to hopefully keep her occupied. I knew she'd wait for my call though. Her number was already memorized.

"Bring your brothers with? I'll have plenty of room at the table. I'll finally let you use the good china."

"Sounds like a plan."

Kimberly had a vise grip on my mom's arm, keeping her upright. Mom was doing an equal amount of comforting by rubbing Kimberly's back.

It was harder than I thought to keep the smile on my face for them, but they needed me to be braver than I'd ever been. Brave like Luke had been for us all those years while his life crumbled. Luke's radiant smile gave me strength when Kimberly squeezed my neck like she'd never let go.

He'd done it for me. I could do it for them.

"Okay, I'll see you across the ocean, then?"

She nodded. I still smiled at her, knowing the next time I saw her she wouldn't be safe.

"You'll find me."

The plane's turbulence snapped me out of the memory, and I went to grip my armrests but both were occupied.

"How long till I see my brothers?" I asked the man beside me.

"About ten hours." The tall one spoke, never once looking at me.

"It's all of them, right? Zach, Luke, and Presley?" I asked. You know, in case I allowed myself to be taken by a different cult that dressed in black and waited for me at the airport.

He simply nodded.

"What else can you tell me?"

"We've been waiting for you," the other one said, staring out the window at the ground below.

That I already knew.

Sixty-Two

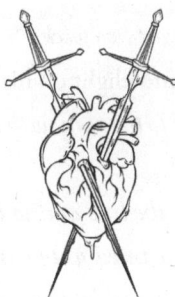

Our time in Alaska was over—at least for now. And as I stared out onto the field of snow, I knew I'd miss it. Though it had been without a doubt the most challenging months of my life and I was tired of snow melting into my socks, leaving brought a lump into my throat.

Aaron actually believed I'd let him go by himself. I smiled at the thought. After a couple hours, I'd felt the hollowness of his absence. Once, I'd grown so accustomed to doing everything on my own, but I looked over my shoulder wishing he were there to wrap his arm around me again. The absence of his support and warmth felt unnatural.

"Are you ready?" Kilian placed a passport in my hand.

I slid my sunglasses on. The illuminating glare from the snow and the metal of the small charter plane would have been enough to put me on my knees a few months ago. Now it was just mildly annoying.

Vera wanted to see me off, but I couldn't do that to her. I begged her to stay with her boyfriend while we were away so she wouldn't be alone. I knew she was waiting, and that was okay because someone would come for her. Even if that someone wasn't me.

"I'm ready."

Echoes of Kilian's and my conversation in his study replayed in my head. After talking with Cecily during the last ritual, I knew my plan had to change.

"I have to go too. I won't wait two weeks."

Kilian flinched and the candlelight on his desk deepened the wrinkles on his face. *"You're referring to the plan with Aaron and Presley... What do you know?"*

"I know Aaron's life is on the line and so is mine. Cecily said I needed to be there on the island if I wanted us to win ... that I might die, but it would save them. I can't wait and let them go alone. I have to go. I know you're going to try to tell me that it's too dangerous or that we're all your valuable little chess pieces and you can't risk it, but this is my family. I made a promise. I need to be there ... to die if that's what has to happen."

"Okay."

"Just like that?"

He nodded. *"I will adjust my plans and see what I can do as far as getting you to the country on your own."*

There was a brief silence between us, and I breathed in a sigh of relief.

"I won't stand in the way of you and your family. I promised I would not again."

The cold wind brought me back to reality.

I was alone again, standing next to a small charter plane while the wind blew fluffy snow onto my lashes.

"You'll arrive close to twenty-four hours after him with the drive and the ride over to the island. All you need to do is not get killed before we arrive."

I had no idea how I would manage that. Kilian needed me to fight . . . but maybe I wasn't even going to make it to the battle. Maybe I'd need to die beforehand.

"Just one." Cecily's words echoed in my head.

I'd have to play it by ear and be smart. I'd know the right time. Oddly enough, I wasn't scared all. I was only a little nervous to get on the plane, but dying . . . I could accept it if it saved my family, and that somehow made everything else feel unimportant.

I was to arrive on the mainland of Ireland and take over the ferry. Kilian mentioned someone would be waiting for me at the airport that could help guide me to the harbor.

"What about all of you?" I asked, staring at our group.

Only a handful had come to see me off. Felix and Halina—I think she made Felix come—Dom and Kilian.

"I promise on my brother's life we will come through for you."

Kilian's words startled me. He never sounded encouraging. Always stern and authoritative but never hopeful. I held out my hand to shake his. I'd finally made peace with our odd relationship.

Dom nodded. "We wouldn't let you go alone."

I hugged him, and Skylar was all I could think of. His body had no give.

He said, "She'd loved to see this."

I would make her proud one way or another. This was the path I'd chosen. I would protect my family, and like Skylar, I had a clear mission. If Aaron was the bait, I was the sacrifice. It would look like a clear surrender. Only, I wasn't sure if She'd let me live more than a few minutes with that decision.

Aaron never would have allowed it if he knew.

"One last thing." Kilian's jaw flexed. "You'll take the dagger along with you."

"What if they take it?"

"We'll know where to find it. It may prove useful to you before our arrival, and I wouldn't want to put you at a disadvantage. Try to keep track of it."

I wondered then if he trusted us to do this. Kilian stayed the same. We hadn't grown closer, and I was okay with that. Aaron had told me what Kilian had gone through with his brother, and though it didn't make me more inclined to trust or like him, I understood him more than I ever had.

Kilian lost his mind for love.

"Won't this be giving Her exactly what She wants?"

"Yes."

Kilian stared through me for a moment. There was more he couldn't say. We'd agreed not to know the plan. I'd also agreed to a suicide mission, which was likely exactly what Kilian needed. Possibly. Maybe.

It didn't matter. It wasn't something I needed to figure out. I needed to trust Aaron and his dream.

"Okay."

"You're the only one who can perform the ritual." Dom gave me an affirming nod.

"You're confident you can remember the transcripts?" Kilian asked.

"Yes, I've been practicing and writing them out daily."

It was imperative to learn the words on my own so I could tap back into the dagger's power and distract the queen while Kilian's men ambushed, whenever that would be. Because of Cecily, we discovered there was still power that could be tapped into during this moon cycle, but how strong it was, was still unknown.

"All right. I'm ready." Felix hadn't stopped swaying.

Halina interjected. "Me too. We'll see you on the other side, then, Burns?

"I . . . my last name is Calem. No matter what happens, please remember me like that. Kimberly Calem."

They nodded with reverence—Halina with a smile that reached her eyes, Dom loosened his shoulders, and even Felix met my eyeline and smirked—while Kilian bowed his head.

I couldn't see the future, but I knew that was the last time I'd ever set eyes on them all together at the same time. With the dagger in hand, I walked onto the plane and toward the fate of the stars.

Sixty-Three

AARON

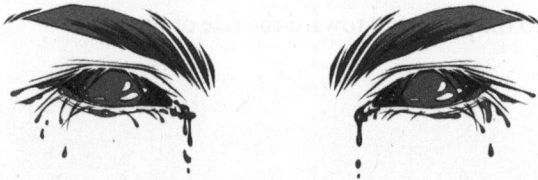

Holy hell. I'd forgotten about the color green. Thick fields of green peppered with little dots of white passed by in the distance.

I was thankful for the information Kilian didn't erase from my memory. The map of the castle was still there. I knew what to expect when the plane landed in Dublin, then we took another smaller plane to the far end of the island. It was all long rolling hills and farmhouses. We passed a town with colorful buildings and followed the road until the iron gate came into view.

Around it were trucks with their trailers filled with dirt and rock. There was a brief conversation with the man at the gate before the driver drove on. I caught a glimpse of a sign:

CLOSED – Attention Visitors and Residents: In order to maintain the island's natural landscape, a coastal erosion control and land preservation project is underway.

All of a sudden, I really hated being alone.

My heartbeat thrummed in my ears as the car winded up the drive and a castle came into view. The gray of the stone matched the sky, and the only color, other than the hills, were the stained-glass windows.

"They know I'm coming, right?" I asked the driver as the door opened for me.

As soon as I said it, I saw him.

Zach strolled across the yard from a large set of burned hedges. His head hung low with a cropped haircut I didn't recognize, but I'd know my brother anywhere.

"Zach." His name caught in my throat.

I smiled. The relief ran over me in waves. He was alive. I'd made my way back to them. All those months of wondering and wishing were done.

He stopped in his tracks.

Our eyes met across the courtyard, and I swallowed. There was no way he knew I was coming because the anger in his eyes made me feel like I was five years old again. *Oh, he's so pissed.*

He stalked toward me, and I had the strangest urge to run and hide. I was unbelievably happy to see my brother, but it didn't matter because he was going to kick my ass.

The men around me bowed as he approached.

"Move," he said, and they all scattered.

"Hi."

He yanked the collar of my shirt and pulled me to walk with him. "Move your fuckin' ass."

"Miss me?"

"Don't talk."

He led me through a large set of doors already propped open and waiting, then down a few halls of ornate wallpaper and lit candles before shoving me into a room that looked to be a small office. And judging by the amount of dust, it wasn't a room they used often.

I opened my mouth to speak, and Zach shoved me into the wall, the plaster cracked beneath.

"Ow."

The pain ran up my spine, and the force drew the breath out of my lungs. When Zach shoved me, it was rarely that hard.

"Why the hell are you here?"

"I thought that was obvious. I came for you."

He scoffed, his eyes boring a hole into me like he wanted to set me on fire. "I should kill you myself for being such a worthless little brother."

I held my hands up while Zach's fingers curled around the edges of my collared shirt, and he shoved me again. Pain ran up my spine, but I said nothing.

He continued, "I should have known you would fuck this up. I mean, what the fuck? How could you let Presley come here?"

"How is he?" I asked, a little too desperately.

"He's fucking fine. No thanks to you!" He pressed his thumb into my arm until I cried out in pain. "He's with Luke."

Luke's name sent a shiver up my spine. "Where are they? I want to see them."

"I'm not done with you yet."

"You going to torture me?"

"I haven't decided yet."

Zach lowered his brow into a deadpan expression, and he got inches from my face. My brother was serious. Kilian was right. That place was changing them, but nothing my brother would say could hurt me. I'd missed my annoying, hotheaded older brother. Even the rage I couldn't stand, I loved as it was being directed at me. I'd missed it so much I wanted him to keep talking.

"Does it make you feel better?" I asked calmly.

"Does what make me feel better?"

"Using me as your punching bag."

He grunted, pulling my shirt tighter.

"You can be mean to me all you want. It doesn't change anything. I came here to save you."

Something in his gaze shifted; his brow softened, and I was dropped to the floor.

"You really piss me off. You know that?"

"You've definitely told me that before, I'm pretty sure."

He shook his head and stared out the window to a charred lawn. "You shouldn't have come. And Pres, why the fuck is he here?"

There was a desperation in his voice, like he was pleading with me to give him a good solid answer beyond the one I had.

"He ran away. He came here for you . . . to be with you."

"Fuck." He rubbed his hands over his eyes and rested his head in his hands.

I'd seen him tired before, but not like this. The castle had been their reality for months. While I'd rested every night in safety with my head on a pillow, what had Zach and Luke done? I'd thought about it every day, but suddenly, I wanted to know even more. Something told me they weren't allowed the same safety I had. The walls weren't warm and inviting. Everything was cold like my brother's expression when he turned to face me again.

"I'm sorry it took so long. But I'm here now and I'm not leaving without you."

"No one ever leaves this place."

This time I smiled. "You underestimate me."

He shook his head. "Stay here. Do. Not. Leave."

"Where am I going to go?"

"I know you. I swear if I come back and you're gone—"

"I'll stay." I looked up at the tall ceilings of the library. "Seems cool in here anyway."

Once he was gone, I moved quickly throughout the room, logging it into my memory.

The walls were white plaster, and at the far end had three glass windows that almost reached the ceilings. A chandelier with faux candles hung overhead.

I was alone in the castle, and I might not be again. I needed to use it to my advantage.

The books lining the shelves were old and worn, much like the books Kilian made us sort through. Only, this library was neater, dusty but well kept, and no books crowded the floor like the ones I'd had to dodge in Kilian's office.

I was used to looking at old books. To the untrained eye, all the books were the same, but there were tells. Foiled lettering on the spine. Deckled edges. The most important books with texts Kilian found interesting were falling apart. Some of them were quickly scribbled notes with ink and bound like the world might crumble if the thoughts weren't put to page in a matter of seconds.

I asked myself where I'd keep the most important books, first scaling the ladder to the second story, but most of those books were too caked with dust, left untouched and likely unimportant.

I sifted through the shelves on the lower end until one caught my eye on a bottom shelf, and the spine was black. No lettering but not a speck of dust. When I pulled it, I stopped to feel the etching in the bottom right of the leather.

Eros.

The pages were plenty worn, like they'd been turned many times over and over. It was a diary. I could tell by the dates barely visible at the top.

No year listed. Just little symbols of the moon scrawled in ink on each page. I grabbed it and brought it by the light of the window. I imagined Eros jotting down his thoughts and gazing out a window at the moon.

I flipped the pages for anything useful. Like all of Kilian's books, it was hard to read, but I landed on a page worn above all the others.

For in death, there is also life. To rid the world of the scourge would be to die encased in ice. But to die would be at the loss of My Love. But to gain My Love is to lose one's lifeblood. My Love will persevere evermore. But my life's blood will die in vain.

My heartbeat was in my ears. There was that word again. *Lifeblood.*

Darkness cleaves on every side. Bonds forged with blood must be put to rest.

~~The dagger. Where is the dagger?~~

The end was scrawled out with rips in the paper.

It wasn't all poems. Some of it was confusing accounts of events that mentioned no names I understood. Times with Her, mostly in Her room, then a garden. He was angry about something. Sometimes he's scribbled at the edge of the page, and he used a lot of exclamations.

Today, I care only of slicing through the heart of My Love.

Hatred taints my soul. She leaves me vacant.

My lifeblood is my only existence left.

Only the next day, it was different.

She called me long before life. She will call to me in death, and I will answer Her every time.

Born to be Her love, but not the lover. I am Her Guardian.

Footsteps were coming down the hall. I flipped in one desperate last attempt until I landed on one of the last entries.

During a New Moon:

Sirius, my lifeblood, remember us—

As the door opened, I'd already placed the book back on the shelf.

Luke entered. The weight of seeing him again almost brought me to the floor. I rushed to pull him into a hug. After imagining it so many times, I expected it to bring me relief, for all that pain I'd felt for months to melt away, but he didn't hug back.

He held me by the shoulders to look at me. "Tell me right now. Why are you here?"

"Hi, brother!" Presley came in and shut the door behind him.

I was trying to take it all in at once. The style of Luke's hair made him almost unrecognizable, along with the gaunt, colorless look of his skin. He wasn't shiny anymore, and that was just Luke. Presley's clothes had changed too. I knew who it reminded me of, and I was too afraid to think of his name.

"Pres." He let me wrap him in a hug, but it was brief. "Tell me you're okay."

A little more than a day, but it was torture not knowing for sure.

"I'm great! Seriously, this place is awesome."

There was something different about him too. Presley was normally fidgety, but he was pulling at the skin of his nails and shifting from one foot to the next.

"Wait. What happened to you?" I knew the answer.

"I went to a church and drank some blood. Lots of it."

It took a beat for me to register it.

"You drank Her blood? When? How?"

"You haven't?" Luke asked.

I ignored him. "Pres, answer me."

"I had another clue."

"They lured you."

"No! They guided me. Akira knew that I would follow the notes. He was right. This whole time, they knew Kilian was trying to get in the way of our destiny. This is fate. She told me so. She said that we're late. That we could have been happier a lot earlier, and She'd seen it so many times, but we never showed up when we were supposed to. We kept Her waiting, but it doesn't matter now because we're all going to be together."

"Do you hear yourself?"

Presley nudged Luke. "He might need to be mind wiped. Kilian's got his claws in deep."

"Pres." I huffed. It was naive of me not to consider the possibility of him having access to more of Her blood, but I hadn't, and he was already so different. I let out a breath to calm the anxiety building in my chest.

"Don't be mad," Presley said.

"I'm not . . . I'm mad at myself."

He shook his head. "You don't get it. You couldn't prevent this. It's our destiny."

"Both of you, be quiet. Answer Luke's question." Zach nudged me again.

"I just explained it."

"Explain it again." Luke pushed me too. There was a lot more pushing than I'd anticipated.

I knew what this looked like to them. Their little brother who didn't understand what we were up against came with no plan. To them, I was still too young to understand anything, but that boy was long gone. I understood the darkness. Even if I hadn't experienced all they'd witnessed, I could sense their protectiveness and see it in the fear in their eyes. They were afraid, but they didn't have to protect me anymore. I had more than a half-baked Calem plan.

"He said he came for us," Zach said.

Luke looked at me with a mixture of fear and anger swirling. He was calculating it in his head of a way to get us out of this, crafting another plan, but he had changed too. He looked like he'd had the flu for weeks.

Thin in the cheeks, even though I wasn't sure that was possible for us.

"You don't have to protect me anymore. I'm here to save you. We're going to leave together."

"You don't know what you're saying."

"I do! It's just like you've always said. We don't give up. There's always a way to turn things around. And now you don't have to do it alone. I can help you now like I wasn't able to before. We can fix this."

"You were supposed to stay home and enjoy your life with Kimberly and Pres and Mom. Everything was fine until Presley and you showed up."

Presley interjected. "Hey."

"No talking," Zach said.

"Liar," I said. Bile built in my throat. Luke wasn't a liar, and the fact he said the words led me to believe he thought it was true. "We felt your pain every day. You left, and everything got worse. We missed you so much. Like it or not, because we drank Akira's blood, we could feel everything you felt. We were connected the whole time."

Luke spoke to Zach with his twin telepathy. I'd missed how annoying it was.

Luke's once warm irises were dark. "This is the prophecy coming true. It's all true. Everything She said."

I expected Zach to protest, but he, too, had that same look of fear.

What had happened to my brothers? I remembered Presley's sobbing on the floor of Mom's cabin and how badly he'd hurt. That pain came from Zach and Luke. I felt guilty for not shouldering the weight, but now I knew why. Because of the bond I had with Kimberly, we had an opening. *I was the opening. And you were the key.*

"We have to get out of here. Do it for our family. Do it for yourself. For Sarah."

Luke flinched like I'd hit him, then looked at Zach. Zach's harder exterior cracked for a moment and anguish flashed on his face.

"What?"

"Nothing. He . . . he doesn't remember."

"You don't remember Sarah . . . How?"

"Long story," Zach said, averting his eyes.

She'd taken his memory of Sarah. No wonder he was acting so strange. Something had happened. Something terrible.

Luke closed his eyes and shook his head. "Doesn't matter. We aren't going anywhere."

"We can fix this. Kilian is coming, and there's going to be a fight."

"We know," Zach growled.

"Teach me how to sound all scary like that," Presley said.

Luke's head shot up. "They'll kill you for siding with him. You're making this worse. Nothing is safe here. I can't protect you from everything."

"And I'm telling you, you don't need to. All I need you to do is follow me. Believe in me."

"I can't," Luke said through gritted teeth.

Okay, things weren't going well, but Kilian had prepared me for that. Sure, I'd hoped they could be convinced with a simple conversation, but that was wishful thinking. It wouldn't be that easy, but I had plenty of time to change their minds.

Presley watched me with a smirk. "Aaron, you don't understand anything. You haven't felt the bond with Her yet. You're gonna flip. There's nothing like it."

"He's right . . . you didn't drink yet. You came on your own, which further proves that this was fate," Luke said.

"No. I came because I wanted to get you so we could get out of here."

"You've always been such a rule follower." Presley snickered.

"Luke?" Zach set his jaw, awaiting Luke's decision on something.

Luke looked down briefly at his hands, then nodded.

"Take him to Her. She'll make him drink."

"What?! Luke!?" I backed up, but Zach and Presley grabbed my arms.

"I know. It won't force the bond, but it will make it easier for you to accept eventually. It will make this entire place easier for you to accept. And She'll be merciful to you."

"What are you talking about? I don't want to accept it! We have to get out."

"I know. I'm sorry, Aaron. But we can't leave. It's impossible. And you're just going to get hurt trying. She'll punish you and . . . it's easier this way. I promise. I'll make sure you and Presley don't struggle like Zach and I did. I'm protecting you. I know it doesn't feel that way—"

"No, it really doesn't!"

They were already dragging me out of the door and into the hallway. I tried to grab the doorframe but three against one was unfair.

"This is for your own good. He's right. I never feel sad here. It's great." Presley was remarkably stronger than I'd remembered.

Even if I could weasel away from his grip, there was nothing breaking Zach's death grip on my arm.

"It doesn't have to be this way." I tried to get my footing, but it was useless.

"It really does. You won't last five seconds here. We're doing you a huge favor," Zach said.

"You'll love Her, Aaron. I'll make sure everything goes smoothly. You won't get hurt. It will be okay." Luke looked back to me with somber eyes.

He was grasping at straws and actually believed he was doing the right thing. I had to keep calm. Even if I drank Her blood, nothing would happen. We expected this. It was all part of the plan.

I felt sick to my stomach, and not just because I was being dragged by my brothers to a demon queen. That wasn't nearly as terrifying as knowing my older brothers had been so traumatized by what had happened they couldn't imagine a better future. I let it fuel me. I would have to lie convincingly.

"I'm sorry, Aaron." Luke swallowed and looked away. "This place will break you. I won't let that happen."

"It's okay, Luke."

I was going to convince my brothers to fight even if it was the last thing I'd ever do.

Sixty-Four

AARON

The steeple of the cathedral grew nearer and nearer. I'd tried to get a feel for the castle, but there wasn't any use because they'd dragged me down the hall and through a door that led outside. The men we passed bowed and averted their gaze at the sight of my brothers. The air smelled of ash and ocean water. I thought I'd spotted a huge pile of ash off in the distance, but I'd had no time to gawk at the landscape in my predicament.

The doors of the cathedral opened, and I stumbled inside. Underneath my feet was a cracked marble floor. Something about it seemed oddly familiar.

My brothers pushed me farther inside until I saw Her. The other two Guard members were at Her side, waiting for me.

"You're late" was the first thing She said with Her eyes on me.

I'd dreaded that moment and secretly wondered if when I set eyes on Her I'd crumble into dust at Her feet, but the woman in front of me wasn't ethereal and otherworldly beautiful. She was a woman whose skin was gaunt and dry from the cold. The closer they brought me, the more of Her flaws I could see: the crepe skin on Her hands and the lines by Her eyes. Like that place, She was a master illusion, a mirage, and now that Her blood didn't affect me at all, I saw Her for what She was. A shell of a woman possessed by something draining the life out of Her barely living body.

"Hi." It was the only word I could recall.

Luke forced my head down to bow.

She spoke. "Our family is finally complete. A momentous occasion."

Neither of the other Guard members smiled. Ezra—I remembered with his piercing eyes—stared me up and down like I might bolt. The person next to him, I guessed, was Sirius.

"What do you mean I'm late?"

"We expected you on another moon." She smiled, and Her arm beckoned me.

My stomach was in my throat. All I had to do was keep everything under wraps. Easy, in theory.

"I already told Her everything," Presley said, with his voice echoing.

"Boy," Sirius cautioned Presley, "what did we discuss about talking out of turn?"

Some deep grumbling came from Zach's chest, and he put himself between the two. "Watch the way you talk to my brother."

She smiled. "Families sometimes take time to understand each other."

"You told Her?"

"He showed me everything. Your childhood. Your time in Blackheart . . . and your secret hideaway with your lover."

I was suddenly thankful Kilian had the caution to keep our heads free of the plan. We didn't know their exact arrival time or their plans to infiltrate, but one thing Kilian hadn't taken . . .

I opened my mouth to speak, and She stopped me.

"Not to worry." She moved Her fingers through my hair, and chills ran up my spine.

"Stop."

Her face fell.

"Luke, please . . . you have to help me. Don't make me do this," I said.

"It's not bad if you don't fight!" Presley said.

Sirius grumbled.

I backed away from Her before I was stopped by Luke's shoulder.

"Is there any way he can have a few days to adjust?" Luke asked.

"We need the information of Kilian's plan," Sirius said.

"But he won't give it up easily," Luke stated.

"Torture it outta him!" Presley said.

Zach held up a finger to silence him.

I let them bicker. If She was in my head, She would know everything about Kimberly. I'd lose my only edge. If I told them Kilian wiped my memory, that might prompt Her to want to check.

"Darling, is something bothering you?" She looked over to Zach who was now pacing in circles.

Darling?

Zach scoffed. "Yes, *Dear*. I am."

He spat Her pet name like an insult. There was real hatred there, yet his eyes softened when he looked to Her.

"I know how this is going to end. You're going to force your way into his head, and it's going to put us all on our ass. They haven't ascended yet. We feel everything that they feel, and that shit hurts."

"He's right. We need to be prepping for The Legion's arrival. We won't be as useful if it's anything like the last few months have been," Luke said.

They still believed we were all bonded. Even if Presley had told them everything, they couldn't have confirmed it.

"Then maybe you'll finally reach your true potential and harden yourself for your queen," Sirius said.

"Fuck you. No one is talking to you either," Zach spat. "I've proven my loyalty over and over."

"He's right to consider it," Ezra said. "But I agree and plead on Luke's behalf for more time."

She watched me. Her hands moved to my arm, and I had to act like it affected me. Like it was anywhere near the feeling of Kimberly's embrace. I had to say something.

"Kilian kept my head clean too. I don't know about their plans."

"He's lying," Sirius said.

"Silence all. Let him speak," She said. Her long slender fingers raked across my cheek.

"I'll take your blood to prove my loyalty. Will that be enough for now?"

I stared into Her light-gray irises. I needed to prove myself with something that would satisfy everyone in the room.

"Luke said . . . it would make everything easier."

"It will." She knit Her hands into the hair at the nape of my neck, then pulled Her hair to the side.

The urge to bolt ran through me. I thought of Kimberly and wanted to go to her. The queen forced me closer till my lips were at the nape of Her neck, and I bit down, letting Her blood into my veins, but nothing good rushed through me. Just the anxiety of knowing I needed to put on a show for Her.

And that I did. I gripped Her cheek and drank deeper. The disgust was the only thing making my hands shake, but it tasted like nothing. I let Her pull away first.

"There. He did it. Can we help him get settled in now?" Zach asked.

My eyes settled on Luke who said nothing. It wasn't like him. Everything was strange and horrible.

"Yes, find him a suitable room."

Presley skipped to sit closest to Her and began stroking Her hair.

"What should we do now? Maybe you want me to wash your hair? I can massage your feet, braid your hair . . ." He traced the skin on Her arms. "Please, anything you want."

My stomach turned.

"Oh! I could paint your nails too."

She placed Her hand on his cheek. "Whatever you want. I'm yours."

Zach grabbed my shirt to drag me again.

"Wait, what about Luke?"

"He's sworn himself to Presley's side. Wherever he goes, Luke will stay. I guess I'm going to have to do the same to you now. Are you all right? After the blood."

"Yeah, I feel . . . like I want more." I thought back to the ravenous hunger I'd felt before. I'd have been consumed and overtaken if not for the bond Kimberly and I had broken. There was a little relief in the thought. *Our opening worked.*

"Get used to it." Zach dragged me out the door.

Sixty-Five

KIMBERLY

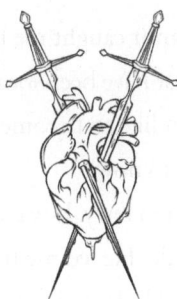

I arrived at the harbor and the fresh scent of dead fish greeted me. The sun peeked through the clouds and a fresh drizzle of rain was soaking the boats and harbor signs. A plane ride to Dublin, then another long car ride over to the ferry was torture. Every minute I didn't have eyes on the boys filled me with dread. I had a vise grip on my backpack strap, and with every step I took, it tightened.

It felt dangerous to have the dagger secured to my back, but Kilian must have some plan for it. Maybe he figured out something about it, like the proximity would weaken Her or something. There was a reason, but I reminded myself I didn't need to figure it out. My job was to go to the island.

A boy greeted me with golden-blond curls and blue eyes. He had to have just turned eighteen. Not much younger than me.

"Kimberly." His eyes widened like he was surprised to see me, and I wasn't the least bit surprised he knew my name. "You came."

"Were you expecting me?"

"She was. Maybe. She said it was likely you could show up today . . . or not at all. The ferry is closed to the public for now, but it's open for you. My name's Connell."

He held out his hand for me to shake, and I did.

"Hi, Connell."

His calm, cheerful demeanor caught me by surprise. His Irish accent was thick, indicating he must have been local. I briefly thought of what his life story must have been like to become a part of The Family, then resolved it was better I didn't know.

I followed him onto a barren ferry. It was a large barge with windows, and seating inside and outside. He led me to the back of the ship, and I looked out along the water. There in the distance, the island sat among gray clouds. It was a relief seeing it, knowing all the people I cared about most were there.

"I, uh . . . I need to bite you," he said.

"What?"

"I should technically just grab you and not give you a choice. This isn't a choice because I have to, but it would be easier if you just let me do it. I'm supposed to weaken you since you're, uh . . . one of us."

I checked we were out of view of any bystanders at the harbor.

"Okay."

I held my arm for him, and he hesitated. I thought he was more nervous than me until he closed the distance between us and grabbed me to sink his teeth into my neck.

It hurt, but it was brief. I gripped the guardrail and counted my way through it. The intimacy of it made my skin crawl. He didn't take everything. Just enough for me to feel human again. Which I didn't mind so much.

"Sorry about that." He pulled a handkerchief from the little pocket on his black blazer, and I used it to wipe the blood from my neck, with one hand still on the guardrail. If someone would have told me last spring that I'd be here, I would have never believed them. It was more unbelievable than vampires existing. I was in another country, far away from Blackheart—a place I thought I'd never leave, and I was going on account of someone else, sailing toward my fate that was more than likely my death. It felt good not to be running anymore and to finally face our problems head-on.

As I peered at the castle coming into view, a strange sense of doom and peace lingered. Like that place had waited for me my entire life. The thick green grass on the rolling hills and the stone wall high in the sky beckoned me forward, yearning to swallow me whole, but I wouldn't be easy prey.

It was amazing how freeing it felt to be a dead girl walking.

When we reached the shore, Connell led me off the boat toward the castle that loomed in the distance. I recalled the map as I walked. There were two harbors on the island. One close to the castle that worked through the island's tour service, and the other was reserved for merchant ship goods. A sparse forest covered a small portion of the grounds, and on the other side of the path, I spotted two black masses. One appeared to be old wood. A structure had burned to nothing but black ash and a few pieces of wood, and closer to the castle was a set of tall leafy hedges. As we walked around the path, most of the hedges were burned and charred. They surrounded a statue I couldn't fully see. A vast expanse of gray ash marked the earth below the hedges.

"There was a fire a few days ago. Pretty wild. Really shook things up." Connell's soft voice made me jump.

A set of hands grabbed me from behind, and I pushed back on my heels and used my weight to throw them off balance. My attacker landed on the grass with a thud.

"Presley," I breathed.

"You. I've been waiting for you."

"What are you doing?" I asked, checking for more of his brothers.

"Hiding from Luke. Come on." He grabbed my hand and pulled me toward the castle. "I've got it from here Connell!"

"But sir—"

"It's fine! Don't tell anyone she's here yet."

Presley's fingernails dug into my palm as he walked me toward the castle. I searched for the sounds of the twins or Aaron. Or the smell of anything familiar. He dragged me through the hallway a little too forcefully. With the blood loss, I could barely keep myself upright. It was all a vivid blur.

Where was Aaron?

Everything about Presley had changed. Not just his clothes that were now all black, with black boots that looked too big for his stature and a long black coat with a tight undershirt. His expression was twisted in an unfamiliar scowl that didn't belong on his face.

He pulled me into a room and locked the door behind us. A dining room. A little like Kilian's with a long table and chairs, but these were ornate and likely expensive. Every design choice, from the rugs to dusty lavender candles in the chandelier above, seemed intentional.

With one arm, he shoved me into a chair.

"I thought you'd know better than to come. You know, because you're the smart one." He stepped onto the table and walked, kicking off the ornate chargers and table runner. *Uh-oh.*

It hadn't occurred to me that Presley could be dangerous. In all the scenarios, I hadn't thought of it once. The Presley I knew wouldn't hurt me. How much could one person change so drastically in a matter of days?

He crouched down to my level. "You look a little scared. There's nothing to be afraid of. This place is amazing. And these people . . . they love me."

The sun from the window cast a long shadow over his face. This wasn't Presley. There was barely any light left in his eyes.

"But I guess this isn't a social call, huh? You being here can mean only one thing . . . you want Her."

"I came for you actually."

"Oh really . . ." He moved behind me and snatched the bag from my shoulder. "What did you bring me as a housewarming gift?"

He pulled out the dagger, and my blood ran cold. With a lightness in his steps, he jumped up and onto the table again.

"Presley . . ."

"Don't say my name like that. You're just trying to manipulate me. That's what She said you'd do. Try to make me feel sorry for you. She said I may not even have to see you again, but I guess . . . this is a different timeline."

A different timeline. A different future than this one.

"I would have preferred the other. But of course you'd want this one. You'd want to hurt me and hurt Her. So that means . . . I have to hurt you."

He stalked toward me, with the dagger gleaming in the light. Was this it? Was this the part where I met my fate? Something about it didn't feel right. I wouldn't hurt Presley. I couldn't, but I also couldn't let Presley do something he'd never be able to forgive himself for. He was making it out of the castle alive. That was nonnegotiable.

"Wait. We can talk about this."

"Why would I waste my time in eternity talking to you when I could be talking to Her instead? You're not even supposed to be here. I could have been with Her way earlier than this, but you just had to come into our lives. You ruined everything. And for that, I have to hurt you."

Presley plunged the dagger into my leg, and every muscle in my body seized. I cried out, and the shock of it caused an agonizing panic in my entire body. I fought to steady my breath so I could remain present.

Something stronger burned in my veins as the adrenaline surged. This was Her fault. She did this to him.

Presley laughed in the wake of my pain. Not his usual chiming laughter that filled every room with a sense of ease. It was hard and forced through his chest.

"She doesn't like you, you know? You're just a blip. A blip in time, and you mean nothing. That's what She said when I asked Her about you. When I showed Her you and everything we've done together."

"You showed Her?"

"I had to. She needed to see everything. I hide nothing from Her. The only way to ascend is to surrender, and She says I'm close. Not long now and I'll ascend just like Zach and Luke."

I tried to move, and a soft cry left my lips.

"You shouldn't move around. You'll just make this harder on everyone. Especially me. Why did you come, knowing this would happen? Knowing I'd be like this and I'd have to eliminate you from my life. Why did you do that to me?" There was a soft pleading in his voice.

"I came to save you. I'd never want to hurt you. You know that."

He shook his head and slammed his hands on the table, making me jolt.

"You're lying!" He reached down, twisting the dagger in my leg. Tears spilled down my cheeks.

I grabbed his hand smeared with my blood, and he didn't pull away.

It was worse than any nightmare. Worse than dying. The pulsing pain in my leg was nothing compared to seeing my best friend change and suffer before my eyes. That pain bubbled over into anger. It replaced the lump in my throat with bile I wanted to spit on the ground.

"It felt right. It made sense. But you're here. I don't understand. Why is this so hard? She said nothing would hurt anymore, but you're crying . . . and now I feel . . . You're not supposed to matter. Why do you matter? You're just a girl. One stupid girl."

Tear after tear fell as the blood from my leg seeped into my pants. Tears gathered in his eyes too. We were still connected somehow.

"This is how it has to be . . . right?" Presley's eyes softened. "We all can't exist here. You knew that, but you came anyway. You came here for me . . . for us."

"I'd always come for you. There's nowhere else I'd rather be than right here with you." I said it slowly, breathing through the blinding pain in my leg.

"You can't mean that. After everything, you don't mean it. Don't lie."

"I'm not lying."

His face grew redder, and his tears turned into sobs. "Stop."

"Remember the patch of land with the little cabins. And you were going to put yours next to mine. And you told me you were going to paint something cool over the door. Daisies and dandelions, we said. We can still do those things. That dream isn't gone forever. I'm still here. And we're going to be together again. Away from this place."

Tears fell from his cheeks and onto the linen. He leaned forward, grabbing the handle of the dagger and pulled it from my leg in one quick swipe. There was a slight relief, but the pain made me tremble.

"Stop, Kim. Stop." Something in me broke at the mention of my name.

"I love you, Presley. It's going to be okay. Don't cry. We can fix this."

It was a relief when the door opened. Luke emerged, and I was sure all the color drained out of the room. He looked ghastly with dark circles under his eyes and a determined, stern expression. My memory of him in the forest, when he'd entrusted me with his brothers, replayed in my head.

"Luke . . ." My voice broke. I'd scarcely realized how much I'd missed seeing him. I'd missed his sureness. His strength. His help. God, I'd missed his help.

But what I remembered of him was long gone. There was no warmth left in his skin or his smile. In three months, he's been gutted from the inside out, leaving someone I didn't recognize.

He didn't look at me. Not even a brief glance. He was less than an arm's distance away. I could have touched his jacket, yet I feared the man standing before me.

"Hey, it's all right." He grabbed Presley's face in his hands.

He sounded like Luke. It was all still in there. The warmth. The love he held for his brothers. So unbelievably real and visceral I almost forgot about the pain in my leg.

"No. No. No. She can't be here. I need to kill her, and I can't. I can't. She's not supposed to be here." He wiped his face, where my blood stained his cheeks.

"You don't need to do anything. It's going to be okay. You'll see." He pulled Presley to his chest and kissed the top of his head.

"Luke." I tried to make my voice stronger this time, but he ignored me.

"Give me the dagger." He pried the knife from Presley's hand.

My heart beat faster as he turned. How far gone was Luke? No. Maybe he just couldn't acknowledge me. She might not like that. He wouldn't hurt me.

He put the dagger in his jacket and moved toward the door. "Pick her up. She belongs to the queen."

"Wait!" I said as Presley lifted me and threw me over my shoulder.

Sixty-Six

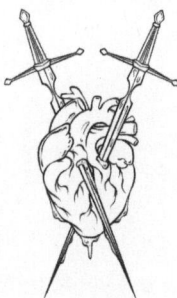

The Legion would come soon. That's the thing I had to recite over and over again as Presley effortlessly carried me over his shoulder. When they slowed, I flew forward, and Presley caught me. His arm wrapped around my neck to cover my mouth.

Ezra's icy blue eyes stared back at me. I'd never forget seeing Ezra's face after the day in the burning forest.

"You have to help me," Luke said. "I don't know what to do."

"This is the girl."

"Yes. I need to take her to the queen . . . but . . . She can't kill her. I can't let that happen. I don't know what to do with her, but I just know that. It's . . . confusing. Doesn't make sense."

"Give her to me. I'll take her. You go get your brothers and bring them

404

into the atrium. Quickly."

"She had this!" Presley grabbed the dagger from Luke and handed it to him.

Luke hesitated, his shoulder rigid, and pulled back.

"I'll take care of it. Just bring them."

Luke nodded and Presley released me. My heart hadn't stopped beating against my ribs since I'd reached the harbor, and in combination with the blood loss, it made me feel lightheaded.

Ezra clutched my arm to steady me.

"Can you walk?"

I nodded.

"Good. Don't talk."

He didn't pull me nearly as fast as Presley, but I still struggled to keep up as we navigated the halls. We stopped in front of a wooden door carved with the sun and the moon. It opened to a room floored in intricate marble bathed in the sun.

"Kimberly Burns. We finally meet."

Her voice cut the air like a blade. Standing next to a man, I guessed to be Sirius, was the queen. I'd often wondered what it might feel like to finally stand in Her presence. Cecily came to mind. The warmth in her cheeks and the green of her eyes had been leached from her. The woman in front of me was a ghost of the girl who once roamed the halls.

"Speak, girl," the man with brown hair and warm skin said.

"Now, Sirius, she's our guest. Let's not be inhospitable."

I guessed right.

"I've heard nothing but terrible things," I said.

Ezra's pressure on my arm tightened.

"Is that so? And here I thought all of the Calem boys were such lovely gentlemen. They're so trusting and sweet." She stepped toward me. Her bare feet made no sound on the floor. "I met your lover not long ago.

He's extraordinary. I see why you're so fond of him. He had quite the appetite."

I bit down on my cheek as the fire reignited in my belly. The image of Aaron drinking from Her was enough to bring me back into the present and ignore the lingering pain in my leg.

It was part of the plan. It was fine.

"What do you want with me?"

"So many things. You see . . . you're quite the pest. We didn't squash you soon enough, and you've turned into a full infestation." Her gown trailed behind Her, and She closed the distance between us. "Infestations must be dealt with accordingly."

I flinched as She reached for my cheek, and the world fell away.

Let's see who Kimberly Burns really is.

Panic burst through my chest. I couldn't feel my hands or my feet. It was just me and Her in my head.

Focus. Show me. Now.

Before I could protest, my memory fluttered by. I was back in foster care, sitting alone on my bed looking out the window. Crying. Sobbing into my hands.

My head pulsed like it was being sawed in half. Flashes of light and images pushed me along in the vast expanse of my mind. She was raking her nails through my childhood. That's what it felt like. Her fingers scratched at the back of my skull and pulled up every memory in Her wake. Excruciating. Unbearable. It had to stop.

"Stop." I barely managed the words.

The world returned, and I crumpled up on the floor, and my face was wet.

She laughed. "You've always been so painfully alone. Longing for bonds . . . It must be terrible knowing you have nothing now."

Her palm rested on my cheek delicately, and She dug her long nails into my face. The blood trickled down my cheek, and I licked it from my lip.

"I'm going to love combing through every single one of your sad little memories. We can have so much fun together."

Ezra interjected. "My queen . . . if I may."

"Yes, you may speak."

"It will not be wise to torture her now, and killing her isn't favorable."

"Ezra," Sirius growled a warning.

"The Legion is nearly at our door. This girl is important to the Calems. Doing anything to interfere with their emotional state at such a vulnerable impasse is ill-advised."

"Ill-advised. You baby them. She is too dangerous to keep alive," Sirius said.

"I'm aware of all the possibilities." She leaned into my ear. "That's the only reason I don't have your pretty little heart in my hands right now."

I swallowed.

"What's this?"

Her attention turned to the ring on my hand. Cold fingers wrapped around my hand and yanked the ring off without mercy.

Her eyes darkened as She examined it in the light from the glass ceiling. "He gave this to you?"

"We're married."

"So you are." Her fingers brushed the gold band. "Such a small delicate little thing."

Without another word, She pushed my ring onto Her finger.

"Fits perfectly. I'll hold on to it for you. You won't be needing it anymore."

Warmth pooled in my cheeks, and my eyes stung. My stomach burned with anger. This was just another one of Her tactics for getting into my head.

"I'll get it back eventually."

"You're so confident."

"I'm alive, aren't I?"

"For now. There are still so many variables at play. *Can't you read the stars?*"

I lifted my head again to meet Her eyeline. She knew.

"You know about the rituals . . ."

"Presley might not have had all the plans, but he remembered you using the dagger to get to me. I guess you could say we're linked now. No matter. I'll be sure to sever that bond." She grabbed the dagger. "I was hoping you'd bring me this."

The Legion were coming, I reminded myself again, but it could be a week . . . weeks . . . longer. I would likely be tortured for as long as I was in Her presence. But maybe that was the right future, maybe that's what would save them.

She handed the dagger to Sirius, and he walked in behind me.

A sharp pain cut through my shoulder. The warmth of my blood slipped down my back.

It's okay. Do it for them.

"Shall we bleed her now?"

"Patience, Sirius. Let's see the lovers' reunion first. Shallow cuts only. I want to hear her sing like a songbird."

Sixty-Seven

AARON

Something was wrong. I could feel it in my gut. Everyone dispersed over the castle grounds. Zach barked orders at the other members. The serious kind—telling them to wait by the harbor and kill anyone they see. We went to the basement and told someone named Henderson he was to secure their blood bag supply and move it upstairs so it could be accessed easier. Everyone seemed to have a job. I caught whisperings of my brothers' names, but mostly, I heard mumblings of something called *The Divine Path*. When I asked Zach about it, he told me to not ask questions. Especially when I asked about the whereabouts of Will and Thane. It was too early to give up.

Presley sat with me on my bed all night long—poking me in the temple.

"Tell me a story."

"No."

"But I'm bored."

"Okay, well, I can't help it."

I'd been given one job. Watch Presley. That was the only way Luke would leave his side, and Zach mine. It was a long night. Presley wouldn't shut up about the queen.

Someone named Connell guarded our door. We'd been given a room in the castle with two beds on either side of a large window. Yet Presley insisted on sitting on mine with me. I didn't mind. At least I could see him with my own eyes and know he was safe from harm, but he wasn't my brother. She'd changed him like She'd changed them all, and every minute we sat together, the fear of the unknown grew. I'd stared at the stars all night trying to absorb the new information, while the northern lights danced across the sky in a bright brilliance display.

The news had said tonight was supposed to be even brighter. It felt like I was stuck in a nightmare.

"Hey, speak when I ask you a question." Zach tugged on my collar and pulled me back to the present. One unpleasant side effect of that place was that my brother was leaning into his worst traits. In Blackheart, my older brother had softened, but no remnants of that progress remained.

"What?"

He dragged me away from Henderson to a garden.

"You're sure your memory isn't feeling a little more jogged today? Nothing you want to tell me about The Legion and their plan."

"Nope."

"She'll get it from you. Sirius and Ezra are hoping you'll feel more cooperative today, which means they're going to go rummaging through your head."

"Let them. Presley was there when Kilian took our memories of the battle plans."

"Doesn't mean you don't know anything that would help us."

"*Us*? So you're definitely siding with The Family?"

"Well, I'm sure as shit not going to help Kilian, am I? That ship sailed a long time ago."

"But—"

"No. We're in this together now whether you like it or not. The Legion are coming to end all of this, and I have people I have to protect, including you. So yeah, I'm going to fight them . . . and so are you."

He was trying to get a rise out of me, but all I wanted to say was sorry. *Sorry I didn't come sooner . . .*

I followed him back toward the castle. It was only seconds after I stepped foot in the door that someone barreled into me.

"You have to come now," Luke said, holding my shoulders.

"What?" I stumbled back.

Presley interjected. "They have Kimberly. I mean . . . we gave her to the queen, technically."

"She wasn't supposed to come this early."

A scream tore through the air, and my blood ran cold.

"You brought her?" Zach said, his nostrils flaring.

I ran with no idea where I was going. Her scream sounded again, and I felt it everywhere in my body. *I'm coming.*

The world was as blur as my brothers led me through a set of double doors. That led to a room with a huge window over the ceiling.

Kimberly was crouched on the floor with blood soaking the back of her shirt and a small pool of it gathered at her feet.

A sudden pulse of red crowded my vision, and I almost let go.

Of everything we worked for.

Of everything I cared about.

Of myself to once and for all let that Thing in my head take over and pull the dagger from Sirius's hand to stick it in his throat.

I fought against the pull of that insanity as Presley backed into me.

"It's not supposed to hurt. She said it wouldn't hurt."

Another swipe of the dagger and we all collapsed to the floor. It was too much at once. Anger and pain hit me so hard I couldn't think.

I had to get to her. I had to stop it.

"Aaron, don't." Luke tried to grab me, but I was faster.

Agony. Pure writhing agony tore through me from head to toe. I went for her, but my older brothers were tugging me to the floor by my arms. I was stronger this time and nearly ducked underneath them and pushed them off.

The bond was tearing them apart from the inside, and her screams were taking me from the outside. All of us were breaking at the same time. I could tell by the way Luke winced and struggled to keep me down and the way Zach let go of my sleeve, giving me the ability to free myself, all while Presley's yelling for us to stop almost drowned out the sounds of Kimberly's torture.

"Please, stop. I'll do any—"

As I fell to my knees in front of her, Kimberly placed her bloody hand over my mouth.

"Don't say it."

The softest gleam of tears almost hid that silent, still determination, but it was flaring in her blue eyes. I could almost read her mind. *Patient. Like we planned.*

This wasn't my plan. She wasn't supposed to get hurt.

I lay my forehead onto hers and took a deep breath. Loving her was trusting her. I longed for our bed together, to hold her again in the safety of the warmth. As I was pulled away again and her skin left mine, I never stopped staring into her eyes. With my heart in my throat, I reached for her, but only the tips of my fingers grazed hers before I was yanked away.

I recognized Zach's tight grip on the back of my neck.

He whispered, "Let Luke fix it."

His hands trembled. My brothers were still visibly shaken. Presley was still on the floor. I was thankful I wasn't connected to the bond anymore. I don't think I'd have been able to get up either, but they felt it, which meant they still felt for Kimberly and were still in there.

"My Love, I'm sorry. I abominate the idea of hurting you. But you know some things must be punished. There are consequences. Your brother has a traitorous heart. You all do. So much feeling for this one insignificant girl. It pains me to see the copious tears you all shed for her . . ."

The queen eyed Luke with a pained expression. Everything about Her seemed to soften around him. I'd thought I'd imagined it before, but I couldn't deny the way She addressed him.

"We just need more time. If you give them more time to adjust, they'll forget about her," Luke said.

Luke reached for Her hand. I couldn't believe what I was hearing, let alone seeing. Was he serious?

"You can't promise it," the queen said, softer this time. Her hand melted over his.

"I can. I'll make sure of it. Lock her up. You have the dagger. If you give me time, I can make sure they forget her, and then you can do whatever you want with her."

"Luke," I said.

"Hush. It's a good deal," Zach said.

Even Presley didn't protest that unacceptable suggestion. This wasn't good. My brothers were more brainwashed than I'd anticipated.

Luke leaned down to kiss Her hand, and my body went rigid. All of it was wrong. It was worse than not seeing Her apparent cruelty, they . . . believed Her. They believed this strange act She was putting on for them, and it was so bad and painfully obvious, but they were hanging on Her every word. Fear slashed through my chest as I realized what I knew since

413

arriving but didn't want to admit—no amount of time would convince them. While the queen lived, they would be tethered to Her.

Her cool eyes settled on me, and I shivered. I couldn't let the full extent of my disgust show.

"And what would you do? How strong is the bond you two share?" She ran Her hands along my chest. "Strong enough for you to plead for her now even with all that blood of mine in your veins. How long will it withstand? Show me what *you'd* do to prove your loyalty. Kiss me."

"What the fuck?" Zach said.

"Not fair," Presley grumbled.

A lump gathered in my throat as I looked at Kimberly. She shook her head.

The queen's lip grazed my ear. "What will you choose? Would you kiss me? Take me to your bed? And how long will she continue to love you after that? How long could she endure seeing you with me night after night?"

"Aaron, don't listen to Her."

Presley shot across the room to put his hand over Kimberly's mouth. "There, there. It's all right. We can be sad and jealous together."

Kimberly squirmed, but he only tightened his grip around her neck and rested his cheek against hers. It was so fucked up. My life had turned into a nightmare. For some odd reason, the queen *really* hated me, but I knew my answer.

"I'll do anything."

Kimberly's cries were stifled, and I had to turn away from her. It would be quick. One kiss. The game the queen was playing would be over before it started. I wasn't going to let any of that happen.

Her hands threaded into my hair, and Her cold lips met mine. It took every bit of control I had to not fling Her off me. Her tongue was like ice, and Her scent was like chili powder in my nostrils—sharp and uncomfortable—but I was acting. I forced my hands to Her waist and pulled Her close while She kissed over my jaw and down my neck. I was so numb from it I could barely feel the pressure of Her. I considered counting like Kimberly had done once in my room. Instead, I imagined that day and how safe it all felt at the beginning before we both knew what we were up against. We sat in my room in Blackheart—her sleeping peacefully and me playing video games in blissful ignorance.

I met Kimberly's gaze. Her eyes were darker than I'd ever seen. She didn't squirm or cry, just watched in silence.

I'm sorry. It's almost over. I had to stay focused. I grabbed the queen's wrist and pulled Her tighter to me. It had to be convincing, or it was all for nothing.

"I think you made your point, *Darling*," Zach said.

I saw something in his eyes I'd never seen before. Jealousy. That pointed scowl was directed at me.

"Soon you'll see it would have been mercy to kill her now before her love turns to hatred."

"It's done, then. You'll leave her alone?"

"We should bleed her before The Legion arrives," Sirius said. "No loose ends."

Something feral from inside me lashed out in the silence of my head. I was confident I wouldn't let him do that. I'd give up everything to stop that from happening.

Presley interjected. "You can't. She said so . . . right?"

"Take hold of your brother's mouth," Sirius said.

"He has more right to talk than you. You're standing in my brother's spot. Warming it up before you croak."

"Keep your mouth shut."

Zach checked his fake watch. "Any minute now, you'll leave this mortal plane and float up into the fucking stars you love so much, and I'll never have to hear your irritating voice again."

"Ah!" Presley cried out and pushed Kimberly to the floor. Licking the blood from his hand, he pouted. "She bit me."

"You can't kill me, and you hate that. You and your stupid prophecy is null and void if I'm dead. How does that make *you* feel?"

Kimberly lifted to her knees, her eyes burning with a new determination, to face the queen. What was she doing?

The queen leaned in close to her face. "I can break you."

"Try."

Of course, she was smarter than me. Kimberly was showing the queen she held power. Torturing her only proved Luke's point further. The queen might be powerful, but all that power was fragile.

The queen reared back and motioned for Sirius. *No.*

I let go before I realized I had. Before my vision went red and my hands went numb.

I let go for her.

Sirius shot to Kimberly in an instant and grabbed her by the hair. Aaron Calem was gone by the time he raised the dagger, poised to slice through Kimberly's back once more.

So gone I didn't feel my body move to grab Sirius by the throat.

"How ... did you ...?" he choked out.

I shouldn't have been able to remember my name. To even hear him or the gasps from my brothers. I'd *let* It take me, but I was still in there, fighting and struggling to get back to the front of my mind.

Take him down, I told the thing inside me, and in less than a second, It replied.

No. Give in. Let her die. Serve your queen.

The red took over, and I was being forced backward. It should have been too much, but I had the control.

No. You'll serve me.

With one easy flick of my arm, I flung Sirius into the wall.

I'd had the control. The effects of all that power lingered in my arm with a dull ache, and I stared at my hand, marveling at the fact I'd stayed grounded.

"My Guardian." The queen gasped.

"Guardian . . . What does it mean?" It was the word I'd seen in Eros's journal.

"It means you're my gift from the stars. You possess the ability to control the power that lingers in the blood that connects us. Eros was the last holder of the gift. I'd hoped Luke would possess it but . . . when he didn't, I wondered if I wouldn't be blessed again by The Divine."

"I don't understand. I thought . . . the Thing in my head was going to take over one day if I let it."

"For others, yes. But you were born as my Guardian. The stars chose you to protect me. You can hold the power in your body and not be overcome. You belong to me."

"Don't listen to anything She says. She lies!" Kim spat blood on the floor, and Ezra moved to gag her with a cloth this time.

The queen frowned. "Eros's thirst became unquenchable after he changed and tasted my blood for the first time. No human blood would sustain him. That was the first sign, but how did you . . . ?"

She looked between Kimberly and me. *Shit.* If She figured out what Kimberly and I had done to break the bond, She'd never let her live.

I'd have to fight them. Guardian bond or not, that was a fight I knew I'd lose.

Still, I braced to free Kimberly first.

A shrill ringing broke through the silence of the atrium. A high-pitched buzzing that felt like a razor blade in my ear.

"Ah!"

All of us covered our ears, except for the queen, Sirius, and Ezra.

Somehow, they were immune. Or more likely our younger sensitive ears weren't accustomed to it.

Kilian would know that. This was a diversion. It wasn't just us. The gasps and groans from the other men outside the atrium were barely audible, and I struggled to adjust.

"They're here." As I said the words, the first explosion rang out.

Sixty-Eight

KIMBERLY

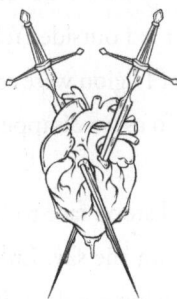

The room erupted into chaos, and some of the lower members of The Family pressed into the atrium. Ezra and Sirius barked their orders, but I reached for Aaron, trying desperately to grab hold of him. The pulsing noise was excruciating. I guessed a drone.

"I'll lock her up," Luke said, wasting no time in grabbing my arm and pushing me toward the door.

"No, let me take her." Aaron grabbed me and pulled off the restraint.

Zach interjected. "So you can run off? No. You don't even know where it is. Stay next to me."

"Get off me!" Aaron reached for me, but Zach yanked him away. My hand barely grazed his again.

"She'll be fine with Luke," Zach said.

"It's okay, Aaron." *Get the dagger*, I mouthed to him.

He nodded with a pained expression. I'd lost sight of it. Sirius could have given it to someone else.

The only solace I had was knowing Aaron would be safe, but what about Zach . . . Luke? They clearly were still not going to fight with us, which meant The Legion would fight them if they stepped in their way.

Luke threw me over his shoulder. I dug my fingers into the cloth of his jacket when he started to run. My head was spinning. The air on my back soothed the sting of the gashes. I moved to look out across the field as we reached the doors that led outside. Yelling. Fighting. It was really happening. A larger group of Legion were coming from the front of the castle, but I lost sight of them as we disappeared into the charred hedge maze.

My feet hit the grass, and I stood face-to-face with a statue I instantly recognized. Icarus falling from the sky. Luke touched the side, then a door opened, and he led me down a dark dusty hallway with stone on either side.

In the barely lit room, I saw a silhouette of a man.

"Will!"

William sat in the corner of a dusty, damp cell, and I ran up to see him. The room was bone-chillingly cold.

He stood up at my words. "Why are you here?"

I hesitated. His eyes, though he'd always had darker irises, were pitch black.

"You've come for Her, haven't you!? You can't have Her!"

I recoiled from the hatred in his voice and fell back into Luke.

"I'm sorry. Can you let me out of here please? I need to get to Her, and they won't let me."

"Will . . ."

"Don't call me that. You don't know me." He slammed his fist into the bars. "If you won't help me, then you can die for all I care."

No. She'd changed him too. Only, he was worse than Presley. This was the consequence of too much of Her blood. I had to fight the lump in my throat at the thought of The Legion and the horror they'd feel seeing him this way. If that's what happened to Will, I was afraid to think about what had happened to Thane.

"I'm sorry you had to see him like this," Luke said. He watched Will, who was now screaming and grabbing the bars to pry his way out. "I . . . I wasn't paying enough attention. This is what happens when you come here. This is likely what will happen to you."

He pointed to the cell beside William's, and I followed.

Luke turned to leave, and I stopped him to wrap my arms around him in a hug. I remembered his hugs. Always reassuring me. Pushing us on and making me believe in something that wasn't there. If I squeezed him hard enough, maybe he'd remember. Maybe he'd cling to himself a little longer. I braced myself for him to push me away, but after a few seconds, he let out a breath, then a few more. His hand moved to my shoulder, and he squeezed me back, soft at first, then hard and comforting.

"Why are you here?" He said it through clenched teeth, but it was a plea.

I stayed clinging to his large frame.

"I'm sorry we didn't come sooner. Everything took so long."

He held me by the shoulders. "I want to tell you that I can save you . . . but I can't. I can't save anybody."

"You don't have to save me. We came to save you."

He shook his head with a furrowed brow. "It's not going to work."

"Did you think no one was coming to help you?"

"I didn't want help . . . not from any of you. I wish you hadn't come." Amid the darkness and the grit, there was still something incredibly soft about Luke. He was in there. Clinging. Holding on. I couldn't see every scar or infliction, but it was written on his face and lived in the dark circles under his eyes.

"I don't know how to help you." His voice wavered from only stoicism to something more. Care.

"You don't need to. We're going to save you this time."

"I've got to go. We'll come get you when this is over."

As he left, I clung to the bars of my cell. Only partly thankful I had a moment to rest. Fear tore into me from every side; Aaron still had a job to do. His brothers needed more convincing, and our time was running out.

Sixty-Nine

AARON

"Move your ass." Zach was fresh on my heels. Presley, Zach, and I followed Ezra to move the queen from the atrium to the cathedral. The loud noise had ended, but there was another explosion somewhere that shook the building. Their plan to disorient everyone had worked, at least on me. I had to focus on the facts. Kimberly was safe for now. Great. Presley was also safe. Perfect. My most important jobs were tended to, so I really needed to find the dagger and drive it through the queen's heart. Problem was, I couldn't do that while hiding.

After a series of hallways and one moved bookcase, we progressed down a stone passageway that smelled of mold and old rotting wood. The warm air of the castle wafted in, and the door shut us into another cold hallway.

"I thought the cathedral and the castle weren't connected," Zach asked.

"We lied," Ezra said.

"Shocker."

"I didn't need you and your brother running around in the walls and sneaking out through the passageways to escape."

They did try to escape. The thought only added to the growing anxiety in my gut. The punishments for escaping in that place were probably nothing I wanted to know about.

After another minute, our secret passageway opened into the cathedral where Luke was already waiting for us.

"I fortified the door."

"Excellent," Ezra said before turning to face my older brothers. "Do you both remember what I told you about the escape plan?"

They nodded.

"Now, we need to split up."

"I want to stay with Her!" Presley said. He'd talked the entire way in the tunnel, but I'd tuned out the whole thing.

"I'd like you to stay too." The queen tugged on Luke's arm. "Please stay next to me, My Love."

It was strange. On one hand, the girl I'd spoken to had seemed evil to the core, but the infliction in Her voice made me wonder if there was more of Cecily still in there than I thought. There was something there between my brother and the queen, something unnatural.

"Well, I'm fighting regardless." Zach rolled his shoulders, like we were boring him more every second.

I interjected. "I want to come with you."

"You'll just get in my way."

"No, I won't. I learned how to fight with Kilian."

Zach and Luke shared a look.

"You'll watch him?" Luke said.

Zach grunted in agreement, then pulled me back through the passage-

424

way.

"You don't have to drag me, you know?"

"You stay close to me. No running off. I need to see you at all times."

"Worried about me?"

He spun on his heels, and I thought for sure he'd slam me into the wall again. "Don't you even try to be a hero out there. You fucking die, I'm going to the afterlife to kick your ass."

I hid my smile. I'd really missed that.

"Got it, brother."

The sky had turned to a burnt orange and red as we stepped out on the lawn. The smell of explosives and smoke carried in the breeze from the ocean cliffside.

"Stay close!" Zach called over the sound of yelling. My ears rang as we moved over fresh bodies gleaming with blood on the lawn. Black blood melted into the grass and dirt. I'd tried to prepare myself for the death for months, but it didn't stop me from feeling nauseated at the sight of it. I tried to orient myself. From what I could tell, the main force had moved in from the west side of the castle, but there were people everywhere.

"Sir!" Connell came bounding toward us, nearly getting taken out by a group of guys grappling.

"What the hell are you doing?" Zach spat.

"Looking for you, sir! I'm supposed to protect you."

"No. You need to hide."

"I can't, sir. I'm supposed to protect The Guard and our queen."

"Fine. Guard the cathedral, and if someone goes for the door, you come tell me. You don't fight."

"But sir—"

"No. You don't fight. If someone goes for you, you run away. Do you understand me? You have no choice. You only exist to serve me. Nod yes as your confirmation."

Connell was hesitant but nodded.

As he disappeared into the fray of people fighting on the lawn, I dodged some men about to ram into me. My brother ignored them. Looking for someone. The Legion saw me and went the other way.

"You were worried about him," I said.

"He's just a fucking kid . . . and he can't fight for shit."

My brother cared. He was still capable of caring even while attached to Her. I wondered if things would be different if I'd taken longer. If months turned into years and things hadn't lined up, would I recognize him at all?

Zach stopped. And I followed his line of sight.

Kilian stood before us with his chest out and his shoulders back. He looked about ten years younger in his combat clothes. His muscles were on display in his cuffed T-shirt. The Legion, too, were dressed in all black, which made the battles circling hard to follow. A good strategy but confusing.

"What are you protecting in the cathedral?" Kilian asked, clearly knowing the answer. He had to have heard the conversation with Connell.

"Kilian. Don't I get a charming greeting? Didn't you miss me at all?"

Kilian cocked his head, but his shoulders stayed alert and ready.

"He's not thinking clearly," I said. "There wasn't enough time."

"Zach, this path you don't need to go down. Fight with us. There's still time to change your fate."

Zach scoffed, and a low laughter leaped from his chest. "Really? That's the angle you want to go with? Too bad you spent all that time manipulating us instead of actually helping."

"Zach."

"No. Kilian doesn't deserve your worship. Everything he says is a lie."

"I'm sorry," Kilian said.

My brother moved a step closer. "Nothing to be sorry about anymore. I don't need your pity."

"I'm sorry I failed you. I was selfish. My brother . . . he would be ashamed of the decisions I made to get here."

The truth of it washed over us, and my brother's stance went rigid. I realized I finally believed Kilian, and in the same moment I forgave him for not being perfect, even in the failure of what was happening in front of me.

"You can tell him all about it when I rip your heart out of your chest."

Zach's expression had fallen, and he braced for Kilian's advance.

Kilian sighed, giving up a breath before his eyes hardened.

"I'm sorry, Aaron."

"No!" I moved in front of my brother. "If you want to kill him, you'll have to kill me first."

"Get off me!" Zach tried to push me away, so I grabbed onto the front of his shirt with everything I had.

"No way, I'm not letting you fight!"

Kilian would win, and I wouldn't let it happen.

"Kilian!" Sirius's voice carried in the breeze. The moon hung between them in the twilight. "I've been waiting for you."

"I know." Kilian squared his shoulders.

"We have a score to settle."

They stood like statues, and silence settled between them like there was nothing else to say.

In the blink of an eye, their bodies collided. I'd never seen anything like it. Full out fighting from the most powerful vampires I'd ever known. Likely some of the strongest left on earth. Kilian flung Sirius into the side of the castle, and the stone cracked. Another blink and Sirius had his arms around Kilian, but he countered quickly and they separated. They were an even match physically, but it was evident Sirius was stronger in technique. As soon as Kilian would get close to Sirius, he'd find himself on the ground. It would be hard for them to get a bite in.

Hands squeezed my shoulders from behind, and I stepped back to knock them off balance. As I spun around to face my attacker, Felix dropped his hand.

"Shit, Aaron, I almost didn't recognize you," Felix said with a toothy smile. It quickly fell from his lips as he spied my brother.

"Felix," Zach said.

"Calem." They circled each other with straightened shoulders. Zach's face went deadpan. All that talk with Kilian didn't help.

"Wait, we want the same things."

We did at the heart of it. We all wanted this to be over. My brother, my actual brother, wanted this to end. The Zach I knew in Blackheart didn't want to care for Her. It was all a lie.

"What if I said I'm going to kill that witch bitch in the cathedral. What do you say to that, Calem?"

"I'd say you'd never even make it in the building." My brother was deadly still.

"That's what I thought."

"Don't do this," I pleaded.

Zach pushed me. "If you're not going to help, move."

Zach would fight for the queen, and Felix was a good fighter, but I'd fought him. He wouldn't beat my brother.

"Felix, he isn't thinking straight. Don't. Just leave."

"Sorry, Aaron. I didn't have the heart to tell you it would probably end up this way. Your brothers were never going to listen. Even if you had the time . . . they're a lost cause. That's what The Family does. They corrupt everyone they touch."

Zach snickered and threw off his jacket. Felix bounced with excitement at the challenge, and I looked out across the field, trying to see past the garden arch. I still didn't see Halina or Dom.

"See, this is the Zach I remember. Cocky smile. No sense of humor."

Zach licked his teeth. "I remember you too. You're weak on your left and you rush too early."

Felix frowned.

"I remember you're not good enough to beat me."

"Let's put it to the test."

I stumbled back as their fighting began. It took seconds for Zach to tear into Felix's shoulder. He wasn't just focused, he was *feral*. I'd never seen him so bloodthirsty. Felix rushed, and with a kick, Zach cracked something in Felix's knee. When he stumbled, Zach kneed him in the back and laughed when he fell.

It was too much.

My brother was a monster.

I had to stop it. I had—

A reflection caught my attention across the field. A man had the dagger in hand and disappeared into the garden.

Shit.

When I looked back, Felix was on his feet again and going blow for blow with my brother. He was already slowing. A punch in the gut. Another knee to the ribs.

I forced my feet to move to the garden. The faster I had the dagger, the faster everything could be over. If my brothers wouldn't listen, I'd have to kill Her, and to do that, I needed that dagger.

I snuck through the rose bushes and walked along the stone path. The sky grew darker by the minute, and the sounds of grunts and yelling filled the air, but the ocean hitting the cliffs almost drowned it out. No one knew about the absolute massacre happening on the island, and I wondered if anyone would find all the bodies when it was over.

I guessed it depended on who won.

The man I followed was tall with big broad shoulders. Taller than Luke even. I could snatch it from him, but he'd likely stop me. No. I had a better idea.

"Sirius wants the dagger taken to him." My words echoed in the air.

"Does he . . . really?" As the man turned around slowly, revealing a muscular fighter build, I realized I knew his name. Henderson. Maybe it would be fine. He seemed agreeable enough.

"Yeah, he needs it right now. Let's go." I walked a step closer. "Or give it to me, and I'll bring it."

"That's interesting because I'm his sworn. And he instructed me specifically to keep it from *you*." He walked in close till our chests were inches apart. "So, tell me, Calem, why would you want this dagger?"

Shit.

"Change of plans." I grabbed the blade of the dagger and tried to wrestle it from his grasp. It was sharp but couldn't break the skin as long as I kept all my blood in my body. With one push, I was down on the ground. I swept his leg, and the dagger flew out of view.

I'd made a mistake. The guy was Luke-level big. When he got me on the ground, he held me down with one arm like a mouse in a trap.

"Are you a traitor, Calem? Because I've been looking for a reason to kill one of you."

Henderson tore into my shoulder, and I ground my teeth from the pain.

I wasn't done. I trapped one of his arms and bridged my hips to destabilize him. He moved off just enough for me to weasel past and stammer to my feet.

"Ah!" Henderson charged me again, and I braced myself to be taken to the ground.

"Stop." Zach emerged bloody, but I saw no physical wounds. Henderson halted midstride. "What the fuck do you think you're doing?"

"He was trying to take the dagger."

"Did I ask? Do you think so highly of yourself that you believed you could touch my brother, a future member of The Guard?"

Henderson hesitated, looking around for the dagger we threw.

"You don't want to be standing next to me in the next few minutes. If I turn around and see you, I'll kill you myself."

"Yes, sir. It will only take a minute. I was ordered by Sirius—"

"Leave now," Zach said. "Unless you feel like fighting me. And you know how that ends for you."

My brother didn't know the importance. I wasn't even sure that Henderson guy knew either. The dagger had to be somewhere close in the flowerbeds. He'd come back for it.

"You're supposed to stay next to me. That's an order."

"An order? These people are my friends. You're fighting on the wrong side. You killed Felix!"

"I'm doing what has to be done. And he's not dead . . . yet."

"What did you do with him?"

"He's bleeding out on the lawn. I noticed you were gone and had to go find you."

"You have to snap out of this. You have to let them kill Her."

"No," Zach snarled. "She's mine to protect."

A blood-curdling scream zipped through the air. The scream of a woman.

In seconds, I was on the lawn in front of the cathedral.

Ezra had Halina on her knees, as well as a few other members of The

Legion.

"I found them ambushing from the north."

"Wait. Don't." I reached for them, but I was too far.

Ezra didn't hesitate. He twisted the heads of them one by one. Their skin was already bloody and torn, and they had no fight left. Zach held onto my shoulder, not letting me move.

Halina's screams sent shivers down my spine, then it stopped. Forever.

I felt . . . nothing. Stumbling back into my brother, I reached for him to steady me.

"No! That's my sister."

A bloody and weak Felix flew forward. I went to stop him. A flash of movement blurred in front of me, then Felix's head rolled from his body and onto the lawn.

I was frozen. Staring at the horror.

There was pressure on my shoulders and the world spun around.

"Look at me," Zach said. His palms were warm against my face. "It's okay. It's going to be all right."

I'd seen death before, but not like this. Not the death of a friend and the end of his family. The end of all their dreaming. All they wanted was for this to end. That's all we ever talked about. It was the only thing we talked about because it's the only thing that mattered.

"This is almost over. Sirius and Ezra will finish off Kilian, and then we'll all be safe."

I nodded.

"Talk."

"Okay . . ." I said, replaying the images of death. "What about Kimberly?"

"We'll figure something out."

He was right. Things were moving in The Family's favor. *We were losing*. Kilian wasn't a match for two members of The Guard *and* my brothers. Kimberly was still locked away. If we lost, she wouldn't be safe. They would torture her, then kill her. Everything would crumble. My brothers and I would stay tethered to Her. The fear of that froze me in place.

"Can I . . . have a minute?" I asked.

"Yeah."

My feet moved on their own. The world slowly came back to me. The sun had set, and the moon was taking hold in the sky. I had two options. Go for the dagger or abandon ship and go find Kimberly and get her out. There was still time. It might be my only opening.

I made my way into the garden, still fighting the disorientation.

My feet hit something hard in the grass, and the dagger stared back at me.

I couldn't give up on our dream. I had to end this once and for all.

I grabbed the dagger and made my way to the cathedral.

Seventy

KIMBERLY

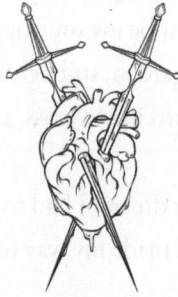

"Will, can you hear me?"

He hadn't said a word or even flinched at the explosions above. I tried not to think about what was happening. Aaron would bring the dagger and be in front of me any minute. He would be fine. They all would be.

Every second that ticked by only added to my restlessness.

"Will," I repeated.

He was at the other side of his cell, scratching something into the wall.

"You have to still be in there somewhere."

"Ah, fuck off. You're so annoying. If you're not going to take me to Her, I don't care what you have to say," he mumbled.

"How did this happen?" I needed him to keep speaking. Anything to distract me from the fact that the people I cared about were above ground, likely fighting for their lives.

"She opened my eyes and then . . . took it away." He hit his head against the wall. "I hate it. It hurts."

It didn't make sense. If Her blood was sacred, why would She give it to someone like Will? Someone She was supposed to hate.

"Why? Why would She give you Her blood?"

"She said it was a punishment. But . . . it made me feel like I was connected." He groaned like he was in pain and rocked on the dirty floor. "Are you sure you can't get me out?"

"I can't even get myself out."

"You're useless," he spat.

I sighed. He didn't deserve it. No one deserved to have the core of who they were stripped away with no thought. It was the opposite of connection. I decided on a different approach.

"What about your sister?"

"I don't have a sister."

"You do. And you love her . . . more than anything. I know that about you, and you didn't even have to tell me."

"I don't! I don't need anything else but Her. You could never understand. She's everywhere. It's everything I have."

I stood at the sound of the door opening. Excitement ran through me at first, then fear. I hoped for a friendly face, but I wasn't expecting the one I saw.

Thane stumbled down the steps and came straight for me.

"Thane! Oh my god. I thought you were dead," I said.

"Yeah, I had to hide for a while. After what She did to Will . . . She was going to kill me, so I hid. I couldn't leave without the others, so I hoped you guys would come, and you did."

Thane smiled a toothy grin, like the world wasn't falling apart. It reminded me of home. His clothes were disheveled and a little bloody but nothing major. He looked radiant in a way the other boys didn't.

"Listen, Kim, I have to apologize to you too. I know you might not believe me, but they cleansed my blood, and everything is different now, but I'm—"

"Please don't. I'm just glad you're okay." It wasn't his fault. It was Hers. Every path led back to Her. "We came for all of you. Did you see Kilian?"

"He hasn't seen me yet. I had a job to do first." He pulled a shiny object from behind his pack and presented it.

The dagger.

"How did you get it back so fast?"

"I didn't. There are two. This is the real one."

My stomach sank.

"Wait, that means . . . Aaron doesn't know the dagger is fake. He's searching for the wrong one."

"I'll go help. Okay, he'll be fine. Halina . . . she wanted to make sure I got this to you specifically. She said you could use it."

"Halina . . . Where is she?"

His expression cracked and his jaw feathered. "She gave it to me before Ezra took her and a few others. She's gone . . . I wanted to help, but she said getting this to you was more important."

I nodded and stuffed the surfacing emotion down. Halina believed in me, and I couldn't let her down.

"They have a plan to evacuate the queen, there's a tunnel that runs from the castle to below the cliffs. Things are moving quickly up there. If you use this, maybe you can keep them on the island and give Kilian more time."

"Okay. I will."

"This is going to work, Kim. We're going to win."

He sounded like Aaron. I grabbed his hand through the bar and squeezed. I needed the boost.

"We're going to win," I repeated.

Seventy-One

AARON

One foot in front of the other, Aaron. I made my way through the passageway from the castle to the cathedral. I had one shot to take Her out, and that would solve everything. Once She was dead, my brothers would remember themselves. Luke would remember Sarah. The tides would change. The thrall everyone was under would disappear.

I had the dagger tucked into my shirt, and it was poking me in the back with every step I took—a sharp reminder that danger was close, but I only needed a second. One good second and this would be over.

Luke greeted me when I entered the cathedral. The sounds of the battle outside were louder than they'd been before. He inspected me with a furrowed brow.

"You're hurt."

"By one of our own actually. Zach took care of it."

"Where is he?"

"He's good. Everything is working. It's almost over I think."

I followed him up the pulpit of dark wood that displayed intricate carved cherubs. At the top, She sat with Presley on the floor. She seemed to be comforting him by running Her hand through his hair and humming.

"What's your favorite flower?" he asked, staring at Her like She was a goddess made only for him.

"Thistle," She answered. "Such a beautiful flower. Painful to touch at times, but a welcome reminder of how strong beauty can be."

With another swipe of Her hand through my brother's hair, I spotted Kimberly's ring. In the shuffle, I hadn't noticed She'd taken it. The queen was actually jealous . . . Maybe I could use that.

She turned to me, and Her attention settled on the blood on my shirt.

"Are you badly injured?"

"I don't know . . . I feel a little lightheaded." I leaned back on the edge of the railing, feigning a dizzy spell.

"Can I see?" She muttered, and crossed the distance to me. My little brother scowled at me.

"Yeah. It's my shoulder."

Luke watched from a little way down the stairs. Still in combat mode and pacing a few steps every few seconds.

"Poor thing." Her cold hands grazed my neck, and Her other moved my shirt down to check the bite that was already closed.

Being The Guardian made me the new shiny toy.

"I missed you," I said. "I mean . . . I was worried about you while I was gone."

"My Guardian. Would you like some of my blood to heal you?"

I considered it for a second. Taking any opportunity to drain Her of blood was a good idea, but I had the dagger. The final piece.

"Can I?" I asked, reaching for Her cheek. There was nothing enjoyable about it. Just a game that determined the life and death of my family. No pressure or anything.

"Of course. We'll become very acquainted. You can have as much as you want, and you won't become overcome. Because you're special, my blood fuels you."

Eros was The Guardian before me. From his journal entries, it seemed like something he had fought at some point too. He'd wanted to leave with his brother.

I moved Her hair from Her neck and crept in. With one hand on Her face, I used that to gain all Her attention. My lips grazed Her neck while I pulled the dagger out with my other hand.

Presley noticed a moment too late to scream a warning.

I thrust the dagger toward through Her heart and—

It fell out of my hand. It didn't pierce Her skin.

Uh-oh.

Her misty eyes bore into mine, and the once soft smile turned sinister. "How?" Her fingers were around my neck.

The pressure grew. Tighter and tighter till I thought my spine would crack, the world was gone.

Panic. Pain. Pressure. My head was splitting. She was in my head. Tearing through everything faster and faster. I think I was screaming, but I couldn't hear it. All I could feel was Her.

Her fingers pulled at my memories. Tearing them up. Her nails were like razor blades.

Show me what you did. Now.

As soon as She said the words in my head, the image of me and Kimberly came up. Of our nights together. I could feel Kimberly's skin on mine again. Smell her. Those moments were ours, and She was scarring them, intruding and making everything hurt. She lingered on the memories of me drinking Kimberly's blood and how it turned into me giving mine.

The memories went by faster and faster till I was sure I would die. It was worse than I remembered when William had made his way into my head. It felt like Her fingers were in my eyes prying open my skull with both hands.

When the world came back, I was on the floor below the pulpit, lying in a scattering of broken wood. Sobbing. Next to me, Luke and Presley were too.

"You changed everything because of that girl." She glared down at me from the pulpit. She'd thrown me off. My brothers must have followed.

I was yanked back against the marble from behind. Sirius had me by the collar, and the dagger in his other hand.

"I knew you were trouble."

Where did he come from? He had to have been alerted somehow.

"Don't, please!" Luke pleaded. Presley sobbed uncontrollably into his hands.

We didn't need Her blood to bind us. Our bond was still there. My pain was killing them.

"Your brother is a traitor and deserves to bleed." He grabbed the fake dagger and thrust it through my chest.

I clutched the hilt and fell back against the marble floor. He missed my heart by two inches. It still hurt. The dagger was a fake. Of course it was. Why else would Kilian send Kimberly here with the dagger?

I groaned. My heartbeat was in my ears. The marble was a welcome salve to my pain. As I turned my head, trying to pull myself up, my gaze settled on a long crack that went all the way to the door.

I can't die here. Not yet.

Not yet.

Not. Yet.

"Aaron, are you okay?" Luke called, but he was still holding Presley who had crumbled to the floor.

"So good," I groaned.

With one swipe, I pulled the dagger from my chest and threw it across the floor. If what She said was true, I had more power than I thought. The fight wasn't over yet. Kilian couldn't do it alone. Ezra had likely been outside fighting Kilian, but Ezra didn't look like he had a scratch on him. No one else would do it. It had to be me.

I stumbled to my feet. "Wait. I'm not finished."

Sirius was next to Her at the stairs of the pulpit, caressing Her and whispering to Her.

"You should kill me. Because I won't stop until She's dead."

"Aaron, stop." Luke worked to get Presley to his feet.

"I can't. I'm not like you. I'm immune to Her blood. Neither of you can see it or even reason with it, but She's manipulating you."

"He's a traitor. He tried to kill me." Her voice shook. "My Love, you can't trust him."

"Luke . . . you can fight with me."

His once concerned expression deteriorated, and his jaw hardened. A second. That's all it took for my brother's image of me to crumble into disgrace.

"That's how it's going to be, huh?"

Luke's voice was cold. "Stay away from Her."

"Yeah, stay away." Presley sniffled.

I met Her eyeline. "Turning my own brothers against me now? That's new."

"You're the one who's manipulating him. Trying to persuade him to go against his true family."

I stepped forward, moving toward them. Sirius craned his neck.

"I will kill you where you stand."

"Good. Try it, then."

Serve Her. Serve Her. Serve Her. The voice was louder than ever, but it didn't matter. I wouldn't listen.

No. I won't. Not now. Not ever.

I walked another step, and Sirius met me there in an instant.

Serve me. Now. I demanded of the Thing inside my head.

My world was red again. I focused on the memory of Akira in the forest and the moment I'd let go for Kimberly. This was different. But similar. Letting go this time felt intentional . . . controlled.

Sirius's fist went for my chest. ***Foolish boy. I don't answer to you.***

I barely dodged it. I needed the Thing's power. I had to get it. Sirius went for me again, and I slipped under his legs.

Help me.

He caught me with an arm around my neck, and I flipped him to the floor. He was faster. Better. I would lose in a matter of seconds.

A force hit me from behind, and Sirius took me by the neck. His other hand was wrapped around the dagger. He went to stab me, and I grabbed the hilt, fighting against him inch by inch.

"Little help here," I said through gritted teeth.

My brothers stayed silent, moving closer to Her and away from me. They wouldn't help me now. Sirius would snap my neck. That or slice me open. I grabbed the dagger and directed it into my side. I cried out at the slicing pain through my gut. My hands were shaking.

We will serve Her.

I was giving in. The Thing would take over and take me with it. I imagined the Thing in my head and all the hatred I'd held for it since it came. I imagined all the pain it caused me. The terror. The fear. And I imagined it engulfing me. Like a pool of black blood was surrounding me. It should drown me. It did nearly every day, but it wouldn't. Not today.

Because I was strong enough.

I imagined drinking all that hate and pain. All that fear and letting it into my body. Accepting it. No more running.

It was finally clear. I had control the entire time. I was always stronger than the Thing inside my head.

It all snapped together, and the tug of war inside me was gone, and I felt . . . powerful.

Powerful, like how I'd felt fighting Akira powerful, but this time I had the reins.

I wrapped my arm around Sirius's neck. He pulled away, but it was useless. I *had* him. My teeth tore the flesh of his neck, and his blood spilled to the floor. He released me, stumbling back, but I didn't give him a second to breathe before I charged him and forced him to the ground. Shock. He was in pure shock at my advancement and strength, but it lasted seconds before he flipped me on my back.

He was still a better fighter, but I used the strength brimming in my body to fling him off me and charge him again. I had to do something. I had to make a dent in his armor.

In seconds, the strength was leaving me and the weakness was returning.

I wasn't much for fighting, but I was good at dodging, and that's all I needed because Sirius was trying to tear me limb from limb. I used that to counter him and get him on the floor. When I retreated, he came back for me.

I chipped away at him. A bite on the forearm. Then another on the arm. The shoulder.

The queen gasped and grabbed Her head. Luke was already there holding Her up.

"What's wrong?"

"I feel . . . strange. Weak."

Sirius's split-second distraction was all I needed. I couldn't get the dagger in his heart. The gut would do. The blade slipped, and I shoved it into his belly. His eyes widened as I used the rest of my strength to push the blade horizontally through tough skin and muscle.

That was it. All I had left. Sirius's blood spilled across the floor. His initial shock wore off, then he worked to stop the bleeding.

Luke held the queen in his arms while She continued to blink slowly. Her eyes were flickering back to green.

"It's okay. I'm here."

"She . . . you have to . . ."

Kimberly had the real dagger, which was great, but Sirius would likely kill me before I ever made it out of the cathedral. I was spent. The burnout of using the Thing's power left my legs wobbly. I had to work to keep upright.

Presley tugged on Luke's shirt, watching me with worried eyes.

Sirius stalked toward me again, and I braced. Maybe it was my time. Maybe I bought Kilian time and weakened Sirius enough for an opening.

No. Not yet.

An explosion blew the door of the cathedral open. The force of it threw us all to the back of the room. I hit something. Many things. Everything hurt. Stone and splinters were stuck to the skin in my arms, and my entire body felt like it was on fire.

"Aaron!" a familiar voice called my name.

"Thane?"

He was a blur as he pulled me to my feet. "Hi, we have to go. Now."

"But . . ." I couldn't open my eyes. My ears were ringing.

"Your brothers are fine. We have to go."

"I can't move."

"You can. It's not over yet. Just a little longer."

With his words, I found my footing and let him drag me through the passageway that led back through the castle.

Seventy-Two

AARON

"Here." Thane shoved a blood bag in my face. He'd tucked us into a place behind some stairs, like he'd been there many times.

"I can't."

"What? Don't tell me you're still afraid to drink."

"No, it's a long story, but I can't. Not while She's still alive. It's okay. You're right. I have to keep going. It's not over yet."

Not yet. The words had come into my head, like a foreign thought that didn't belong to me. The voice was mine, but how did I know?

I was the opening, and you were the key. I am the key.

"It's good to see you, Thane." It really was. Seeing him alive and well was a welcome surprise I hadn't expected.

He smiled and squeezed my shoulder. The only one that wasn't covered in blood. "I wish it was under different circumstances. I need to go help Kilian. Will you be okay?"

446

"I can make it. Where is she?"

"In the middle of the maze, there is a statue with a hidden latch at the foot of it."

I nodded.

"Listen, Aaron..." Thane looked down at his hands, but I didn't need his apology. I never did.

"It wasn't your fault."

"It doesn't matter. I'm still sorry."

"Consider us even."

He hugged me, and I winced at the very real pain coursing through my veins. We said our brief goodbye, and he disappeared from my sight.

I continued down the hallway toward Kimberly and the real dagger, but first I had to make a stop. *I was the opening, and you were the key.* The answer was right on the edge of my tongue.

The west side of the castle had seen better days. A hole was blown into the side, and I could see the stars shining in the periwinkle sky outside. With one hand on the wound to my side, I walked. It was slow, but it gave me time to process it all as it came together.

The library Zach had shoved me into when we arrived remained untouched. I went for the little black book again, immediately flipping through to the back.

Dear Sirius,

It's too late for you to get this letter. Ascension is upon us, and any minute they will fetch me.

I've fought for us as long as I could, brother. Though you were lost long ago.

Our hope is gone. I can no longer imagine a future in another place that does not include Her.

My only regret is that I did not die for you sooner. Then we could run and never look back.

Then it all made sense. The prophecy. Sirius and his brother. Eros had loved his brother as I loved mine, and he ended up enthralled with Her. All the poems made sense. Lifeblood goes on forever.

I could break my brother's thrall to the queen. *I was the key.*

Seventy-Three

KIMBERLY

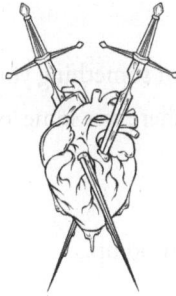

I opened my eyes. The dirty cell slowly came into view. Aaron was on the other side of the bars, rubbing my back.

"Did it work?" I asked. "I couldn't see anything. It wasn't the same as before, but the chanting was correct, I think."

"It worked," he muttered while tracing along my jaw. "That's how I knew where to find the real dagger."

My world was expanding, and I finally took in his condition. Blood stained his shirt at his side and his chest. His arms had rubble and sticks embedded in them.

"Oh my god, are you okay? I told Thane to get to you."

"He did. He blew up the cathedral door, and I was able to escape. Otherwise, Sirius would have definitely killed me."

"You fought Sirius?"

"Yeah. It's a long story. But I need that dagger."

I handed it to him without another thought.

"Right. We need to go and finish this. Did you get the key to let me out?" I asked, knowing what was coming next.

My time was almost up. It was too fast. I needed more time with him. To tell him all the things I didn't know I needed to say yet. To show how much I wanted this life with him. But I had to die. I didn't know why my death needed to happen. It didn't matter. I finally had a family, and they were worth dying for.

"Kim, I think I figured out something you're not going to like."

I think I knew too. That there was some loophole somewhere I hadn't accounted for.

"What is it?"

He took the dagger and stood up.

"What are you doing?"

"Please don't be mad at me."

"Aaron, let me out. I have to go to the battle. It's the only way this ends well. I have to. Cecily said—"

He reached for me between the bars, and even through the roaring of blood in my head and the anger, I let him grab me and pull me close.

"I know. But I figured out the message. The visions the stars gave you. It wasn't a warning. It was showing you the right path. The thing that was supposed to happen. I know how to save my brothers."

He didn't say it, but I knew. My heart was tearing. I was breaking from the inside.

"No. No. No. Let me out. I'll go with you. We'll do it together."

"You know I can't let you go with me because you'll try to stop me. And I love that about you, but this time I have to do this. You have to let me do this."

"You can't go. You know what will happen."

Nothing could have prepared me for the grief. I think I always knew but wouldn't admit it to myself. I wanted it to be me. It would have been easier to die than to live without him.

"It's going to work out. This is going to be over, and we'll be free. I still think it's going to be okay. Somehow, this is going to work out, and we're going to go home. Believe with me."

I couldn't. The price was too high. The tears poured down my cheeks, and I reached for him, like it would stop time. Like I'd have more time with him. Like it wasn't the end.

He pulled a crumpled piece of paper from his pocket and handed it to me. Through tears, I straightened it. Our forever list.

"Promise me you'll try."

He had a place he needed to be, and I had to let him. As much as I wanted to scream and beg him to stay, I couldn't say a word. We'd agreed on our mission. One that was just and right with the world, even if it didn't feel right to the emotion threatening to cave in my chest.

"Don't say goodbye to me, Aaron Calem."

"Never. I don't think we were ever meant to say goodbye anyway. Probably why it's been impossibly hard."

"I think you're right."

He kissed me through the bars, and the swirl of emotions threatened to topple me to the ground. Not goodbye. A see you later. My mind screamed at me in desperation, forcefully playing tug of war and fighting the urge to beg him to stay. I wanted to beg. To plead.

"I love you." I staggered out a breath. Trying to keep my voice steady and not let the grief keep me from him. I opened myself further. "I'll try. I promise."

"I love you, Mrs. Calem." He leaned his head onto the bars until our foreheads touched. "I'll find you."

He didn't shed a single tear. Somehow, he was still smiling. The bright kind of smile that only eternally optimistic people do. That kind that made me want to believe this wasn't our last moment together. That maybe just maybe when he disappeared from my sight it wouldn't be the last time I looked at that golden hair and the light in his eyes.

He broke away from me and disappeared into the corridor, running.

Our time was up.

Seventy-Four

AARON

This time, I ran. Slow at first, but I picked up speed into a full sprint. I knew what I needed to do. My body didn't hurt anymore. With the dagger in one hand, I rushed toward the cathedral where the sounds of another fight raged on.

Luke had Presley nestled with the queen on the altar while he stood guarding them. Next to him, Presley was moving his hands along the wall under the pulpit stairs like he was searching for something,

A larger fight had unfolded. Ezra, Sirius, and Kilian fought in a collective bloody mess.

Kilian—still remarkably resilient—fought blow for blow. Sirius was slower now. Sloppy. Still, Kilian wouldn't last long. He needed help.

There were others, the last of our forces were battling it out on the floor.

Zach grabbed my shoulder. "There you are. Fuck. Don't scare me like that."

"Wait, you're not shunning me like Luke and Presley?"

"She wants you alive."

"Comforting."

"We're here!" Thane came crashing into the room, effectively ending our conversation, with another familiar face. Dom.

"Dom had something we needed." He held up more blood bags.

"Thane. You're not dead." Zach's voice stayed at an even level with no excitement.

"We're going to fix this. Remember what we talked about." Thane was instantly pleading. "The Legion came just like I said they would, and we can help them."

"There's nothing to talk about anymore. You're too late. I'm glad you're alive, but . . . if you're trying to get to Her, I'm going to fight you."

"Zach. Come on, dude. It's me."

"Move out of my way, Thane."

Thane panned to me, and I shook my head.

"Go, get Kilian his blood. I'll keep him busy," Dom said, staring down my brother. "Then you need to go get the injured and start helping them to the chopper."

"I'm not leaving you. I'm fighting," Thane said.

"They need someone that can fly the chopper."

Thane hesitated, then promptly ran into the battle filled with screams and anguish. I was happy he would avoid my brother's wrath, but Dom—

"Dom. Don't. He won't listen."

"It's okay. Not much for talking."

Dom shed his shirt, and Zach loosened the collar of his.

Zach tilted his head, with his eyes darkening. "You saved my family."

"I did."

"There's still time for you to run."

"Not much for running either."

"Then let's not." Zach readied himself.

"The sad thing is . . . a couple more years in this place and I think Her words might actually be true. You'd be unstoppable," Dom said.

"Flattery won't stop me from fighting you."

"It's not supposed to. I'm going to fight you. And I'm going to do it for my sister."

Zach nodded. "I respect that. I'll make it quick."

"Dom, please."

Dom's stance was set. There was no convincing him. "Aaron, you have your own job to do. Go do it. Keep your promises to your loved ones, and I will keep mine."

He was right. I hated that he was right.

"May fate guide you." Zach lowered his head briefly for a bow.

Dom bowed without skipping a beat. "May fate guide you."

They moved at the same time and collided in a flurry of fists. My brother didn't have a scratch on him and neither did Dom, which meant their fight would be even. I needed to hurry.

The fight with Kilian and The Guard had reached a peak. Sirius was on the ground bleeding out. Not moving. While Kilian sucked down the blood bag and dodged another advance from Ezra. I couldn't spot Thane.

"Got it!" Presley's voice echoed into the ceiling. The bricks had moved, revealing a door. The smell of mold and sea water wafted in. Their escape route was open.

"Come on, Luke. Let's go." Presley had one arm on the queen and the other extended toward my brother.

Luke hesitated, watching me, then Zach.

"My Love, it's time," the queen called to him, and he stepped back toward the door.

This was it.

They would escape, and we would all be separated. In an instant, I imagined the agony of all the possibilities. Us losing. The entire battle being for nothing while She continued to live and keep my brothers under Her spell.

We couldn't separate. I knew what I needed to do.

I moved toward the steps to Her, and Luke blocked the way—one hulking mass staring down at me. With strong shoulders and that serious expression, he looked like Ezra. And there in that place, he would turn into him. He'd usher me and my brothers around and make us follow the rules.

"I can't let you hurt Her."

"My Love, please. Come with me," She pleaded.

I scoffed. "You've resigned to kill me now?"

When She looked at Luke, She melted him with her timid voice. "Don't let him come any closer."

"Presley, stay close to Her," Luke said.

"Would you really kill me for Her?"

"If I have to."

His eyes were set and cold. Darker than the ones I'd known growing up. Luke's eyes lit up with radiant joy when he was a kid, one he'd passed on to all of us. She'd taken it from him, but I would give it back.

"I'm sorry you don't remember Sarah, but she meant a lot to you."

His face fell. "What are you talking about?"

"Sarah Garanger was your best friend. She was what Kimberly is to me for you. You loved her. You spent all your free time with her."

"Stop."

"You took her to prom. And she wore a purple dress, and we had a picture on the wall of her where she kissed you on the cheek. You pretended to be embarrassed about it, but you never stopped talking about her. She liked butterflies and baking cookies. She was so amazing and cool, and no one knew her better than you did."

"I said stop."

"You loved her. And this place made you forget her, but I'm gonna fix it. You're going to remember."

I stepped forward, and he squared his shoulders.

"You're not going to get near Her."

"My Love, leave him," She called.

"But don't you need this?" I pulled the dagger from behind my back. "Without it, you're still connected to Kimberly, and your queen will be weakened by it. We'll use it to find you again and kill Her."

That got his attention. He stepped forward till we were feet away. "Give me the dagger."

"Come and get it. Kill me and take it."

He stepped forward. "Stop messing around."

"I'm not. Do it, Luke. Kill me for Her."

"Don't make me fight you. You know I'll win." He stood, wavering, and anger flashed in his eyes that I'd even dare to try.

"You're underestimating me." A smile curled my lips. "You didn't think I'd come unprepared to die, did you?"

The dagger was heavy in my hand.

Luke's eyes narrowed at the sight. "What are you doing?"

I stepped toward the altar.

Then I stopped.

"Saving you."

With one heaving blow, I plunged the dagger into the center of my chest.

A sharp pain followed by a lightness brought me to my knees, but I kept my eyes on my brother. Waiting. Hoping.

His angry scowl turned into wide-eyed surprise, then . . . to grief.

Bond breaker.

I was the key. Without Kimberly, we never would have made it that far—she was the opening, but I was the only one with the missing piece.

My brother was my lifeblood, and it was stronger than Her blood. Our bond would go on forever, and Hers would die. A price to pay to carve the way. Eros figured it out too late.

Lifeblood gave way, a high price to pay.

Fate does not guide us.

We carve our way.

I carved Her out of our story. Their bond with Her was finally severed.

"Oh fuck." I already felt dizzy. My chest was warm with the blood as it spread across my chest. I gripped at the hilt and fell back across the marble.

Luke pulled off his shirt to cover my wounds and bring me into his reach.

"Why would you do that?!" His hands trembled as he tried to cover the blood spreading farther and farther. "You're okay. You're fine. I can fix this. I can."

"Luke."

"I can fix this. It's not too late."

"*Luke.* Tell me you remember."

"What?"

"Tell me you remember Sarah."

He was panicking, biting his wrist and trying to give me his blood.

"Luke. Stop." With bloody hands and the only strength I had, I grabbed his face and pulled him closer. "Tell me your favorite memory of Sarah."

I had to know it worked. That all Her mysticism had left my brothers for good. I had to know they were finally free.

He spoke in a sob. "When she told me she loved me."

"I knew it." I chuckled, and despite the heaviness on my chest, relief rushed over me.

It was done. My part in all of it was over. I wanted to stay and fight, but I was going.

"You're free, Luke. You've got to get them all out. You have to fight."

"This is wrong. This is all wrong." He gripped at my chest, trying desperately to stop the bleeding. "You were supposed to stay home. You were supposed to live."

"No, this is right. This is how it's supposed to be. I'm saving you this time."

"This is my fault."

"No way. You've done everything right. You've been such a great big brother."

All that trying not to cry was catching up to me, and my eyes went wet when I spoke.

"Why? Why would you do that for me?" Luke pressed his forehead to me between sobs, and I struggled to keep my eyes open.

"You'd have done it for me." I coughed. Black blood filled my mouth and splattered on the floor. "You deserve to make your own choices. You need to live. They'll need you."

"I need you."

I shook my head. "Go be free, Luke. Live."

"I can't."

"Yes, you can. Make your five-year plan. Get all of them and go. I know you'll take care of Kim."

It was never my story. I was never hero material—way too soft to ever be strong enough to take down this coven—and not smart enough either, but I broke the curse holding my brothers in bondage, the thing forcing us against each other. That was enough for me.

"Promise me you'll fight."

My vision was going, and I was thinking of her. Finally, the sadness of leaving Kimberly hit me. I kept my promises, but it would have been nice to build her that cabin . . . and I bet she'd have looked breathtaking in a wedding dress. Maybe it wasn't in the cards this time around.

"Luke, promise."

"I promise."

The relief of his words held me as I drifted into the peaceful bliss pulling my eyes closed.

Chaos broke out in front of me. Yelling. Screaming. Crying. *I wanted to stay.*

The funny thing was, even with a dagger through the chest, I still had hope things would work out.

Seventy-Five

I couldn't leave him there. I'd poured my blood into his wounds, and he still wasn't awake. My brother's blood soaked my pant legs. His skin had gone pale, and seconds later, he let go of my hand.

It was usually the part where I'd crumble. Cry. Resign to the grief and the hopelessness and the weight of all the emotion that had fallen back over me, but my brother had believed in me. His belief was the only thing that got me to my feet.

And I *promised* to fight.

I looked behind me. Zach hadn't realized yet. I needed to go. I'd given almost all my blood to my brother, but I had to try to live for him.

I didn't look at Her as I turned to the battle. The fire in my blood sang higher and higher until I was engulfed completely.

461

Without Her, I was whole again.
Finally free.

Seventy-Six

ZACH

Something inside me broke.

I dodged Dom's advance and stumbled back, clutching my chest. He hadn't landed a hit, but something burst. I'd wondered for a split second if my heart had exploded.

"What is it?" Dom stopped, his breath heaving. He was looking at something behind me, but I stayed bent over. Not understanding. It was the opposite of being out of breath. Instead, I felt like I was filled with it. Like I'd gained some time of strength. Like my body was mine again.

"What did you do to me?"

"It wasn't me."

I couldn't stop staring at my hand and moving it around in the candlelight. I almost forgot where I was. All that pain. All that weight sitting in my chest was gone. For years, I'd been bonded to Her, and now—

I looked to the altar where the queen stood overlooking the battle and retreating toward the pulpit. The need to protect Her had vanished. All my feelings for Her had disappeared in an instant. She caught my eyeline, and for the first time, I saw Her panic.

I was finally free of that bitch.

I waited for Her voice in my head, but there was only sweet silence. She was so fucking dead.

"I . . . don't want to fight you anymore," I said.

"Good. Because we need to help Kilian."

"Help Kilian, and then you'll help me kill that bitch?"

Dom smirked. "Yeah."

Seventy-Seven

PRESLEY

Holy shit.

That was the first thought that entered my head when I realized where I was. I was in the cathedral, along with knowledge of the building I didn't remember learning. Weird.

Aaron.

I'd seen the whole thing below. The moment he shoved the dagger into his chest, my world came back into view. My brother just had to be the hero. It took Zach a few minutes to realize it when Luke joined him in the fray. But when he did, all the light left his eyes.

I had felt nothing. The shock of it kept me numb enough to move with no tears or theatrics. I could still help him. I knew where the blood was. Rushing through the secret passageway, I went for the halls to search

465

for our stash.

"Thane?"

"Presley." His eyes widened when he saw me, and he used his body to guard the remaining stash of blood that was almost depleted. Around him were wounded men I hardly remembered.

"Oh. I'm me again. I'm normal."

"Is She dead? I still feel the same."

"No, it's a long story, but I need that blood for Aaron."

"Here." He handed me some. "He wouldn't take it earlier, but maybe things are different. Hurry."

He didn't need to tell me twice. In seconds, I arrived back in the cathedral where Zach and Luke were fighting alongside Kilian. Aaron wasn't moving. I bit into the blood bag to pour down his throat. He couldn't be dead. No. He would get up and be annoying any second. It wasn't the end. It couldn't be.

We had done nothing on our forever list. Not a single thing. At every attempt for grief to find its way through my panic, I pushed it further down. I'd had so much practice with it, it was a reflex. His skin was cold. My brain wouldn't stop reminding me.

Someone slammed into me from the side, and I reared back to see that prick Henderson stalking toward me.

"Uh, can I help you?"

"Yeah, you and your brother can die."

"Jeez. Holding in some anger there, huh, buddy?"

He charged me, and in seconds, his fingers dug into my throat as he lifted me off the ground.

"You . . . really . . . don't like us."

"I don't like traitors."

Zach tackled him, and we all tumbled to the ground. I sat up long enough to see Luke and Dom fighting Sirius. They were nearly spent.

Super bloody.

"Ah!"

Henderson hit me again, and Zach flung him across the room into the wall. A scattering of lit candles fell over him and singed his clothes. The collective lot lit the gathering bodies closer to the wall and sent them ablaze.

"Don't touch my brother."

Our fights collided till we all stumbled back to look at each other. Kilian was clutching his side. One of his eyes was gone. Sirius's arm was broken, practically hanging there. Ezra was the least beat up, but his gaze flitted to the pulpit every few seconds. I knew that look. The look of a fellow bolter.

"How did this happen?" Ezra looked at my brothers. "I don't understand."

"I told you they're traitors," Sirius spat.

"No. Their brother paid a high price to break the bond of your queen," Kilian said.

Ezra shook his head. "That's not possible."

"Guess you didn't see this one coming?" Zach said.

"It can be remade. It's not too late," Ezra said.

A shiver of fear fell over me. Something told me if we didn't beat The Guard here, they weren't against holding us all down to remake that bond.

And with that bond, Aaron's sacrifice would be for nothing. This was it. He was right. Losing was not an option.

I shifted my thoughts back to Aaron, whose blood was pooling onto the floor. All the fighting was taking too long. Aaron needed help. He needed blood.

Ezra bolted, and I lunged for him. The others collided with shouts and grunts. He tried to fling me off, but I held onto his arm till he bit my wrist.

"Ah, fuck," I groaned. I really shouldn't have spent all that time moping instead of learning to fight. *Bad Presley.*

Zach slid next to me and grabbed Henderson as he tried to ambush me from behind.

"Are you okay?" he asked.

"Been better."

Suddenly, Sirius and Henderson fixated on me while Luke and Kilian barred Ezra from leaving. I had to hand it to them. It was a good strategy—I was useless.

"Not so strong now, huh, Calem?"

I tried to dodge but even with the blood loss, they were too fast. Zach shoved me out of the way to take every hit and keep them from me. Any attempt to move ended the same way.

Sirius got Zach by the neck and tore a chunk of his shoulder out with his teeth. It was agonizing watching him wither from Sirius's grasp, but Sirius had lost a lot of blood and the use of an arm—it wasn't enough alone.

Sirius charged again while Henderson came up behind. Zach didn't see it while all his attention was on me. He would not dodge both.

It was kinda like the movies. My body moved without thinking.

"No!" I fell in front of him, and excruciating pain tore through my chest. A sickening wet tearing noise filled my ears. When he pulled his arm away, there was a hole clean through my chest and shoulder.

"What the fuck did you just do?" Zach's eyes went wide, then completely dark.

I always said I wanted to be there when my brother went off like a nuclear bomb, but not like this. As I crumbled to the ground in a pool of my own blood, Zach held Henderson down before crushing his head with his foot. There wasn't a lot of fun about any of it. He wasn't ever going to stop. I wondered what would have made it more fun. Less blood? Less death?

Sirius tried to retreat.

"Stop him!" Zach snarled.

Luke's head snapped up. His large frame towered over Sirius, who was barely on his feet.

"Times up," Luke said, lunging. He won the brief struggle, snapping his neck and ripping it from his body. *Good riddance.*

Zach was drenched when he was finished with his rampage, and my limbs were heavy when he pulled me to his lap.

"Come on. I'm going to get you blood." His voice broke, and his eyes, once dark, were back to the brown I knew.

"No, you gotta stay. You have to finish this. You gotta make sure She's dead."

"I can't, Pres."

"Why?"

"Because it doesn't matter! None of this fucking matters if you're dead. And Aaron . . . I can't."

"You're such an idiot."

"What?"

"You're just as important as I am." It was so obvious, but he still didn't get it.

"Stop talking, you're making it worse." He worked to patch my wound with his shirt, but my blood was everywhere. It clung to my shirt, and now I was cold too.

The room blurred, and I remembered I was close to Aaron. I reached for him. Maybe I couldn't save him, but at least we'd die together. That wasn't *so* bad.

"No. Fuck. No."

"It's true, dude. Sorry I had to die for you to see it."

"Fuck you," Zach said with a choked sob.

I smiled for what had to be the first real smile in months. "I love you too."

I did it. I helped. I smiled at the thought, then the world went dark.

Seventy-Eight

KIMBERLY

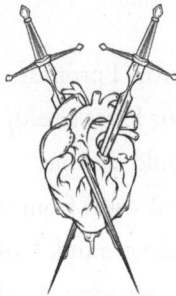

With my heart racing, I shook the bars of my iron cage. I wasn't strong enough to bend them by myself, and no amount of sure will was budging them.

"Will, can you hear me?"

Will busied himself with scratching at the wall, not paying attention in the slightest.

"I need your help."

"Fuck off."

"Please help me. Look. I've already bent the bar a little. If you just help me, I'll get you out. I'll make sure you get to Her. Wouldn't that be great?"

He stopped carving into the stone. "You'll take me to Her?"

"Yes! And you can have all the blood you want. Just come over here and reach into my cage and pull on this bar while I pull this other one."

I blinked, then William was in front of me on the other side of the bars. "I'll kill you if you touch Her."

"I don't care about Her. I have to get to Aaron. Just help me."

William reached for the other bar, and I pulled with all my might on mine. The hole to fit in was tight, but I slipped out.

"Okay. Help me now," he said.

William had more energy than I'd seen all day as he pulled at the bars of his enclosure.

"Sorry. I'll come back for you. I promise."

"You bitch!" he called, but I was already up at the top of the stairs running as fast as my feet would take me.

The only light left in the sky was from the moon and the northern lights overhead. I scanned the ground, looking at all the fallen. They could be anywhere, but my body seemed to know where to go. The top of the cathedral served as my beacon in the night. All I could hear was my breath while the strong scent of blood hung in the air.

The front of the cathedral had been blown open, and the rubble was all over the lawn. From inside, the remnants of flickering candlelight illuminated my path.

My eyes settled on an image I'd never be able to scrub from my memory.

Zach and Luke leaned over two bodies on the floor.

My heart wasn't beating.

It wasn't real.

Aaron lay against the tile with a dagger straight through his chest. Eyes closed. Pale. Next to him, lay Presley. Unmoving.

A scream curdled in my throat. I wanted it to shake the building and tear down every stone and paned window until every piece crumpled into dust.

I was too late.

In less than a second, I was there, but Aaron's warmth was already gone. I placed my hand on his chest and felt nothing. For minutes, I sobbed, unable to control the grief. It was just as I'd feared . . . I'd lost everything.

I pulled the dagger from his chest and went to work biting my wrist to pour my blood into his open wound. Then Presley's. Nothing. No sound. I bit my other wrist. More blood. It had to work. Our blood was the same. Why wouldn't it work?

"Kim." Someone was talking to me and trying to grab me. I pushed them away.

How had I been too late to fix this? I'd done everything I was supposed to. It was all for nothing. They were gone. Along with every dream we had of leaving this place behind. I missed something. There was a solution I didn't find. It had to be my fault somehow.

I clenched the bloody dagger in my hand and imagined shoving it through my own heart to be done with it all. There was nothing left.

Zach, Luke, and I were all together but utterly alone. Everything that meant anything was gone. Up at the altar, Ezra held the queen. She was offering Her blood to heal him.

I didn't care about Her anymore. She could have the ring. She could have anything She wanted. I just wanted them back.

It would be easy to leave the cruel world behind. One dagger to the heart, then it would be over, and we'd be together again.

Then Aaron's words echoed in my mind. *Promise me you'll try.*

"Aaron did it so we wouldn't be connected to Her anymore. I'm sorry." I think it was Luke speaking.

I couldn't stop staring at Aaron, caressing his cheek as he'd done to me so many times.

No, this is right. It was exactly right. The Calem boys were free. Those wonderful free boys that sang, laughed, and danced together in Blackheart—that loved more fiercely than I could have ever hoped to—were finally free.

As I stared up at that altar, I knew it was where I was meant to be. Not in Blackheart or Alaska, but there with them. We did it, and even though this was the end to us, all the love and happiness we'd shared, somehow, it still felt right. The true ending. It was Aaron's dream . . . our dream, and I had to see it through.

Only the five of us remained. Ezra stood next to the queen at the altar. Bloody but alive. Clinging to Her. While the twins wept next to me.

Our family was gone, and our world lay lifeless on the marble.

"We can remake the bond. Save your brothers. But we have to do it now," Ezra said, eyeing me like he still wanted me dead. He likely would kill me, and I didn't have the desire to fight it. I almost wanted him to come closer and get it over with. "We have to leave."

"We can all be together again." The queen spoke, walking closer and leaning in front of Zach and Luke and beckoning them. "We can start over."

The twins weren't answering. They, too, were staring at our dead with the same vacant longing and shock.

"My Love, this isn't the end. It's only the beginning. We still have centuries. So many happy memories to look forward to." She moved Her hand over Luke's cheek and ran Her fingers into Zach's hair. "Let me show you. Let me ease your pain."

Aaron had passed his hope to Presley and me . . . and I was the last one standing. I had to keep it alive, even if I felt like dying. Even if living in a world without Aaron Calem was like living in a world without sunlight.

"You can't have them." My voice was barely a whisper. I leaned on blind faith they could hear me and tried to push the words out louder.

"Don't do it."

The Calem boys didn't belong to them. They were meant to be free from that wretched place. We belonged to no one.

"Aaron wanted you all to be free. That's his dream. You promised to protect and to love this family . . . to fight. Until the very end. I promised you and you promised me."

That was the oath we'd all made. *Our dream.*

Ezra ignored me and extended his arm to pick them off the floor. I gripped the dagger, ready to defend Aaron's and Presley's bodies. Till my heart stopped beating, I would fight for our dream. I wouldn't give up. *I would try.*

The twins slowly dissolved from their frozen stares and exchanged a brief charged glance. In the same second, they lunged at Ezra.

The queen's gasp cut the air, and She retreated to the edge of the altar. I should have been scared . . . or broken, but I was neither. In my chest, fury burned ablaze. I hadn't realized the incipient fire growing in my belly until it was a wildfire of rage and abhorrence.

I'd let it burn until She was dust in my hands.

Our eyes met. She knew. A promise was a promise. That Thing had taken Cecily's body and tricked her, and she needed me to free her once and for all. I gripped the dagger covered with Aaron's blood and staggered to my feet.

I, Kimberly Calem, am brave. I will finish this. I believe because he believed.

She went to run, but I was faster. I grabbed Her by the collar of Her dress and flung Her to the floor. With my hand firmly pressed to the dagger and my blood and Aaron's mixed, I chanted. As I felt the dagger's pull, I lunged. She was stronger than me, but it didn't matter if I separated the power from Her body. She missed and pushed me against the altar. Candles flew and crumbled to the floor as She hoisted me into the air.

There I saw the twins battling with Ezra . . . losing. Luke was a bloody mess barely able to keep on his feet.

She tried to thrust a hand through my chest, and I recited the words again, still clutching the dagger with all my might. She dropped me, and I jumped on top of Her, and my teeth ripped into Her shoulder. Her blood filled my body like tar. Our blood was never supposed to mesh, yet there I was.

With a kick, She flung me into the railing of the pulpit, and it cracked under my weight. Nothing could take my hand from the dagger. She'd have to rip my arm off before I allowed Her to take it.

The twin's battle almost fell into mine. Luke had fallen, and it was just Zach and Ezra. Zach had his arm around Ezra's throat before he weaseled out.

I had to finish it. I willed my body to move toward Her. One clear shot with the dagger was all I needed. I caught the back of Her hair as She tried to run. Her grip on my arm could break me, but I wouldn't let Her shake me off. I bit into Her neck again, letting Her putrid blood fill my mouth, and in turn, She forced Her hand through my shoulder. A soft cry left my throat.

She'd been aiming for my heart, but Her body was finally weak. My vision blurred. A sticky wetness drenched my shirt. I didn't know how I willed myself past the darkness taking over my vision, but whatever I did, I was taking Her with me one way or another.

Her hands wrapped around my throat, and I smiled despite the crushing pressure.

She couldn't get away from me.

I let my body fall dead weight into Her. She wasn't strong enough to keep me up.

"No!" Ezra exclaimed, and I glanced up in just enough time to see

Zach shove his arm through Ezra's chest and seize his heart in his hand.

I wrapped my arms around Her in a hug and pushed the dagger through the center of Her back through Her heart.

"How's this for nothing?"

I twisted the dagger, forfeiting a bit of myself as it tore through flesh, and Her skin poured black ink.

My ears were ringing, and She was thrashing, but I had Her pinned with the last of my strength. I wouldn't let Her get up. When She weaseled from my grasp, I dove forward, taking Her to the ground, then shoved the dagger into Her chest.

I was finishing this. Then death could take me.

It sliced through Her rib cage with ease.

It should have disgusted me, but I was high on the fire engulfing me from head to toe. I didn't feel a damn thing. She'd killed him. She'd killed them all, and now She had to die for everything She took from me.

"Don't—" Her final word as I pulled open Her ribcage with both hands and grabbed Her beating heart from Her chest.

I watched it stop moving in my hands. It was finally done. I sliced the heart through for good measure and smiled.

We did it. We won. And now Cecily was free. I kept my promises too.

On Her hand laid my ring, and I struggled to pull it off and slip it back onto my finger.

Once the rage was gone, I had nothing left.

I tried to make my way down the stairs, but I lost my footing and tumbled to the floor.

No physical pain could touch my grief. I landed next to Aaron. My hand stretched to him. His golden hair gleamed in the candlelight, and I hoped wherever he was I'd soon be following. I imagined it to be warm and sunny, a place to pry the cold out of my bones.

When I looked to the ceiling, I realized there was no more movement.

Zach was down too. It was over, and there was no one left fighting, even me.

I admired Aaron's face. It was serene despite the usual blush in his cheeks being a far memory. My fingers twitched, longing to inch closer. His hand was so close. *If only I could reach a little more.*

A fear like I'd never known ripped through me. I was dying. My body screamed at me to get up and to fight, but everything I had to fight for was dead on the floor around me. Carnal terror sent my heartbeat up a few paces and pumped what remaining blood I had onto the cold floor. What if this was the last time I saw Aaron? I knew where I'd hoped I'd be when I died, but I'd never know for sure until I was there.

Black blood stained my fingers and fell to the floor in slow, oozing droplets. *Drip. Drip. Drip.*

A black puddle formed around me. Whether it was mine or Aaron's blood, I didn't know. My vision was going, and my body felt light as a feather. I thought one last time on the Calem boys and the love that they shared. That love wasn't gone, it was somewhere floating in the air of the cathedral waiting for me to follow it, and I wanted to. Tears stung my eyes as I took in the last sight of him. Internally, I prayed that when I finally closed my eyes, I'd open them and see him.

I replayed it all. All the best parts. Hiking. Meeting Aaron. My birthday. The feeling of his lips on mine. The laughter our family shared.

I willed my eyelids open. A few more minutes with him was all I needed. To memorize every soft detail, to remember every laugh and celebration. Just in case it was truly the last time I would. In case wherever I was going I would be alone.

Thump . . . thump . . . thump . . . th—

Seventy-Nine

AARON

Find her again.

I was at peace in the In-Between. Not quite gone but not solid any-more.

You have to find her. I kept thinking it. Over and over again.

Thump, thump.

Find her. You promised.

Thump, thump ... thump.

I want to stay. Let me stay with her.

Thump, thump . . . thump, thump . . . thump, thump.

"Fucker. Wake up." Will's voice pulled me out of the void and . . . toward the sound of sobbing.

As I got closer to the sound, I felt pain. Sweet pain searing and aching in my chest. It was hot and cold at the same time. My stomach was sick, and my limbs felt like they weren't attached to my body anymore. I tried to move my fingers but had no luck.

"Will, what are you doing?" Thane spoke. His voice was an echo.

Someone squeezed my hand, and I tried to move it again.

"He needs more."

"But—"

"Not up for arguing right now. Just focus. Keep packing that wound. Dom still needs a tourniquet over there."

"I can do it!" Another voice. The name wasn't coming easily. "I don't really know how though."

"Switch with me," Thane said.

"Yes, sir."

The sobbing was getting louder and louder and was making me feel more than the pain in my body. It made me sad. Somehow, I knew that crying was for me.

"Alright. Alright. You two, try talking to him. Maybe that will make him move his ass," Will said. "His heart restarted."

Something hot and wet traveled down my throat. Once he mentioned another, I felt the tight grip of someone on my other arm.

"Please . . . w-wake up. Y-you to get up." It was Kimberly. She was crying so hard I could barely understand her. "It's over. All of it is over."

"Yeah, dude, Zach and Luke aren't up yet. Me and Kim really, *really* need you."

Their words grounded me. I fought the invisible cloud keeping me down, and forced my eyelids to open. They needed me. That's all I required to fight past the disorientation.

"Fucking finally." Will leaned over me. He looked tired. Sick. Dying. He was paler than usual. His eyes sunken and hollow. He pat the side of my face with a relieved chuckle. "Good boy."

A strong set of arms tackled me. Kimberly kissed my forehead, and my little brother had a death grip on my arm. I still felt light. Far away. I was back but on the edge.

"Keep pressure here. It's already starting to close, but he can't lose more."

"What are you doing?" I mumbled, fighting to keep my eyes open.

"Saving you."

I could barely move my arms to embrace Presley and Kimberly, who were both weeping in a collective howling echo. One was on my stomach and the other on my chest. I used the only strength in my arms to rub their heads to get them to stop.

"It's okay now. Don't cry."

Their hair and bodies were covered in thick black smudges everywhere. My chest and my back were sticky.

William fell to his knees in front of Zach and made a long cut down his wrist with the dagger to drain the blood from his arm. With blood dripping, he brought it up to Zach's mouth pouring it in.

"He's . . ."

"Saving all you assholes. Someone's gotta do it," Will said.

"Will."

"It's fine, Thane."

When the gash no longer produced blood, he'd cut another. Will's hands were shaking, but he didn't stop. He meticulously added his blood into my brother's wounds. Next to him, sat Connell. His name finally came back to me. He was giving Luke blood and wrapping a cloth around one of his arms.

"Maybe we should help," I said, trying to move my elbows.

"Fuck no. Lay down like I told you," William snapped. "If your wound opens and your *precious* blood spills out, you're dead, and I'm the one who has to bury you and comfort your blubbering loved ones. Give your body time to close up that wound."

"Nice to know you care." I barely moved, and searing pain sent my chest on fire. "Ah . . . Ow."

"Yeah, that's what you get for shoving a dagger in your chest."

"He's right. You'd totally kill me if I did something like that," Presley said.

I lay my head back on the tile and mustered a smile. It was nice to hear his voice return to normal. "Worth it."

"I feel really tired," Connell said.

"It's fine. Stop. You're going to need to help Thane carry Dom out of here," Will said.

"What about you?"

"Don't worry about it."

Zach's gasped echoed through to the ceiling. He moved to stand, but Will held him down.

"Hey, fucker. Enjoy your nap?" Will asked.

"Fuck you," Zach said, then reached for Luke. "Luke. I have to help Luke."

"I got it. Hold here. Do. Not. Move."

Will could barely use his legs anymore. It was agonizing watching. Something burned in my chest when I tried to move again, and I winced.

Will spun around. "Aaron fucking Calem, listen to me for once in your life."

"Let me help." Presley grabbed Will's arm to help him over.

"No. You're going to need your legs to carry some of the others out.

You'll all need blood fast."

Every second, I saw more. Felt more. Life was coming back to me. Kimberly's scent filled my nostrils.

"Hey, Mrs. Calem," I said, trying to reach her face and wipe the tears from her eyes. "I'm sorry I scared you."

She grabbed my hand and stared back at me with her blue eyes and a strained smile. "Are you okay?"

"Yeah, I'm here."

Thane appeared with Dom draped across his arm. "I've got Dom. I need to take him. But . . ."

"Go. I got this." Will didn't look up while he continued to tend to Luke.

"No, I'm not leaving without you."

"I'm not arguing."

"No. I won't go."

"Fucking why not?" Will asked.

"Because you know why."

William sighed.

Connell stepped forward. "I-I can take him. I don't know if you trust me . . . but I want to help."

Thane nodded. "You can take him. You know the land."

Dom groaned, with his eyes still closed. "I know the way."

William worked while they argued, forcing blood in Luke's mouth, but my brother was still dead with no heartbeat.

"Let me do it," Zach said, barely keeping himself up.

"You don't have any blood to give," Will said as he cut another gash on his skin to pour the blood into Luke's wounds and mouth.

"Well, neither do you."

"Do you ever fucking shut up?"

"Move. You're doing it wrong," Zach spat.

"I'm giving my life to save your brother; how could I do that *wrong*?"

"Yeah, it's supposed to be me. It *has* to be me."

Zach said the words with a desperate heaving breath. His gaze locked with Will's, which was more than anger. He was pleading. They'd grown closer. That much was certain.

Will shook his head. His whole demeanor softened. "No. It doesn't. Not this time."

Thane fell to his knees beside Luke and bit his wrist.

"Fuck. No. Someone needs to fly the helicopter out of there. Do you think dumbass can?"

Will motioned to Connell who was struggling under the weight of Dom's body draped across his shoulder.

"Oh, I don't know how to fly. I can't even drive," Connell said.

"Exactly. You're going to take Connell and Dom and this dagger and get out of here with any of the remaining members that are alive. And the Calems are going to take their little happy family and go to the harbor, and you'll go separate ways."

"So you just planned it all out? That fast." Thane glared at Will.

"Yeah. I did. And you're gonna listen one last time. Kilian might be dead, but I'm still your superior."

Kilian. Dead. It made me wonder who else was dead.

"Kilian's dead?" I turned my head to see, but all I saw was a wall of bodies.

"Stay still," Will said.

He was saving us instead of Kilian. The thought was unbelievable even as I watched him tend to my brother.

William swayed, but I had to get up to Luke's side. He had to get up.

"I can't let you do this," Thane said. "Let me."

"Will everybody shut up and trust me for a minute? He's going to wake up. He's . . . just . . . taking his sweet ass time." Will continued his work on my brother. "The angels, or whatever the fuck, are probably trying to convince him to stay."

"He has to get up." Zach groaned holding his side. "I can't—"

"I *know*," Will said through gritted teeth while he poured more blood in Luke's mouth.

"Let's do it together. Then we both die," Thane said.

Will scoffed. "You have a lot left to do. You can't die here. Plus, you're not the one who owes them a favor. I do."

"I promised I'd get us all out," Thane said.

"And they will. You're keeping that promise."

Luke's eyes fluttered open. His heart reacted with thundering loudness, and relief fell from my eyes. I could barely see what was happening. Kimberly helped lift my head.

"I'm up. I'm up," he said it like a dad being pestered by his children, and I barely laughed. He took a minute to sit up.

My whole chest felt like pins and needles.

"Took you long enough." Will smiled, wider than I'd ever seen.

Then he fell to the ground, and Thane and Zach grabbed him.

"Come on. We can make it to the chopper still." Thane tried to pull William up with his arm.

"He's right. We all can," Zach said.

"No." William pushed his hand away. "You're not going together. You're going to take all your brothers and Kimberly and go to the mainland from the harbor and get someone to drink. Thane, Connell, and Dom will take the dagger and give it to Anzola. You need to go separately."

"How do you know about that?" Kimberly gasped.

"Because I know Kilian. He wouldn't plan something like this without consulting her." Will had his eyes closed but continued on. "I bet she loved you, huh? A girl who can use the dagger."

"Yeah . . . She liked Aaron too."

"She's not dangerous, but you don't want her to know you're alive. She'll try to recruit all of you, and she won't stop. Don't give them the chance. You died here. That's what you need to tell them." He groaned.

"I can still carry you," Thane said.

"You can barely stand, and the boy over there is about to drop Dom any second. I'll be dead by the time you reach the chopper. Now move for a second, I need to talk to the leader there. I have requests, and I need to talk to the person I know who can keep his promises."

He motioned for Luke, and Zach helped him scoot closer.

Luke spoke in a strained whisper, "I'm here, brother."

William shivered, and we pressed in around him the best we could. The wound in my chest was closed. Every second, I felt more coherent. The sound came back, but it was the rapid beats of hearts echoing in the silence of the night and the crackling of small fires that lingered on the marble floor.

"I need you to promise me that you're going to get the fuck out of here. No more cults. Of any kind. Live your fucking ridiculously long lives being annoying somewhere. Everywhere. And maybe get a hobby. A selfish one. No volunteering or shit like that."

"I promise." Luke squeezed his hand, his face red. "You're sure you don't want me to try to carry you?"

Will chuckled. "No, fucker. Don't you dare."

"I won't let you down," Luke said.

"I know you won't. And now we're even." He smiled and turned to Presley. "Presley . . ."

"Yeah, dude."

"Try to be less annoying."

Presley wiped the tears from his cheeks. "I'll try."

I laughed, holding my aching chest and leaning into Kimberly for support. Tears rolled down my face as he said his final goodbyes. I never thought I'd cry about William. The man who terrorized me a year ago, saved my life. He saved us all.

"Hey love." He motioned to Kim. "I have a tiny request for you."

"Hi," Kimberly said with a sob but smiled. "I'll allow it."

"Plant some flowers for my sister in that big, beautiful garden your lover boy will undoubtedly make for you."

She nodded, wiping her face with a smile. "What kind did she like?"

"Primrose. She loved yellow." William's heartbeat slowed. "Aaron, I know you'll take good care of her. Have that fuckin' wedding with the peonies."

"I will," I said. "And thank you . . . for everything." For saving my life. For saving my family.

"And you . . ." Will turned to Zach and reached for his hand.

Zach clenched his jaw as a tear fell. "Fuck me, right?"

Will shook his head with a wide smile. "No. Try to be happy. Whatever the fuck that means. Don't argue. Just try."

"I don't think I know how."

"You'll figure it out. You've got this lot here to help ya."

Zach didn't let go of his hand as Will groaned and moved to look at Thane. His eyelids stayed heavy, but he kept them open.

"Saved the best for last."

Thane shook his head, and his chest heaved in a soft sob.

"It's okay, Thane."

"But I just got you back. And I'm . . . not ready. I know you want to go and you'll be fine. But I won't. I still don't know what the hell I'm doing."

"You're ready. The Legion needs ya. Without Kilian, they'll need someone with some sense. I know you won't be alone. If I thought you would, I'd have found another solution. But I'm tired . . . It's done."

Thane nodded. "You're right. Your and Kilian's dream is done. She's dead."

Once he said the words, I realized it should have been obvious, but I blame it on the blood loss. The queen was finally dead.

"You know what I'm going to ask you . . ."

"I'll protect them. Forever."

"You're gonna do a lot of good shit, Thane. I'm really . . . proud of . . . you."

William struggled to get the words out. There was a pool of blood surrounding him, and he grew more and more pale.

"I hate this." Presley said.

William's voice grew soft and quiet. "Tell me, all of you . . . how was death?"

"Peaceful," I said.

"Warm," Presley said. "Like a bath."

"Quiet," Zach said.

"I didn't feel lonely." Kimberly squeezed my hand.

"I won't be either. I've got three girls who are waiting for me."

"If your little sister is anything like my brothers, she'll probably give you an earful for keeping her waiting," Luke said.

Will chuckled. "I can't wait. I swear . . . I . . . I can hear her. Singing. She loved to sing."

William hummed softly to himself, his face stayed relaxed and blissful till the humming slowed and his head fell. He was gone but still smiling. We cried, taking in the scene of carnage around us. The queen was dead, and Her Guard was no more.

And somehow, like I planned, we were free.

"What do we do now?" Presley sniffled.

There was a pause among us. The birds chirped outside. The sound of the night was alive. Bugs. The bugs of spring were singing.

"We live," Luke said.

Eighty

PRESLEY

Zach and Luke were really heavy. William was right, we wouldn't have been able to carry him. I could barely keep my brothers from falling into the street. Aaron reopened his wound, and well—

"Where the heck is it!?"

"This is the right street." Kimberly huffed, studying the colored buildings that lined the street. Everything looked the same color at night. None of my senses were working the way they should. We'd somehow gotten off the island. Zach explained the basics of how to drive the speed boat. I almost crashed. It was fine.

"I can't see anything!"

"Me neither!"

Kim and I were panicking a tiny bit. The other three were in and out of consciousness, and we'd gotten too far to lose one of them. I was about two seconds away from a frustration cry but was trying to keep it together.

"I think it's that one. He said it had a red door."

"Kim, half the houses on this street have a red door."

"Let's just try one." Kimberly was holding pressure to Aaron's chest.

"What if you're wrong? We're covered in blood!"

"We'll tell them it's oil."

"Why are you two fighting?" Luke asked.

"Because you're all going to die here in the street, and me and Kim are going to go back to Alaska alone and become sad, young, forever hermits."

"Wow. Creative," Zach said.

"Don't panic or anything." Aaron coughed. He was being sarcastic, and sarcastic was better than dead.

"That's it." Luke lifted his head and pointed to the same house Kimberly was eyeing.

I rang the doorbell on a pink townhouse. It was past midnight at least, and I'd seen only one person walking on the other side of the street.

When a few seconds passed, I rang again.

"Presley, don't." Aaron groaned. Kimberly's hand was wet with his blood as she firmly held scraps of her crumpled shirt to cover it.

"Well, we're bleeding out here. Kinda need her to hurry the hell up," I said, trying to hide the stress in my voice.

"It's okay. Take a deep breath. It will work out," Luke said. His best attempt at comfort in our current situation. I missed that.

"Says the guy that's currently bleeding all over me! Ugh!" I pressed the doorbell a couple more times while struggling not to drop him on the cobblestone.

There was a soft stirring inside before the door swung open and the one named Aine appeared. "Fuck. Who is—"

Her eyes widened at the sight of all five of us bloody on her doorstep.

"Hi," Luke croaked out.

There was black on the edges of my vision—I'd chosen to simply *ignore* it—but I could make out her red hair.

"What is this?" she asked.

"Heard you had blood. We're going to need it," I said.

"Let Luke do the talking, Pres." Zach groaned, clutching his side.

"What is all over you?" Her eyes remained wide.

"Wait, she doesn't know?!" I scoffed in frustration, and we all almost fell to the ground.

"Know what?"

Luke opened his mouth to speak, but he was taking too long.

"We're vampires. We're dying and bleeding out. Yep, the black stuff is blood, and we just got back from killing the cult members on that island, and we really need the blood that you have. Luke said you're the blood bank lady. If you don't, we're all *literally* going to die on your doorstep. So can you please let us in?"

"Subtle," Aaron muttered.

Kimberly cleared her throat. "Please, we don't mean any harm. We just need a little help. This was the only place Luke knew to go."

Aine's eyes were huge. "It was real. The rumors were true."

"Yes," Luke said. "And it's done. It's over."

"Yeah. See. Can we hurry? My brothers are super heavy, and I can't hold them much longer," I said.

"These are your little brothers you mentioned?" She appeared to still be in shock, which I didn't have the time to entertain because my grip was slipping under Zach's arm.

"Here in the flesh." I bit my tongue. "Can we come in or not?"

I didn't want to have to pick people off the street to drink, but I'd do it.

She nodded and held open the door. "Fine."

Her house kind of reminded me of our house in Brooklyn, but I was too busy dying to admire the furniture. She led us through a hall into what looked like a guest room with two simple bedside tables and a large bed.

"You can all rest here tonight, but I need you out by the morning. I'll go see what I can do about the blood."

I dropped the twins on the bed and collapsed onto the floor while Kimberly did the same with Aaron.

My entire body was shaking. The slow sense of safety and exhaustion nearly took me to the floor. I made myself get up, refusing to let go of the little energy I had left. I needed to make sure my brothers got blood and that everything was truly over.

"All of you get up till I know you're okay. If you die now, I'm going to be so pissed."

"We're okay, Pres," Luke said, sitting up slowly. He did that for me, I think. "Come here. Let me look at you."

I froze at Luke's eyes on me. He moved the blood-soaked hair from my eyes, inspecting me for any signs of damage. Everything else in the room blurred.

"Where are you hurt?" he asked.

I wanted to speak, but something was weighing me down. My chest was tight.

"Check his chest. Henderson got him in the chest," Zach said, still lying on the bed with his eyes closed.

"Here, let me see." Luke inspected my torn clothes. As I stared at him, everything came crashing down on me. He looked so different yet the same. His skin was warm.

We did it. It really was over.

"Pres, are you okay?" Luke shook me urgently.

How long was I staring?

"Am *I*? Are you?" I finally said, tears running down my face.

"Yeah. I'm okay." He nodded. "Thanks to you. All three of you."

"I waited for you to come home, and you didn't. I thought . . . maybe you forgot about me."

"I wanted to come, Pres. I tried. I promise I tried."

He wrapped me in a hug that was oddly soft in comparison to the ones I remembered, but it was still good.

"I know. I just missed you so much, and I couldn't tell you. It was terrible. So much stuff happened, and a lot of it sucked. And I wasn't that good while you were gone. I'm sorry. I was really close to robbing a bank."

It was like seeing him for the first time in months. All my memories after the blood in the church were foggy. I couldn't remember if I'd told him how much I'd missed or if he even remembered.

Tears formed in my brother's eyes.

"Don't cry, Luke."

"No, it's a good cry." He wiped his face, wearing a toothy smile. "I still can't believe this is real. Is this really happening?"

"It's real, dude." I squeezed him harder.

I turned to Zach and punched his only good leg. "And you. Get up."

He groaned and pulled himself up to his elbows, and I fell onto him. Hugging him and relishing it and not caring about the embarrassment of it all.

"Did you miss me a little?"

He rubbed my back, and his voice cracked. "Yeah, Pres, I did."

"Are you mad I came?"

"No. You came at the perfect time."

I tried to push back and remember. It was hazy, but I vaguely remembered Zach leaning over Luke covered in blood.

"You were . . . fighting."

He rubbed my head. "It doesn't matter now. None of it matters."

"You're right. You're free. Shit, Mom is going to be so happy to see you."

"Mom," Zach and Luke said simultaneously.

I couldn't wait for them to see her and her to see them. It would be like getting her the best Christmas gift ever. There was no topping something like that.

Then we were all crying, and every tear made me feel lighter. Like all that time we were apart and the pain had melted away. I'd dreamed of that moment so many times.

"Wait, I'm not dead, am I?" I sat up, wiping my face of the blood and tears.

"If this is death, I'm pissed it hurts so much," Zach said, unable to get up with the wound in his side.

"You." Luke was focused on Aaron who was still barely conscious in Kimberly's arms. They'd been whispering back and forth too low for me to concentrate on.

"Don't ever do that again."

"Don't make me ever have to." Aaron smiled, spotting me and winking.

I loved that sweet bastard with all my heart.

"You're okay. You'll stay awake till she gets us blood?" Luke had his forehead pressed to Aaron's like he might die any minute.

"Yeah. I've got people who need me."

The swift image of me slamming a freaking dagger in Kim's leg shot me to my feet. "Oh, my god. Kim, I'm so sorry. Let me see your leg."

"I'm fine. I'm in a lot better shape than most of you. It's okay."

"You did amazing back there," Luke said with tears in his eyes, smiling at her.

"She did it. She finished it." Aaron leaned up to kiss her. "It's over because of her."

"Because of you." She kissed him again, and her voice cracked. "I couldn't have done it without you."

"I'm sorry you all had to do this," Luke said.

"No apologies needed. We're all family. That's what families do, I hear," she said, and I glimpsed the ring on her finger.

"You got engaged without me!? What the hell?" I moved to stare at the perfect ring on Kimberly's hand. I hated to give my brother kudos, but since he literally died for all of us, I'd probably have to start handing it out more. Plus, the ring was perfect for her.

"We're kind of . . . married."

"What!?"

"We said our vows before we came."

"If that wasn't the cutest thing ever, it would be terrible news."

"That's what you get for running off. Don't scare me like that," he said.

"I second what Luke said. Don't kill yourself for us, then. Let's all agree. No more sacrifices. No more dying. And no more running away."

"Deal," we all said together.

"Don't worry, Pres. You'll still get your wedding," Aaron said.

"Thank god."

There was a knock on the doorframe. "Here. I don't know how much you need, but it's all I could spare at the clinic. I can try to get more tomorrow morning. I also found you all a change of clothes since you all look like you've been rolling around in oil."

"Thank you." Luke nodded.

"Don't leave my bathroom looking like a crime scene."

We nodded and inspected the clothes she gave us.

"These fucking shorts." Zach held up a small set of shorts. "There's one set of sweatpants."

"Can I have them? I'm so cold," Kimberly said.

"You can have anything you want, Kim," I said. "The queen has spoken."

I said it loudly, and we all juggled the weirdness of that sentence, then the strangest laughter trickled out of us one by one. We laughed together for the first time in months. Everything would be different, but I wasn't scared anymore because we were together again. Now and forever.

Epilogue

KIMBERLY

Two springs passed before we were ready to leave the gray clouds and cold behind. To feel the sun on our faces and let the warmth in. Something about the frigid air and the dark winters of Alaska gave us a place to hide. To mourn and heal in the shelter of the cold. It was a safe place that allowed us to stay covered and bundled together night after night sitting by the fireplace. Sometimes we sat in complete silence, sometimes with tears, but still together.

"It's bad luck to see the bride in her dress," I whispered in Aaron's ear. My bare feet warmed in the sun while I snuggled closer to him as he carried me up the mountain on his back.

His smile was radiant. "You know I don't believe in that stuff."

"Kim, I don't think a dress with a big tulle train was really the move for this mountain wedding," Presley said.

"Maybe you should have thought about that before you teared up at the fitting."

I smiled back at Presley as he struggled to tame the train behind me and carry it. It took me a year to save for a dress, and another half year for Vera to teach me how to sew floral appliqués over it.

"You're right, this was the best one." Presley wiped some dirt from his face. "It's perfect."

Our procession consisted of the entire Calem family, including Vera, who was being carried on Luke's back. Next to him, Zach was in charge of holding my flower crown and veil. He hadn't complained once.

As we waded through fallen branches and toward the trail head, I laid my head on Aaron's shoulder. The sun was high in the sky and warmed the entirety of my back and cheek.

After Ireland, I'd never believed I'd be whole again . . . that none of us would. We'd never be the same. That much was true. We couldn't return to that time in Blackheart—that summer and fall when everything was whole and knit together. There was before Ireland and after.

Some things I'd never be able to unsee or feel, like the sight of everyone I loved dead on the floor. The feeling of no heartbeat in Aaron's chest, and the queen's blood coating my hands. Those things were part of me now.

I squeezed Aaron's arm and played with the ends of his hair at the nape of his neck.

"Comfortable?" His voice vibrated his chest, and I savored it with my cheek still resting on him.

"Mm-hm. I'm very relaxed."

"Good, because it's your day."

"It's our day," I whispered back to him.

A day I thought maybe we'd never see. It was true we couldn't go back, but just because we couldn't go back to the people we were, didn't mean everything that came after had to be worse than before. We made new memories. Things could be *better* than they were before, and in a lot of ways, they were.

"Are we almost there?" Presley mumbled.

"No complaining on Kim's day," Luke said. The sunshine reflected in his hair that was back to the same mullet he had in Blackheart.

"*I like it long*," He'd said shortly after returning home, and grew it back out along with his facial hair. Luke was the first person I convinced to get up and hike with me in the mornings. Hiking was healing for me, and I wondered if it could be for them too. After a month, Luke convinced Zach to join. Because of that, I could see the highlights in their hair from the sun.

Even in the warmth, I remembered the cold night we'd finally made it home to Vera's cabin. She'd ran out into the snow and the twins fell into her arms in a collective sob.

"Sorry we took so long, Mom."

We'd all cried together that night and we'd refused to part ways for even a minute. Instead, we'd made a pallet on her living room floor.

Just when I thought our eternal winter would be forevermore, there were glimmers of hope. My time with The Family was brief in comparison to Zach's and Luke's, but I still found myself looking over my shoulder, waiting for the other shoe to fall. When things were good, I feared a thief in the night would steal it away, and when things were bad, I wondered if we'd ever heal.

It took a long time to feel safe. Like maybe somehow someone would find us and rip us apart again. We were each other's life source now.

Breaking us apart would spell death. I'd never known such a bond, but I think we finally started to see the rhythm when Luke baked cakes for birthdays and we'd all finally convinced Zach to do somatic yoga with us. Or when Aaron stopped waiting by the door every night just in case.

And finally, when yet another year passed and nothing but silence followed us, we all collectively made the decision to finally put it behind us. We were still bound to that castle, but not forever.

Aaron dropped me to the ground at our destination. The once barren icy cliff was covered in a lush green and a plethora of wildflowers.

Our spot had waited for us to return, and in those two years, the sky seemed bluer and the sparkling water below did too.

"Okay, everyone assume your positions while I set up the tripod," Presley said as he slung his backpack on the ground and pulled out his set up.

I tried to brush my hair from drifting into my eyes.

"Here. Let me," Vera said. She smiled endlessly the entire day. She wore a light-blue dress, and her hair was pinned up out of her face. "Do you want me to pull it up?"

"Would you?"

She winked and gathered her stash of hair supplies from Presley's backpack, then went to work pulling up half of my hair to get out of my eyes. We'd worked to cut the darker ends off, but some of it was still there as my reminder of what once was.

I took it in. The smell of fresh blooms and the sound of the bugs and birds.

Once she was done and retreated over to the twins to do her final check of their suits, I turned my attention back to my husband. He stood in his sky-blue suit and his hands shoved in his pockets, while his warm gaze brushed over me from head to toe.

"Why are you looking at me like that?" I asked.

THIS BLOOD THAT BONDS US

Aaron's gaze was heavy on my face, and he moved in closer. His hands stayed glued to my hips. I didn't mind it. His scent was all over me. It had been a whole week since we'd had a night alone together. Presley insisted it would be "fun" to make us spend our nights apart before our wedding night. And it was fun having sleepovers in Presley's room with Sarah, the dog, snuggled next to me. But in a week I craved my husband, and every brush of his hands felt like a promise for the coming night.

"I'm just soaking it in. I get to marry you more than once. I'm literally the luckiest man alive."

"Ew," Presley called.

His smile was radiant. Aaron was beautiful and all mine.

"And what could you be thinking about?" I forfeited a breath when his fingers grazed my cheek. "Anything you want to share?"

I shook my head and leaned into him to bathe in the warmth and comfort. Nothing I wouldn't *show* him later.

"No kissing!" Zach and Luke interjected.

Another one of their "fun" ideas. It had been the sweetest torture.

"Don't you guys have better things to do than to watch me?" Aaron grunted.

"Not really. We literally hiked all the way up here to watch you guys kiss."

Zach nudged Luke with a snicker. He'd grown his hair back out too. The sun complemented the glow in their cheeks. The winter had been the harshest on them, but something new had bloomed. I was excited to watch it form.

"When you get married one of these days, payback is going to be a bitch." Aaron wrapped an arm around me while flipping off his brothers.

"You'll be waiting a long time for that one, buddy," Luke said.

Vera spun around. "We'll see about that. You boys are full of surprises."

"Okay, it's set. Let's say a few words so you guys can kiss, I'll take a picture, then we can party."

We moved in front of the cliffside, and Luke handed me my bouquet—a flurry of fluffy peonies and wildflowers—while Zach helped me put on my flower crown and veil. I couldn't take my eyes off Aaron as he hugged his mom and whispered something that made her laugh just so she'd stop crying.

I'd never thought someone like him could exist. His hands found mine, and he pulled me close to him at the edge of our natural altar. The sounds of birds and the buzz of the insects was a dull roar in my ears as Presley came up from behind us and took his stance. The twins stood at the side of the aisle with their arms around their mother.

"We gather here today . . ."

"Keep it short, Pres," Aaron said.

"Do I seem like the kinda guy that would drone on?"

There was a brief silence, and I tried to hide my laughter. I'd never felt so light and utterly empty of all negative emotion. It was like living on a cloud. Nothing could touch me.

"Damn. I had this whole bit about how you guys met and how it was love at first bite—"

Aaron shook his head with a wide smile. "Don't do it."

"Fine. Family, we gather today to celebrate the love of two star-crossed lovers whose love was doomed by the fates for tragedy and despite all odds have come together in the most glorious, amazing, spectacular, out-of-this-world love story."

Aaron and I shared a look of amusement at Presley's exaggeration. His golden hair glimmered in the sun's rays, and his skin was nearly glowing.

"Aaron, do you promise to love Kimberly for the rest of eternity and vow to never let anything separate you?"

Our gaze stayed fixed. I wanted to etch it all into my brain so I could

504

replay it forever. The way his hair laid across his forehead, the affectionate smirk on his lips, and the love and adoration in his eyes.

"I do."

"And do you Kimberly, promise to love my brother for the rest of eternity and vow to never let anything separate you?"

"I do." My cheeks hurt from smiling.

"Do we have rings?"

"We do!" Zach and Luke each handed us our rings. Simple little things we'd been able to afford.

"Please exchange rings as a symbol of your everlasting love and commitment."

Aaron took his time to open my hand and place the ring on my finger. I'd stared at his hands many hours of the night and had memorized the lines in his palms and the veins in his forearms. I placed the ring on his finger with thankfulness brimming in my eyes. All of our dreams had come true. Will would have loved to see it. Skylar too.

"By the power invested in me, I now pronounce you husband and wife. You may kiss your wife again."

Aaron pulled me to his lips, wrapped his hands in my hair, and dipped me.

It already felt official. I hadn't needed a wedding, but the sight of our family overlooking the cliffside felt like it might be the highest, most perfect moment of my life.

"God, I missed that." Aaron pressed his forehead to mine.

"Wait! Stay there." Presley bolted to the camera, then back to the edge of the altar, which was just a patch of dirt.

The flash caught in my eye, and I turned around to admire the ones I held dear. I had a family for photos. We'd already taken so many in a short amount of time, but it would grow and grow. Somehow, I knew there would be scrapbook after scrapbook of our memories. Quilts would be made and videos taken.

Our world had ended, yet we'd survived.

———— ⚘ ————

Vera handed me a fistful of primrose as we waited by the waterfall's edge.

We'd killed it the spring before, but this year we had a beautiful spoil of yellow flowers sprouting in the garden beds in front of the cabin.

I eyed the yellow petals while we waited at the water's edge.

"What a beautiful bride indeed. They did warn me." Thane stepped into the clearing of trees, overdressed in a three-piece suit. Dom walked in beside him with a simple nod of affirmation.

"I'm so glad you both came." I greeted them with a hug. Vera and Luke had worn off on me. I was officially a hugger.

"Wouldn't miss it."

Thane looked well, and mostly the same. His long hair was half up, and Dom's was slightly shorter.

I handed my fist full of flowers to Thane. "We were just about to start."

With a heavy sigh, he grabbed the flowers, and his jaw feathered. Tears formed in his eyes, but he blinked them away. "Let's do it."

I handed some to Dom too. "You've been well?"

He nodded. "Very."

Another familiar face fluttered into view. Connell waved to me with vigor. His blond hair was grown out like Thane's, and his eyes were bright blue in the light of the sun.

"Hi, thanks for inviting me. I can't believe it's been two years already."

We hadn't seen them since Ireland. Before we went our separate ways, Thane gave Luke a good number to reach him. Luke had checked in a few months later, but Thane let us know he'd only call or visit when he knew it was safest. He kept his promises—to The Legion, we were dead.

"How is work?" I asked.

"The Legion keeps me busy." He winked.

Aaron and his brothers came through the trees, their laughter and happiness fell from them in waves. He found me instantly, with a bundle of primrose already in his hand. The sun warmed the trees though it was late in the day. In Alaska when the winters turned into spring with long sunny days, the sun didn't set till after 10:00 p.m.

Aaron nodded to me in silent affirmation, then spoke, "Thank you guys for coming. One reason Kim and I wanted to have a wedding was to take time to remember the people who we're leaving behind. We wouldn't be here today without their sacrifices, and more than that, we want to celebrate them every year and tell their stories by the fire so they'll never be forgotten. Will and his sister, Skylar, Sarah, Halina, Felix, Kilian, and so many more. Today we honor them, and we say thank you. May we live every day in remembrance of the life they gave up."

We gathered by the water with a soft chatter back and forth. Talk of Will and how he'd hate we were doing something like this brought up some laughter from the boys. I feathered the yellow petals in my hand. On my finger sat a small blue butterfly ring, given to me by Vera for my something blue. I'd heard more stories of Sarah since Zach and Luke returned. Tales of her laughter and keen baking skills, but mostly her vigor and her dimpled smile. She felt like an old friend. And as I kneeled in my wedding dress at the water's edge, I imagined in another life she'd have been here too. My new family was hers first and always would be.

I plucked the flowers from their stems and sat them in the rolling, ever-moving water. The sound was vivid and gushing and the force of it sent a mist in the air. Aaron crouched beside me and placed his in too. As the flowers disappeared into the water, I thought of each of our fallen.

We couldn't move forward without looking back. And for the first time in two years, looking back didn't have quite the sting.

Aaron's fingers intertwined with mine reminded me that the best days were still ahead.

———————— ✦ ————————

The boys started the party when we reached the campsite at the foot of the mountain. The long sunny day continued, but I didn't mind the feeling of it on my skin. I settled in Aaron's lap with my arms around his neck while we watched his brothers usher the others into conversation.

I was *trying* to pay attention to them more than Aaron tracing light featherlike circles on my arm.

Thane and Connell told a few stories of their new adventures in The Legion. They kept most of the details to themselves. It was mostly quiet, but they mentioned some activity in another country and made us promise to consult with them before we started traveling. Connell said he was happy it was warm there. Dom mostly stayed quiet but had agreed to a beer.

"You guys seem good." Thane smiled and lifted his beer to the sky. "Enjoying being dead?"

"It has its moments," Aaron said, his soft laughter shook me.

"I like that no one asks me to do anything." Zach stood up to go get a beer from the cooler.

Presley shot to his feet. "Wait, I'm coming with you!"

"Jeez. Fine."

They disappeared into the brush.

"Codependent much?" Thane snickered and motioned to Luke. "Still working on that in therapy?"

"Yeah . . . we're making progress. Slow progress," Luke said.

Therapy was a nonnegotiable for all of us. Vera prompted us to try at first, but I think we all learned to enjoy it for our own reasons. The twins still went twice a week, and the rest of us were down to every two weeks. Codependency was a hard habit to break. But we'd all almost lost each other, and we'd hadn't had much time apart since what happened in Ireland. I think we all liked it that way.

Presley and Zach reappeared through the trees all smiles.

"I want to give a speech." Luke stood up.

"We said no speeches," Aaron said. Presley had begged.

"I know. But this one is important."

"It's okay." I squeezed Aaron's arm. "Go ahead."

Luke walked in next to the fire and waited for Zach and Presley to take their seats.

"I kinda prepared this a couple months ago, and I wasn't going to say it, but I can't think of a more perfect moment . . . There are a lot of things I could say about the bride and the groom. Aaron, my little brother, it's an honor to know you know as a man. You have always been such a vital connector of our family, and that's never been clearer to me. Despite everything, you've grown into someone I admire. And every day, I think about how I want to be more like you. I know you'll take great care of Kimberly. And Kimberly, I can honestly say when I met you, I didn't know the extent of how important you would become to our family. You were the missing piece I didn't know we needed."

I already felt the tears well in my eyes.

"You both are the reason we're all here tonight. Your bravery and your love that you share for each other is the reason I'm standing here now. You loved even knowing that you might lose everything, and that's the bravest thing anyone could ever do. That's something I was afraid to do .

. . So this is to you, my brave little brother, and to Kim, my kickass sister, I can't believe we're all stuck together till the end of the world. But I wouldn't want it any other way. I love you both."

He raised his glass, and Aaron was there to wipe the tears from my cheek. Love was brimming inside me and spilling from my eyes.

"All because Aaron just had to talk to the human girl." Presley smiled.

"I guess it's a good thing you're the soft one, huh." Zach raised his beer to us, and I swear I saw him wipe his eyes.

Vera raised her drink. "To the beautiful couple."

After that the night dragged on slowly, and the sun started to fade behind the trees leaving us in darkness and quiet stillness while the fire cracked and spoke incoherent sounds. Vera, Connell, Thane, and Dom retreated to their campsite cabins for the night, then it was just the five of us staring into the light of the fire.

"So where are we going first?" Zach said, pulling his hands through his hair.

It took two years to heal but also two years to save up enough money for us to start traveling. A daunting task but something we were finally ready for. We had a forever list filled out front and back, and it was time to start crossing things off. There was a lot left to work through within us, but after two years in Alaska, we realized we could only heal it by living.

Presley pointed to me. "We let Kimberly decide because she's the bride."

"I don't want to pick. I have literally everything I could ever want right now. I'll go anywhere you guys want to."

I didn't care where in the slightest. I could stay in Alaska and be happy as long as we were all together. Home was wherever they were.

"Then I pick! And we're going to Italy," Presley said.

Aaron stood up and grabbed my hand to guide me toward the trees.

"How about all three of you each pick a place, and we'll start there. Kimberly and I are just along for the ride, I think."

He was right. I didn't want to plan another thing. No more detailed lists or things to do. I wanted to lay my bare feet on the earth and watch the flowers bloom every spring and catch every sunset and sunrise wherever that might be. The slow monotony was calling my name and lulling me into safety.

"As long as it's not cold," Zach said, and we'd all agreed.

Luke was the only one quiet enough to spot us leaving as we neared the tree line. He leaned back in his chair. "And where are you two going?"

"Just taking a moment over here. Don't worry." Aaron guided me through to the edge of the campsite and out of sight into the trees.

"Ah. I finally have you all to myself."

Our faces would never age, but I swear there was something different in the eyes of the boy I met in the forest. He'd grown up before my very eyes.

"Will you dance with me, Mrs. Calem?"

"Right now?"

"Humor me." He kissed my cheek and ushered me into the opening in the trees. I was still barefoot and the cool dirt beneath my feet was soft and clean of debris.

"We're dancing again," I said as Aaron grabbed me by the waist and pulled me to him.

"Mm-hm." His voice hummed next to my ear, and we swayed in a natural cadence.

The crickets were back to occupy our dance, only this time Aaron was more sure footed than before. The night was quiet except for the bugs and the laughter of the people we loved most in the world a few feet away. It was almost midnight, and the stars peppered the sky in an endless sparkling blanket. And the light from the fire danced and illuminated our shadows on the trees. A few strands of fairy lights lit up our dance floor.

"I won't step on your feet this time." He smiled and twirled me under the twinkling of lights. His hands were strong as he gripped the small of my back and squeezed my hand.

The stars shimmered above, and when I laid my head on his shoulder, I was sure I heard singing. Thane's laughter echoed in the trees, and I thought of The Legion and the work we'd once done and would never have to do again. I pondered the postmortem meeting of our battle and of how the Calem name was stricken from the story. We were dead to the world but so very alive. To them we'd lost, but in our deaths we'd gained everything.

Our freedom.

And that never would have happened without Aaron Calem. If he'd left me in the forest to die, we'd have never broken that curse over his brothers. They'd be with Her, and I'd be dead or alone.

Aaron changed it.

"I just realized . . . you did it. You rearranged the stars."

"I know," he said confidently.

"When you saved me in the forest, it changed everything. You saved us before you even realized what you were doing."

There was one good ending to their story, and he found it like he'd found me. Because he was kind and pure of heart, he'd saved me, a complete stranger. And even after that night when he'd stood in front of me in the courtyard of our college campus and offered to turn himself in, he'd rearranged the stars and changed the story.

"I know." He moved his lips to my ear. "You underestimated me. I'm a secret mastermind. Once I found you, there was no way I was letting you go."

He dipped me under the glow of the lights and kissed his way up my

512

neck. With each dizzying second, I gave a little more of myself to him. He had all of me safely tucked away in his own heart.

"And I'm not done showing you the world and all the amazing things it has to offer, not by a long shot."

Aaron's thumb traced my bottom lip, and I moved my head to his chest to listen to his vibrant, pulsing heartbeat. There was no sound more perfect.

People always said good things must come to an end, but I think that's because death is the inevitable end. But we were blessed with the true gift of the stars. We would never die, and all our dreaming and hope would continue to grow with each passing year. There would be no goodbyes. Our good things would go on forever.

Author's Note

I cried a lot writing this book. I even cried formatting it and writing this note. This isn't the end of this story. These characters have a lot of story left to tell. Granted, it will be a little less exciting. This was just one moment for them in a very long lifetime. Most of this story is the worst time in their lives. They have a lot to look forward to. And so do you. My ultimate hope in writing this story is that it helps you look ahead and find the light. That even when the worst thing happens, you still *try to* believe your best days are ahead. Even if it's different, that doesn't mean it has to be *worse* than before.

If you're my family and you're reading this, first, I love you. Second, I'm going to keep writing adult vampire books. I'm sorry if that makes things a little awkward.

If you're a reader reading this, thank you for being on this journey. This series grew up with me and these characters will continue to grow with me as I get older. Thank you for reading. I hope this gives you the courage to follow your dreams. I almost let the first book sit on my shelf and now it's been read by more people than I'd ever imagined it would. And because I did, This Blood that Binds Us will live on forever.

S.l. Cokeley

Samantha Cokeley was raised in a small town in Oklahoma. Growing up, she always had an active imagination and an interest in crafting stories. She developed a love for writing after college when she discovered anime and fan fiction. If she isn't spending time painting colorful sea creatures or crocheting, you can find her with family, including her pug named Kylo. The This Blood that Binds Us series is complete. But you can expect many more stories with vampires, heart warming found family, and fluff to come.

Follow Me

Links to my newsletter so you can stay up to date.

Follow me on Amazon so you never miss a release.

Facebook Reader Group

Instagram

The This Blood that Binds Us Series

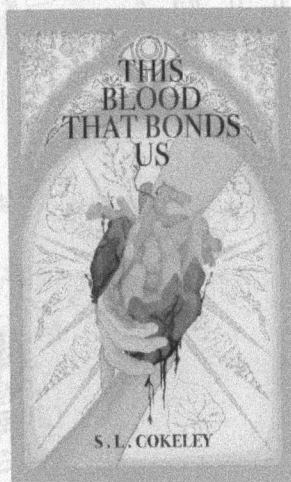

THIS BLOOD THAT BINDS US

S. L. COKELEY

THIS BLOOD THAT BURNS US

S. L. COKELEY

THIS BLOOD THAT BREAKS US

S. L. COKELEY

THIS BLOOD THAT BONDS US

S. L. COKELEY

A complete series

This series is available in different formats including the omnibuses that have combined 40k words of extra content.

This Blood that Binds Us Omnibuses

vol. 1

vol. 2

These can be found on Barnes and Noble, Waterstones, and more

This Blood that Binds Us Omnibus Vol. 1

Kimberly and Aaron's first "date"

"You're not following the rules." She was still flirting. *God, help me.*

I stared at the outline of her lips in the shadow of the broken streetlamp overhead. The cascading of lights around us illuminated the side of her face.

"I haven't kissed you yet."

"Yet?" Her breath caught in her chest, and she licked her lips while staring up at me. "Rules."

"Rules," I said.

We agreed, lingering there for a few more beats, letting ourselves draw a little closer with each passing second. I'd never been much of a rule follower, but I'd do it for her.

preview of "Now or Never" in vol. 1

For those looking for a little more color
on their shelves...

This Blood that Binds Us
Bare Cover edition paperbacks

These feature the hardcover design in
paperback form with the blurb on the back.
I do monthly signed copy drops on my
Tik Tok shop as well.

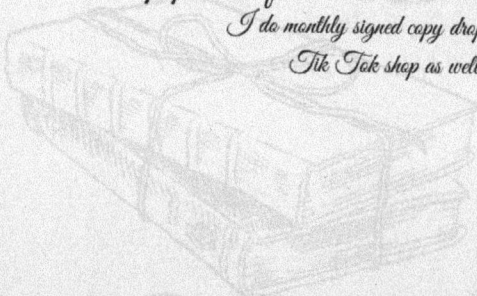